THE VIKING CRITICAL LIBRARY

THE CRUCIBLE

Text and Criticism

ARTHUR MILLER was born in New York City in 1915 and studied at the University of Michigan. His plays include *All My Sons* (1947), *Death of a Salesman* (1949), *The Crucible* (1953), *A View from the Bridge* and *A Memory of Two Mondays* (1955), *After the Fall* (1964), *Incident at Vichy* (1964), *The Price* (1968), *The Creation of the World and Other Business* (1972), and *The American Clock* (1980). He has also written two novels, *Focus* (1945) and *The Misfits*, which was filmed in 1960, and the text for *In Russia* (1969), *Chinese Encounters* (1979), and *In the Country* (1977), three books of photographs by his wife, Inge Morath. His most recent works are *Salesman in Beijing* (1984); *Danger: Memory! Two Plays* (1987); *Timebends*, a memoir (1988); the three plays *The Ride Down Mt. Morgan* (1991), *The Last Yankee* (1993), and *Broken Glass* (1994), which won the 1995 Olivier Award for best play; and a novella, *Homely Girl, a Life* (1995). He has twice won the New York Drama Critics Circle Award, and in 1949 he was awarded the Pulitzer Prize.

GERALD WEALES is Emeritus Professor of English at the University of Pennsylvania. He is the author of *Religion in Modern English Drama*, *American Drama Since World War II*, *The Play and Its Parts*, *Tennessee Williams*, *The Jumping-Off Place*, *Clifford Odets*, and *Canned Goods as Caviar: American Film Comedy of the 1930s*. Mr. Weales is the editor of *Edwardian Plays*, *The Complete Plays of William Wycherley*, and The Viking Critical Library edition of Arthur Miller's *Death of a Salesman*. He has written a novel, *Tale for the Bluebird*, and two books for children. Mr. Weales won the George Jean Nathan Award for Drama Criticism in 1965.

The Viking Critical Library

Winesburg, Ohio
Sherwood Anderson
Edited by John H. Ferres

The Quiet American
Graham Greene
Edited by John Clark Pratt

A Portrait of the Artist as a Young Man
James Joyce
Edited by Chester G. Anderson

Dubliners
James Joyce
Edited by Robert Scholes and A. Walton Litz

One Flew Over the Cuckoo's Nest
Ken Kesey
Edited by John Clark Pratt

Sons and Lovers
D. H. Lawrence
Edited by Julian Moynahan

The Crucible
Arthur Miller
Edited by Gerald Weales

Death of a Salesman
Arthur Miller
Edited by Gerald Weales

The Grapes of Wrath
John Steinbeck
Edited by Peter Lisca
Updated with Kevin Hearle

THE VIKING CRITICAL LIBRARY

ARTHUR MILLER

The Crucible

TEXT AND CRITICISM

EDITED BY

Gerald Weales

PENGUIN BOOKS

PENGUIN BOOKS
Published by the Penguin Group
Penguin Group (USA) Inc., 375 Hudson Street, New York, New York 10014, U.S.A.
Penguin Group (Canada), 90 Eglinton Avenue East, Suite 700, Toronto, Ontario,
Canada M4P 2Y3 (a division of Pearson Penguin Canada Inc.)
Penguin Books Ltd, 80 Strand, London WC2R 0RL, England
Penguin Ireland, 25 St Stephen's Green, Dublin 2, Ireland (a division of Penguin Books Ltd)
Penguin Group (Australia), 250 Camberwell Road, Camberwell, Victoria 3124,
Australia (a division of Pearson Australia Group Pty Ltd)
Penguin Books India Pvt Ltd, 11 Community Centre, Panchsheel Park,
New Delhi – 110 017, India
Penguin Group (NZ), 67 Apollo Drive, Rosedale, North Shore 0632,
New Zealand (a division of Pearson New Zealand Ltd)
Penguin Books (South Africa) (Pty) Ltd, 24 Sturdee Avenue, Rosebank,
Johannesburg 2196, South Africa

Penguin Books Ltd, Registered Offices: 80 Strand, London WC2R 0RL, England

The Crucible first published in the United States of America by The Viking Press 1953
The Viking Critical Library *The Crucible* first published in the United States of America
by The Viking Press 1971
Published in Penguin Books 1977
This edition published in Penguin Books 1996

17 19 21 23 25 26 24 22 20 18 16

Copyright Arthur Miller, 1952, 1953, 1954
Copyright renewed Arthur Miller, 1980, 1981, 1982
Copyright © The Viking Press, Inc., 1971
All rights reserved

An earlier version of this drama was copyrighted under the title *Those Familiar Spirits*.

ISBN 978-0-14-024772-5
(CIP data available)

Printed in the United States of America
Set in Linotype Electra and Times Roman

Contents

v

Introduction

I

The Crucible belongs on the stage. That may seem an odd way to begin an introduction to a printed play, but it is just as well to get the categories straight at the beginning. There are plays—Arthur Miller's *Death of a Salesman*, for instance—which are wonderfully rich and allusive, difficult to pin down, impossible to label. Such plays, impressively produced, provide theatre at its most exciting, but an ordinary, workaday, just-learn-your-lines-and-walk-through production can kill much of the play's subtlety; one might as well read the play and stage it in one's mind, catching all those nuances that imagined actors never miss. There are other plays which are extremely direct, designed to overwhelm, and the means to that end is a sequence of highly charged scenes which really come alive only in performance. These plays include all kinds of melodrama—the suspense play, the ghost story, the romance—but they also take in plays like *The Crucible*, in which the very directness can be used to carry a social, a political, a moral point.

I do not want to suggest that *The Crucible* cannot be read with pleasure, that one cannot feel on the page the mounting excitement and anxiety that the play provides, but to recognize what is going on in a scene is not the same as actually seeing it. Take the scene in which Elizabeth lies to protect John's name; even a bad actress can, by her physical presence alone, make us see that scene as one in which the character is thrust suddenly into an expectant circle and left to grope for the right response to the undefined demands that surround her. Nor am I suggesting that the quality of the production is unimportant; obviously it is better to watch first-rate performers, well directed, in an imaginatively designed set. Still, *The Crucible* is almost actor-proof. Although I have reservations about the play—as my essay later in the volume indicates—I admire Miller's ability to construct scenes with such theatrical vitality that they cannot be killed onstage. I once saw a college production in which Giles Corey was plainly eighteen, not eighty, under his badly drawn age lines and his obviously powdered hair, and even the actor's fake old-man quivers could not destroy the truculent humor of Giles in Act I or the darkening of that quality in Act III. The virtues of *The Crucible* were made clear to me back in 1963, when I saw the National Repertory Theatre do the play. The production was a mediocre one; only Denholm Elliott, as John Hale, gave a performance interesting in its own right and he was clearly fighting a bad cold the afternoon I saw him. The audience, however, was superb. It was a matinee for high-school students, and as Miller's play, with minimal help from the actors, pulled the spectators in, manipulated them, absorbed them, made them cry out—like the man Jean Selz describes in his review of the Paris production—I knew that *The Crucible* was undeniably a stage piece of great power.

Such a virtue can be a difficulty—not for the playwright, but for the editor who sets out to put together a critical edition of the play, an anthology of comment to accompany the text. The people who know the play best, who might be in the most advantageous position to talk about how the effects are achieved, are the directors and performers who have staged it, but such practitioners are not much given to writing essays. The more conventional academic critics, the ones who descended on *Death of a Salesman* so enthusiastically, those who like to play with psychological nuances and aesthetic niceties, have a tendency to shy away from plays that are too theatrical—perhaps because they are afraid to tackle a discussion of stage technique, more likely because they suspect that the play's very efficiency is an indication that it lacks High Seriousness. Of course, a play of ideas, one that grows out of a particular moral or political attitude, is bound to attract those critics who want to argue ideology—often, alas, at the expense of the play itself. So, I approached the making of this book somewhat reluctantly and, like that matinee audience at *The Crucible*, I got sucked in, in the process. If there was a limited number of critical articles from which I could choose, there was a world of other material out there that might turn out to be relevant to what is going on in *The Crucible*. In I plunged, now lost in old Salem, now wandering through the American landscape of the 1950s. The result rather pleases me. It is—I hope—a book that can be read not only as comment on *The Crucible*, but for the sake of the selections themselves. Let me, like a pitchman outside a carnival tent, explain what you can expect to find inside.

To begin with, there is Arthur Miller himself. The play, of course, followed by some of his nondramatic prose—an essay he wrote while *The Crucible* was in the making and a sampling of his retrospective thoughts on the play. It is a good rule of thumb never to take an author's word about what he has done, to question his assumptions as you would those of any critic, but even a defensive comment can be revealing. Since a playwright's best statements are dramatic ones, I have also included an excerpt from *After the Fall*, a passage that touches on some of the problems with which Miller is concerned in *The Crucible*.

The essays on the play are divided into two groups. First, those that concern the play in production, not only in New York, but in England, in San Francisco, in Paris. There are comments by the men involved, some written at the time of production, such as Marcel Aymé's charming essay; others remembered years after the event, such as Herbert Blau's long thoughts. The responses to the play onstage vary from daily reviews—Walter Kerr, Brooks Atkinson—to extended articles —Robert Warshow, Jean Selz. The second group consists of essays that were written with the printed play in hand, the immediacy of production at best a memory. These include both detailed studies of the play and essays, like my own, in which the play is considered in relation to a body of the dramatist's work.

Then come the contexts. A selection of the documents relating to the Salem trials—examinations, testimony, charges —and excerpts from several contemporary books on the witchcraft phenomenon give a hint of the play's historical setting. An essay, a speech, a confession, and a reporter's note come together to suggest the play's immediate background, the political climate of the early 1950s.

Finally, spin-offs and analogues. Scenes from the opera and movie versions of *The Crucible* show Robert Ward and Bernard Stambler, in one instance, and Jean-Paul Sartre, in the other, following clues in Miller's original and pushing suggestions—of Abigail's attachment to John, of the anger at Andover—far beyond their treatment in the play. The analogues—the scene from *Saint Joan* and the excerpts from *Tom Sawyer* and *Waterfront*—all touch (each in its idiosyncratic way) on situations and ideas central to *The Crucible* and its reception. I must admit that the selections in the last group cause me a certain amount of aesthetic anguish. I am not fond of snippets. I generally avoid theatres in which superannuated stars turn up doing bits-and-pieces of Shakespeare. I have a feeling that a play or a novel or an opera or a movie is best read or seen or heard as an artistic whole, uncut and unexcerpted. But there it is. There was hardly room in this volume for an unsnipped novel or all of *Saint Joan* ("Including Shaw's

preface?" asked a friend). It was either samples or nothing, and you can always make it up to Shaw or Schulberg by going on to the complete work.

II

Does *The Crucible* portray the Salem witchcraft trials accurately? Does its use of Salem provide a workable analogy for the American political situation in the early 1950s? These are the two questions most often asked about *The Crucible*. Inevitably, they are bound together. The second implies that the play has an immediate political point to make, and such an implication suggests that the material on which the play is based has been manipulated to that end. *And why not?* you might well ask. The emphasis on the play's historical accuracy or lack of it stems from two things. First, from Miller's own insistence on the validity of his research, apparent not only in his comments on the play but in the novelistic notes he worked into the published text. That man does have a way of starting false hares, leading people away from his play into thickets of abstraction. Thus the controversy over whether or not *Death of a Salesman* is a tragedy finds its analogy in the concern about *The Crucible* as true history. Which brings us to the second contributing factor in the historical discussion—the assumption of some people that artists are sources of information. Cecil B. De Mille kept a large research staff so that he could be sure his Biblical warriors wore the right kind of bronze breastplate. Yet if you have seen *Samson and Delilah* (1949) on television recently, you must have noticed that Samson sounds more like a post-World War II idealist than a hero out of the Book of Judges. Nor is it only the movie historians who have to be taken with care. Anyone who goes to Arthur Miller to learn about Salem, to Bernard Shaw to learn about Saint Joan, to Peter Weiss to learn about either Marat or Sade is in trouble. A playwright may be drawn to a historical subject for any number of

reasons, from the aesthetic assumption that a particular type
of character can best be explored through a familiar figure,
to the crassly commercial hope that a famous love story
or a bloody battle will draw an audience. More often, among
serious playwrights, the past is attractive as a means to saying
something about the present. Thus, in 1938, Robert E. Sherwood, in *Abe Lincoln in Illinois*, could use Lincoln as a vehicle
to ask the American audience to face the necessity of the
approaching war. Thus Bertolt Brecht could keep rewriting
his *Galileo* so that it reflected his changing opinion about
the role of science in social and political upheaval. Thus Arthur
Miller . . . but that is one of the questions you will be considering as you read. Even though I have dismissed the concept
of the play as history lesson, such a dismissal does not do
away with the need to consider the historical background of a
play and the way it is used. Some playwrights attempt to
re-create the past, others simply put historical characters into
an obviously modern play; some attempt to find the events
they need in the past, others invent them. *The Crucible* as a
play about Salem raises a host of questions somewhat more
subtle than the blunt one with which this paragraph begins.

The Crucible as a play about the United States in the early
1950s provides a problem today that no one—playwright, critics,
audience—had to face when it was written. When Eric Bentley
and Robert Warshow sat down to deal with Miller's play,
they accepted it as an immediate political fact. To most of
the readers of this volume, *The Crucible* as a product of
the age of McCarthyism is also a historical play. There have,
after all, been other Senator McCarthys since 1953, and of
quite a different character. To understand what *The Crucible*
meant in its own time requires a historical reconstruction for
the reader in 1970; for that reason, this volume contains not
only reviews and documents from the period, but a busy band
of footnotes that turn into a kind of Who's Who of hysteria,
pointing to names that are almost unknown today although

once they caused tempers to flare and hearts to beat high.
Some reviewers supposed that Miller was making specific
analogies; Howard Fast, for instance, thought *The Crucible*
was about the Rosenbergs. I assume that a more general comment was intended. Had Miller wanted to be specific, he
surely would not have passed up a chance to use a character
like William Barker. A confessed witch from Andover, Barker
gave details on the witchcraft conspiracy in Massachusetts,
testifying to "about 307 witches in the country" and "about
an hundred five blades" who gathered at the Devil's call.
Such pseudo-precision, an avoidance of round numbers, gives
a credibility to his testimony which recalls Senator McCarthy's
famous speech at Wheeling on February 9, 1950, in which
he said he had the names of 57 Communists in the State
Department (or was it 205? the number became a bone of
contention on the Senate floor).

The chief reason why Miller did not go for a one-to-one
analogy between the Salem trials and the loyalty hearings of
the 1950s is that beyond whatever immediate point he wanted
to make as a political man he hoped, as an artist, to create a
play that might outlast the moment. It was difficult for *The
Crucible* to shake itself loose from the political context in
which it was written. As late as March 24, 1959, John McClain
reported in his "Man About Manhattan" column in the New
York *Journal-American* that he had received a letter from an
angry reader berating him politically for having mentioned in
an earlier column that the Off Broadway revival of *The Crucible*
had run for more than a year. By that time, presumably, it
was only the lunatic fringe who still conceived of *The Crucible*
as a *parti pris* political document. It had begun to lead an
artistic life of its own. Although my curiosity is strong enough
to make me worry about what *The Crucible* has to say about
Salem and Senator McCarthy, the questions that open this
section of the introduction are not the kind that I ordinarily
ask about a play. I want to know what it is, what it does, what

it says right now. Interviewed in *Theatre World* in 1965, Miller said, "McCarthyism may have been the historical occasion of the play, not its theme." The important questions—at least, those about the play's meaning—should inquire into theme. What are the implications of John Proctor's final willingness to hang? of Danforth's need to hang him? of Elizabeth's acceptance of the death? of Parris's fear? of Hale's conversion? These are questions that do not depend on either of the play's historical contexts for an answer. Considered carefully, they may even explain the continued popularity of the play, its appeal to young men and women who have real or imagined Danforths of their own.

It would be unfortunate, however, if a consideration of *The Crucible* stopped with its themes. The *how* of a play always seems to me as important as the *what*. In his long interview with Richard I. Evans, Miller reported that one playwright, after seeing *The Crucible*, said, "This play's about marriage." One might ask how much truth there is in that reaction, and then look with clearer eyes at the assumptions behind Marcel Aymé's comic chronicle of his difficulties as an adapter. What, after all, does an old-fashioned triangle plot have to do with a political play? Structure and theme, as Miller implies in his Introduction to the play, are different if not separate things.

The critics of *The Crucible*—including the ones reprinted in this book—have not given enough attention to plot and structure. You will have to read the selections carefully, finding a sentence here, a phrase there—accidental comments in the middle of another kind of argument altogether—that help you to establish what is happening in the play. In the same way, the other elements that go into the construction of the play have been touched on only lightly. Character is sometimes elucidated, casually, in a remark about a particular performer. Both Stephen Fender and Penelope Curtis have taken first steps toward a consideration of Miller's language, although

Miss Curtis's own vocabulary—her discussion of the "muscularity" of language—is a bit too vague for my taste. For the most part, the reader will have to imagine the theatrical environment in which the play takes place, although comments, such as those of Jean Selz, on sets and costumes may provide ways of thinking about the characters as something more tangible than disembodied lines on a page. A colleague of mine stopped me one day: "I'm on my way to teach *The Crucible*. Give me a good question to start the class." My suggestion was that he ask how Elizabeth walked in Act II after she got the news that she was accused as a witch. I was not joking. If you can imagine how Elizabeth moves, you can accept the physical fact of her as a woman, which should lead you to an understanding of her conflict with John; that perception is a necessary first step if you are to appreciate the impact of the play, if you are to see how so ideational a drama can give an audience so emotional a charge.

Anyone with a touch of conscience, a hint of political interest, a whisper of moral concern will be drawn to *The Crucible*. Its big ideas are just right to set a classroom in motion, to turn it toward the kind of meaningful discussion which, in my youth, was called a bull session. Let the play carry you along, then, but stop now and then, for discipline's sake, and look at the details. Remember that Miller is a skilled playwright who can use the simplest incident for a multiple purpose. For example, look at the stewing rabbit at the beginning of Act II. The business in which Proctor tastes the rabbit, adds salt, and then compliments his wife on her seasoning lets us know that they have different tastes, that he is capable of at least a mild deception, and that he wants to please her. All that, with a pinch of salt.

A pinch? A grain, at least. That's how most generalizations should be taken.

1970
November   G.W.

Chronology

1915   Arthur Miller born in New York City.

1936   *Honors at Dawn*, first play, produced at the University of Michigan. Wins university's Avery Hopwood Award.

1937   *No Villain* produced at university.

1938   *No Villain*, revised and entitled *They Too Arise*, produced at the university. Wins another Hopwood Award and a prize of the Theater Guild Bureau of New Plays. Graduates from the University of Michigan. Joins the Federal Theater Project.

1944   During war, writes radio plays. *The Man Who Had All the Luck* produced in New York. Miller gathers material in Army camps, which becomes basis for a book of reportage, *Situation Normal*.

1945   *Focus*, a novel, published.

1947   *All My Sons* produced and published. Wins New York Drama Critics' Circle Award and Donaldson Award.

1948   Film version of *All My Sons* produced.

1949   *Death of a Salesman* produced and published. Wins Pulitzer Prize, New York Drama Critics' Circle Award, Antoinette Perry Award, American Newspaper Guild Award, Theater Club Award, and Donaldson Award.

1950   *An Enemy of the People*, Miller's adaption of Ibsen's play, produced and published.

1951   Film version of *Death of a Salesman* produced.

1953   *The Crucible* produced and published. Wins Antoinette Perry Award.

1955   A *Memory of Two Mondays* and *A View from the Bridge* produced and published. Wins New York Drama Critics' Circle Award for *View*.

1956   Miller appears before House Un-American Activities Committee; refuses to inform on others. *A View from the Bridge*, revised, produced in London. Miller receives honorary degree from University of Michigan.

1957   Prosecution and conviction for contempt of Congress. *Collected Plays* published. Film version of *The Crucible* produced in France.

1958   Contempt conviction reversed by higher court. Miller elected to The National Institute of Arts and Letters.

1959   Miller wins Gold Medal for Drama from The National Institute of Arts and Letters.

1961   *The Misfits*, a movie, produced and screenplay published.

1962   Film version of *A View from the Bridge* produced.

1964   *After the Fall*, commissioned as the first production of the Lincoln Center Repertory Company, produced at the ANTA–Washington Square Theatre. *After the Fall* published. *Incident at Vichy* produced in December.

1965   *Incident at Vichy* published. Miller elected International President of P.E.N.

1967   *I Don't Need You Any More*, a collection of short stories, published. Television production of *The Crucible*.

1968   *The Price* produced and published.

1969   *In Russia* (with photographs by Inge Morath) published.

I

THE TEXT

CONTENTS

A NOTE ON THE HISTORICAL ACCURACY
OF THIS PLAY

This play is not history in the sense in which the word is used by the academic historian. Dramatic purposes have sometimes required many characters to be fused into one; the number of girls involved in the "crying out" has been reduced; Abigail's age has been raised; while there were several judges of almost equal authority, I have symbolized them all in Hathorne and Danforth. However, I believe that the reader will discover here the essential nature of one of the strangest and most awful chapters in human history. The fate of each character is exactly that of his historical model, and there is no one in the drama who did not play a similar—and in some cases exactly the same—role in history.

As for the characters of the persons, little is known about most of them excepting what may be surmised from a few letters, the trial record, certain broadsides written at the time, and references to their conduct in sources of varying reliability. They may therefore be taken as creations of my own, drawn to the best of my ability in conformity with their known behavior, except as indicated in the commentary I have written for this text.

ACT ONE

(AN OVERTURE)

A small upper bedroom in the home of Reverend Samuel Parris, Salem, Massachusetts, in the spring of the year 1692.

There is a narrow window at the left. Through its leaded panes the morning sunlight streams. A candle still burns near the bed, which is at the right. A chest, a chair, and a small table are the other furnishings. At the back a door opens on the landing of the stairway to the ground floor. The room gives off an air of clean spareness. The roof rafters are exposed, and the wood colors are raw and unmellowed.

As the curtain rises, Reverend Parris is discovered kneeling beside the bed, evidently in prayer. His daughter, Betty Parris, aged ten, is lying on the bed, inert.

At the time of these events Parris was in his middle forties. In history he cut a villainous path, and there is very little good to be said for him. He believed he was being persecuted wherever he went, despite his best efforts to win people and God to his side. In meeting, he felt insulted if someone rose to shut the door without first asking his permission. He was a widower with no interest in children, or talent with them. He regarded them as

3

young adults, and until this strange crisis he, like the rest of
Salem, never conceived that the children were anything but
thankful for being permitted to walk straight, eyes slightly lowered, arms at the sides, and mouths shut until bidden to speak.

His house stood in the "town"—but we today would hardly
call it a village. The meeting house was nearby, and from this
point outward—toward the bay or inland—there were a few
small-windowed, dark houses snuggling against the raw Massachusetts winter. Salem had been established hardly forty years
before. To the European world the whole province was a bar-
baric frontier inhabited by a sect of fanatics who, nevertheless,
were shipping out products of slowly increasing quantity and
value.

No one can really know what their lives were like. They had
no novelists—and would not have permitted anyone to read
a novel if one were handy. Their creed forbade anything re-
sembling a theater or "vain enjoyment." They did not celebrate
Christmas, and a holiday from work meant only that they must
concentrate even more upon prayer.

Which is not to say that nothing broke into this strict and
somber way of life. When a new farmhouse was built, friends
assembled to "raise the roof," and there would be special foods
cooked and probably some potent cider passed around. There
was a good supply of ne'er-do-wells in Salem, who dallied at
the shovelboard in Bridget Bishop's tavern. Probably more than
the creed, hard work kept the morals of the place from spoiling,
for the people were forced to fight the land like heroes for every
grain of corn, and no man had very much time for fooling
around.

That there were some jokers, however, is indicated by the
practice of appointing a two-man patrol whose duty was to
"walk forth in the time of God's worship to take notice of such
as either lye about the meeting house, without attending to the
word and ordinances, or that lye at home or in the fields without giving good account thereof, and to take the names of such

persons, and to present them to the magistrates, whereby they may be accordingly proceeded against." This predilection for minding other people's business was time-honored among the people of Salem, and it undoubtedly created many of the suspicions which were to feed the coming madness. It was also, in my opinion, one of the things that a John Proctor would rebel against, for the time of the armed camp had almost passed, and since the country was reasonably—although not wholly—safe, the old disciplines were beginning to rankle. But, as in all such matters, the issue was not clear-cut, for danger was still a possibility, and in unity still lay the best promise of safety.

The edge of the wilderness was close by. The American continent stretched endlessly west, and it was full of mystery for them. It stood, dark and threatening, over their shoulders night and day, for out of it Indian tribes marauded from time to time, and Reverend Parris had parishioners who had lost relatives to these heathen.

The parochial snobbery of these people was partly responsible for their failure to convert the Indians. Probably they also preferred to take land from heathens rather than from fellow Christians. At any rate, very few Indians were converted, and the Salem folk believed that the virgin forest was the Devil's last preserve, his home base and the citadel of his final stand. To the best of their knowledge the American forest was the last place on earth that was not paying homage to God.

For these reasons, among others, they carried about an air of innate resistance, even of persecution. Their fathers had, of course, been persecuted in England. So now they and their church found it necessary to deny any other sect its freedom, lest their New Jerusalem be defiled and corrupted by wrong ways and deceitful ideas.

They believed, in short, that they held in their steady hands the candle that would light the world. We have inherited this belief, and it has helped and hurt us. It helped them with the discipline it gave them. They were a dedicated folk, by and large, and they had to be to survive the life they had chosen or been born into in this country.

The proof of their belief's value to them may be taken from the opposite character of the first Jamestown settlement, farther south, in Virginia. The Englishmen who landed there were motivated mainly by a hunt for profit. They had thought to pick off the wealth of the new country and then return rich to England. They were a band of individualists, and a much more ingratiating group than the Massachusetts men. But Virginia destroyed them. Massachusetts tried to kill off the Puritans, but they combined; they set up a communal society which, in the beginning, was little more than an armed camp with an autocratic and very devoted leadership. It was, however, an autocracy by consent, for they were united from top to bottom by a commonly held ideology whose perpetuation was the reason and justification for all their sufferings. So their self-denial, their purposefulness, their suspicion of all vain pursuits, their hardhanded justice, were altogether perfect instruments for the conquest of this space so antagonistic to man.

But the people of Salem in 1692 were not quite the dedicated folk that arrived on the *Mayflower*. A vast differentiation had taken place, and in their own time a revolution had unseated the royal government and substituted a junta which was at this moment in power. The times, to their eyes, must have been out of joint, and to the common folk must have seemed as insoluble and complicated as do ours today. It is not hard to see how easily many could have been led to believe that the time of confusion had been brought upon them by deep and darkling forces. No hint of such speculation appears on the court record, but social disorder in any age breeds such mystical suspicions, and when, as in Salem, wonders are brought forth from below the social surface, it is too much to expect people to hold back very long from laying on the victims with all the force of their frustrations.

The Salem tragedy, which is about to begin in these pages,

developed from a paradox. It is a paradox in whose grip we still live, and there is no prospect yet that we will discover its resolution. Simply, it was this: for good purposes, even high purposes, the people of Salem developed a theocracy, a combine of state and religious power whose function was to keep the community together, and to prevent any kind of disunity that might open it to destruction by material or ideological enemies. It was forged for a necessary purpose and accomplished that purpose. But all organization is and must be grounded on the idea of exclusion and prohibition, just as two objects cannot occupy the same space. Evidently the time came in New England when the repressions of order were heavier than seemed warranted by the dangers against which the order was organized. The witch-hunt was a perverse manifestation of the panic which set in among all classes when the balance began to turn toward greater individual freedom.

When one rises above the individual villainy displayed, one can only pity them all, just as we shall be pitied someday. It is still impossible for man to organize his social life without repressions, and the balance has yet to be struck between order and freedom.

The witch-hunt was not, however, a mere repression. It was also, and as importantly, a long overdue opportunity for everyone so inclined to express publicly his guilt and sins, under the cover of accusations against the victims. It suddenly became possible—and patriotic and holy—for a man to say that Martha Corey had come into his bedroom at night, and that, while his wife was sleeping at his side, Martha laid herself down on his chest and "nearly suffocated him." Of course it was her spirit only, but his satisfaction at confessing himself was no lighter than if it had been Martha herself. One could not ordinarily speak such things in public.

Long-held hatreds of neighbors could now be openly expressed, and vengeance taken, despite the Bible's charitable injunctions. Land-lust which had been expressed before by constant bickering over boundaries and deeds, could now be elevated to the arena of morality; one could cry witch against one's neighbor and feel perfectly justified in the bargain. Old scores could be settled on a plane of heavenly combat between Lucifer and the Lord; suspicions and the envy of the miserable toward the happy could and did burst out in the general revenge.

Reverend Parris is praying now, and, though we cannot hear his words, a sense of his confusion hangs about him. He mumbles, then seems about to weep; then he weeps, then prays again; but his daughter does not stir on the bed.

The door opens, and his Negro slave enters. Tituba is in her forties. Parris brought her with him from Barbados, where he spent some years as a merchant before entering the ministry. She enters as one does who can no longer bear to be barred from the sight of her beloved, but she is also very frightened because her slave sense has warned her that, as always, trouble in this house eventually lands on her back.

TITUBA, *already taking a step backward:* My Betty be hearty soon?

PARRIS: Out of here!

TITUBA, *backing to the door:* My Betty not goin' die . . .

PARRIS, *scrambling to his feet in a fury:* Out of my sight! *She is gone.* Out of my— *He is overcome with sobs. He clamps his teeth against them and closes the door and leans against it, exhausted.* Oh, my God! God help me! *Quaking with fear, mumbling to himself through his sobs, he goes to the bed and gently takes Betty's hand.* Betty. Child. Dear child. Will you wake, will you open up your eyes! Betty, little one . . .

He is bending to kneel again when his niece, Abigail Williams, seventeen, enters—a strikingly beautiful girl, an orphan, with an

*endless capacity for dissembling. Now she is all worry and appre-
hension and propriety.*

ABIGAIL: Uncle? *He looks to her.* Susanna Walcott's here from
Doctor Griggs.

PARRIS: Oh? Let her come, let her come.

ABIGAIL, *leaning out the door to call to Susanna, who is down
the hall a few steps:* Come in, Susanna.

*Susanna Walcott, a little younger than Abigail, a nervous, hur-
ried girl, enters.*

PARRIS, *eagerly:* What does the doctor say, child?

SUSANNA, *craning around Parris to get a look at Betty:* He bid
me come and tell you, reverend sir, that he cannot discover no
medicine for it in his books.

PARRIS: Then he must search on.

SUSANNA: Aye, sir, he have been searchin' his books since he left
you, sir. But he bid me tell you, that you might look to unnatural things for the cause of it.

PARRIS, *his eyes going wide:* No—no. There be no unnatural
cause here. Tell him I have sent for Reverend Hale of Beverly,
and Mr. Hale will surely confirm that. Let him look to medicine
and put out all thought of unnatural causes here. There be none.

SUSANNA: Aye, sir. He bid me tell you. *She turns to go.*

ABIGAIL: Speak nothin' of it in the village, Susanna.

PARRIS: Go directly home and speak nothing of unnatural
causes.

SUSANNA: Aye, sir. I pray for her. *She goes out.*

ABIGAIL: Uncle, the rumor of witchcraft is all about; I think you'd best go down and deny it yourself. The parlor's packed with people, sir. I'll sit with her.

PARRIS, *pressed, turns on her:* And what shall I say to them? That my daughter and my niece I discovered dancing like heathen in the forest?

ABIGAIL: Uncle, we did dance; let you tell them I confessed it —and I'll be whipped if I must be. But they're speakin' of witch-craft. Betty's not witched.

PARRIS: Abigail, I cannot go before the congregation when I know you have not opened with me. What did you do with her in the forest?

ABIGAIL: We did dance, uncle, and when you leaped out of the bush so suddenly, Betty was frightened and then she fainted. And there's the whole of it.

PARRIS: Child. Sit you down.

ABIGAIL, *quavering, as she sits:* I would never hurt Betty. I love her dearly.

PARRIS: Now look you, child, your punishment will come in its time. But if you trafficked with spirits in the forest I must know it now, for surely my enemies will, and they will ruin me with it.

ABIGAIL: But we never conjured spirits.

PARRIS: Then why can she not move herself since midnight? This child is desperate! *Abigail lowers her eyes.* It must come out—my enemies will bring it out. Let me know what you done there. Abigail, do you understand that I have many enemies?

ABIGAIL: I have heard of it, uncle.

PARRIS: There is a faction that is sworn to drive me from my pulpit. Do you understand that?

ABIGAIL: I think so, sir.

PARRIS: Now then, in the midst of such disruption, my own household is discovered to be the very center of some obscene practice. Abominations are done in the forest—

ABIGAIL: It were sport, uncle!

PARRIS, *pointing at Betty:* You call this sport? *She lowers her eyes. He pleads:* Abigail, if you know something that may help the doctor, for God's sake tell it to me. *She is silent.* I saw Tituba waving her arms over the fire when I came on you. Why was she doing that? And I heard a screeching and gibberish coming from her mouth. She were swaying like a dumb beast over that fire!

ABIGAIL: She always sings her Barbados songs, and we dance.

PARRIS: I cannot blink what I saw, Abigail, for my enemies will not blink it. I saw a dress lying on the grass.

ABIGAIL, *innocently:* A dress?

PARRIS—*it is very hard to say:* Aye, a dress. And I thought I saw—someone naked running through the trees!

ABIGAIL, *in terror:* No one was naked! You mistake yourself, uncle!

PARRIS, *with anger:* I saw it! *He moves from her. Then, resolved:* Now tell me true, Abigail. And I pray you feel the weight of truth upon you, for now my ministry's at stake, my ministry and perhaps your cousin's life. Whatever abomination you have done, give me all of it now, for I dare not be taken unaware when I go before them down there.

ABIGAIL: There is nothin' more. I swear it, uncle.

PARRIS, *studies her, then nods, half convinced:* Abigail, I have fought here three long years to bend these stiff-necked people to me, and now, just now when some good respect is rising for me in the parish, you compromise my very character. I have given you a home, child, I have put clothes upon your back—now give me upright answer. Your name in the town—it is entirely white, is it not?

ABIGAIL, *with an edge of resentment:* Why, I am sure it is, sir. There be no blush about my name.

PARRIS, *to the point:* Abigail, is there any other cause than you have told me, for your being discharged from Goody Proctor's service? I have heard it said, and I tell you as I heard it, that she comes so rarely to the church this year for she will not sit so close to something soiled. What signified that remark?

ABIGAIL: She hates me, uncle, she must, for I would not be her slave. It's a bitter woman, a lying, cold, sniveling woman, and I will not work for such a woman!

PARRIS: She may be. And yet it has troubled me that you are now seven month out of their house, and in all this time no other family has ever called for your service.

ABIGAIL: They want slaves, not such as I. Let them send to Barbados for that. I will not black my face for any of them! *With ill-concealed resentment at him:* Do you begrudge my bed, uncle?

PARRIS: No—no.

ABIGAIL, *in a temper:* My name is good in the village! I will not have it said my name is soiled! Goody Proctor is a gossiping liar!

Enter Mrs. Ann Putnam. She is a twisted soul of forty-five, a death-ridden woman, haunted by dreams.

PARRIS, *as soon as the door begins to open:* No—no, I cannot have anyone. *He sees her, and a certain deference springs into him, although his worry remains.* Why, Goody Putnam, come in.

MRS. PUTNAM, *full of breath, shiny-eyed:* It is a marvel. It is surely a stroke of hell upon you.

PARRIS: No, Goody Putnam, it is—

MRS. PUTNAM, *glancing at Betty:* How high did she fly, how high?

PARRIS: No, no, she never flew—

MRS. PUTNAM, *very pleased with it:* Why, it's sure she did. Mr. Collins saw her goin' over Ingersoll's barn, and come down light as bird, he says!

PARRIS: Now, look you, Goody Putnam, she never— *Enter Thomas Putnam, a well-to-do, hard-handed landowner, near fifty.* Oh, good morning, Mr. Putnam.

PUTNAM: It is a providence the thing is out now! It is a providence. *He goes directly to the bed.*

PARRIS: What's out, sir, what's—?

Mrs. Putnam goes to the bed.

PUTNAM, *looking down at Betty:* Why, *her* eyes is closed! Look you, Ann.

MRS. PUTNAM: Why, that's strange. *To Parris:* Ours is open.

PARRIS, *shocked:* Your Ruth is sick?

MRS. PUTNAM, *with vicious certainty:* I'd not call it sick; the Devil's touch is heavier than sick. It's death, y'know, it's death drivin' into them, forked and hoofed.

PARRIS: Oh, pray not! Why, how does Ruth ail?

MRS. PUTNAM: She ails as she must—she never waked this morning, but her eyes open and she walks, and hears naught, sees naught, and cannot eat. Her soul is taken, surely.

Parris is struck.

PUTNAM, *as though for further details:* They say you've sent for Reverend Hale of Beverly?

PARRIS, *with dwindling conviction now:* A precaution only. He has much experience in all demonic arts, and I—

MRS. PUTNAM: He has indeed; and found a witch in Beverly last year, and let you remember that.

PARRIS: Now, Goody Ann, they only thought that were a witch, and I am certain there be no element of witchcraft here.

PUTNAM: No witchcraft! Now look you, Mr. Parris—

PARRIS: Thomas, Thomas, I pray you, leap not to witchcraft. I know that you—you least of all, Thomas, would ever wish so disastrous a charge laid upon me. We cannot leap to witchcraft. They will howl me out of Salem for such corruption in my house.

A word about Thomas Putnam. He was a man with many grievances, at least one of which appears justified. Some time before, his wife's brother-in-law, James Bayley, had been turned down as minister of Salem. Bayley had all the qualifications, and a two-thirds vote into the bargain, but a faction stopped his acceptance, for reasons that are not clear.

Thomas Putnam was the eldest son of the richest man in the village. He had fought the Indians at Narragansett, and was deeply interested in parish affairs. He undoubtedly felt it poor payment that the village should so blatantly disregard his candidate for one of its more important offices, especially since he regarded himself as the intellectual superior of most of the people around him.

His vindictive nature was demonstrated long before the witchcraft began. Another former Salem minister, George Burroughs, had had to borrow money to pay for his wife's funeral, and, since the parish was remiss in his salary, he was soon bankrupt. Thomas and his brother John had Burroughs jailed for debts the man did not owe. The incident is important only in that Burroughs succeeded in becoming minister where Bayley,

Thomas Putnam's brother-in-law, had been rejected; the motif of resentment is clear here. Thomas Putnam felt that his own name and the honor of his family had been smirched by the village, and he meant to right matters however he could.

Another reason to believe him a deeply embittered man was his attempt to break his father's will, which left a disproportionate amount to a stepbrother. As with every other public cause in which he tried to force his way, he failed in this.

So it is not surprising to find that so many accusations against people are in the handwriting of Thomas Putnam, or that his name is so often found as a witness corroborating the supernatural testimony, or that his daughter led the crying-out at the most opportune junctures of the trials, especially when— But we'll speak of that when we come to it.

PUTNAM—*at the moment he is intent upon getting Parris, for whom he has only contempt, to move toward the abyss:* Mr. Parris, I have taken your part in all contention here, and I would continue; but I cannot if you hold back in this. There are hurtful, vengeful spirits layin' hands on these children.

PARRIS: But, Thomas, you cannot—

PUTNAM: Ann! Tell Mr. Parris what you have done.

MRS. PUTNAM: Reverend Parris, I have laid seven babies unbaptized in the earth. Believe me, sir, you never saw more hearty babies born. And yet, each would wither in my arms the very night of their birth. I have spoke nothin', but my heart has clamored intimations. And now, this year, my Ruth, my only— I see her turning strange. A secret child she has become this year, and shrivels like a sucking mouth were pullin' on her life too. And so I thought to send her to your Tituba—

PARRIS: To Tituba! What may Tituba—?

MRS. PUTNAM: Tituba knows how to speak to the dead, Mr. Parris.

PARRIS: Goody Ann, it is a formidable sin to conjure up the dead!

MRS. PUTNAM: I take it on my soul, but who else may surely tell us what person murdered my babies?

PARRIS, *horrified:* Woman!

MRS. PUTNAM: They were murdered, Mr. Parris! And mark this proof! Mark it! Last night my Ruth were ever so close to their little spirits; I know it, sir. For how else is she struck dumb now except some power of darkness would stop her mouth? It is a marvelous sign, Mr. Parris!

PUTNAM: Don't you understand it, sir? There is a murdering witch among us, bound to keep herself in the dark. *Parris turns to Betty, a frantic terror rising in him.* Let your enemies make of it what they will, you cannot blink it more.

PARRIS, *to Abigail:* Then you were conjuring spirits last night.

ABIGAIL, *whispering:* Not I, sir—Tituba and Ruth.

PARRIS *turns now, with new fear, and goes to Betty, looks down at her, and then, gazing off:* Oh, Abigail, what proper payment for my charity! Now I am undone.

PUTNAM: You are not undone! Let you take hold here. Wait for no one to charge you—declare it yourself. You have discovered witchcraft—

PARRIS: In my house? In my house, Thomas? They will topple me with this! They will make of it a—

Enter Mercy Lewis, the Putnams' servant, a fat, sly, merciless girl of eighteen.

MERCY: Your pardons. I only thought to see how Betty is.

PUTNAM: Why aren't you home? Who's with Ruth?

MERCY: Her grandma come. She's improved a little, I think—she give a powerful sneeze before.

MRS. PUTNAM: Ah, there's a sign of life!

MERCY: I'd fear no more, Goody Putnam. It were a grand sneeze; another like it will shake her wits together, I'm sure. *She goes to the bed to look.*

PARRIS: Will you leave me now, Thomas? I would pray a while alone.

ABIGAIL: Uncle, you've prayed since midnight. Why do you not go down and—

PARRIS: No—no. *To Putnam:* I have no answer for that crowd. I'll wait till Mr. Hale arrives. *To get Mrs. Putnam to leave:* If you will, Goody Ann . . .

PUTNAM: Now look you, sir. Let you strike out against the Devil, and the village will bless you for it! Come down, speak to them—pray with them. They're thirsting for your word, Mister! Surely you'll pray with them.

PARRIS, *swayed:* I'll lead them in a psalm, but let you say nothing of witchcraft yet. I will not discuss it. The cause is yet unknown. I have had enough contention since I came; I want no more.

MRS. PUTNAM: Mercy, you go home to Ruth, d'y'hear?

MERCY: Aye, mum.

Mrs. Putnam goes out.

PARRIS, *to Abigail:* If she starts for the window, cry for me at once.

ABIGAIL: I will, uncle.

PARRIS, *to Putnam:* There is a terrible power in her arms today. *He goes out with Putnam.*

ABIGAIL, *with hushed trepidation:* How is Ruth sick?

MERCY: It's weirdish, I know not—she seems to walk like a dead one since last night.

ABIGAIL, *turns at once and goes to Betty, and now, with fear in her voice:* Betty? *Betty doesn't move. She shakes her.* Now stop this! Betty! Sit up now!

Betty doesn't stir. Mercy comes over.

MERCY: Have you tried beatin' her? I gave Ruth a good one and it waked her for a minute. Here, let me have her.

ABIGAIL, *holding Mercy back:* No, he'll be comin' up. Listen, now; if they be questioning us, tell them we danced—I told him as much already.

MERCY: Aye. And what more?

ABIGAIL: He knows Tituba conjured Ruth's sisters to come out of the grave.

MERCY: And what more?

ABIGAIL: He saw you naked.

MERCY, *clapping her hands together with a frightened laugh:* Oh, Jesus!

Enter Mary Warren, breathless. She is seventeen, a subservient, naive, lonely girl.

MARY WARREN: What'll we do? The village is out! I just come from the farm; the whole country's talkin' witchcraft! They'll be callin' us witches, Abby!

MERCY, *pointing and looking at Mary Warren:* She means to tell, I know it.

MARY WARREN: Abby, we've got to tell. Witchery's a hangin' error, a hangin' like they done in Boston two year ago! We must tell the truth, Abby! You'll only be whipped for dancin', and the other things!

ABIGAIL: Oh, *we'll* be whipped!

MARY WARREN: I never done none of it, Abby. I only looked!

MERCY, *moving menacingly toward Mary:* Oh, you're a great one for lookin', aren't you, Mary Warren? What a grand peeping courage you have!

Betty, on the bed, whimpers. Abigail turns to her at once.

ABIGAIL: Betty? *She goes to Betty.* Now, Betty, dear, wake up now. It's Abigail. *She sits Betty up and furiously shakes her.* I'll beat you, Betty! *Betty whimpers.* My, you seem improving. I talked to your papa and I told him everything. So there's nothing to——

BETTY, *darts off the bed, frightened of Abigail, and flattens herself against the wall:* I want my mama!

ABIGAIL, *with alarm, as she cautiously approaches Betty:* What ails you, Betty? Your mama's dead and buried.

BETTY: I'll fly to Mama. Let me fly! *She raises her arms as though to fly, and streaks for the window, gets one leg out.*

ABIGAIL, *pulling her away from the window:* I told him everything; he knows now, he knows everything we——

BETTY: You drank blood, Abby! You didn't tell him that!

ABIGAIL: Betty, you never say that again! You will never——

BETTY: You did, you did! You drank a charm to kill John Proctor's wife! You drank a charm to kill Goody Proctor!

ABIGAIL, *smashes her across the face:* Shut it! Now shut it!

BETTY, *collapsing on the bed:* Mama, Mama! *She dissolves into sobs.*

ABIGAIL: Now look you. All of you. We danced. And Tituba conjured Ruth Putnam's dead sisters. And that is all. And mark this. Let either of you breathe a word, or the edge of a word, about the other things, and I will come to you in the black of some terrible night and I will bring a pointy reckoning that will shudder you. And you know I can do it; I saw Indians smash my dear parents' heads on the pillow next to mine, and I have seen some reddish work done at night, and I can make you wish you had never seen the sun go down! *She goes to Betty and roughly sits her up.* Now, you—sit up and stop this!

But Betty collapses in her hands and lies inert on the bed.

MARY WARREN, *with hysterical fright:* What's got her? *Abigail stares in fright at Betty.* Abby, she's going to die! It's a sin to conjure, and we—

ABIGAIL, *starting for Mary:* I say shut it, Mary Warren!

Enter John Proctor. On seeing him, Mary Warren leaps in fright.

Proctor was a farmer in his middle thirties. He need not have been a partisan of any faction in the town, but there is evidence to suggest that he had a sharp and biting way with hypocrites. He was the kind of man—powerful of body, even-tempered, and not easily led—who cannot refuse support to partisans without drawing their deepest resentment. In Proctor's presence a fool felt his foolishness instantly—and a Proctor is always marked for calumny therefore.

But as we shall see, the steady manner he displays does not spring from an untroubled soul. He is a sinner, a sinner not only against the moral fashion of the time, but against his own vision of decent conduct. These people had no ritual for the washing away of sins. It is another trait we inherited from them, and it has helped to discipline us as well as to breed hypocrisy among us. Proctor, respected and even feared in Salem, has come to regard himself as a kind of fraud. But no hint of this has yet appeared on the surface, and as he enters from the crowded parlor below it is a man in his prime we see, with a quiet confidence and an unexpressed, hidden force. Mary Warren, his servant, can barely speak for embarrassment and fear.

MARY WARREN: Oh! I'm just going home, Mr. Proctor.

PROCTOR: Be you foolish, Mary Warren? Be you deaf? I forbid you leave the house, did I not? Why shall I pay you? I am looking for you more often than my cows!

MARY WARREN: I only come to see the great doings in the world.

PROCTOR: I'll show you a great doin' on your arse one of these days. Now get you home; my wife is waitin' with your work! *Trying to retain a shred of dignity, she goes slowly out.*

MERCY LEWIS, *both afraid of him and strangely titillated:* I'd best be off. I have my Ruth to watch. Good morning, Mr. Proctor.

Mercy sidles out. Since Proctor's entrance, Abigail has stood as though on tiptoe, absorbing his presence, wide-eyed. He glances at her, then goes to Betty on the bed.

ABIGAIL: Gah! I'd almost forgot how strong you are, John Proctor!

PROCTOR, *looking at Abigail now, the faintest suggestion of a knowing smile on his face:* What's this mischief here?

ABIGAIL, *with a nervous laugh:* Oh, she's only gone silly somehow.

PROCTOR: The road past my house is a pilgrimage to Salem all morning. The town's mumbling witchcraft.

ABIGAIL: Oh, posh! *Winningly she comes a little closer, with a confidential, wicked air.* We were dancin' in the woods last night, and my uncle leaped in on us. She took fright, is all.

PROCTOR, *his smile widening:* Ah, you're wicked yet, aren't y'! *A trill of expectant laughter escapes her, and she dares come closer, feverishly looking into his eyes.* You'll be clapped in the stocks before you're twenty.

He takes a step to go, and she springs into his path.

ABIGAIL: Give me a word, John. A soft word. *Her concentrated desire destroys his smile.*

PROCTOR: No, no, Abby. That's done with.

ABIGAIL, *tauntingly:* You come five mile to see a silly girl fly? I know you better.

PROCTOR, *setting her firmly out of his path:* I come to see what mischief your uncle's brewin' now. *With final emphasis:* Put it out of mind, Abby.

ABIGAIL, *grasping his hand before he can release her:* John— I am waitin' for you every night.

PROCTOR: Abby, I never give you hope to wait for me.

ABIGAIL, *now beginning to anger—she can't believe it:* I have something better than hope, I think!

PROCTOR: Abby, you'll put it out of mind. I'll not be comin' for you more.

ABIGAIL: You're surely sportin' with me.

PROCTOR: You know me better.

ABIGAIL: I know how you clutched my back behind your house and sweated like a stallion whenever I come near! Or did I dream that? It's she put me out, you cannot pretend it were you. I saw your face when she put me out, and you loved me then and you do now!

PROCTOR: Abby, that's a wild thing to say—

ABIGAIL: A wild thing may say wild things. But not so wild, I think. I have seen you since she put me out; I have seen you nights.

PROCTOR: I have hardly stepped off my farm this sevenmonth.

ABIGAIL: I have a sense for heat, John, and yours has drawn me to my window, and I have seen you looking up, burning in your loneliness. Do you tell me you've never looked up at my window?

PROCTOR: I may have looked up.

ABIGAIL, *now softening:* And you must. You are no wintry man. I know you, John. I *know* you. *She is weeping.* I cannot sleep for dreamin'; I cannot dream but I wake and walk about the house as though I'd find you comin' through some door. *She clutches him desperately.*

PROCTOR, *gently pressing her from him, with great sympathy but firmly:* Child—

ABIGAIL, *with a flash of anger:* How do you call me child!

PROCTOR: Abby, I may think of you softly from time to time. But I will cut off my hand before I'll ever reach for you again. Wipe it out of mind. We never touched, Abby.

ABIGAIL: Aye, but we did.

PROCTOR: Aye, but we did not.

ABIGAIL, *with a bitter anger:* Oh, I marvel how such a strong man may let such a sickly wife be—

PROCTOR, *angered—at himself as well:* You'll speak nothin' of Elizabeth!

ABIGAIL: She is blackening my name in the village! She is telling lies about me! She is a cold, sniveling woman, and you bend to her! Let her turn you like a—

PROCTOR, *shaking her:* Do you look for whippin'?

A psalm is heard being sung below.

ABIGAIL, *in tears:* I look for John Proctor that took me from my sleep and put knowledge in my heart! I never knew what pretense Salem was, I never knew the lying lessons I was taught by all these Christian women and their covenanted men! And now you bid me tear the light out of my eyes? I will not, I cannot! You loved me, John Proctor, and whatever sin it is, you love me yet! *He turns abruptly to go out. She rushes to him.* John, pity me, pity me!

The words "going up to Jesus" are heard in the psalm, and Betty claps her ears suddenly and whines loudly.

ABIGAIL: Betty? *She hurries to Betty, who is now sitting up and screaming. Proctor goes to Betty as Abigail is trying to pull her hands down, calling "Betty!"*

PROCTOR, *growing unnerved:* What's she doing? Girl, what ails you? Stop that wailing!

The singing has stopped in the midst of this, and now Parris rushes in.

PARRIS: What happened? What are you doing to her? Betty! *He rushes to the bed, crying, "Betty, Betty!" Mrs. Putnam enters, feverish with curiosity, and with her Thomas Putnam and Mercy Lewis. Parris, at the bed, keeps lightly slapping Betty's face, while she moans and tries to get up.*

ABIGAIL: She heard you singin' and suddenly she's up and screamin'.

MRS. PUTNAM: The psalm! The psalm! She cannot bear to hear the Lord's name!

PARRIS: No, God forbid. Mercy, run to the doctor! Tell him what's happened here! *Mercy Lewis rushes out.*

MRS. PUTNAM: Mark it for a sign, mark it!

Rebecca Nurse, seventy-two, enters. She is white-haired, leaning upon her walking-stick.

PUTNAM, *pointing at the whimpering Betty:* That is a notorious sign of witchcraft afoot, Goody Nurse, a prodigious sign!

MRS. PUTNAM: My mother told me that! When they cannot bear to hear the name of—

PARRIS, *trembling:* Rebecca, Rebecca, go to her, we're lost. She suddenly cannot bear to hear the Lord's—

Giles Corey, eighty-three, enters. He is knotted with muscle, canny, inquisitive, and still powerful.

REBECCA: There is hard sickness here, Giles Corey, so please to keep the quiet.

GILES: I've not said a word. No one here can testify I've said a word. Is she going to fly again? I hear she flies.

PUTNAM: Man, be quiet now!

Everything is quiet. Rebecca walks across the room to the bed. Gentleness exudes from her. Betty is quietly whimpering, eyes shut. Rebecca simply stands over the child, who gradually quiets.

And while they are so absorbed, we may put a word in for Rebecca. Rebecca was the wife of Francis Nurse, who, from all accounts, was one of those men for whom both sides of the argument had to have respect. He was called upon to arbitrate disputes as though he were an unofficial judge, and Rebecca also enjoyed the high opinion most people had for him. By the time of the delusion, they had three hundred acres, and their children were settled in separate homesteads within the same estate. However, Francis had originally rented the land, and one theory has it that, as he gradually paid for it and raised his social status, there were those who resented his rise.

Another suggestion to explain the systematic campaign against Rebecca, and inferentially against Francis, is the land war he fought with his neighbors, one of whom was a Putnam. This squabble grew to the proportions of a battle in the woods between partisans of both sides, and it is said to have lasted for two days. As for Rebecca herself, the general opinion of her character was so high that to explain how anyone dared cry her out for a witch—and more, how adults could bring themselves to lay hands on her—we must look to the fields and boundaries of that time.

As we have seen, Thomas Putnam's man for the Salem ministry was Bayley. The Nurse clan had been in the faction that prevented Bayley's taking office. In addition, certain families allied to the Nurses by blood or friendship, and whose farms were contiguous with the Nurse farm or close to it, combined to break away from the Salem town authority and set up Topsfield, a new and independent entity whose existence was resented by old Salemites.

That the guiding hand behind the outcry was Putnam's is indicated by the fact that, as soon as it began, this Topsfield-Nurse faction absented themselves from church in protest and disbelief. It was Edward and Jonathan Putnam who signed the first complaint against Rebecca; and Thomas Putnam's little daughter was the one who fell into a fit at the hearing and pointed to Rebecca as her attacker. To top it all, Mrs. Putnam—who is now staring at the bewitched child on the bed—soon accused Rebecca's spirit of "tempting her to iniquity," a charge that had more truth in it than Mrs. Putnam could know.

MRS. PUTNAM, *astonished:* What have you done?

Rebecca, in thought, now leaves the bedside and sits.

PARRIS, *wondrous and relieved:* What do you make of it, Rebecca?

PUTNAM, *eagerly:* Goody Nurse, will you go to my Ruth and see if you can wake her?

REBECCA, *sitting:* I think she'll wake in time. Pray calm yourselves. I have eleven children, and I am twenty-six times a grandma, and I have seen them all through their silly seasons, and when it come on them they will run the Devil bowlegged keeping up with their mischief. I think she'll wake when she tires of it. A child's spirit is like a child, you can never catch it by running after it; you must stand still, and, for love, it will soon itself come back.

PROCTOR: Aye, that's the truth of it, Rebecca.

MRS. PUTNAM: This is no silly season, Rebecca. My Ruth is bewildered, Rebecca; she cannot eat.

REBECCA: Perhaps she is not hungered yet. *To Parris:* I hope you are not decided to go in search of loose spirits, Mr. Parris. I've heard promise of that outside.

PARRIS: A wide opinion's running in the parish that the Devil may be among us, and I would satisfy them that they are wrong.

PROCTOR: Then let you come out and call them wrong. Did you consult the wardens before you called this minister to look for devils?

PARRIS: He is not coming to look for devils!

PROCTOR: Then what's he coming for?

PUTNAM: There be children dyin' in the village, Mister!

PROCTOR: I seen none dyin'. This society will not be a bag to swing around your head, Mr. Putnam. *To Parris:* Did you call a meeting before you—?

PUTNAM: I am sick of meetings; cannot the man turn his head without he have a meeting?

PROCTOR: He may turn his head, but not to Hell!

REBECCA: Pray, John, be calm. *Pause. He defers to her.* Mr. Parris, I think you'd best send Reverend Hale back as soon as he come. This will set us all to arguin' again in the society, and we thought to have peace this year. I think we ought rely on the doctor now, and good prayer.

MRS. PUTNAM: Rebecca, the doctor's baffled!

REBECCA: If so he is, then let us go to God for the cause of it. There is prodigious danger in the seeking of loose spirits. I fear it, I fear it. Let us rather blame ourselves and—

PUTNAM: How may we blame ourselves? I am one of nine sons; the Putnam seed have peopled this province. And yet I have but one child left of eight—and now she shrivels!

REBECCA: I cannot fathom that.

MRS. PUTNAM, *with a growing edge of sarcasm:* But I must! You think it God's work you should never lose a child, nor grandchild either, and I bury all but one? There are wheels within wheels in this village, and fires within fires!

PUTNAM, *to Parris:* When Reverend Hale comes, you will proceed to look for signs of witchcraft here.

PROCTOR, *to Putnam:* You cannot command Mr. Parris. We vote by name in this society, not by acreage.

PUTNAM: I never heard you worried so on this society, Mr. Proctor. I do not think I saw you at Sabbath meeting since snow flew.

PROCTOR: I have trouble enough without I come five mile to hear him preach only hellfire and bloody damnation. Take it to heart, Mr. Parris. There are many others who stay away from church these days because you hardly ever mention God any more.

PARRIS, *now aroused:* Why, that's a drastic charge!

REBECCA: It's somewhat true; there are many that quail to bring their children—

PARRIS: I do not preach for children, Rebecca. It is not the children who are unmindful of their obligations toward this ministry.

REBECCA: Are there really those unmindful?

PARRIS: I should say the better half of Salem village—

PUTNAM: And more than that!

PARRIS: Where is my wood? My contract provides I be supplied with all my firewood. I am waiting since November for a stick, and even in November I had to show my frostbitten hands like some London beggar!

GILES: You are allowed six pound a year to buy your wood, Mr. Parris.

PARRIS: I regard that six pound as part of my salary. I am paid little enough without I spend six pound on firewood.

PROCTOR: Sixty, plus six for firewood—

PARRIS: The salary is sixty-six pound, Mr. Proctor! I am not some preaching farmer with a book under my arm; I am a graduate of Harvard College.

GILES: Aye, and well instructed in arithmetic!

PARRIS· Mr. Corey, you will look far for a man of my kind at sixty pound a year! I am not used to this poverty; I left a thrifty business in the Barbados to serve the Lord. I do not fathom it, why am I persecuted here? I cannot offer one proposition but there be a howling riot of argument. I have often wondered if the Devil be in it somewhere; I cannot understand you people otherwise.

PROCTOR: Mr. Parris, you are the first minister ever did demand the deed to this house—

PARRIS: Man! Don't a minister deserve a house to live in?

PROCTOR: To live in, yes. But to ask ownership is like you shall own the meeting house itself; the last meeting I were at you spoke so long on deeds and mortgages I thought it were an auction.

PARRIS: I want a mark of confidence, is all! I am your third preacher in seven years. I do not wish to be put out like the cat whenever some majority feels the whim. You people seem not to comprehend that a minister is the Lord's man in the parish; a minister is not to be so lightly crossed and contradicted—

PUTNAM: Aye!

PARRIS: There is either obedience or the church will burn like Hell is burning!

PROCTOR: Can you speak one minute without we land in Hell again? I am sick of Hell!

PARRIS: It is not for you to say what is good for you to hear!

PROCTOR: I may speak my heart, I think!

PARRIS, *in a fury:* What, are we Quakers? We are not Quakers here yet, Mr. Proctor. And you may tell that to your followers!

PROCTOR: My followers!

PARRIS—*now he's out with it:* There is a party in this church. I am not blind; there is a faction and a party.

PROCTOR: Against you?

PUTNAM: Against him and all authority!

PROCTOR: Why, then I must find it and join it.

There is shock among the others.

REBECCA: He does not mean that.

PUTNAM: He confessed it now!

PROCTOR: I mean it solemnly, Rebecca; I like not the smell of this "authority."

REBECCA: No, you cannot break charity with your minister. You are another kind, John. Clasp his hand, make your peace.

PROCTOR: I have a crop to sow and lumber to drag home. *He goes angrily to the door and turns to Corey with a smile.* What say you, Giles, let's find the party. He says there's a party.

GILES: I've changed my opinion of this man, John. Mr. Parris, I beg your pardon. I never thought you had so much iron in you.

PARRIS, *surprised:* Why, thank you, Giles!

GILES: It suggests to the mind what the trouble be among us all these years. *To all:* Think on it. Wherefore is everybody suing everybody else? Think on it now, it's a deep thing, and dark as a pit. I have been six time in court this year—

PROCTOR, *familiarly, with warmth, although he knows he is approaching the edge of Giles' tolerance with this:* Is it the Devil's fault that a man cannot say you good morning without you clap him for defamation? You're old, Giles, and you're not hearin' so well as you did.

GILES—*he cannot be crossed:* John Proctor, I have only last month collected four pound damages for you publicly sayin' I burned the roof off your house, and I—

PROCTOR, *laughing:* I never said no such thing, but I've paid you for it, so I hope I can call you deaf without charge. Now come along, Giles, and help me drag my lumber home.

PUTNAM: A moment, Mr. Proctor. What lumber is that you're draggin', if I may ask you?

PROCTOR: My lumber. From out my forest by the riverside.

PUTNAM: Why, we are surely gone wild this year. What anarchy is this? That tract is in my bounds, it's in my bounds, Mr. Proctor.

PROCTOR: In your bounds! *Indicating Rebecca:* I bought that tract from Goody Nurse's husband five months ago.

PUTNAM: He had no right to sell it. It stands clear in my grand-father's will that all the land between the river and—

PROCTOR: Your grandfather had a habit of willing land that never belonged to him, if I may say it plain.

GILES: That's God's truth; he nearly willed away my north pasture but he knew I'd break his fingers before he'd set his name to it. Let's get your lumber home, John. I feel a sudden will to work coming on.

PUTNAM: You load one oak of mine and you'll fight to drag it home!

GILES: Aye, and we'll win too, Putnam—this fool and I. Come on! *He turns to Proctor and starts out.*

PUTNAM: I'll have my men on you, Corey! I'll clap a writ on you!

Enter Reverend John Hale of Beverly.

Mr. Hale is nearing forty, a tight-skinned, eager-eyed intellectual. This is a beloved errand for him; on being called here to ascertain witchcraft he felt the pride of the specialist whose unique knowledge has at last been publicly called for. Like almost all men of learning, he spent a good deal of his time pondering the invisible world, especially since he had himself encountered a witch in his parish not long before. That woman, however, turned into a mere pest under his searching scrutiny, and the child she had allegedly been afflicting recovered her normal behavior after Hale had given her his kindness and a few days of rest in his own house. However, that experience never raised a doubt in his mind as to the reality of the under-world or the existence of Lucifer's many-faced lieutenants. And his belief is not to his discredit. Better minds than Hale's were—and still are—convinced that there is a society of spirits beyond our ken. One cannot help noting that one of his lines has never yet raised a laugh in any audience that has seen this play; it is his assurance that "We cannot look to superstition in this. The Devil is precise." Evidently we are not quite certain even now whether diabolism is holy and not to be scoffed at. And it is no accident that we should be so bemused.

Like Reverend Hale and the others on this stage, we conceive the Devil as a necessary part of a respectable view of cosmology. Ours is a divided empire in which certain ideas and emotions and actions are of God, and their opposites are of Lucifer. It is as impossible for most men to conceive of a morality without sin as of an earth without "sky." Since 1692 a great but super-ficial change has wiped out God's beard and the Devil's horns, but the world is still gripped between two diametrically opposed absolutes. The concept of unity, in which positive and negative are attributes of the same force, in which good and evil are relative, ever-changing, and always joined to the same phenom-enon—such a concept is still reserved to the physical sciences and to the few who have grasped the history of ideas. When it is recalled that until the Christian era the underworld was never regarded as a hostile area, that all gods were useful and es-sentially friendly to man despite occasional lapses; when we see the steady and methodical inculcation into humanity of the idea of man's worthlessness—until redeemed—the necessity of the Devil may become evident as a weapon, a weapon designed and used time and time again in every age to whip men into a surrender to a particular church or church-state.

Our difficulty in believing the—for want of a better word—political inspiration of the Devil is due in great part to the fact that he is called up and damned not only by our social antagonists but by our own side, whatever it may be. The Catholic Church, through its Inquisition, is famous for cultivating Lucifer as the arch-fiend, but the Church's enemies relied no less upon the Old Boy to keep the human mind enthralled. Luther was himself accused of alliance with Hell, and he in turn accused his enemies. To complicate matters further, he believed that he had had contact with the Devil and had argued theology with him. I am not surprised at this, for at my own university a professor of history—a Lutheran, by the way—used to assemble his graduate students, draw the shades, and commune in the classroom with Erasmus. He was never, to my knowledge, officially scoffed at for this, the reason being that the university officials, like most of us, are the children of a history which still sucks at the Devil's teats. At this writing, only England has held back before the temptations of contemporary diabolism. In the countries of the Communist ideology, all resistance of any import is linked to the totally malign capitalist succubi, and in America any man who is not reactionary in his views is open to the charge of alliance with the Red hell. Political opposition, thereby, is given an inhumane overlay which then justifies the abrogation of all normally applied customs of civilized intercourse. A political policy is equated with moral right, and opposition to it with diabolical malevolence. Once such an equation is effectively made, society becomes a congerie of plots and counterplots, and the main role of government changes from that of the arbiter to that of the scourge of God.

The results of this process are no different now from what

they ever were, except sometimes in the degree of cruelty
inflicted, and not always even in that department. Normally the
actions and deeds of a man were all that society felt comfortable in judging. The secret intent of an action was left to
the ministers, priests, and rabbis to deal with. When diabolism
rises, however, actions are the least important manifests of the
true nature of a man. The Devil, as Reverend Hale said, is a
wily one, and, until an hour before he fell, even God thought
him beautiful in Heaven.

The analogy, however, seems to falter when one considers
that, while there were no witches then, there are Communists
and capitalists now, and in each camp there is certain proof
that spies of each side are at work undermining the other. But
this is a snobbish objection and not at all warranted by the
facts. I have no doubt that people *were* communing with, and
even worshiping, the Devil in Salem, and if the whole truth
could be known in this case, as it is in others, we should discover a regular and conventionalized propitiation of the dark
spirit. One certain evidence of this is the confession of Tituba,
the slave of Reverend Parris, and another is the behavior of the
children who were known to have indulged in sorceries with her.

There are accounts of similar *klatches* in Europe, where the
daughters of the towns would assemble at night and, sometimes
with fetishes, sometimes with a selected young man, give themselves to love, with some bastardly results. The Church, sharp-
eyed as it must be when gods long dead are brought to life,
condemned these orgies as witchcraft and interpreted them,
rightly, as a resurgence of the Dionysiac forces it had crushed
long before. Sex, sin, and the Devil were early linked, and so
they continued to be in Salem, and are today. From all accounts
there are no more puritanical mores in the world than those
enforced by the Communists in Russia, where women's fashions,
for instance, are as prudent and all-covering as any American
Baptist would desire. The divorce laws lay a tremendous responsibility on the father for the care of his children. Even the

laxity of divorce regulations in the early years of the revolution was undoubtedly a revulsion from the nineteenth-century Victorian immobility of marriage and the consequent hypocrisy that developed from it. If for no other reasons, a state so powerful, so jealous of the uniformity of its citizens, cannot long tolerate the atomization of the family. And yet, in American eyes at least, there remains the conviction that the Russian attitude toward women is lascivious. It is the Devil working again, just as he is working within the Slav who is shocked at the very idea of a woman's disrobing herself in a burlesque show. Our opposites are always robed in sexual sin, and it is from this unconscious conviction that demonology gains both its attractive sensuality and its capacity to infuriate and frighten.

Coming into Salem now, Reverend Hale conceives of himself much as a young doctor on his first call. His painfully acquired armory of symptoms, catchwords, and diagnostic procedures are now to be put to use at last. The road from Beverly is unusually busy this morning, and he has passed a hundred rumors that make him smile at the ignorance of the yeomanry in this most precise science. He feels himself allied with the best minds of Europe—kings, philosophers, scientists, and ecclesiasts of all churches. His goal is light, goodness and its preservation, and he knows the exaltation of the blessed whose intelligence, sharpened by minute examinations of enormous tracts, is finally called upon to face what may be a bloody fight with the Fiend himself.

He appears loaded down with half a dozen heavy books.

HALE: Pray you, someone take these!

PARRIS, *delighted:* Mr. Hale! Oh! it's good to see you again! *Taking some books:* My, they're heavy!

HALE, *setting down his books:* They must be; they are weighted with authority.

PARRIS, *a little scared:* Well, you do come prepared!

HALE: We shall need hard study if it comes to tracking down the Old Boy. *Noticing Rebecca:* You cannot be Rebecca Nurse?

REBECCA: I am, sir. Do you know me?

HALE: It's strange how I knew you, but I suppose you look as such a good soul should. We have all heard of your great charities in Beverly.

PARRIS: Do you know this gentleman? Mr. Thomas Putnam. And his good wife Ann.

HALE: Putnam! I had not expected such distinguished company, sir.

PUTNAM, *pleased:* It does not seem to help us today, Mr. Hale. We look to you to come to our house and save our child.

HALE: Your child ails too?

MRS. PUTNAM: Her soul, her soul seems flown away. She sleeps and yet she walks . . .

PUTNAM: She cannot eat.

HALE: Cannot eat! *Thinks on it. Then, to Proctor and Giles Corey:* Do you men have afflicted children?

PARRIS: No, no, these are farmers. John Proctor—

GILES COREY: He don't believe in witches.

PROCTOR, *to Hale:* I never spoke on witches one way or the other. Will you come, Giles?

GILES: No—no, John, I think not. I have some few queer questions of my own to ask this fellow.

PROCTOR: I've heard you to be a sensible man, Mr. Hale. I hope you'll leave some of it in Salem.

Proctor goes. Hale stands embarrassed for an instant.

PARRIS, *quickly:* Will you look at my daughter, sir? *Leads Hale to the bed.* She has tried to leap out the window; we discovered her this morning on the highroad, waving her arms as though she'd fly.

HALE, *narrowing his eyes:* Tries to fly.

PUTNAM: She cannot bear to hear the Lord's name, Mr. Hale; that's a sure sign of witchcraft afloat.

HALE, *holding up his hands:* No, no. Now let me instruct you. We cannot look to superstition in this. The Devil is precise; the marks of his presence are definite as stone, and I must tell you all that I shall not proceed unless you are prepared to believe me if I should find no bruise of hell upon her.

PARRIS: It is agreed, sir—it is agreed—we will abide by your judgment.

HALE: Good then. *He goes to the bed, looks down at Betty. To Parris:* Now, sir, what were your first warning of this strangeness?

PARRIS: Why, sir—I discovered her—*indicating Abigail*—and my niece and ten or twelve of the other girls, dancing in the forest last night.

HALE, *surprised:* You permit dancing?

PARRIS: No, no, it were secret—

MRS. PUTNAM, *unable to wait:* Mr. Parris's slave has knowledge of conjurin', sir.

PARRIS, *to Mrs. Putnam:* We cannot be sure of that, Goody Ann—

MRS. PUTNAM, *frightened, very softly:* I know it, sir. I sent my child—she should learn from Tituba who murdered her sisters.

REBECCA, *horrified:* Goody Ann! You sent a child to conjure up the dead?

MRS. PUTNAM: Let God blame me, not you, not you, Rebecca! I'll not have you judging me any more! *To Hale:* Is it a natural work to lose seven children before they live a day?

PARRIS: Sssh!

Rebecca, with great pain, turns her face away. There is a pause.

HALE: Seven dead in childbirth.

MRS. PUTNAM, *softly:* Aye. *Her voice breaks; she looks up at him. Silence. Hale is impressed. Parris looks to him. He goes to his books, opens one, turns pages, then reads. All wait, avidly.*

PARRIS, *hushed:* What book is that?

MRS. PUTNAM: What's there, sir?

HALE, *with a tasty love of intellectual pursuit:* Here is all the invisible world, caught, defined, and calculated. In these books the Devil stands stripped of all his brute disguises. Here are all your familiar spirits—your incubi and succubi; your witches that go by land, by air, and by sea; your wizards of the night and of the day. Have no fear now—we shall find him out if he has come among us, and I mean to crush him utterly if he has shown his face! *He starts for the bed.*

REBECCA: Will it hurt the child, sir?

HALE: I cannot tell. If she is truly in the Devil's grip we may have to rip and tear to get her free.

REBECCA: I think I'll go, then. I am too old for this. *She rises.*

PARRIS, *striving for conviction:* Why, Rebecca, we may open up the boil of all our troubles today!

REBECCA: Let us hope for that. I go to God for you, sir.

PARRIS, *with trepidation—and resentment:* I hope you do not mean we go to Satan here! *Slight pause.*

REBECCA: I wish I knew. *She goes out; they feel resentful of her note of moral superiority.*

PUTNAM, *abruptly:* Come, Mr. Hale, let's get on. Sit you here.

GILES: Mr. Hale, I have always wanted to ask a learned man—what signifies the readin' of strange books?

HALE: What books?

GILES: I cannot tell; she hides them.

HALE: Who does this?

GILES: Martha, my wife. I have waked at night many a time and found her in a corner, readin' of a book. Now what do you make of that?

HALE: Why, that's not necessarily—

GILES: It discomfits me! Last night—mark this—I tried and tried and could not say my prayers. And then she close her book and walks out of the house, and suddenly—mark this—I could pray again!

Old Giles must be spoken for, if only because his fate was to be so remarkable and so different from that of all the others. He was in his early eighties at this time, and was the most comical hero in the history. No man has ever been blamed for so much. If a cow was missed, the first thought was to look for her around Corey's house; a fire blazing up at night brought suspicion of arson to his door. He didn't give a hoot for public opinion, and only in his last years—after he had married Martha—did he bother much with the church. That she stopped his prayer is very probable, but he forgot to say that he'd only recently learned any prayers and it didn't take much to make him stumble over them. He was a crank and a nuisance, but withal a deeply innocent and brave man. In court once, he was asked if it were true that he had been frightened by the strange behavior of a hog and had then said he knew it to be the Devil in an animal's shape. "What frighted you?" he was asked. He forgot everything but the word "frighted," and instantly replied, "I do not know that I ever spoke that word in my life."

HALE: Ah! The stoppage of prayer—that is strange. I'll speak further on that with you.

GILES: I'm not sayin' she's touched the Devil, now, but I'd admire to know what books she reads and why she hides them. She'll not answer me, y' see.

HALE: Aye, we'll discuss it. *To all:* Now mark me, if the Devil is in her you will witness some frightful wonders in this room, so please to keep your wits about you. Mr. Putnam, stand close in case she flies. Now, Betty, dear, will you sit up? *Putnam comes in closer, ready-handed. Hale sits Betty up, but she hangs limp in his hands.* Hmmm. *He observes her carefully. The others watch breathlessly.* Can you hear me? I am John Hale, minister of Beverly. I have come to help you, dear. Do you remember my two little girls in Beverly? *She does not stir in his hands.*

PARRIS, *in fright:* How can it be the Devil? Why would he choose my house to strike? We have all manner of licentious people in the village!

HALE: What victory would the Devil have to win a soul already bad? It is the best the Devil wants, and who is better than the minister?

GILES: That's deep, Mr. Parris, deep, deep!

PARRIS, *with resolution now:* Betty! Answer Mr. Hale! Betty!

HALE: Does someone afflict you, child? It need not be a woman, mind you, or a man. Perhaps some bird invisible to others comes to you—perhaps a pig, a mouse, or any beast at all. Is there some figure bids you fly? *The child remains limp in his hands. In silence he lays her back on the pillow. Now, holding out his hands toward her, he intones:* In nomine Domini Sabaoth sui filiique ite ad infernos. *She does not stir. He turns to Abigail, his eyes narrowing.* Abigail, what sort of dancing were you doing with her in the forest?

ABIGAIL: Why—common dancing is all.

PARRIS: I think I ought to say that I—I saw a kettle in the grass where they were dancing.

ABIGAIL: That were only soup.

HALE: What sort of soup were in this kettle, Abigail?

ABIGAIL: Why, it were beans—and lentils, I think, and—

HALE: Mr. Parris, you did not notice, did you, any living thing in the kettle? A mouse, perhaps, a spider, a frog—?

PARRIS, *fearfully:* I—do believe there were some movement—in the soup.

ABIGAIL: That jumped in, we never put it in!

HALE, *quickly:* What jumped in?

ABIGAIL: Why, a very little frog jumped—

PARRIS: A frog, Abby!

HALE, *grasping Abigail:* Abigail, it may be your cousin is dying. Did you call the Devil last night?

ABIGAIL: I never called him! Tituba, Tituba . . .

PARRIS, *blanched:* She called the Devil?

HALE: I should like to speak with Tituba.

PARRIS: Goody Ann, will you bring her up? *Mrs. Putnam exits.*

HALE: How did she call him?

ABIGAIL: I know not—she spoke Barbados.

HALE: Did you feel any strangeness when she called him? A sudden cold wind, perhaps? A trembling below the ground?

ABIGAIL: I didn't see no Devil! *Shaking Betty:* Betty, wake up. Betty! Betty!

HALE: You cannot evade me, Abigail. Did your cousin drink any of the brew in that kettle?

ABIGAIL: She never drank it!

HALE: Did you drink it?

ABIGAIL: No, sir!

HALE: Did Tituba ask you to drink it?

ABIGAIL: She tried, but I refused.

HALE: Why are you concealing? Have you sold yourself to Lucifer?

ABIGAIL: I never sold myself! I'm a good girl! I'm a proper girl!

Mrs. Putnam enters with Tituba, and instantly Abigail points at Tituba.

ABIGAIL: She made me do it! She made Betty do it!

TITUBA, *shocked and angry:* Abby!

ABIGAIL: She makes me drink blood!

PARRIS: Blood!!

MRS. PUTNAM: My baby's blood?

TITUBA: No, no, chicken blood. I give she chicken blood!

HALE: Woman, have you enlisted these children for the Devil?

TITUBA: No, no, sir, I don't truck with no Devil!

HALE: Why can she not wake? Are you silencing this child?

TITUBA: I love me Betty!

HALE: You have sent your spirit out upon this child, have you not? Are you gathering souls for the Devil?

ABIGAIL: She sends her spirit on me in church; she makes me laugh at prayer!

PARRIS: She have often laughed at prayer!

ABIGAIL: She comes to me every night to go and drink blood!

TITUBA: You beg *me* to conjure! She beg *me* make charm—

ABIGAIL: Don't lie! *To Hale:* She comes to me while I sleep; she's always making me dream corruptions!

TITUBA: Why you say that, Abby?

ABIGAIL: Sometimes I wake and find myself standing in the open doorway and not a stitch on my body! I always hear her laughing in my sleep. I hear her singing her Barbados songs and tempting me with—

TITUBA: Mister Reverend, I never—

HALE, *resolved now:* Tituba, I want you to wake this child.

TITUBA: I have no power on this child, sir.

HALE: You most certainly do, and you will free her from it now! When did you compact with the Devil?

TITUBA: I don't compact with no Devil!

PARRIS: You will confess yourself or I will take you out and whip you to your death, Tituba!

PUTNAM: This woman must be hanged! She must be taken and hanged!

TITUBA, *terrified, falls to her knees:* No, no, don't hang Tituba! I tell him I don't desire to work for him, sir.

PARRIS: The Devil?

HALE: Then you saw him! *Tituba weeps.* Now Tituba, I know that when we bind ourselves to Hell it is very hard to break with it. We are going to help you tear yourself free—

TITUBA, *frightened by the coming process:* Mister Reverend, I do believe somebody else be witchin' these children.

HALE: Who?

TITUBA: I don't know, sir, but the Devil got him numerous witches.

HALE: Does he! *It is a clue.* Tituba, look into my eyes. Come, look into me. *She raises her eyes to his fearfully.* You would be a good Christian woman, would you not, Tituba?

TITUBA: Aye, sir, a good Christian woman.

HALE: And you love these little children?

TITUBA: Oh, yes, sir, I don't desire to hurt little children.

HALE: And you love God, Tituba?

TITUBA: I love God with all my bein'.

HALE: Now, in God's holy name—

TITUBA: Bless Him. Bless Him. *She is rocking on her knees, sobbing in terror.*

HALE: And to His glory—

TITUBA: Eternal glory. Bless Him—bless God . . .

HALE: Open yourself, Tituba—open yourself and let God's holy light shine on you.

TITUBA: Oh, bless the Lord.

HALE: When the Devil comes to you does he ever come—with another person? *She stares up into his face.* Perhaps another person in the village? Someone you know.

PARRIS: Who came with him?

PUTNAM: Sarah Good? Did you ever see Sarah Good with him? Or Osburn?

PARRIS: Was it man or woman came with him?

TITUBA: Man or woman. Was—was woman.

PARRIS: What woman? A woman, you said. What woman?

TITUBA: It was black dark, and I—

PARRIS: You could see him, why could you not see her?

TITUBA: Well, they was always talking; they was always runnin' round and carryin' on—

PARRIS: You mean out of Salem? Salem witches?

TITUBA: I believe so, yes, sir.

Now Hale takes her hand. She is surprised.

HALE: Tituba. You must have no fear to tell us who they are, do you understand? We will protect you. The Devil can never overcome a minister. You know that, do you not?

TITUBA, *kisses Hale's hand:* Aye, sir, oh, I do.

HALE: You have confessed yourself to witchcraft, and that speaks a wish to come to Heaven's side. And we will bless you, Tituba.

TITUBA, *deeply relieved:* Oh, God bless you, Mr. Hale!

HALE, *with rising exaltation:* You are God's instrument put in our hands to discover the Devil's agents among us. You are selected, Tituba, you are chosen to help us cleanse our village. So speak utterly, Tituba, turn your back on him and face God— face God, Tituba, and God will protect you.

TITUBA, *joining with him:* Oh, God, protect Tituba!

HALE, *kindly:* Who came to you with the Devil? Two? Three? Four? How many?

Tituba pants, and begins rocking back and forth again, staring ahead.

TITUBA: There was four. There was four.

PARRIS, *pressing in on her:* Who? Who? Their names, their names!

TITUBA, *suddenly bursting out:* Oh, how many times he bid me kill you, Mr. Parris!

PARRIS: Kill me!

TITUBA, *in a fury:* He say Mr. Parris must be kill! Mr. Parris no goodly man, Mr. Parris mean man and no gentle man, and he bid me rise out of my bed and cut your throat! *They gasp.* But I tell him "No! I don't hate that man. I don't want kill that man." But he say, "You work for me, Tituba, and I make you free! I give you pretty dress to wear, and put you way high up in the air, and you gone fly back to Barbados!" And I say, "You lie, Devil, you lie!" And then he come one stormy night to me, and he say, "Look! I have *white* people belong to me." And I look—and there was Goody Good.

PARRIS: Sarah Good!

TITUBA, *rocking and weeping:* Aye, sir, and Goody Osburn.

MRS. PUTNAM: I knew it! Goody Osburn were midwife to me three times. I begged you, Thomas, did I not? I begged him not to call Osburn because I feared her. My babies always shriveled in her hands!

HALE: Take courage, you must give us all their names. How can you bear to see this child suffering? Look at her, Tituba. *He is indicating Betty on the bed.* Look at her God-given innocence; her soul is so tender; we must protect her, Tituba; the Devil is out and preying on her like a beast upon the flesh of the pure lamb. God will bless you for your help.

Abigail rises, staring as though inspired, and cries out.

ABIGAIL: I want to open myself! *They turn to her, startled. She is enraptured, as though in a pearly light.* I want the light of God, I want the sweet love of Jesus! I danced for the Devil; I saw him; I wrote in his book; I go back to Jesus; I kiss His hand. I saw Sarah Good with the Devil! I saw Goody Osburn with the Devil! I saw Bridget Bishop with the Devil!

As she is speaking, Betty is rising from the bed, a fever in her eyes, and picks up the chant.

BETTY, *staring too:* I saw George Jacobs with the Devil! I saw Goody Howe with the Devil!

PARRIS: She speaks! *He rushes to embrace Betty.* She speaks!

HALE: Glory to God! It is broken, they are free!

BETTY, *calling out hysterically and with great relief:* I saw Martha Bellows with the Devil!

ABIGAIL: I saw Goody Sibber with the Devil! *It is rising to a great glee.*

PUTNAM: The marshal, I'll call the marshal!

Parris is shouting a prayer of thanksgiving.

BETTY: I saw Alice Barrow with the Devil!

The curtain begins to fall.

HALE, *as Putnam goes out:* Let the marshal bring irons!

ABIGAIL: I saw Goody Hawkins with the Devil!

BETTY: I saw Goody Bibber with the Devil!

ABIGAIL: I saw Goody Booth with the Devil!

On their ecstatic cries

THE CURTAIN FALLS

ACT TWO

The common room of Proctor's house, eight days later.

At the right is a door opening on the fields outside. A fireplace is at the left, and behind it a stairway leading upstairs. It is the low, dark, and rather long living room of the time. As the curtain rises, the room is empty. From above, Elizabeth is heard softly singing to the children. Presently the door opens and John Proctor enters, carrying his gun. He glances about the room as he comes toward the fireplace, then halts for an instant as he hears her singing. He continues on to the fireplace, leans the gun against the wall as he swings a pot out of the fire and smells it. Then he lifts out the ladle and tastes. He is not quite pleased. He reaches to a cupboard, takes a pinch of salt, and drops it into the pot. As he is tasting again, her footsteps are heard on the stair. He swings the pot into the fireplace and goes to a basin and washes his hands and face. Elizabeth enters.

ELIZABETH: What keeps you so late? It's almost dark.

PROCTOR: I were planting far out to the forest edge.

ELIZABETH: Oh, you're done then.

PROCTOR: Aye, the farm is seeded. The boys asleep?

ELIZABETH: They will be soon. *And she goes to the fireplace, proceeds to ladle up stew in a dish.*

PROCTOR: Pray now for a fair summer.

ELIZABETH: Aye.

PROCTOR: Are you well today?

ELIZABETH: I am. *She brings the plate to the table, and, indicating the food:* It is a rabbit.

PROCTOR, *going to the table:* Oh, is it! In Jonathan's trap?

ELIZABETH: No, she walked into the house this afternoon; I found her sittin' in the corner like she come to visit.

PROCTOR: Oh, that's a good sign walkin' in.

ELIZABETH: Pray God. It hurt my heart to strip her, poor rabbit. *She sits and watches him taste it.*

PROCTOR: It's well seasoned.

ELIZABETH, *blushing with pleasure:* I took great care. She's tender?

PROCTOR: Aye. *He eats. She watches him.* I think we'll see green fields soon. It's warm as blood beneath the clods.

ELIZABETH: That's well.

Proctor eats, then looks up.

PROCTOR: If the crop is good I'll buy George Jacob's heifer. How would that please you?

ELIZABETH: Aye, it would.

PROCTOR, *with a grin:* I mean to please you, Elizabeth.

ELIZABETH—*it is hard to say:* I know it, John.

He gets up, goes to her, kisses her. She receives it. With a certain disappointment, he returns to the table.

PROCTOR, *as gently as he can:* Cider?

ELIZABETH, *with a sense of reprimanding herself for having forgot:* Aye! *She gets up and goes and pours a glass for him. He now arches his back.*

PROCTOR: This farm's a continent when you go foot by foot droppin' seeds in it.

ELIZABETH, *coming with the cider:* It must be.

PROCTOR, *drinks a long draught, then, putting the glass down:* You ought to bring some flowers in the house.

ELIZABETH: Oh! I forgot! I will tomorrow.

PROCTOR: It's winter in here yet. On Sunday let you come with me, and we'll walk the farm together; I never see such a load of flowers on the earth. *With good feeling he goes and looks up at the sky through the open doorway.* Lilacs have a purple smell. Lilac is the smell of nightfall, I think. Massachusetts is a beauty in the spring!

ELIZABETH: Aye, it is.

There is a pause. She is watching him from the table as he stands there absorbing the night. It is as though she would speak but cannot. Instead, now, she takes up his plate and glass and fork and goes with them to the basin. Her back is turned to him. He turns to her and watches her. A sense of their separation rises.

PROCTOR: I think you're sad again. Are you?

ELIZABETH—*she doesn't want friction, and yet she must:* You come so late I thought you'd gone to Salem this afternoon.

PROCTOR: Why? I have no business in Salem.

ELIZABETH: You did speak of going, earlier this week.

PROCTOR—*he knows what she means:* I thought better of it since.

ELIZABETH: Mary Warren's there today.

PROCTOR: Why'd you let her? You heard me forbid her go to Salem any more!

ELIZABETH: I couldn't stop her.

PROCTOR, *holding back a full condemnation of her:* It is a fault, it is a fault, Elizabeth—you're the mistress here, not Mary Warren.

ELIZABETH: She frightened all my strength away.

PROCTOR: How may that mouse frighten you, Elizabeth? You—

ELIZABETH: It is a mouse no more. I forbid her go, and she raises up her chin like the daughter of a prince and says to me, "I must go to Salem, Goody Proctor; I am an official of the court!"

PROCTOR: Court! What court?

ELIZABETH: Aye, it is a proper court they have now. They've sent four judges out of Boston, she says, weighty magistrates of the General Court, and at the head sits the Deputy Governor of the Province.

PROCTOR, *astonished:* Why, she's mad.

ELIZABETH: I would to God she were. There be fourteen people in the jail now, she says. *Proctor simply looks at her, unable to grasp it.* And they'll be tried, and the court have power to hang them too, she says.

PROCTOR, *scoffing, but without conviction:* Ah, they'd never hang—

ELIZABETH: The Deputy Governor promise hangin' if they'll not confess, John. The town's gone wild, I think. She speak of Abigail, and I thought she were a saint, to hear her. Abigail brings the other girls into the court, and where she walks the crowd will part like the sea for Israel. And folks are brought before them, and if they scream and howl and fall to the floor—the person's clapped in the jail for bewitchin' them.

PROCTOR, *wide-eyed:* Oh, it is a black mischief.

ELIZABETH: I think you must go to Salem, John. *He turns to her.* I think so. You must tell them it is a fraud.

PROCTOR, *thinking beyond this:* Aye, it is, it is surely.

ELIZABETH: Let you go to Ezekiel Cheever—he knows you well. And tell him what she said to you last week in her uncle's house. She said it had naught to do with witchcraft, did she not?

PROCTOR, *in thought:* Aye, she did, she did. *Now, a pause.*

ELIZABETH, *quietly, fearing to anger him by prodding:* God forbid you keep that from the court, John. I think they must be told.

PROCTOR, *quietly, struggling with his thought:* Aye, they must, they must. It is a wonder they do believe her.

ELIZABETH: I would go to Salem now, John—let you go tonight.

PROCTOR: I'll think on it.

ELIZABETH, *with her courage now:* You cannot keep it, John.

PROCTOR, *angering:* I know I cannot keep it. I say I will think on it!

ELIZABETH, *hurt, and very coldly:* Good, then, let you think on it. *She stands and starts to walk out of the room.*

PROCTOR: I am only wondering how I may prove what she told me, Elizabeth. If the girl's a saint now, I think it is not easy to prove she's fraud, and the town gone so silly. She told it to me in a room alone—I have no proof for it.

ELIZABETH: You were alone with her?

PROCTOR, *stubbornly:* For a moment alone, aye.

ELIZABETH: Why, then, it is not as you told me.

PROCTOR, *his anger rising:* For a moment, I say. The others come in soon after.

ELIZABETH, *quietly—she has suddenly lost all faith in him:* Do as you wish, then. *She starts to turn.*

PROCTOR: Woman. *She turns to him.* I'll not have your suspicion any more.

ELIZABETH, *a little loftily: I* have no—

PROCTOR: I'll not have it!

ELIZABETH: Then let you not earn it.

PROCTOR, *with a violent undertone:* You doubt me yet?

ELIZABETH, *with a smile, to keep her dignity:* John, if it were not Abigail that you must go to hurt, would you falter now? I think not.

PROCTOR: Now look you—

ELIZABETH: I see what I see, John.

PROCTOR, *with solemn warning:* You will not judge me more, Elizabeth. I have good reason to think before I charge fraud on Abigail, and I will think on it. Let you look to your own improvement before you go to judge your husband any more. I have forgot Abigail, and—

ELIZABETH: And I.

PROCTOR: Spare me! You forget nothin' and forgive nothin'. Learn charity, woman. I have gone tiptoe in this house all seven month since she is gone. I have not moved from there to there without I think to please you, and still an everlasting funeral marches round your heart. I cannot speak but I am doubted, every moment judged for lies, as though I come into a court when I come into this house!

ELIZABETH: John, you are not open with me. You saw her with a crowd, you said. Now you—

PROCTOR: I'll plead my honesty no more, Elizabeth.

ELIZABETH—*now she would justify herself:* John, I am only—

PROCTOR: No more! I should have roared you down when first you told me your suspicion. But I wilted, and, like a Christian, I confessed. Confessed! Some dream I had must have mistaken you for God that day. But you're not, you're not, and let you remember it! Let you look sometimes for the goodness in me, and judge me not.

ELIZABETH: I do not judge you. The magistrate sits in your heart that judges you. I never thought you but a good man, John —*with a smile*—only somewhat bewildered.

PROCTOR, *laughing bitterly:* Oh, Elizabeth, your justice would freeze beer! *He turns suddenly toward a sound outside. He starts for the door as Mary Warren enters. As soon as he sees her, he goes directly to her and grabs her by her cloak, furious.* How do you go to Salem when I forbid it? Do you mock me? *Shaking her.* I'll whip you if you dare leave this house again!

Strangely, she doesn't resist him, but hangs limply by his grip.

MARY WARREN: I am sick, I am sick, Mr. Proctor. Pray, pray, hurt me not. *Her strangeness throws him off, and her evident pallor and weakness. He frees her.* My insides are all shuddery; I am in the proceedings all day, sir.

PROCTOR, *with draining anger—his curiosity is draining it:* And what of these proceedings here? When will you proceed to keep this house, as you are paid nine pound a year to do—and my wife not wholly well?

*As though to compensate, Mary Warren goes to Elizabeth with
a small rag doll.*

MARY WARREN: I made a gift for you today, Goody Proctor. I
had to sit long hours in a chair, and passed the time with sewing.

ELIZABETH, *perplexed, looking at the doll:* Why, thank you,
it's a fair poppet.

MARY WARREN, *with a trembling, decayed voice:* We must all
love each other now, Goody Proctor.

ELIZABETH, *amazed at her strangeness:* Aye, indeed we must.

MARY WARREN, *glancing at the room:* I'll get up early in the
morning and clean the house. I must sleep now. *She turns and
starts off.*

PROCTOR: Mary. *She halts.* Is it true? There be fourteen women
arrested?

MARY WARREN: No, sir. There be thirty-nine now— *She suddenly breaks off and sobs and sits down, exhausted.*

ELIZABETH: Why, she's weepin'! What ails you, child?

MARY WARREN: Goody Osburn—will hang!

There is a shocked pause, while she sobs.

PROCTOR: Hang! *He calls into her face.* Hang, y'say?

MARY WARREN, *through her weeping:* Aye.

PROCTOR: The Deputy Governor will permit it?

MARY WARREN: He sentenced her. He must. *To ameliorate it:*
But not Sarah Good. For Sarah Good confessed, y'see.

PROCTOR: Confessed! To what?

MARY WARREN: That she—*in horror at the memory*—she sometimes made a compact with Lucifer, and wrote her name in his

black book—with her blood—and bound herself to torment
Christians till God's thrown down—and we all must worship
Hell forevermore.

Pause.

PROCTOR: But—surely you know what a jabberer she is. Did
you tell them that?

MARY WARREN: Mr. Proctor, in open court she near to choked
us all to death.

PROCTOR: How, choked you?

MARY WARREN: She sent her spirit out.

ELIZABETH: Oh, Mary, Mary, surely you—

MARY WARREN, *with an indignant edge:* She tried to kill me
many times, Goody Proctor!

ELIZABETH: Why, I never heard you mention that before.

MARY WARREN: I never knew it before. I never knew anything
before. When she come into the court I say to myself, I must
not accuse this woman, for she sleep in ditches, and so very old
and poor. But then—then she sit there, denying and denying,
and I feel a misty coldness climbin' up my back, and the skin
on my skull begin to creep, and I feel a clamp around my neck
and I cannot breathe air; and then—*entranced*—I hear a voice,
a screamin' voice, and it were my voice—and all at once I remembered everything she done to me!

PROCTOR: Why? What did she do to you?

MARY WARREN, *like one awakened to a marvelous secret insight:* So many time, Mr. Proctor, she come to this very door,
beggin' bread and a cup of cider—and mark this: whenever I
turned her away empty, she *mumbled.*

ELIZABETH: Mumbled! She may mumble if she's hungry.

MARY WARREN: But *what* does she mumble? You must remember, Goody Proctor. Last month—a Monday, I think—she walked away, and I thought my guts would burst for two days after. Do you remember it?

ELIZABETH: Why—I do, I think, but—

MARY WARREN: And so I told that to Judge Hathorne, and he asks her so. "Sarah Good," says he, "what curse do you mumble that this girl must fall sick after turning you away?" And then she replies—*mimicking an old crone*—"Why, your excellence, no curse at all. I only say my commandments; I hope I may say my commandments," says she!

ELIZABETH: And that's an upright answer.

MARY WARREN: Aye, but then Judge Hathorne say, "Recite for us your commandments!"—*leaning avidly toward them*—and of all the ten she could not say a single one. She never knew no commandments, and they had her in a flat lie!

PROCTOR: And so condemned her?

MARY WARREN, *now a little strained, seeing his stubborn doubt:* Why, they must when she condemned herself.

PROCTOR: But the proof, the proof!

MARY WARREN, *with greater impatience with him:* I told you the proof. It's hard proof, hard as rock, the judges said.

PROCTOR, *pauses an instant, then:* You will not go to court again, Mary Warren.

MARY WARREN: I must tell you, sir, I will be gone every day now. I am amazed you do not see what weighty work we do.

PROCTOR: What work you do! It's strange work for a Christian girl to hang old women!

MARY WARREN: But, Mr. Proctor, they will not hang them if

they confess. Sarah Good will only sit in jail some time—*recalling*—and here's a wonder for you; think on this. Goody Good is pregnant!

ELIZABETH: Pregnant! Are they mad? The woman's near to sixty!

MARY WARREN: They had Doctor Griggs examine her, and she's full to the brim. And smokin' a pipe all these years, and no husband either! But she's safe, thank God, for they'll not hurt the innocent child. But be that not a marvel? You must see it, sir, it's God's work we do. So I'll be gone every day for some time. I'm—I am an official of the court, they say, and I— *She has been edging toward offstage.*

PROCTOR: I'll official you! *He strides to the mantel, takes down the whip hanging there.*

MARY WARREN, *terrified, but coming erect, striving for her authority:* I'll not stand whipping any more!

ELIZABETH, *hurriedly, as Proctor approaches:* Mary, promise now you'll stay at home—

MARY WARREN, *backing from him, but keeping her erect posture, striving, striving for her way:* The Devil's loose in Salem, Mr. Proctor; we must discover where he's hiding!

PROCTOR: I'll whip the Devil out of you! *With whip raised he reaches out for her, and she streaks away and yells.*

MARY WARREN, *pointing at Elizabeth:* I saved her life today!

Silence. His whip comes down.

ELIZABETH, *softly:* I am accused?

MARY WARREN, *quaking:* Somewhat mentioned. But I said I never see no sign you ever sent your spirit out to hurt no one, and seeing I do live so closely with you, they dismissed it.

ELIZABETH: Who accused me?

MARY WARREN: I am bound by law, I cannot tell it. *To Proctor:* I only hope you'll not be so sarcastical no more. Four judges and the King's deputy sat to dinner with us but an hour ago. I—I would have you speak civilly to me, from this out.

PROCTOR, *in horror, muttering in disgust at her:* Go to bed.

MARY WARREN, *with a stamp of her foot:* I'll not be ordered to bed no more, Mr. Proctor! I am eighteen and a woman, however single!

PROCTOR: Do you wish to sit up? Then sit up.

MARY WARREN: I wish to go to bed!

PROCTOR, *in anger:* Good night, then!

MARY WARREN: Good night. *Dissatisfied, uncertain of herself, she goes out. Wide-eyed, both, Proctor and Elizabeth stand staring.*

ELIZABETH, *quietly:* Oh, the noose, the noose is up!

PROCTOR: There'll be no noose.

ELIZABETH: She wants me dead. I knew all week it would come to this!

PROCTOR, *without conviction:* They dismissed it. You heard her say—

ELIZABETH: And what of tomorrow? She will cry me out until they take me!

PROCTOR: Sit you down.

ELIZABETH: She wants me dead, John, you know it!

PROCTOR: I say sit down! *She sits, trembling. He speaks quietly, trying to keep his wits.* Now we must be wise, Elizabeth.

ELIZABETH, *with sarcasm, and a sense of being lost:* Oh, indeed, indeed!

PROCTOR: Fear nothing. I'll find Ezekiel Cheever. I'll tell him she said it were all sport.

ELIZABETH: John, with so many in the jail, more than Cheever's help is needed now, I think. Would you favor me with this? Go to Abigail.

PROCTOR, *his soul hardening as he senses* . . . : What have I to say to Abigail?

ELIZABETH, *delicately:* John—grant me this. You have a faulty understanding of young girls. There is a promise made in any bed—

PROCTOR, *striving against his anger:* What promise!

ELIZABETH: Spoke or silent, a promise is surely made. And she may dote on it now—I am sure she does—and thinks to kill me, then to take my place.

Proctor's anger is rising; he cannot speak.

ELIZABETH: It is her dearest hope, John, I know it. There be a thousand names; why does she call mine? There be a certain danger in calling such a name—I am no Goody Good that sleeps in ditches, nor Osburn, drunk and half-witted. She'd dare not call out such a farmer's wife but there be monstrous profit in it. She thinks to take my place, John.

PROCTOR: She cannot think it! *He knows it is true.*

ELIZABETH, *"reasonably":* John, have you ever shown her somewhat of contempt? She cannot pass you in the church but you will blush—

PROCTOR: I may blush for my sin.

ELIZABETH: I think she sees another meaning in that blush.

PROCTOR: And what see you? What see you, Elizabeth?

ELIZABETH, *"conceding":* I think you be somewhat ashamed, for I am there, and she so close.

PROCTOR: When will you know me, woman? Were I stone I would have cracked for shame this seven month!

ELIZABETH: Then go and tell her she's a whore. Whatever promise she may sense—break it, John, break it.

PROCTOR, *between his teeth:* Good, then. I'll go. *He starts for his rifle.*

ELIZABETH, *trembling, fearfully:* Oh, how unwillingly!

PROCTOR, *turning on her, rifle in hand:* I will curse her hotter than the oldest cinder in hell. But pray, begrudge me not my anger!

ELIZABETH: Your anger! I only ask you—

PROCTOR: Woman, am I so base? Do you truly think me base?

ELIZABETH: I never called you base.

PROCTOR: Then how do you charge me with such a promise? The promise that a stallion gives a mare I gave that girl!

ELIZABETH: Then why do you anger with me when I bid you break it?

PROCTOR: Because it speaks deceit, and I am honest! But I'll plead no more! I see now your spirit twists around the single error of my life, and I will never tear it free!

ELIZABETH, *crying out:* You'll tear it free—when you come to know that I will be your only wife, or no wife at all! She has an arrow in you yet, John Proctor, and you know it well!

Quite suddenly, as though from the air, a figure appears in the doorway. They start slightly. It is Mr. Hale. He is different now —drawn a little, and there is a quality of deference, even of guilt, about his manner now.

HALE: Good evening.

PROCTOR, *still in his shock:* Why, Mr. Hale! Good evening to you, sir. Come in, come in.

HALE, *to Elizabeth:* I hope I do not startle you.

ELIZABETH: No, no, it's only that I heard no horse—

HALE: You are Goodwife Proctor.

PROCTOR: Aye; Elizabeth.

HALE, *nods, then:* I hope you're not off to bed yet.

PROCTOR, *setting down his gun:* No, no. *Hale comes further into the room. And Proctor, to explain his nervousness:* We are not used to visitors after dark, but you're welcome here. Will you sit you down, sir?

HALE: I will. *He sits.* Let you sit, Goodwife Proctor.

She does, never letting him out of her sight. There is a pause as Hale looks about the room.

PROCTOR, *to break the silence:* Will you drink cider, Mr. Hale?

HALE: No, it rebels my stomach; I have some further traveling yet tonight. Sit you down, sir. *Proctor sits.* I will not keep you long, but I have some business with you.

PROCTOR: Business of the court?

HALE: No—no, I come of my own, without the court's authority. Hear me. *He wets his lips.* I know not if you are aware, but your wife's name is—mentioned in the court.

PROCTOR: We know it, sir. Our Mary Warren told us. We are entirely amazed.

HALE: I am a stranger here, as you know. And in my ignorance I find it hard to draw a clear opinion of them that come accused before the court. And so this afternoon, and now tonight, I go from house to house—I come now from Rebecca Nurse's house and—

ELIZABETH, *shocked:* Rebecca's charged!

HALE: God forbid such a one be charged. She is, however—mentioned somewhat.

ELIZABETH, *with an attempt at a laugh:* You will never believe, I hope, that Rebecca trafficked with the Devil.

HALE: Woman, it is possible.

PROCTOR, *taken aback:* Surely you cannot think so.

HALE: This is a strange time, Mister. No man may longer doubt the powers of the dark are gathered in monstrous attack upon this village. There is too much evidence now to deny it. You will agree, sir?

PROCTOR, *evading:* I—have no knowledge in that line. But it's hard to think so pious a woman be secretly a Devil's bitch after seventy year of such good prayer.

HALE: Aye. But the Devil is a wily one, you cannot deny it. However, she is far from accused, and I know she will not be. *Pause.* I thought, sir, to put some questions as to the Christian character of this house, if you'll permit me.

PROCTOR, *coldly, resentful:* Why, we—have no fear of questions, sir.

HALE: Good, then. *He makes himself more comfortable.* In the book of record that Mr. Parris keeps, I note that you are rarely in the church on Sabbath Day.

PROCTOR: No, sir, you are mistaken.

HALE: Twenty-six time in seventeen month, sir. I must call that rare. Will you tell me why you are so absent?

PROCTOR: Mr. Hale, I never knew I must account to that man

for I come to church or stay at home. My wife were sick this winter.

HALE: So I am told. But you, Mister, why could you not come alone?

PROCTOR: I surely did come when I could, and when I could not I prayed in this house.

HALE: Mr. Proctor, your house is not a church; your theology must tell you that.

PROCTOR: It does, sir, it does; and it tells me that a minister may pray to God without he have golden candlesticks upon the altar.

HALE: What golden candlesticks?

PROCTOR: Since we built the church there were pewter candlesticks upon the altar; Francis Nurse made them, y'know, and a sweeter hand never touched the metal. But Parris came, and for twenty week he preach nothin' but golden candlesticks until he had them. I labor the earth from dawn of day to blink of night, and I tell you true, when I look to heaven and see my money glaring at his elbows—it hurt my prayer, sir, it hurt my prayer. I think, sometimes, the man dreams cathedrals, not clapboard meetin' houses.

HALE, *thinks, then:* And yet, Mister, a Christian on Sabbath Day must be in church. *Pause.* Tell me—you have three children?

PROCTOR: Aye. Boys.

HALE: How comes it that only two are baptized?

PROCTOR, *starts to speak, then stops, then, as though unable to restrain this:* I like it not that Mr. Parris should lay his hand upon my baby. I see no light of God in that man. I'll not conceal it.

HALE: I must say it, Mr. Proctor; that is not for you to decide. The man's ordained, therefore the light of God is in him.

PROCTOR, *flushed with resentment but trying to smile:* What's your suspicion, Mr. Hale?

HALE: No, no, I have no—

PROCTOR: I nailed the roof upon the church, I hung the door—

HALE: Oh, did you! That's a good sign, then.

PROCTOR: It may be I have been too quick to bring the man to book, but you cannot think we ever desired the destruction of religion. I think that's in your mind, is it not?

HALE, *not altogether giving way:* I—have—there is a softness in your record, sir, a softness.

ELIZABETH: I think, maybe, we have been too hard with Mr. Parris. I think so. But sure we never loved the Devil here.

HALE, *nods, deliberating this. Then, with the voice of one administering a secret test:* Do you know your Commandments, Elizabeth?

ELIZABETH, *without hesitation, even eagerly:* I surely do. There be no mark of blame upon my life, Mr. Hale. I am a covenanted Christian woman.

HALE: And you, Mister?

PROCTOR, *a trifle unsteadily:* I—am sure I do, sir.

HALE, *glances at her open face, then at John, then:* Let you repeat them, if you will.

PROCTOR: The Commandments.

HALE: Aye.

PROCTOR, *looking off, beginning to sweat:* Thou shalt not kill.

HALE: Aye.

PROCTOR, *counting on his fingers:* Thou shalt not steal. Thou shalt not covet thy neighbor's goods, nor make unto thee any graven image. Thou shalt not take the name of the Lord in vain; thou shalt have no other gods before me. *With some hesitation:* Thou shalt remember the Sabbath Day and keep it holy. *Pause. Then:* Thou shalt honor thy father and mother. Thou shalt not bear false witness. *He is stuck. He counts back on his fingers, knowing one is missing.* Thou shalt not make unto thee any graven image.

HALE: You have said that twice, sir.

PROCTOR, *lost:* Aye. *He is flailing for it.*

ELIZABETH, *delicately:* Adultery, John.

PROCTOR, *as though a secret arrow had pained his heart:* Aye. *Trying to grin it away—to Hale:* You see, sir, between the two of us we do know them all. *Hale only looks at Proctor, deep in his attempt to define this man. Proctor grows more uneasy.* I think it be a small fault.

HALE: Theology, sir, is a fortress; no crack in a fortress may be accounted small. *He rises; he seems worried now. He paces a little, in deep thought.*

PROCTOR: There be no love for Satan in this house, Mister.

HALE: I pray it, I pray it dearly. *He looks to both of them, an attempt at a smile on his face, but his misgivings are clear.* Well, then—I'll bid you good night.

ELIZABETH, *unable to restrain herself:* Mr. Hale. *He turns.* I do think you are suspecting me somewhat? Are you not?

HALE, *obviously disturbed—and evasive:* Goody Proctor, I do not judge you. My duty is to add what I may to the godly wisdom of the court. I pray you both good health and good fortune. *To John:* Good night, sir. *He starts out.*

ELIZABETH, *with a note of desperation:* I think you must tell him, John.

HALE: What's that?

ELIZABETH, *restraining a call:* Will you tell him?

Slight pause. Hale looks questioningly at John.

PROCTOR, *with difficulty:* I—I have no witness and cannot prove it, except my word be taken. But I know the children's sickness had naught to do with witchcraft.

HALE, *stopped, struck:* Naught to do—?

PROCTOR: Mr. Parris discovered them sportin' in the woods. They were startled and took sick.

Pause.

HALE: Who told you this?

PROCTOR, *hesitates, then:* Abigail Williams.

HALE: Abigail!

PROCTOR: Aye.

HALE, *his eyes wide:* Abigail Williams told you it had naught to do with witchcraft!

PROCTOR: She told me the day you came, sir.

HALE, *suspiciously:* Why—why did you keep this?

PROCTOR: I never knew until tonight that the world is gone daft with this nonsense.

HALE: Nonsense! Mister, I have myself examined Tituba, Sarah Good, and numerous others that have confessed to dealing with the Devil. They have *confessed* it.

PROCTOR: And why not, if they must hang for denyin' it? There are them that will swear to anything before they'll hang; have you never thought of that?

HALE: I have. I—I have indeed. *It is his own suspicion, but he resists it. He glances at Elizabeth, then at John.* And you— would you testify to this in court?

PROCTOR: I—had not reckoned with goin' into court. But if I must I will.

HALE: Do you falter here?

PROCTOR: I falter nothing, but I may wonder if my story will be credited in such a court. I do wonder on it, when such a steady-minded minister as you will suspicion such a woman that never lied, and cannot, and the world knows she cannot! I may falter somewhat, Mister; I am no fool.

HALE, *quietly—it has impressed him:* Proctor, let you open with me now, for I have a rumor that troubles me. It's said you hold no belief that there may even be witches in the world. Is that true, sir?

PROCTOR—*he knows this is critical, and is striving against his disgust with Hale and with himself for even answering:* I know not what I have said, I may have said it. I have wondered if there be witches in the world—although I cannot believe they come among us now.

HALE: Then you do not believe—

PROCTOR: I have no knowledge of it; the Bible speaks of witches, and I will not deny them.

HALE: And you, woman?

ELIZABETH: I—I cannot believe it.

HALE, *shocked:* You cannot!

PROCTOR: Elizabeth, you bewilder him!

ELIZABETH, *to Hale:* I cannot think the Devil may own a woman's soul, Mr. Hale, when she keeps an upright way, as I have. I am a good woman, I know it; and if you believe I may do only good work in the world, and yet be secretly bound to Satan, then I must tell you, sir, I do not believe it.

HALE: But, woman, you do believe there are witches in—

ELIZABETH: If you think that I am one, then I say there are none.

HALE: You surely do not fly against the Gospel, the Gospel—

PROCTOR: She believe in the Gospel, every word!

ELIZABETH: Question Abigail Williams about the Gospel, not myself!

Hale stares at her.

PROCTOR: She do not mean to doubt the Gospel, sir, you cannot think it. This be a Christian house, sir, a Christian house.

HALE: God keep you both; let the third child be quickly baptized, and go you without fail each Sunday in to Sabbath prayer; and keep a solemn, quiet way among you. I think—

Giles Corey appears in doorway.

GILES: John!

PROCTOR: Giles! What's the matter?

GILES: They take my wife.

Francis Nurse enters.

GILES: And his Rebecca!

PROCTOR, *to Francis:* Rebecca's in the *jail!*

FRANCIS: Aye, Cheever come and take her in his wagon. We've

only now come from the jail, and they'll not even let us in to see them.

ELIZABETH: They've surely gone wild now, Mr. Hale!

FRANCIS, *going to Hale:* Reverend Hale! Can you not speak to the Deputy Governor? I'm sure he mistakes these people—

HALE: Pray calm yourself, Mr. Nurse.

FRANCIS: My wife is the very brick and mortar of the church, Mr. Hale—*indicating Giles*—and Martha Corey, there cannot be a woman closer yet to God than Martha.

HALE: How is Rebecca charged, Mr. Nurse?

FRANCIS, *with a mocking, half-hearted laugh:* For murder, she's charged! *Mockingly quoting the warrant:* "For the marvelous and supernatural murder of Goody Putnam's babies." What am I to do, Mr. Hale?

HALE, *turns from Francis, deeply troubled, then:* Believe me, Mr. Nurse, if Rebecca Nurse be tainted, then nothing's left to stop the whole green world from burning. Let you rest upon the justice of the court; the court will send her home, I know it.

FRANCIS: You cannot mean she will be tried in court!

HALE, *pleading:* Nurse, though our hearts break, we cannot flinch; these are new times, sir. There is a misty plot afoot so subtle we should be criminal to cling to old respects and ancient friendships. I have seen too many frightful proofs in court—the Devil is alive in Salem, and we dare not quail to follow wherever the accusing finger points!

PROCTOR, *angered:* How may such a woman murder children?

HALE, *in great pain:* Man, remember, until an hour before the Devil fell, God thought him beautiful in Heaven.

GILES: I never said my wife were a witch, Mr. Hale; I only said she were reading books!

HALE: Mr. Corey, exactly what complaint were made on your wife?

GILES: That bloody mongrel Walcott charge her. Y'see, he buy a pig of my wife four or five year ago, and the pig died soon after. So he come dancin' in for his money back. So my Martha, she says to him, "Walcott, if you haven't the wit to feed a pig properly, you'll not live to own many," she says. Now he goes to court and claims that from that day to this he cannot keep a pig alive for more than four weeks because my Martha bewitch them with her books!

Enter Ezekiel Cheever. A shocked silence.

CHEEVER: Good evening to you, Proctor.

PROCTOR: Why, Mr. Cheever. Good evening.

CHEEVER: Good evening, all. Good evening, Mr. Hale.

PROCTOR: I hope you come not on business of the court.

CHEEVER: I do, Proctor, aye. I am clerk of the court now, y'know.

Enter Marshal Herrick, a man in his early thirties, who is some-what shamefaced at the moment.

GILES: It's a pity, Ezekiel, that an honest tailor might have gone to Heaven must burn in Hell. You'll burn for this, do you know it?

CHEEVER: You know yourself I must do as I'm told. You surely know that, Giles. And I'd as lief you'd not be sending me to Hell. I like not the sound of it, I tell you; I like not the sound of it. *He fears Proctor, but starts to reach inside his coat.* Now believe me, Proctor, how heavy be the law, all its tonnage I do carry on my back tonight. *He takes out a warrant.* I have a warrant for your wife.

PROCTOR, *to Hale:* You said she were not charged!

HALE: I know nothin' of it. *To Cheever:* When were she charged?

CHEEVER: I am given sixteen warrant tonight, sir, and she is one.

PROCTOR: Who charged her?

CHEEVER: Why, Abigail Williams charge her.

PROCTOR: On what proof, what proof?

CHEEVER, *looking about the room:* Mr. Proctor, I have little time. The court bid me search your house, but I like not to search a house. So will you hand me any poppets that your wife may keep here?

PROCTOR: Poppets?

ELIZABETH: I never kept no poppets, not since I were a girl.

CHEEVER, *embarrassed, glancing toward the mantel where sits Mary Warren's poppet:* I spy a poppet, Goody Proctor.

ELIZABETH: Oh! *Going for it:* Why, this is Mary's.

CHEEVER, *shyly:* Would you please to give it to me?

ELIZABETH, *handing it to him, asks Hale:* Has the court discovered a text in poppets now?

CHEEVER, *carefully holding the poppet:* Do you keep any others in this house?

PROCTOR: No, nor this one either till tonight. What signifies a poppet?

CHEEVER: Why, a poppet—*he gingerly turns the poppet over*—a poppet may signify— Now, woman, will you please to come with me?

PROCTOR: She will not! *To Elizabeth:* Fetch Mary here.

CHEEVER, *ineptly reaching toward Elizabeth:* No, no, I am forbid to leave her from my sight.

PROCTOR, *pushing his arm away:* You'll leave her out of sight and out of mind, Mister. Fetch Mary, Elizabeth. *Elizabeth goes upstairs.*

HALE: What signifies a poppet, Mr. Cheever?

CHEEVER, *turning the poppet over in his hands:* Why, they say it may signify that she— *He has lifted the poppet's skirt, and his eyes widen in astonished fear.* Why, this, this—

PROCTOR, *reaching for the poppet:* What's there?

CHEEVER: Why— *He draws out a long needle from the poppet* —it is a needle! Herrick, Herrick, it is a needle!

Herrick comes toward him.

PROCTOR, *angrily, bewildered:* And what signifies a needle!

CHEEVER, *his hands shaking:* Why, this go hard with her, Proctor, this—I had my doubts, Proctor, I had my doubts, but here's calamity. *To Hale, showing the needle:* You see it, sir, it is a needle!

HALE: Why? What meanin' has it?

CHEEVER, *wide-eyed, trembling:* The girl, the Williams girl, Abigail Williams, sir. She sat to dinner in Reverend Parris's house tonight, and without word nor warnin' she falls to the floor. Like a struck beast, he says, and screamed a scream that a bull would weep to hear. And he goes to save her, and, stuck two inches in the flesh of her belly, he draw a needle out. And demandin' of her how she come to be so stabbed, she—*to Proctor now* —testify it were your wife's familiar spirit pushed it in.

PROCTOR: Why, she done it herself! *To Hale:* I hope you're not takin' this for proof, Mister!

Hale, struck by the proof, is silent.

CHEEVER: 'Tis hard proof! *To Hale:* I find here a poppet Goody Proctor keeps. I have found it, sir. And in the belly of the poppet a needle's stuck. I tell you true, Proctor, I never warranted to see such proof of Hell, and I bid you obstruct me not, for I—

Enter Elizabeth with Mary Warren. Proctor, seeing Mary Warren, draws her by the arm to Hale.

PROCTOR: Here now! Mary, how did this poppet come into my house?

MARY WARREN, *frightened for herself, her voice very small:* What poppet's that, sir?

PROCTOR, *impatiently, pointing at the doll in Cheever's hand:* This poppet, this poppet.

MARY WARREN, *evasively, looking at it:* Why, I—I think it is mine.

PROCTOR: It is your poppet, is it not?

MARY WARREN, *not understanding the direction of this:* It—is, sir.

PROCTOR: And how did it come into this house?

MARY WARREN, *glancing about at the avid faces:* Why—I made it in the court, sir, and—give it to Goody Proctor tonight.

PROCTOR, *to Hale:* Now, sir—do you have it?

HALE: Mary Warren, a needle have been found inside this poppet.

MARY WARREN, *bewildered:* Why, I meant no harm by it, sir.

PROCTOR, *quickly:* You stuck that needle in yourself?

MARY WARREN: I—I believe I did, sir, I—

PROCTOR, *to Hale:* What say you now?

HALE, *watching Mary Warren closely:* Child, you are certain this be your natural memory? May it be, perhaps, that someone conjures you even now to say this?

MARY WARREN: Conjures me? Why, no, sir, I am entirely myself, I think. Let you ask Susanna Walcott—she saw me sewin' it in court. *Or better still:* Ask Abby, Abby sat beside me when I made it.

PROCTOR, *to Hale, of Cheever:* Bid him begone. Your mind is surely settled now. Bid him out, Mr. Hale.

ELIZABETH: What signifies a needle?

HALE: Mary—you charge a cold and cruel murder on Abigail.

MARY WARREN: Murder! I charge no—

HALE: Abigail were stabbed tonight; a needle were found stuck into her belly—

ELIZABETH: And she charges me?

HALE: Aye.

ELIZABETH, *her breath knocked out:* Why—! The girl is murder! She must be ripped out of the world!

CHEEVER, *pointing at Elizabeth:* You've heard that, sir! Ripped out of the world! Herrick, you heard it!

PROCTOR, *suddenly snatching the warrant out of Cheever's hands:* Out with you.

CHEEVER: Proctor, you dare not touch the warrant.

PROCTOR, *ripping the warrant:* Out with you!

CHEEVER: You've ripped the Deputy Governor's warrant, man!

PROCTOR: Damn the Deputy Governor! Out of my house!

HALE: Now, Proctor, Proctor!

PROCTOR: Get y'gone with them! You are a broken minister.

HALE: Proctor, if she is innocent, the court—

PROCTOR: If *she* is innocent! Why do you never wonder if Parris be innocent, or Abigail? Is the accuser always holy now? Were they born this morning as clean as God's fingers? I'll tell you what's walking Salem—vengeance is walking Salem. We are what we always were in Salem, but now the little crazy children are jangling the keys of the kingdom, and common vengeance writes the law! This warrant's vengeance! I'll not give my wife to vengeance!

ELIZABETH: I'll go, John—

PROCTOR: You will not go!

HERRICK: I have nine men outside. You cannot keep her. The law binds me, John, I cannot budge.

PROCTOR, *to Hale, ready to break him:* Will you see her taken?

HALE: Proctor, the court is just—

PROCTOR: Pontius Pilate! God will not let you wash your hands of this!

ELIZABETH: John—I think I must go with them. *He cannot bear to look at her.* Mary, there is bread enough for the morning; you will bake, in the afternoon. Help Mr. Proctor as you were his daughter—you owe me that, and much more. *She is fighting her weeping. To Proctor:* When the children wake, speak nothing of witchcraft—it will frighten them. *She cannot go on.*

PROCTOR: I will bring you home. I will bring you soon.

ELIZABETH: Oh, John, bring me soon!

PROCTOR: I will fall like an ocean on that court! Fear nothing, Elizabeth.

ELIZABETH, *with great fear:* I will fear nothing. *She looks about the room, as though to fix it in her mind.* Tell the children I have gone to visit someone sick.

She walks out the door, Herrick and Cheever behind her. For a moment, Proctor watches from the doorway. The clank of chain is heard.

PROCTOR: Herrick! Herrick, don't chain her! *He rushes out the door. From outside:* Damn you, man, you will not chain her! Off with them! I'll not have it! I will not have her chained!

There are other men's voices against his. Hale, in a fever of guilt and uncertainty, turns from the door to avoid the sight; Mary Warren bursts into tears and sits weeping. Giles Corey calls to Hale.

GILES: And yet silent, minister? It is fraud, you know it is fraud! What keeps you, man?

Proctor is half braced, half pushed into the room by two deputies and Herrick.

PROCTOR: I'll pay you, Herrick, I will surely pay you!

HERRICK, *panting:* In God's name, John, I cannot help myself. I must chain them all. Now let you keep inside this house till I am gone! *He goes out with his deputies.*

Proctor stands there, gulping air. Horses and a wagon creaking are heard.

HALE, *in great uncertainty:* Mr. Proctor—

PROCTOR: Out of my sight!

HALE: Charity, Proctor, charity. What I have heard in her favor, I will not fear to testify in court. God help me, I cannot judge her guilty or innocent—I know not. Only this consider: the world goes mad, and it profit nothing you should lay the cause to the vengeance of a little girl.

PROCTOR: You are a coward! Though you be ordained in God's own tears, you are a coward now!

HALE: Proctor, I cannot think God be provoked so grandly by such a petty cause. The jails are packed—our greatest judges sit in Salem now—and hangin's promised. Man, we must look to cause proportionate. Were there murder done, perhaps, and never brought to light? Abomination? Some secret blasphemy that stinks to Heaven? Think on cause, man, and let you help me to discover it. For there's your way, believe it, there is your only way, when such confusion strikes upon the world. *He goes to Giles and Francis.* Let you counsel among yourselves; think on your village and what may have drawn from heaven such thundering wrath upon you all. I shall pray God open up our eyes.

Hale goes out.

FRANCIS, *struck by Hale's mood:* I never heard no murder done in Salem.

PROCTOR—*he has been reached by Hale's words:* Leave me, Francis, leave me.

GILES, *shaken:* John—tell me, are we lost?

PROCTOR: Go home now, Giles. We'll speak on it tomorrow.

GILES: Let you think on it. We'll come early, eh?

PROCTOR: Aye. Go now, Giles.

GILES: Good night, then.

Giles Corey goes out. After a moment:

MARY WARREN, *in a fearful squeak of a voice:* Mr. Proctor,

very likely they'll let her come home once they're given proper
evidence.

PROCTOR: You're coming to the court with me, Mary. You will
tell it in the court.

MARY WARREN: I cannot charge murder on Abigail.

PROCTOR, *moving menacingly toward her:* You will tell the
court how that poppet come here and who stuck the needle in.

MARY WARREN: She'll kill me for sayin' that! *Proctor continues
toward her.* Abby'll charge lechery on you, Mr. Proctor!

PROCTOR, *halting:* She's told you!

MARY WARREN: I have known it, sir. She'll ruin you with it, I
know she will.

PROCTOR, *hesitating, and with deep hatred of himself:* Good.
Then her saintliness is done with. *Mary backs from him.* We will
slide together into our pit; you will tell the court what you
know.

MARY WARREN, *in terror:* I cannot, they'll turn on me—

*Proctor strides and catches her, and she is repeating, "I cannot,
I cannot!"*

PROCTOR: My wife will never die for me! I will bring your guts
into your mouth but that goodness will not die for me!

MARY WARREN, *struggling to escape him:* I cannot do it, I
cannot!

PROCTOR, *grasping her by the throat as though he would strangle
her:* Make your peace with it! Now Hell and Heaven grapple
on our backs, and all our old pretense is ripped away—make
your peace! *He throws her to the floor, where she sobs, "I
cannot, I cannot . . ." And now, half to himself, staring, and*

turning to the open door: Peace. It is a providence, and no great change; we are only what we always were, but naked now. *He walks as though toward a great horror, facing the open sky.* Aye, naked! And the wind, God's icy wind, will blow!

And she is over and over again sobbing, "I cannot, I cannot, I cannot," as

THE CURTAIN FALLS*

* See A Note on the Text, p. 153, and Appendix, p. 148.

ACT THREE

The vestry room of the Salem meeting house, now serving as the anteroom of the General Court.

As the curtain rises, the room is empty, but for sunlight pouring through two high windows in the back wall. The room is solemn, even forbidding. Heavy beams jut out, boards of random widths make up the walls. At the right are two doors leading into the meeting house proper, where the court is being held. At the left another door leads outside.

There is a plain bench at the left, and another at the right. In the center a rather long meeting table, with stools and a considerable armchair snugged up to it.

Through the partitioning wall at the right we hear a prosecutor's voice, Judge Hathorne's, asking a question; then a woman's voice, Martha Corey's, replying.

HATHORNE'S VOICE: Now, Martha Corey, there is abundant evidence in our hands to show that you have given yourself to the reading of fortunes. Do you deny it?

MARTHA COREY'S VOICE: I am innocent to a witch. I know not what a witch is.

HATHORNE'S VOICE: How do you know, then, that you are not a witch?

MARTHA COREY'S VOICE: If I were, I would know it.

HATHORNE'S VOICE: Why do you hurt these children?

MARTHA COREY'S VOICE: I do not hurt them. I scorn it!

GILES' VOICE, *roaring:* I have evidence for the court!

Voices of townspeople rise in excitement.

DANFORTH'S VOICE: You will keep your seat!

GILES' VOICE: Thomas Putnam is reaching out for land!

DANFORTH'S VOICE: Remove that man, Marshal!

GILES' VOICE: You're hearing lies, lies!

A roaring goes up from the people.

HATHORNE'S VOICE: Arrest him, excellency!

GILES' VOICE: I have evidence. Why will you not hear my evidence?

The door opens and Giles is half carried into the vestry room by Herrick.

GILES: Hands off, damn you, let me go!

HERRICK: Giles, Giles!

GILES: Out of my way, Herrick! I bring evidence—

HERRICK: You cannot go in there, Giles; it's a court!

Enter Hale from the court.

HALE: Pray be calm a moment.

GILES: You, Mr. Hale, go in there and demand I speak.

HALE: A moment, sir, a moment.

GILES: They'll be hangin' my wife!

Judge Hathorne enters. He is in his sixties, a bitter, remorseless Salem judge.

HATHORNE: How do you dare come roarin' into this court! Are you gone daft, Corey?

GILES: You're not a Boston judge yet, Hathorne. You'll not call me daft!

Enter Deputy Governor Danforth and, behind him, Ezekiel Cheever and Parris. On his appearance, silence falls. Danforth is a grave man in his sixties, of some humor and sophistication that does not, however, interfere with an exact loyalty to his position and his cause. He comes down to Giles, who awaits his wrath.

DANFORTH, *looking directly at Giles:* Who is this man?

PARRIS: Giles Corey, sir, and a more contentious—

GILES, *to Parris:* I am asked the question, and I am old enough to answer it! *To Danforth, who impresses him and to whom he smiles through his strain:* My name is Corey, sir, Giles Corey. I have six hundred acres, and timber in addition. It is my wife you be condemning now. *He indicates the courtroom.*

DANFORTH: And how do you imagine to help her cause with such contemptuous riot? Now be gone. Your old age alone keeps you out of jail for this.

GILES, *beginning to plead:* They be tellin' lies about my wife, sir, I—

DANFORTH: Do you take it upon yourself to determine what this court shall believe and what it shall set aside?

GILES: Your Excellency, we mean no disrespect for—

DANFORTH: Disrespect indeed! It is disruption, Mister. This is the highest court of the supreme government of this province, do you know it?

GILES, *beginning to weep:* Your Excellency, I only said she were readin' books, sir, and they come and take her out of my house for—

DANFORTH, *mystified:* Books! What books?

GILES, *through helpless sobs:* It is my third wife, sir; I never had no wife that be so taken with books, and I thought to find the cause of it, d'y'see, but it were no witch I blamed her for. *He is openly weeping.* I have broke charity with the woman, I have broke charity with her. *He covers his face, ashamed. Danforth is respectfully silent.*

HALE: Excellency, he claims hard evidence for his wife's defense. I think that in all justice you must—

DANFORTH: Then let him submit his evidence in proper affidavit. You are certainly aware of our procedure here, Mr. Hale. *To Herrick:* Clear this room.

HERRICK: Come now, Giles. *He gently pushes Corey out.*

FRANCIS: We are desperate, sir; we come here three days now and cannot be heard.

DANFORTH: Who is this man?

FRANCIS: Francis Nurse, Your Excellency.

HALE: His wife's Rebecca that were condemned this morning.

DANFORTH: Indeed! I am amazed to find you in such uproar. I have only good report of your character, Mr. Nurse.

HATHORNE: I think they must both be arrested in contempt, sir.

DANFORTH, *to Francis:* Let you write your plea, and in due time I will—

FRANCIS: Excellency, we have proof for your eyes; God forbid you shut them to it. The girls, sir, the girls are frauds.

DANFORTH: What's that?

FRANCIS: We have proof of it, sir. They are all deceiving you.

Danforth is shocked, but studying Francis.

HATHORNE: This is contempt, sir, contempt!

DANFORTH: Peace, Judge Hathorne. Do you know who I am, Mr. Nurse?

FRANCIS: I surely do, sir, and I think you must be a wise judge to be what you are.

DANFORTH: And do you know that near to four hundred are in the jails from Marblehead to Lynn, and upon my signature?

FRANCIS: I—

DANFORTH: And seventy-two condemned to hang by that signature?

FRANCIS: Excellency, I never thought to say it to such a weighty judge, but you are deceived.

Enter Giles Corey from left. All turn to see as he beckons in Mary Warren with Proctor. Mary is keeping her eyes to the ground; Proctor has her elbow as though she were near collapse.

PARRIS, *on seeing her, in shock:* Mary Warren! *He goes directly to bend close to her face.* What are you about here?

PROCTOR, *pressing Parris away from her with a gentle but firm motion of protectiveness:* She would speak with the Deputy Governor.

DANFORTH, *shocked by this, turns to Herrick:* Did you not tell me Mary Warren were sick in bed?

HERRICK: She were, Your Honor. When I go to fetch her to the court last week, she said she were sick.

GILES: She has been strivin' with her soul all week, Your Honor; she comes now to tell the truth of this to you.

DANFORTH: Who is this?

PROCTOR: John Proctor, sir. Elizabeth Proctor is my wife.

PARRIS: Beware this man, Your Excellency, this man is mischief.

HALE, *excitedly:* I think you must hear the girl, sir, she—

DANFORTH, *who has become very interested in Mary Warren and only raises a hand toward Hale:* Peace. What would you tell us, Mary Warren?

Proctor looks at her, but she cannot speak.

PROCTOR: She never saw no spirits, sir.

DANFORTH, *with great alarm and surprise, to Mary:* Never saw no spirits!

GILES, *eagerly:* Never.

PROCTOR, *reaching into his jacket:* She has signed a deposition, sir—

DANFORTH, *instantly:* No, no, I accept no depositions. *He is rapidly calculating this; he turns from her to Proctor.* Tell me, Mr. Proctor, have you given out this story in the village?

PROCTOR: We have not.

PARRIS: They've come to overthrow the court, sir! This man is—

DANFORTH: I pray you, Mr. Parris. Do you know, Mr. Proctor, that the entire contention of the state in these trials is that the voice of Heaven is speaking through the children?

PROCTOR: I know that, sir.

DANFORTH, *thinks, staring at Proctor, then turns to Mary Warren:* And you, Mary Warren, how came you to cry out people for sending their spirits against you?

MARY WARREN: It were pretense, sir.

DANFORTH: I cannot hear you.

PROCTOR: It were pretense, she says.

DANFORTH: Ah? And the other girls? Susanna Walcott, and— the others? They are also pretending?

MARY WARREN: Aye, sir.

DANFORTH, *wide-eyed:* Indeed. *Pause. He is baffled by this. He turns to study Proctor's face.*

PARRIS, *in a sweat:* Excellency, you surely cannot think to let so vile a lie be spread in open court!

DANFORTH: Indeed not, but it strike hard upon me that she will dare come here with such a tale. Now, Mr. Proctor, before I decide whether I shall hear you or not, it is my duty to tell you this. We burn a hot fire here; it melts down all concealment.

PROCTOR: I know that, sir.

DANFORTH: Let me continue. I understand well, a husband's tenderness may drive him to extravagance in defense of a wife. Are you certain in your conscience, Mister, that your evidence is the truth?

PROCTOR: It is. And you will surely know it.

DANFORTH: And you thought to declare this revelation in the open court before the public?

PROCTOR: I thought I would, aye—with your permission.

DANFORTH, *his eyes narrowing:* Now, sir, what is your purpose in so doing?

PROCTOR: Why, I—I would free my wife, sir.

DANFORTH: There lurks nowhere in your heart, nor hidden in your spirit, any desire to undermine this court?

PROCTOR, *with the faintest faltering:* Why, no, sir.

CHEEVER, *clears his throat, awakening:* I— Your Excellency.

DANFORTH: Mr. Cheever.

CHEEVER: I think it be my duty, sir— *Kindly, to Proctor:* You'll not deny it, John. *To Danforth:* When we come to take his wife, he damned the court and ripped your warrant.

PARRIS: Now you have it!

DANFORTH: He did that, Mr. Hale?

HALE, *takes a breath:* Aye, he did.

PROCTOR: It were a temper, sir. I knew not what I did.

DANFORTH, *studying him:* Mr. Proctor.

PROCTOR: Aye, sir.

DANFORTH, *straight into his eyes:* Have you ever seen the Devil?

PROCTOR: No, sir.

DANFORTH: You are in all respects a Gospel Christian?

PROCTOR: I am, sir.

PARRIS: Such a Christian that will not come to church but once in a month!

DANFORTH, *restrained—he is curious:* Not come to church?

PROCTOR: I—I have no love for Mr. Parris. It is no secret. But God I surely love.

CHEEVER: He plow on Sunday, sir.

DANFORTH: Plow on Sunday!

CHEEVER, *apologetically:* I think it be evidence, John. I am an official of the court, I cannot keep it.

PROCTOR: I—I have once or twice plowed on Sunday. I have three children, sir, and until last year my land give little.

GILES: You'll find other Christians that do plow on Sunday if the truth be known.

HALE: Your Honor, I cannot think you may judge the man on such evidence.

DANFORTH: I judge nothing. *Pause. He keeps watching Proctor, who tries to meet his gaze.* I tell you straight, Mister—I have seen marvels in this court. I have seen people choked before my eyes by spirits; I have seen them stuck by pins and slashed by daggers. I have until this moment not the slightest reason to suspect that the children may be deceiving me. Do you understand my meaning?

PROCTOR: Excellency, does it not strike upon you that so many of these women have lived so long with such upright reputation, and—

PARRIS: Do you read the Gospel, Mr. Proctor?

PROCTOR: I read the Gospel.

PARRIS: I think not, or you should surely know that Cain were an upright man, and yet he did kill Abel.

PROCTOR: Aye, God tells us that. *To Danforth:* But who tells us Rebecca Nurse murdered seven babies by sending out her spirit on them? It is the children only, and this one will swear she lied to you.

Danforth considers, then beckons Hathorne to him. Hathorne leans in, and he speaks in his ear. Hathorne nods.

HATHORNE: Aye, she's the one.

DANFORTH: Mr. Proctor, this morning, your wife send me a claim in which she states that she is pregnant now.

PROCTOR: My wife pregnant!

DANFORTH: There be no sign of it—we have examined her body.

PROCTOR: But if she say she is pregnant, then she must be! That woman will never lie, Mr. Danforth.

DANFORTH: She will not?

PROCTOR: Never, sir, never.

DANFORTH: We have thought it too convenient to be credited. However, if I should tell you now that I will let her be kept another month; and if she begin to show her natural signs, you shall have her living yet another year until she is delivered— what say you to that? *John Proctor is struck silent.* Come now. You say your only purpose is to save your wife. Good, then, she is saved at least this year, and a year is long. What say you, sir? It is done now. *In conflict, Proctor glances at Francis and Giles.* Will you drop this charge?

PROCTOR: I—I think I cannot.

DANFORTH, *now an almost imperceptible hardness in his voice:* Then your purpose is somewhat larger.

PARRIS: He's come to overthrow this court, Your Honor!

PROCTOR: These are my friends. Their wives are also accused—

DANFORTH, *with a sudden briskness of manner:* I judge you not, sir. I am ready to hear your evidence.

PROCTOR: I come not to hurt the court; I only—

DANFORTH, *cutting him off:* Marshal, go into the court and bid

Judge Stoughton and Judge Sewall declare recess for one hour. And let them go to the tavern, if they will. All witnesses and prisoners are to be kept in the building.

HERRICK: Aye, sir. *Very deferentially:* If I may say it, sir, I know this man all my life. It is a good man, sir.

DANFORTH—*it is the reflection on himself he resents:* I am sure of it, Marshal. *Herrick nods, then goes out.* Now, what deposition do you have for us, Mr. Proctor? And I beg you be clear, open as the sky, and honest.

PROCTOR, *as he takes out several papers:* I am no lawyer, so I'll—

DANFORTH: The pure in heart need no lawyers. Proceed as you will.

PROCTOR, *handing Danforth a paper:* Will you read this first, sir? It's a sort of testament. The people signing it declare their good opinion of Rebecca, and my wife, and Martha Corey. *Danforth looks down at the paper.*

PARRIS, *to enlist Danforth's sarcasm:* Their good opinion! *But Danforth goes on reading, and Proctor is heartened.*

PROCTOR: These are all landholding farmers, members of the church. *Delicately, trying to point out a paragraph:* If you'll notice, sir—they've known the women many years and never saw no sign they had dealings with the Devil.

Parris nervously moves over and reads over Danforth's shoulder.

DANFORTH, *glancing down a long list:* How many names are here?

FRANCIS: Ninety-one, Your Excellency.

PARRIS, *sweating:* These people should be summoned. *Danforth looks up at him questioningly.* For questioning.

FRANCIS, *trembling with anger:* Mr. Danforth, I gave them all my word no harm would come to them for signing this.

PARRIS: This is a clear attack upon the court!

HALE, *to Parris, trying to contain himself:* Is every defense an attack upon the court? Can no one—?

PARRIS: All innocent and Christian people are happy for the courts in Salem! These people are gloomy for it. *To Danforth directly:* And I think you will want to know, from each and every one of them, what discontents them with you!

HATHORNE: I think they ought to be examined, sir.

DANFORTH: It is not necessarily an attack, I think. Yet—

FRANCIS: These are all covenanted Christians, sir.

DANFORTH: Then I am sure they may have nothing to fear. *Hands Cheever the paper.* Mr. Cheever, have warrants drawn for all of these—arrest for examination. *To Proctor:* Now, Mister, what other information do you have for us? *Francis is still standing, horrified.* You may sit, Mr. Nurse.

FRANCIS: I have brought trouble on these people; I have—

DANFORTH: No, old man, you have not hurt these people if they are of good conscience. But you must understand, sir, that a person is either with this court or he must be counted against it, there be no road between. This is a sharp time, now, a precise time—we live no longer in the dusky afternoon when evil mixed itself with good and befuddled the world. Now, by God's grace, the shining sun is up, and them that fear not light will surely praise it. I hope you will be one of those. *Mary Warren suddenly sobs.* She's not hearty, I see.

PROCTOR: No, she's not, sir. *To Mary, bending to her, holding her hand, quietly:* Now remember what the angel Raphael said to the boy Tobias. Remember it.

MARY WARREN, *hardly audible:* Aye.

PROCTOR: "Do that which is good, and no harm shall come to thee."

MARY WARREN: Aye.

DANFORTH: Come, man, we wait you.

Marshal Herrick returns, and takes his post at the door.

GILES: John, my deposition, give him mine.

PROCTOR: Aye. *He hands Danforth another paper.* This is Mr. Corey's deposition.

DANFORTH: Oh? *He looks down at it. Now Hathorne comes behind him and reads with him.*

HATHORNE, *suspiciously:* What lawyer drew this, Corey?

GILES: You know I never hired a lawyer in my life, Hathorne.

DANFORTH, *finishing the reading:* It is very well phrased. My compliments. Mr. Parris, if Mr. Putnam is in the court, will you bring him in? *Hathorne takes the deposition, and walks to the window with it. Parris goes into the court.* You have no legal training, Mr. Corey?

GILES, *very pleased:* I have the best, sir—I am thirty-three time in court in my life. And always plaintiff, too.

DANFORTH: Oh, then you're much put-upon.

GILES: I am never put-upon; I know my rights, sir, and I will have them. You know, your father tried a case of mine—might be thirty-five year ago, I think.

DANFORTH: Indeed.

GILES: He never spoke to you of it?

DANFORTH: No, I cannot recall it.

GILES: That's strange, he give me nine pound damages. He were a fair judge, your father. Y'see, I had a white mare that time, and this fellow come to borrow the mare— *Enter Parris with Thomas Putnam. When he sees Putnam, Giles' ease goes; he is hard.* Aye, there he is.

DANFORTH: Mr. Putnam, I have here an accusation by Mr. Corey against you. He states that you coldly prompted your daughter to cry witchery upon George Jacobs that is now in jail.

PUTNAM: It is a lie.

DANFORTH, *turning to Giles:* Mr. Putnam states your charge is a lie. What say you to that?

GILES, *furious, his fists clenched:* A fart on Thomas Putnam, that is what I say to that!

DANFORTH: What proof do you submit for your charge, sir?

GILES: My proof is there! *Pointing to the paper.* If Jacobs hangs for a witch he forfeit up his property—that's law! And there is none but Putnam with the coin to buy so great a piece. This man is killing his neighbors for their land!

DANFORTH: But proof, sir, proof.

GILES, *pointing at his deposition:* The proof is there! I have it from an honest man who heard Putnam say it! The day his daughter cried out on Jacobs, he said she'd given him a fair gift of land.

HATHORNE: And the name of this man?

GILES, *taken aback:* What name?

HATHORNE: The man that give you this information.

GILES, *hesitates, then:* Why, I—I cannot give you his name.

HATHORNE: And why not?

GILES, *hesitates, then bursts out:* You know well why not! He'll lay in jail if I give his name!

HATHORNE: This is contempt of the court, Mr. Danforth!

DANFORTH, *to avoid that:* You will surely tell us the name.

GILES: I will not give you no name. I mentioned my wife's name once and I'll burn in hell long enough for that. I stand mute.

DANFORTH: In that case, I have no choice but to arrest you for contempt of this court, do you know that?

GILES: This is a hearing; you cannot clap me for contempt of a hearing.

DANFORTH: Oh, it is a proper lawyer! Do you wish me to declare the court in full session here? Or will you give me good reply?

GILES, *faltering:* I cannot give you no name, sir, I cannot.

DANFORTH: You are a foolish old man. Mr. Cheever, begin the record. The court is now in session. I ask you, Mr. Corey—

PROCTOR, *breaking in:* Your Honor—he has the story in confidence, sir, and he—

PARRIS: The Devil lives on such confidences! *To Danforth:* Without confidences there could be no conspiracy, Your Honor!

HATHORNE. I think it must be broken, sir.

DANFORTH, *to Giles:* Old man, if your informant tells the truth let him come here openly like a decent man. But if he hide in anonymity I must know why. Now sir, the government and central church demand of you the name of him who reported Mr. Thomas Putnam a common murderer.

HALE: Excellency—

DANFORTH: Mr. Hale.

HALE: We cannot blink it more. There is a prodigious fear of this court in the country—

DANFORTH: Then there is a prodigious guilt in the country. Are *you* afraid to be questioned here?

HALE: I may only fear the Lord, sir, but there is fear in the country nevertheless.

DANFORTH, *angered now:* Reproach me not with the fear in the country; there is fear in the country because there is a moving plot to topple Christ in the country!

HALE: But it does not follow that everyone accused is part of it.

DANFORTH: No uncorrupted man may fear this court, Mr. Hale! None! *To Giles:* You are under arrest in contempt of this court. Now sit you down and take counsel with yourself, or you will be set in the jail until you decide to answer all questions.

Giles Corey makes a rush for Putnam. Proctor lunges and holds him.

PROCTOR: No, Giles!

GILES, *over Proctor's shoulder at Putnam:* I'll cut your throat, Putnam, I'll kill you yet!

PROCTOR, *forcing him into a chair:* Peace, Giles, peace. *Releasing him.* We'll prove ourselves. Now we will. *He starts to turn to Danforth.*

GILES: Say nothin' more, John. *Pointing at Danforth:* He's only playin' you! He means to hang us all!

Mary Warren bursts into sobs.

DANFORTH: This is a court of law, Mister. I'll have no effrontery here!

PROCTOR: Forgive him, sir, for his old age. Peace, Giles, we'll prove it all now. *He lifts up Mary's chin.* You cannot weep,

Mary. Remember the angel, what he say to the boy. Hold to it, now; there is your rock. *Mary quiets. He takes out a paper, and turns to Danforth.* This is Mary Warren's deposition. I—I would ask you remember, sir, while you read it, that until two week ago she were no different than the other children are today. *He is speaking reasonably, restraining all his fears, his anger, his anxiety.* You saw her scream, she howled, she swore familiar spirits choked her; she even testified that Satan, in the form of women now in jail, tried to win her soul away, and then when she refused—

DANFORTH: We know all this.

PROCTOR: Aye, sir. She swears now that she never saw Satan; nor any spirit, vague or clear, that Satan may have sent to hurt her. And she declares her friends are lying now.

Proctor starts to hand Danforth the deposition, and Hale comes up to Danforth in a trembling state.

HALE: Excellency, a moment. I think this goes to the heart of the matter.

DANFORTH, *with deep misgivings:* It surely does.

HALE: I cannot say he is an honest man; I know him little. But in all justice, sir, a claim so weighty cannot be argued by a farmer. In God's name, sir, stop here; send him home and let him come again with a lawyer—

DANFORTH, *patiently:* Now look you, Mr. Hale—

HALE: Excellency, I have signed seventy-two death warrants; I am a minister of the Lord, and I dare not take a life without there be a proof so immaculate no slightest qualm of conscience may doubt it.

DANFORTH: Mr. Hale, you surely do not doubt my justice.

HALE: I have this morning signed away the soul of Rebecca

Nurse, Your Honor. I'll not conceal it, my hand shakes yet as with a wound! I pray you, sir, *this* argument let lawyers present to you.

DANFORTH: Mr. Hale, believe me; for a man of such terrible learning you are most bewildered—I hope you will forgive me. I have been thirty-two year at the bar, sir, and I should be confounded were I called upon to defend these people. Let you consider, now— *To Proctor and the others:* And I bid you all do likewise. In an ordinary crime, how does one defend the accused? One calls up witnesses to prove his innocence. But witchcraft is *ipso facto,* on its face and by its nature, an invisible crime, is it not? Therefore, who may possibly be witness to it? The witch and the victim. None other. Now we cannot hope the witch will accuse herself; granted? Therefore, we must rely upon her victims—and they do testify, the children certainly do testify. As for the witches, none will deny that we are most eager for all their confessions. Therefore, what is left for a lawyer to bring out? I think I have made my point. Have I not?

HALE: But this child claims the girls are not truthful, and if they are not—

DANFORTH: That is precisely what I am about to consider, sir. What more may you ask of me? Unless you doubt my probity?

HALE, *defeated:* I surely do not, sir. Let you consider it, then.

DANFORTH: And let you put your heart to rest. Her deposition, Mr. Proctor.

Proctor hands it to him. Hathorne rises, goes beside Danforth, and starts reading. Parris comes to his other side. Danforth looks at John Proctor, then proceeds to read. Hale gets up, finds position near the judge, reads too. Proctor glances at Giles. Francis prays silently, hands pressed together. Cheever waits placidly, the sublime official, dutiful. Mary Warren sobs once. John Proctor touches her head reassuringly. Presently Danforth lifts his eyes, stands up, takes out a kerchief and blows his nose. The others stand aside as he moves in thought toward the window.

PARRIS, *hardly able to contain his anger and fear:* I should like to question—

DANFORTH—*his first real outburst, in which his contempt for Parris is clear:* Mr. Parris, I bid you be silent! *He stands in silence, looking out the window. Now, having established that he will set the gait:* Mr. Cheever, will you go into the court and bring the children here? *Cheever gets up and goes out upstage. Danforth now turns to Mary.* Mary Warren, how came you to this turnabout? Has Mr. Proctor threatened you for this deposition?

MARY WARREN: No, sir.

DANFORTH: Has he ever threatened you?

MARY WARREN, *weaker:* No, sir.

DANFORTH, *sensing a weakening:* Has he threatened you?

MARY WARREN: No, sir.

DANFORTH: Then you tell me that you sat in my court, callously lying, when you knew that people would hang by your evidence? *She does not answer.* Answer me!

MARY WARREN, *almost inaudibly:* I did, sir.

DANFORTH: How were you instructed in your life? Do you not know that God damns all liars? *She cannot speak.* Or is it now that you lie?

MARY WARREN: No, sir—I am with God now.

DANFORTH: You are with God now.

MARY WARREN: Aye, sir.

DANFORTH, *containing himself:* I will tell you this—you are either lying now, or you were lying in the court, and in either case you have committed perjury and you will go to jail for it. You cannot lightly say you lied, Mary. Do you know that?

MARY WARREN: I cannot lie no more. I am with God, I am with God.

But she breaks into sobs at the thought of it, and the right door opens, and enter Susanna Walcott, Mercy Lewis, Betty Parris, and finally Abigail. Cheever comes to Danforth.

CHEEVER: Ruth Putnam's not in the court, sir, nor the other children.

DANFORTH: These will be sufficient. Sit you down, children. *Silently they sit.* Your friend, Mary Warren, has given us a deposition. In which she swears that she never saw familiar spirits, apparitions, nor any manifest of the Devil. She claims as well that none of you have seen these things either. *Slight pause.* Now, children, this is a court of law. The law, based upon the Bible, and the Bible, writ by Almighty God, forbid the practice of witchcraft, and describe death as the penalty thereof. But likewise, children, the law and Bible damn all bearers of false witness. *Slight pause.* Now then. It does not escape me that this deposition may be devised to blind us; it may well be that Mary Warren has been conquered by Satan, who sends her here to distract our sacred purpose. If so, her neck will break for it. But if she speak true, I bid you now drop your guile and confess your pretense, for a quick confession will go easier with you. *Pause.* Abigail Williams, rise. *Abigail slowly rises.* Is there any truth in this?

ABIGAIL: No, sir.

DANFORTH, *thinks, glances at Mary, then back to Abigail:* Children, a very augur bit will now be turned into your souls until your honesty is proved. Will either of you change your positions now, or do you force me to hard questioning?

ABIGAIL: I have naught to change, sir. She lies.

DANFORTH, *to Mary:* You would still go on with this?

MARY WARREN, *faintly:* Aye, sir.

DANFORTH, *turning to Abigail:* A poppet were discovered in Mr. Proctor's house, stabbed by a needle. Mary Warren claims that you sat beside her in the court when she made it, and that you saw her make it and witnessed how she herself stuck her needle into it for safe-keeping. What say you to that?

ABIGAIL, *with a slight note of indignation:* It is a lie, sir.

DANFORTH, *after a slight pause:* While you worked for Mr. Proctor, did you see poppets in that house?

ABIGAIL: Goody Proctor always kept poppets.

PROCTOR: Your Honor, my wife never kept no poppets. Mary Warren confesses it was her poppet.

CHEEVER: Your Excellency.

DANFORTH: Mr. Cheever.

CHEEVER: When I spoke with Goody Proctor in that house, she said she never kept no poppets. But she said she did keep poppets when she were a girl.

PROCTOR: She has not been a girl these fifteen years, Your Honor.

HATHORNE: But a poppet will keep fifteen years, will it not?

PROCTOR: It will keep if it is kept, but Mary Warren swears she never saw no poppets in my house, nor anyone else.

PARRIS: Why could there not have been poppets hid where no one ever saw them?

PROCTOR, *furious:* There might also be a dragon with five legs in my house, but no one has ever seen it.

PARRIS: We are here, Your Honor, precisely to discover what no one has ever seen.

PROCTOR: Mr. Danforth, what profit this girl to turn herself about? What may Mary Warren gain but hard questioning and worse?

DANFORTH: You are charging Abigail Williams with a marvelous cool plot to murder, do you understand that?

PROCTOR: I do, sir. I believe she means to murder.

DANFORTH, *pointing at Abigail, incredulously:* This child would murder your wife?

PROCTOR: It is not a child. Now hear me, sir. In the sight of the congregation she were twice this year put out of this meetin' house for laughter during prayer.

DANFORTH, *shocked, turning to Abigail:* What's this? Laughter during—!

PARRIS: Excellency, she were under Tituba's power at that time, but she is solemn now.

GILES: Aye, now she is solemn and goes to hang people!

DANFORTH: Quiet, man.

HATHORNE: Surely it have no bearing on the question, sir. He charges contemplation of murder.

DANFORTH: Aye. *He studies Abigail for a moment, then:* Continue, Mr. Proctor.

PROCTOR: Mary. Now tell the Governor how you danced in the woods.

PARRIS, *instantly:* Excellency, since I come to Salem this man is blackening my name. He—

DANFORTH: In a moment, sir. *To Mary Warren, sternly, and surprised:* What is this dancing?

MARY WARREN: I— *She glances at Abigail, who is staring down at her remorselessly. Then, appealing to Proctor:* Mr. Proctor—

PROCTOR, *taking it right up:* Abigail leads the girls to the woods, Your Honor, and they have danced there naked—

PARRIS: Your Honor, this—

PROCTOR, *at once:* Mr. Parris discovered them himself in the dead of night! There's the "child" she is!

DANFORTH—*it is growing into a nightmare, and he turns, astonished, to Parris:* Mr. Parris—

PARRIS: I can only say, sir, that I never found any of them naked, and this man is—

DANFORTH: But you discovered them dancing in the woods? *Eyes on Parris, he points at Abigail.* Abigail?

HALE: Excellency, when I first arrived from Beverly, Mr. Parris told me that.

DANFORTH: Do you deny it, Mr. Parris?

PARRIS: I do not, sir, but I never saw any of them naked.

DANFORTH: But she have *danced?*

PARRIS, *unwillingly:* Aye, sir.

Danforth, as though with new eyes, looks at Abigail.

HATHORNE: Excellency, will you permit me? *He points at Mary Warren.*

DANFORTH, *with great worry:* Pray, proceed.

HATHORNE: You say you never saw no spirits, Mary, were never threatened or afflicted by any manifest of the Devil or the Devil's agents.

MARY WARREN, *very faintly:* No, sir.

HATHORNE, *with a gleam of victory:* And yet, when people accused of witchery confronted you in court, you would faint, saying their spirits came out of their bodies and choked you—

MARY WARREN: That were pretense, sir.

DANFORTH: I cannot hear you.

MARY WARREN: Pretense, sir.

PARRIS: But you did turn cold, did you not? I myself picked you up many times, and your skin were icy. Mr. Danforth, you—

DANFORTH: I saw that many times.

PROCTOR: She only pretended to faint, Your Excellency. They're all marvelous pretenders.

HATHORNE: Then can she pretend to faint now?

PROCTOR: Now?

PARRIS: Why not? Now there are no spirits attacking her, for none in this room is accused of witchcraft. So let her turn herself cold now, let her pretend she is attacked now, let her faint. *He turns to Mary Warren.* Faint!

MARY WARREN: Faint?

PARRIS: Aye, faint. Prove to us how you pretended in the court so many times.

MARY WARREN, *looking to Proctor:* I—cannot faint now, sir.

PROCTOR, *alarmed, quietly:* Can you not pretend it?

MARY WARREN: I— *She looks about as though searching for the passion to faint.* I—have no *sense* of it now, I—

DANFORTH: Why? What is lacking now?

MARY WARREN: I—cannot tell, sir, I—

DANFORTH: Might it be that here we have no afflicting spirit loose, but in the court there were some?

MARY WARREN: I never saw no spirits.

PARRIS: Then see no spirits now, and prove to us that you can faint by your own will, as you claim.

MARY WARREN, *stares, searching for the emotion of it, and then shakes her head:* I—cannot do it.

PARRIS: Then you will confess, will you not? It were attacking spirits made you faint!

MARY WARREN: No, sir, I—

PARRIS: Your Excellency, this is a trick to blind the court!

MARY WARREN: It's not a trick! *She stands.* I—I used to faint because I—I thought I saw spirits.

DANFORTH: *Thought* you saw them!

MARY WARREN: But I did not, Your Honor.

HATHORNE: How could you think you saw them unless you saw them?

MARY WARREN: I—I cannot tell how, but I did. I—I heard the other girls screaming, and you, Your Honor, you seemed to believe them, and I— It were only sport in the beginning, sir, but then the whole world cried spirits, spirits, and I—I promise you, Mr. Danforth, I only thought I saw them but I did not.

Danforth peers at her.

PARRIS, *smiling, but nervous because Danforth seems to be struck by Mary Warren's story:* Surely Your Excellency is not taken by this simple lie.

DANFORTH, *turning worriedly to Abigail:* Abigail. I bid you now search your heart and tell me this—and beware of it, child, to God every soul is precious and His vengeance is terrible on them that take life without cause. Is it possible, child, that the spirits you have seen are illusion only, some deception that may cross your mind when—

ABIGAIL: Why, this—this—is a base question, sir.

DANFORTH: Child, I would have you consider it—

ABIGAIL: I have been hurt, Mr. Danforth; I have seen my blood runnin' out! I have been near to murdered every day because I done my duty pointing out the Devil's people—and this is my reward? To be mistrusted, denied, questioned like a—

DANFORTH, *weakening:* Child, I do not mistrust you—

ABIGAIL, *in an open threat:* Let *you* beware, Mr. Danforth. Think you to be so mighty that the power of Hell may not turn *your* wits? Beware of it! There is— *Suddenly, from an accusatory attitude, her face turns, looking into the air above—it is truly frightened.*

DANFORTH, *apprehensively:* What is it, child?

ABIGAIL, *looking about in the air, clasping her arms about her as though cold:* I—I know not. A wind, a cold wind, has come. *Her eyes fall on Mary Warren.*

MARY WARREN, *terrified, pleading:* Abby!

MERCY LEWIS, *shivering:* Your Honor, I freeze!

PROCTOR: They're pretending!

HATHORNE, *touching Abigail's hand:* She is cold, Your Honor, touch her!

MERCY LEWIS, *through chattering teeth:* Mary, do you send this shadow on me?

MARY WARREN: Lord, save me!

SUSANNA WALCOTT: I freeze, I freeze!

ABIGAIL, *shivering visibly:* It is a wind, a wind!

MARY WARREN: Abby, don't do that!

DANFORTH, *himself engaged and entered by Abigail:* Mary Warren, do you witch her? I say to you, do you send your spirit out?

With a hysterical cry Mary Warren starts to run. Proctor catches her.

MARY WARREN, *almost collapsing:* Let me go, Mr. Proctor, I cannot, I cannot—

ABIGAIL, *crying to Heaven:* Oh, Heavenly Father, take away this shadow!

Without warning or hesitation, Proctor leaps at Abigail and, grabbing her by the hair, pulls her to her feet. She screams in pain. Danforth, astonished, cries, "What are you about?" and Hathorne and Parris call, "Take your hands off her!" and out of it all comes Proctor's roaring voice.

PROCTOR: How do you call Heaven! Whore! Whore!

Herrick breaks Proctor from her.

HERRICK: John!

DANFORTH: Man! Man, what do you—

PROCTOR, *breathless and in agony:* It is a whore!

DANFORTH, *dumfounded:* You charge—?

ABIGAIL: Mr. Danforth, he is lying!

PROCTOR: Mark her! Now she'll suck a scream to stab me with, but—

DANFORTH: You will prove this! This will not pass!

PROCTOR, *trembling, his life collapsing about him:* I have known her, sir. I have known her.

DANFORTH: You—you are a lecher?

FRANCIS, *horrified:* John, you cannot say such a—

PROCTOR: Oh, Francis, I wish you had some evil in you that you might know me! *To Danforth:* A man will not cast away his good name. You surely know that.

DANFORTH, *dumfounded:* In—in what time? In what place?

PROCTOR, *his voice about to break, and his shame great:* In the proper place—where my beasts are bedded. On the last night of my joy, some eight months past. She used to serve me in my house, sir. *He has to clamp his jaw to keep from weeping.* A man may think God sleeps, but God sees everything, I know it now. I beg you, sir, I beg you—see her what she is. My wife, my dear good wife, took this girl soon after, sir, and put her out on the highroad. And being what she is, a lump of vanity, sir— *He is being overcome.* Excellency, forgive me, forgive me. *Angrily against himself, he turns away from the Governor for a moment. Then, as though to cry out is his only means of speech left:* She thinks to dance with me on my wife's grave! And well she might, for I thought of her softly. God help me, I lusted, and there *is* a promise in such sweat. But it is a whore's vengeance, and you must see it; I set myself entirely in your hands. I know you must see it now.

DANFORTH, *blanched, in horror, turning to Abigail:* You deny every scrap and tittle of this?

ABIGAIL: If I must answer that, I will leave and I will not come back again!

Danforth seems unsteady.

PROCTOR: I have made a bell of my honor! I have rung the doom of my good name—you will believe me, Mr. Danforth! My wife is innocent, except she knew a whore when she saw one!

ABIGAIL, *stepping up to Danforth:* What look do you give me? *Danforth cannot speak.* I'll not have such looks! *She turns and starts for the door.*

DANFORTH: You will remain where you are! *Herrick steps into her path. She comes up short, fire in her eyes.* Mr. Parris, go into the court and bring Goodwife Proctor out.

PARRIS, *objecting:* Your Honor, this is all a—

DANFORTH, *sharply to Parris:* Bring her out! And tell her not one word of what's been spoken here. And let you knock before you enter. *Parris goes out.* Now we shall touch the bottom of this swamp. *To Proctor:* Your wife, you say, is an honest woman.

PROCTOR: In her life, sir, she have never lied. There are them that cannot sing, and them that cannot weep—my wife cannot lie. I have paid much to learn it, sir.

DANFORTH: And when she put this girl out of your house, she put her out for a harlot?

PROCTOR: Aye, sir.

DANFORTH: And knew her for a harlot?

PROCTOR: Aye, sir, she knew her for a harlot.

DANFORTH: Good then. *To Abigail:* And if she tell me, child, it were for harlotry, may God spread His mercy on you! *There is a knock. He calls to the door.* Hold! *To Abigail:* Turn your back. Turn your back. *To Proctor:* Do likewise. *Both turn their backs—Abigail with indignant slowness.* Now let neither of you turn to face Goody Proctor. No one in this room is to speak one word, or raise a gesture aye or nay. *He turns toward the door, calls:* Enter! *The door opens. Elizabeth enters with Parris. Parris leaves her. She stands alone, her eyes looking for Proctor.* Mr. Cheever, report this testimony in all exactness. Are you ready?

CHEEVER: Ready, sir.

DANFORTH: Come here, woman. *Elizabeth comes to him, glancing at Proctor's back.* Look at me only, not at your husband. In my eyes only.

ELIZABETH, *faintly:* Good, sir.

DANFORTH: We are given to understand that at one time you dismissed your servant, Abigail Williams.

ELIZABETH: That is true, sir.

DANFORTH: For what cause did you dismiss her? *Slight pause. Then Elizabeth tries to glance at Proctor.* You will look in my eyes only and not at your husband. The answer is in your memory and you need no help to give it to me. Why did you dismiss Abigail Williams?

ELIZABETH, *not knowing what to say, sensing a situation, wetting her lips to stall for time:* She—dissatisfied me. *Pause.* And my husband.

DANFORTH: In what way dissatisfied you?

ELIZABETH: She were— *She glances at Proctor for a cue.*

DANFORTH: Woman, look at me! *Elizabeth does.* Were she slovenly? Lazy? What disturbance did she cause?

ELIZABETH: Your Honor, I—in that time I were sick. And I— My husband is a good and righteous man. He is never drunk as some are, nor wastin' his time at the shovelboard, but always at his work. But in my sickness—you see, sir, I were a long time sick after my last baby, and I thought I saw my husband somewhat turning from me. And this girl— *She turns to Abigail.*

DANFORTH: Look at me.

ELIZABETH: Aye, sir. Abigail Williams— *She breaks off.*

DANFORTH: What of Abigail Williams?

ELIZABETH: I came to think he fancied her. And so one night I lost my wits, I think, and put her out on the highroad.

DANFORTH: Your husband—did he indeed turn from you?

ELIZABETH, *in agony:* My husband—is a goodly man, sir.

DANFORTH: Then he did not turn from you.

ELIZABETH, *starting to glance at Proctor:* He—

DANFORTH, *reaches out and holds her face, then:* Look at me! To your own knowledge, has John Proctor ever committed the crime of lechery? *In a crisis of indecision she cannot speak.* Answer my question! Is your husband a lecher!

ELIZABETH, *faintly:* No, sir.

DANFORTH: Remove her, Marshal.

PROCTOR: Elizabeth, tell the truth!

DANFORTH: She has spoken. Remove her!

PROCTOR, *crying out:* Elizabeth, I have confessed it!

ELIZABETH: Oh, God! *The door closes behind her.*

PROCTOR: She only thought to save my name!

HALE: Excellency, it is a natural lie to tell; I beg you, stop now before another is condemned! I may shut my conscience to it no more—private vengeance is working through this testimony! From the beginning this man has struck me true. By my oath to Heaven, I believe him now, and I pray you call back his wife before we—

DANFORTH: She spoke nothing of lechery, and this man has lied!

HALE: I believe him! *Pointing at Abigail:* This girl has always struck me false! She has—

Abigail, with a weird, wild, chilling cry, screams up to the ceiling.

ABIGAIL: You will not! Begone! Begone, I say!

DANFORTH: What is it, child? *But Abigail, pointing with fear, is now raising up her frightened eyes, her awed face, toward the ceiling—the girls are doing the same—and now Hathorne, Hale, Putnam, Cheever, Herrick, and Danforth do the same.* What's there? *He lowers his eyes from the ceiling, and now he is frightened; there is real tension in his voice.* Child! *She is transfixed —with all the girls, she is whimpering open-mouthed, agape at the ceiling.* Girls! Why do you—?

MERCY LEWIS, *pointing:* It's on the beam! Behind the rafter!

DANFORTH, *looking up:* Where!

ABIGAIL: Why—? *She gulps.* Why do you come, yellow bird?

PROCTOR: Where's a bird? I see no bird!

ABIGAIL, *to the ceiling:* My face? My face?

PROCTOR: Mr. Hale—

DANFORTH: Be quiet!

PROCTOR, *to Hale:* Do you see a bird?

DANFORTH: Be quiet!!

ABIGAIL, *to the ceiling, in a genuine conversation with the "bird," as though trying to talk it out of attacking her:* But God made my face; you cannot want to tear my face. Envy is a deadly sin, Mary.

MARY WARREN, *on her feet with a spring, and horrified, pleading:* Abby!

ABIGAIL, *unperturbed, continuing to the "bird":* Oh, Mary, this is a black art to change your shape. No, I cannot, I cannot stop my mouth; it's God's work I do.

MARY WARREN: Abby, I'm *here!*

PROCTOR, *frantically:* They're pretending, Mr. Danforth!

ABIGAIL—*now she takes a backward step, as though in fear the bird will swoop down momentarily:* Oh, please, Mary! Don't come down.

SUSANNA WALCOTT: Her claws, she's stretching her claws!

PROCTOR: Lies, lies.

ABIGAIL, *backing further, eyes still fixed above:* Mary, please don't hurt me!

MARY WARREN, *to Danforth:* I'm not hurting her!

DANFORTH, *to Mary Warren:* Why does she see this vision?

MARY WARREN: She sees nothin'!

ABIGAIL, *now staring full front as though hypnotized, and mimicking the exact tone of Mary Warren's cry:* She sees nothin'!

MARY WARREN, *pleading:* Abby, you mustn't!

ABIGAIL AND ALL THE GIRLS, *all transfixed:* Abby, you mustn't!

MARY WARREN, *to all the girls:* I'm here, I'm here!

GIRLS: I'm here, I'm here!

DANFORTH, *horrified:* Mary Warren! Draw back your spirit out of them!

MARY WARREN: Mr. Danforth!

GIRLS, *cutting her off:* Mr. Danforth!

DANFORTH: Have you compacted with the Devil? Have you?

MARY WARREN: Never, never!

GIRLS: Never, never!

DANFORTH, *growing hysterical:* Why can they only repeat you?

PROCTOR: Give me a whip—I'll stop it!

MARY WARREN: They're sporting. They—!

GIRLS: They're sporting!

MARY WARREN, *turning on them all hysterically and stamping her feet:* Abby, stop it!

GIRLS, *stamping their feet:* Abby, stop it!

MARY WARREN: Stop it!

GIRLS: Stop it!

MARY WARREN, *screaming it out at the top of her lungs, and raising her fists:* Stop it!!

GIRLS, *raising their fists:* Stop it!!

Mary Warren, utterly confounded, and becoming overwhelmed by Abigail's—and the girls'—utter conviction, starts to whimper, hands half raised, powerless, and all the girls begin whimpering exactly as she does.

DANFORTH: A little while ago you were afflicted. Now it seems you afflict others; where did you find this power?

MARY WARREN, *staring at Abigail:* I—have no power.

GIRLS: I have no power.

PROCTOR: They're gulling you, Mister!

DANFORTH: Why did you turn about this past two weeks? You have seen the Devil, have you not?

HALE, *indicating Abigail and the girls:* You cannot believe them!

MARY WARREN: I—

PROCTOR, *sensing her weakening:* Mary, God damns all liars!

DANFORTH, *pounding it into her:* You have seen the Devil, you have made compact with Lucifer, have you not?

PROCTOR: God damns liars, Mary!

Mary utters something unintelligible, staring at Abigail, who keeps watching the "bird" above.

DANFORTH: I cannot hear you. What do you say? *Mary utters again unintelligibly.* You will confess yourself or you will hang! *He turns her roughly to face him.* Do you know who I am? I say you will hang if you do not open with me!

PROCTOR: Mary, remember the angel Raphael—do that which is good and—

ABIGAIL, *pointing upward:* The wings! Her wings are spreading! Mary, please, don't, don't—!

HALE: I see nothing, Your Honor!

DANFORTH: Do you confess this power! *He is an inch from her face.* Speak!

ABIGAIL: She's going to come down! She's walking the beam!

DANFORTH: Will you speak!

MARY WARREN, *staring in horror:* I cannot!

GIRLS: I cannot!

PARRIS: Cast the Devil out! Look him in the face! Trample him! We'll save you, Mary, only stand fast against him and——

ABIGAIL, *looking up:* Look out! She's coming down!

She and all the girls run to one wall, shielding their eyes. And now, as though cornered, they let out a gigantic scream, and Mary, as though infected, opens her mouth and screams with them. Gradually Abigail and the girls leave off, until only Mary is left there, staring up at the "bird," screaming madly. All watch her, horrified by this evident fit. Proctor strides to her.

PROCTOR: Mary, tell the Governor what they— *He has hardly got a word out, when, seeing him coming for her, she rushes out of his reach, screaming in horror.*

MARY WARREN: Don't touch me—don't touch me! *At which the girls halt at the door.*

PROCTOR, *astonished*: Mary!

MARY WARREN, *pointing at Proctor:* You're the Devil's man!

He is stopped in his tracks.

PARRIS: Praise God!

GIRLS: Praise God!

PROCTOR, *numbed:* Mary, how—?

MARY WARREN: I'll not hang with you! I love God, I love God.

DANFORTH, *to Mary:* He bid you do the Devil's work?

MARY WARREN, *hysterically, indicating Proctor:* He come at me by night and every day to sign, to sign, to—

DANFORTH: Sign what?

PARRIS: The Devil's book? He come with a book?

MARY WARREN, *hysterically, pointing at Proctor, fearful of him:* My name, he want my name. "I'll murder you," he says, "if my wife hangs! We must go and overthrow the court," he says!

Danforth's head jerks toward Proctor, shock and horror in his face.

PROCTOR, *turning, appealing to Hale:* Mr. Hale!

MARY WARREN, *her sobs beginning:* He wake me every night, his eyes were like coals and his fingers claw my neck, and I sign, I sign . . .

HALE: Excellency, this child's gone wild!

PROCTOR, *as Danforth's wide eyes pour on him:* Mary, Mary!

MARY WARREN, *screaming at him:* No, I love God; I go your way no more. I love God, I bless God. *Sobbing, she rushes to Abigail.* Abby, Abby, I'll never hurt you more! *They all watch, as Abigail, out of her infinite charity, reaches out and draws the sobbing Mary to her, and then looks up to Danforth.*

DANFORTH, *to Proctor:* What are you? *Proctor is beyond speech in his anger.* You are combined with anti-Christ, are you not? I have seen your power; you will not deny it! What say you, Mister?

HALE: Excellency—

DANFORTH: I will have nothing from you, Mr. Hale! *To Proctor:* Will you confess yourself befouled with Hell, or do you keep that black allegiance yet? What say you?

PROCTOR, *his mind wild, breathless:* I say—I say—God is dead!

PARRIS: Hear it, hear it!

PROCTOR, *laughs insanely, then:* A fire, a fire is burning! I hear the boot of Lucifer, I see his filthy face! And it is my face, and yours, Danforth! For them that quail to bring men out of ignorance, as I have quailed, and as you quail now when you know in all your black hearts that this be fraud—God damns our kind especially, and we will burn, we will burn together!

DANFORTH: Marshal! Take him and Corey with him to the jail!

HALE, *starting across to the door:* I denounce these proceedings!

PROCTOR: You are pulling Heaven down and raising up a whore!

HALE: I denounce these proceedings, I quit this court! *He slams the door to the outside behind him.*

DANFORTH, *calling to him in a fury:* Mr. Hale! Mr. Hale!

THE CURTAIN FALLS

ACT FOUR

A cell in Salem jail, that fall.

At the back is a high barred window; near it, a great, heavy door. Along the walls are two benches.

The place is in darkness but for the moonlight seeping through the bars. It appears empty. Presently footsteps are heard coming down a corridor beyond the wall, keys rattle, and the door swings open. Marshal Herrick enters with a lantern.

He is nearly drunk, and heavy-footed. He goes to a bench and nudges a bundle of rags lying on it.

HERRICK: Sarah, wake up! Sarah Good! *He then crosses to the other bench.*

SARAH GOOD, *rising in her rags:* Oh, Majesty! Comin', comin'! Tituba, he's here, His Majesty's come!

HERRICK: Go to the north cell; this place is wanted now. *He hangs his lantern on the wall. Tituba sits up.*

TITUBA: That don't look to me like His Majesty; look to me like the marshal.

HERRICK, *taking out a flask:* Get along with you now, clear this

121

place. *He drinks, and Sarah Good comes and peers up into his face.*

SARAH GOOD: Oh, is it you, Marshal! I thought sure you be the devil comin' for us. Could I have a sip of cider for me goin'-away?

HERRICK, *handing her the flask:* And where are you off to, Sarah?

TITUBA, *as Sarah drinks:* We goin' to Barbados, soon the Devil gits here with the feathers and the wings.

HERRICK: Oh? A happy voyage to you.

SARAH GOOD: A pair of bluebirds wingin' southerly, the two of us! Oh, it be a grand transformation, Marshal! *She raises the flask to drink again.*

HERRICK, *taking the flask from her lips:* You'd best give me that or you'll never rise off the ground. Come along now.

TITUBA: I'll speak to him for you, if you desires to come along, Marshal.

HERRICK: I'd not refuse it, Tituba; it's the proper morning to fly into Hell.

TITUBA: Oh, it be no Hell in Barbados. Devil, him be pleasure-man in Barbados, him be singin' and dancin' in Barbados. It's you folks—you riles him up 'round here; it be too cold 'round here for that Old Boy. He freeze his soul in Massachusetts, but in Barbados he just as sweet and— *A bellowing cow is heard, and Tituba leaps up and calls to the window:* Aye, sir! That's him, Sarah!

SARAH GOOD: I'm here, Majesty! *They hurriedly pick up their rags as Hopkins, a guard, enters.*

HOPKINS: The Deputy Governor's arrived.

HERRICK, *grabbing Tituba:* Come along, come along.

TITUBA, *resisting him:* No, he comin' for me. I goin' home!

HERRICK, *pulling her to the door:* That's not Satan, just a poor old cow with a hatful of milk. Come along now, out with you!

TITUBA, *calling to the window:* Take me home, Devil! Take me home!

SARAH GOOD, *following the shouting Tituba out:* Tell him I'm goin', Tituba! Now you tell him Sarah Good is goin' too!

In the corridor outside Tituba calls on—"Take me home, Devil; Devil take me home!" and Hopkins' voice orders her to move on. Herrick returns and begins to push old rags and straw into a corner. Hearing footsteps, he turns, and enter Danforth and Judge Hathorne. They are in greatcoats and wear hats against the bitter cold. They are followed in by Cheever, who carries a dispatch case and a flat wooden box containing his writing materials.

HERRICK: Good morning, Excellency.

DANFORTH: Where is Mr. Parris?

HERRICK: I'll fetch him. *He starts for the door.*

DANFORTH: Marshal. *Herrick stops.* When did Reverend Hale arrive?

HERRICK: It were toward midnight, I think.

DANFORTH, *suspiciously:* What is he about here?

HERRICK: He goes among them that will hang, sir. And he prays with them. He sits with Goody Nurse now. And Mr. Parris with him.

DANFORTH: Indeed. That man have no authority to enter here, Marshal. Why have you let him in?

HERRICK: Why, Mr. Parris command me, sir. I cannot deny him.

DANFORTH: Are you drunk, Marshal?

HERRICK: No, sir; it is a bitter night, and I have no fire here.

DANFORTH, *containing his anger:* Fetch Mr. Parris.

HERRICK: Aye, sir.

DANFORTH: There is a prodigious stench in this place.

HERRICK: I have only now cleared the people out for you.

DANFORTH: Beware hard drink, Marshal.

HERRICK: Aye, sir. *He waits an instant for further orders. But Danforth, in dissatisfaction, turns his back on him, and Herrick goes out. There is a pause. Danforth stands in thought.*

HATHORNE: Let you question Hale, Excellency; I should not be surprised he have been preaching in Andover lately.

DANFORTH: We'll come to that; speak nothing of Andover. Parris prays with him. That's strange. *He blows on his hands, moves toward the window, and looks out.*

HATHORNE: Excellency, I wonder if it be wise to let Mr. Parris so continuously with the prisoners. *Danforth turns to him, interested.* I think, sometimes, the man has a mad look these days.

DANFORTH: Mad?

HATHORNE: I met him yesterday coming out of his house, and I bid him good morning—and he wept and went his way. I think it is not well the village sees him so unsteady.

DANFORTH: Perhaps he have some sorrow.

CHEEVER, *stamping his feet against the cold:* I think it be the cows, sir.

DANFORTH: Cows?

CHEEVER: There be so many cows wanderin' the highroads, now their masters are in the jails, and much disagreement who they will belong to now. I know Mr. Parris be arguin' with farmers all yesterday—there is great contention, sir, about the cows. Contention make him weep, sir; it were always a man that weep for contention. *He turns, as do Hathorne and Danforth, hearing someone coming up the corridor. Danforth raises his head as Parris enters. He is gaunt, frightened, and sweating in his greatcoat.*

PARRIS, *to Danforth, instantly:* Oh, good morning, sir, thank you for coming, I beg your pardon wakin' you so early. Good morning, Judge Hathorne.

DANFORTH: Reverend Hale have no right to enter this—

PARRIS: Excellency, a moment. *He hurries back and shuts the door.*

HATHORNE: Do you leave him alone with the prisoners?

DANFORTH: What's his business here?

PARRIS, *prayerfully holding up his hands:* Excellency, hear me. It is a providence. Reverend Hale has returned to bring Rebecca Nurse to God.

DANFORTH, *surprised:* He bids her confess?

PARRIS, *sitting:* Hear me. Rebecca have not given me a word this three month since she came. Now she sits with him, and her sister and Martha Corey and two or three others, and he pleads with them, confess their crimes and save their lives.

DANFORTH: Why—this is indeed a providence. And they soften, they soften?

PARRIS: Not yet, not yet. But I thought to summon you, sir, that we might think on whether it be not wise, to— *He dares not say it.* I had thought to put a question, sir, and I hope you will not—

DANFORTH: Mr. Parris, be plain, what troubles you?

PARRIS: There is news, sir, that the court—the court must reckon with. My niece, sir, my niece—I believe she has vanished.

DANFORTH: Vanished!

PARRIS: I had thought to advise you of it earlier in the week, but—

DANFORTH: Why? How long is she gone?

PARRIS: This be the third night. You see, sir, she told me she would stay a night with Mercy Lewis. And next day, when she does not return, I send to Mr. Lewis to inquire. Mercy told him she would sleep in *my* house for a night.

DANFORTH: They are both gone?!

PARRIS, *in fear of him:* They are, sir.

DANFORTH, *alarmed:* I will send a party for them. Where may they be?

PARRIS: Excellency, I think they be aboard a ship. *Danforth stands agape.* My daughter tells me how she heard them speaking of ships last week, and tonight I discover my—my strongbox is broke into. *He presses his fingers against his eyes to keep back tears.*

HATHORNE, *astonished:* She have robbed you?

PARRIS: Thirty-one pound is gone. I am penniless. *He covers his face and sobs.*

DANFORTH: Mr. Parris, you are a brainless man! *He walks in thought, deeply worried.*

PARRIS: Excellency, it profit nothing you should blame me. I cannot think they would run off except they fear to keep in Salem any more. *He is pleading.* Mark it, sir, Abigail had close knowledge of the town, and since the news of Andover has broken here—

DANFORTH: Andover is remedied. The court returns there on Friday, and will resume examinations.

PARRIS: I am sure of it, sir. But the rumor here speaks rebellion in Andover, and it—

DANFORTH: There is no rebellion in Andover!

PARRIS: I tell you what is said here, sir. Andover have thrown out the court, they say, and will have no part of witchcraft. There be a faction here, feeding on that news, and I tell you true, sir, I fear there will be riot here.

HATHORNE: Riot! Why at every execution I have seen naught but high satisfaction in the town.

PARRIS: Judge Hathorne—it were another sort that hanged till now. Rebecca Nurse is no Bridget that lived three year with Bishop before she married him. John Proctor is not Isaac Ward that drank his family to ruin. *To Danforth:* I would to God it were not so, Excellency, but these people have great weight yet in the town. Let Rebecca stand upon the gibbet and send up some righteous prayer, and I fear she'll wake a vengeance on you.

HATHORNE: Excellency, she is condemned a witch. The court have—

DANFORTH, *in deep concern, raising a hand to Hathorne:* Pray you. *To Parris:* How do you propose, then?

PARRIS: Excellency, I would postpone these hangin's for a time.

DANFORTH: There will be no postponement.

PARRIS: Now Mr. Hale's returned, there is hope, I think—for if he bring even one of these to God, that confession surely damns the others in the public eye, and none may doubt more that they are all linked to Hell. This way, unconfessed and claiming innocence, doubts are multiplied, many honest people will weep for them, and our good purpose is lost in their tears.

DANFORTH, *after thinking a moment, then going to Cheever:* Give me the list.

Cheever opens the dispatch case, searches.

PARRIS: It cannot be forgot, sir, that when I summoned the congregation for John Proctor's excommunication there were hardly thirty people come to hear it. That speak a discontent, I think, and—

DANFORTH, *studying the list:* There will be no postponement.

PARRIS: Excellency—

DANFORTH: Now, sir—which of these in your opinion may be brought to God? I will myself strive with him till dawn. *He hands the list to Parris, who merely glances at it.*

PARRIS: There is not sufficient time till dawn.

DANFORTH: I shall do my utmost. Which of them do you have hope for?

PARRIS, *not even glancing at the list now, and in a quavering voice, quietly:* Excellency—a dagger— *He chokes up.*

DANFORTH: What do you say?

PARRIS: Tonight, when I open my door to leave my house—a dagger clattered to the ground. *Silence. Danforth absorbs this. Now Parris cries out:* You cannot hang this sort. There is danger for me. I dare not step outside at night!

Reverend Hale enters. They look at him for an instant in silence.

He is steeped in sorrow, exhausted, and more direct than he ever was.

DANFORTH: Accept my congratulations, Reverend Hale; we are gladdened to see you returned to your good work.

HALE, *coming to Danforth now:* You must pardon them. They will not budge.

Herrick enters, waits.

DANFORTH, *conciliatory:* You misunderstand, sir; I cannot pardon these when twelve are already hanged for the same crime. It is not just.

PARRIS, *with failing heart:* Rebecca will not confess?

HALE: The sun will rise in a few minutes. Excellency, I must have more time.

DANFORTH: Now hear me, and beguile yourselves no more. I will not receive a single plea for pardon or postponement. Them that will not confess will hang. Twelve are already executed; the names of these seven are given out, and the village expects to see them die this morning. Postponement now speaks a floundering on my part; reprieve or pardon must cast doubt upon the guilt of them that died till now. While I speak God's law, I will not crack its voice with whimpering. If retaliation is your fear, know this—I should hang ten thousand that dared to rise against the law, and an ocean of salt tears could not melt the resolution of the statutes. Now draw yourselves up like men and help me, as you are bound by Heaven to do. Have you spoken with them all, Mr. Hale?

HALE: All but Proctor. He is in the dungeon.

DANFORTH, *to Herrick:* What's Proctor's way now?

HERRICK: He sits like some great bird; you'd not know he lived except he will take food from time to time.

DANFORTH, *after thinking a moment:* His wife—his wife must be well on with child now.

HERRICK: She is, sir.

DANFORTH: What think you, Mr. Parris? You have closer knowledge of this man; might her presence soften him?

PARRIS: It is possible, sir. He have not laid eyes on her these three months. I should summon her.

DANFORTH, *to Herrick:* Is he yet adamant? Has he struck at you again?

HERRICK: He cannot, sir, he is chained to the wall now.

DANFORTH, *after thinking on it:* Fetch Goody Proctor to me. Then let you bring him up.

HERRICK: Aye, sir. *Herrick goes. There is silence.*

HALE: Excellency, if you postpone a week and publish to the town that you are striving for their confessions, that speak mercy on your part, not faltering.

DANFORTH: Mr. Hale, as God have not empowered me like Joshua to stop this sun from rising, so I cannot withhold from them the perfection of their punishment.

HALE, *harder now:* If you think God wills you to raise rebellion, Mr. Danforth, you are mistaken!

DANFORTH, *instantly:* You have heard rebellion spoken in the town?

HALE: Excellency, there are orphans wandering from house to house; abandoned cattle bellow on the highroads, the stink of rotting crops hangs everywhere, and no man knows when the harlots' cry will end his life—and you wonder yet if rebellion's spoke? Better you should marvel how they do not burn your province!

DANFORTH: Mr. Hale, have you preached in Andover this month?

HALE: Thank God they have no need of me in Andover.

DANFORTH: You baffle me, sir. Why have you returned here?

HALE: Why, it is all simple. I come to do the Devil's work. I come to counsel Christians they should belie themselves. *His sarcasm collapses.* There is blood on my head! Can you not see the blood on my head!!

PARRIS: Hush! *For he has heard footsteps. They all face the door. Herrick enters with Elizabeth. Her wrists are linked by heavy chain, which Herrick now removes. Her clothes are dirty; her face is pale and gaunt. Herrick goes out.*

DANFORTH, *very politely:* Goody Proctor. *She is silent.* I hope you are hearty?

ELIZABETH, *as a warning reminder:* I am yet six month before my time.

DANFORTH: Pray be at your ease, we come not for your life. We—*uncertain how to plead, for he is not accustomed to it.* Mr. Hale, will you speak with the woman?

HALE: Goody Proctor, your husband is marked to hang this morning.

Pause.

ELIZABETH, *quietly:* I have heard it.

HALE: You know, do you not, that I have no connection with the court? *She seems to doubt it.* I come of my own, Goody Proctor. I would save your husband's life, for if he is taken I count myself his murderer. Do you understand me?

ELIZABETH: What do you want of me?

HALE: Goody Proctor, I have gone this three month like our Lord into the wilderness. I have sought a Christian way, for damnation's doubled on a minister who counsels men to lie.

HATHORNE: It is no lie, you cannot speak of lies.

HALE: It is a lie! They are innocent!

DANFORTH: I'll hear no more of that!

HALE, *continuing to Elizabeth:* Let you not mistake your duty as I mistook my own. I came into this village like a bridegroom to his beloved, bearing gifts of high religion; the very crowns of holy law I brought, and what I touched with my bright confidence, it died; and where I turned the eye of my great faith, blood flowed up. Beware, Goody Proctor—cleave to no faith when faith brings blood. It is mistaken law that leads you to sacrifice. Life, woman, life is God's most precious gift; no principle, however glorious, may justify the taking of it. I beg you, woman, prevail upon your husband to confess. Let him give his lie. Quail not before God's judgment in this, for it may well be God damns a liar less than he that throws his life away for pride. Will you plead with him? I cannot think he will listen to another.

ELIZABETH, *quietly:* I think that be the Devil's argument.

HALE, *with a climactic desperation:* Woman, before the laws of God we are as swine! We cannot read His will!

ELIZABETH: I cannot dispute with you, sir; I lack learning for it.

DANFORTH, *going to her:* Goody Proctor, you are not summoned here for disputation. Be there no wifely tenderness within you? He will die with the sunrise. Your husband. Do you understand it? *She only looks at him.* What say you? Will you contend with him? *She is silent.* Are you stone? I tell you true, woman, had I no other proof of your unnatural life, your dry eyes now would be sufficient evidence that you delivered up your soul to

Hell! A very ape would weep at such calamity! Have the devil
dried up any tear of pity in you? *She is silent.* Take her out. It
profit nothing she should speak to him!

ELIZABETH, *quietly:* Let me speak with him, Excellency.

PARRIS, *with hope:* You'll strive with him? *She hesitates.*

DANFORTH: Will you plead for his confession or will you not?

ELIZABETH: I promise nothing. Let me speak with him.

*A sound—the sibilance of dragging feet on stone. They turn.
A pause. Herrick enters with John Proctor. His wrists are
chained. He is another man, bearded, filthy, his eyes misty as
though webs had overgrown them. He halts inside the doorway,
his eye caught by the sight of Elizabeth. The emotion flowing
between them prevents anyone from speaking for an instant.
Now Hale, visibly affected, goes to Danforth and speaks quietly.*

HALE: Pray, leave them, Excellency.

DANFORTH, *pressing Hale impatiently aside:* Mr. Proctor, you
have been notified, have you not? *Proctor is silent, staring at
Elizabeth.* I see light in the sky, Mister; let you counsel with
your wife, and may God help you turn your back on Hell.
Proctor is silent, staring at Elizabeth.

HALE, *quietly:* Excellency, let—

*Danforth brushes past Hale and walks out. Hale follows. Cheever
stands and follows, Hathorne behind. Herrick goes. Parris, from
a safe distance, offers:*

PARRIS: If you desire a cup of cider, Mr. Proctor, I am sure
I— *Proctor turns an icy stare at him, and he breaks off. Parris
raises his palms toward Proctor.* God lead you now. *Parris goes
out.*

*Alone. Proctor walks to her, halts. It is as though they stood in
a spinning world. It is beyond sorrow, above it. He reaches out*

*his hand as though toward an embodiment · ot quite real, and
as he touches her, a strange soft sound, half laughter, half
amazement, comes from his throat. He pats her hand. She covers
his hand with hers. And then, weak, he sits. Then she sits,
facing him.*

PROCTOR: The child?

ELIZABETH: It grows.

PROCTOR: There is no word of the boys?

ELIZABETH: They're well. Rebecca's Samuel keeps them.

PROCTOR: You have not seen them?

ELIZABETH: I have not. *She catches a weakening in herself and
downs it.*

PROCTOR: You are a—marvel, Elizabeth.

ELIZABETH: You—have been tortured?

PROCTOR: Aye. *Pause. She will not let herself be drowned in
the sea that threatens her.* They come for my life now.

ELIZABETH: I know it.

Pause.

PROCTOR: None—have yet confessed?

ELIZABETH: There be many confessed.

PROCTOR: Who are they?

ELIZABETH: There be a hundred or more, they say. Goody
Ballard is one; Isaiah Goodkind is one. There be many.

PROCTOR: Rebecca?

ELIZABETH: Not Rebecca. She is one foot in Heaven now;
naught may hurt her more.

PROCTOR: And Giles?

ELIZABETH: You have not heard of it?

PROCTOR: I hear nothin', where I am kept.

ELIZABETH: Giles is dead.

He looks at her incredulously.

PROCTOR: When were he hanged?

ELIZABETH, *quietly, factually:* He were not hanged. He would not answer aye or nay to his indictment; for if he denied the charge they'd hang him surely, and auction out his property. So he stand mute, and died Christian under the law. And so his sons will have his farm. It is the law, for he could not be condemned a wizard without he answer the indictment, aye or nay.

PROCTOR: Then how does he die?

ELIZABETH, *gently:* They press him, John.

PROCTOR: Press?

ELIZABETH: Great stones they lay upon his chest until he plead aye or nay. *With a tender smile for the old man:* They say he give them but two words. "More weight," he says. And died.

PROCTOR, *numbed—a thread to weave into his agony:* "More weight."

ELIZABETH: Aye. It were a fearsome man, Giles Corey.

Pause.

PROCTOR, *with great force of will, but not quite looking at her:* I have been thinking I would confess to them, Elizabeth. *She shows nothing.* What say you? If I give them that?

ELIZABETH: I cannot judge you, John.

Pause.

PROCTOR, *simply—a pure question:* What would you have me do?

ELIZABETH: As you will, I would have it. *Slight pause:* I want you living, John. That's sure.

PROCTOR, *pauses, then with a flailing of hope:* Giles' wife? Have she confessed?

ELIZABETH: She will not.

Pause.

PROCTOR: It is a pretense, Elizabeth.

ELIZABETH: What is?

PROCTOR: I cannot mount the gibbet like a saint. It is a fraud. I am not that man. *She is silent.* My honesty is broke, Elizabeth; I am no good man. Nothing's spoiled by giving them this lie that were not rotten long before.

ELIZABETH: And yet you've not confessed till now. That speak goodness in you.

PROCTOR: Spite only keeps me silent. It is hard to give a lie to dogs. *Pause, for the first time he turns directly to her.* I would have your forgiveness, Elizabeth.

ELIZABETH: It is not for me to give, John, I am—

PROCTOR: I'd have you see some honesty in it. Let them that never lied die now to keep their souls. It is pretense for me, a vanity that will not blind God nor keep my children out of the wind. *Pause.* What say you?

ELIZABETH, *upon a heaving sob that always threatens:* John, it come to naught that I should forgive you, if you'll not forgive yourself. *Now he turns away a little, in great agony.* It is not my soul, John, it is yours. *He stands, as though in physical pain, slowly rising to his feet with a great immortal longing to find his answer. It is difficult to say, and she is on the verge of tears.* Only be sure of this, for I know it now: Whatever you will do, it is a good man does it. *He turns his doubting, searching gaze upon her.* I have read my heart this three month, John. *Pause.* I have sins of my own to count. It needs a cold wife to prompt lechery.

PROCTOR, *in great pain:* Enough, enough—

ELIZABETH, *now pouring out her heart:* Better you should know me!

PROCTOR: I will not hear it! I know you!

ELIZABETH: You take my sins upon you, John—

PROCTOR, *in agony:* No, I take my own, my own!

ELIZABETH: John, I counted myself so plain, so poorly made, no honest love could come to me! Suspicion kissed you when I did; I never knew how I should say my love. It were a cold house I kept! *In fright, she swerves, as Hathorne enters.*

HATHORNE: What say you, Proctor? The sun is soon up.

Proctor, his chest heaving, stares, turns to Elizabeth. She comes to him as though to plead, her voice quaking.

ELIZABETH: Do what you will. But let none be your judge. There be no higher judge under Heaven than Proctor is! Forgive me, forgive me, John—I never knew such goodness in the world! *She covers her face, weeping.*

Proctor turns from her to Hathorne; he is off the earth, his voice hollow.

PROCTOR: I want my life.

HATHORNE, *electrified, surprised:* You'll confess yourself?

PROCTOR: I will have my life.

HATHORNE, *with a mystical tone:* God be praised! It is a providence! *He rushes out the door, and his voice is heard calling down the corridor:* He will confess! Proctor will confess!

PROCTOR, *with a cry, as he strides to the door:* Why do you cry it? *In great pain he turns back to her.* It is evil, is it not? It is evil.

ELIZABETH, *in terror, weeping:* I cannot judge you, John, I cannot!

PROCTOR: Then who will judge me? *Suddenly clasping his hands:* God in Heaven, what is John Proctor, what is John Proctor? *He moves as an animal, and a fury is riding in him, a tantalized search.* I think it is honest, I think so; I am no saint. *As though she had denied this he calls angrily at her:* Let Rebecca go like a saint; for me it is fraud!

Voices are heard in the hall, speaking together in suppressed excitement.

ELIZABETH: I am not your judge, I cannot be. *As though giving him release:* Do as you will, do as you will!

PROCTOR: Would you give them such a lie? Say it. Would you ever give them this? *She cannot answer.* You would not; if tongs of fire were singeing you you would not! It is evil. Good, then—it is evil, and I do it!

Hathorne enters with Danforth, and, with them, Cheever, Parris, and Hale. It is a businesslike, rapid entrance, as though the ice had been broken.

DANFORTH, *with great relief and gratitude:* Praise to God, man, praise to God; you shall be blessed in Heaven for this. *Cheever has hurried to the bench with pen, ink, and paper. Proctor watches him.* Now then, let us have it. Are you ready, Mr. Cheever?

PROCTOR, *with a cold, cold horror at their efficiency:* Why must it be written?

DANFORTH: Why, for the good instruction of the village, Mister; this we shall post upon the church door! *To Parris, urgently:* Where is the marshal?

PARRIS, *runs to the door and calls down the corridor:* Marshal! Hurry!

DANFORTH: Now, then, Mister, will you speak slowly, and directly to the point, for Mr. Cheever's sake. *He is on record now, and is really dictating to Cheever, who writes.* Mr. Proctor, have you seen the Devil in your life? *Proctor's jaws lock.* Come, man, there is light in the sky; the town waits at the scaffold; I would give out this news. Did you see the Devil?

PROCTOR: I did.

PARRIS: Praise God!

DANFORTH: And when he come to you, what were his demand? *Proctor is silent. Danforth helps.* Did he bid you to do his work upon the earth?

PROCTOR: He did.

DANFORTH: And you bound yourself to his service? *Danforth turns, as Rebecca Nurse enters, with Herrick helping to support her. She is barely able to walk.* Come in, come in, woman!

REBECCA, *brightening as she sees Proctor:* Ah, John! You are well, then, eh?

Proctor turns his face to the wall.

DANFORTH: Courage, man, courage—let her witness your good example that she may come to God herself. Now hear it, Goody Nurse! Say on, Mr. Proctor. Did you bind yourself to the Devil's service?

REBECCA, *astonished:* Why, John!

PROCTOR, *through his teeth, his face turned from Rebecca:* I did.

DANFORTH: Now, woman, you surely see it profit nothin' to keep this conspiracy any further. Will you confess yourself with him?

REBECCA: Oh, John—God send his mercy on you!

DANFORTH: I say, will you confess yourself, Goody Nurse?

REBECCA: Why, it is a lie, it is a lie; how may I damn myself? I cannot, I cannot.

DANFORTH: Mr. Proctor. When the Devil came to you did you see Rebecca Nurse in his company? *Proctor is silent.* Come, man, take courage—did you ever see her with the Devil?

PROCTOR, *almost inaudibly:* No.

Danforth, now sensing trouble, glances at John and goes to the table, and picks up a sheet—the list of condemned.

DANFORTH: Did you ever see her sister, Mary Easty, with the Devil?

PROCTOR: No, I did not.

DANFORTH, *his eyes narrow on Proctor:* Did you ever see Martha Corey with the Devil?

PROCTOR: I did not.

DANFORTH, *realizing, slowly putting the sheet down:* Did you ever see anyone with the Devil?

PROCTOR: I did not.

DANFORTH: Proctor, you mistake me. I am not empowered to trade your life for a lie. You have most certainly seen some person with the Devil. *Proctor is silent.* Mr. Proctor, a score of people have already testified they saw this woman with the Devil.

PROCTOR: Then it is proved. Why must I say it?

DANFORTH: Why "must" you say it! Why, you should rejoice to say it if your soul is truly purged of any love for Hell!

PROCTOR: They think to go like saints. I like not to spoil their names.

DANFORTH, *inquiring, incredulous:* Mr. Proctor, do you think they go like saints?

PROCTOR, *evading:* This woman never thought she done the Devil's work.

DANFORTH: Look you, sir. I think you mistake your duty here. It matters nothing what she thought—she is convicted of the unnatural murder of children, and you for sending your spirit out upon Mary Warren. Your soul alone is the issue here, Mister, and you will prove its whiteness or you cannot live in a Christian country. Will you tell me now what persons conspired with you in the Devil's company? *Proctor is silent.* To your knowledge was Rebecca Nurse ever—

PROCTOR: I speak my own sins; I cannot judge another. *Crying out, with hatred:* I have no tongue for it.

HALE, *quickly to Danforth:* Excellency, it is enough he confess himself. Let him sign it, let him sign it.

PARRIS, *feverishly:* It is a great service, sir. It is a weighty name; it will strike the village that Proctor confess. I beg you, let him sign it. The sun is up, Excellency!

DANFORTH, *considers; then with dissatisfaction:* Come, then, sign your testimony. *To Cheever:* Give it to him. *Cheever goes to Proctor, the confession and a pen in hand. Proctor does not look at it.* Come, man, sign it.

PROCTOR, *after glancing at the confession:* You have all witnessed it—it is enough.

DANFORTH: You will not sign it?

PROCTOR: You have all witnessed it; what more is needed?

DANFORTH: Do you sport with me? You will sign your name or it is no confession, Mister! *His breast heaving with agonized breathing, Proctor now lays the paper down and signs his name.*

PARRIS: Praise be to the Lord!

Proctor has just finished signing when Danforth reaches for the paper. But Proctor snatches it up, and now a wild terror is rising in him, and a boundless anger.

DANFORTH, *perplexed, but politely extending his hand:* If you please, sir.

PROCTOR: No.

DANFORTH, *as though Proctor did not understand:* Mr. Proctor, I must have—

PROCTOR: No, no. I have signed it. You have seen me. It is done! You have no need for this.

PARRIS: Proctor, the village must have proof that—

PROCTOR: Damn the village! I confess to God, and God has seen my name on this! It is enough!

DANFORTH: No, sir, it is—

PROCTOR: You came to save my soul, did you not? Here! I have confessed myself; it is enough!

DANFORTH: You have not con—

PROCTOR: I have confessed myself! Is there no good penitence but it be public? God does not need my name nailed upon the church! God sees my name; God knows how black my sins are! It is enough!

DANFORTH: Mr. Proctor—

PROCTOR: You will not use me! I am no Sarah Good or Tituba,

I am John Proctor! You will not use me! It is no part of salvation that you should use me!

DANFORTH: I do not wish to—

PROCTOR: I have three children—how may I teach them to walk like men in the world, and I sold my friends?

DANFORTH: You have not sold your friends—

PROCTOR: Beguile me not! I blacken all of them when this is nailed to the church the very day they hang for silence!

DANFORTH: Mr. Proctor, I must have good and legal proof that you—

PROCTOR: You are the high court, your word is good enough! Tell them I confessed myself; say Proctor broke his knees and wept like a woman; say what you will, but my name cannot—

DANFORTH, *with suspicion:* It is the same, is it not? If I report it or you sign to it?

PROCTOR—*he knows it is insane:* No, it is not the same! What others say and what I sign to is not the same!

DANFORTH: Why? Do you mean to deny this confession when you are free?

PROCTOR: I mean to deny nothing!

DANFORTH: Then explain to me, Mr. Proctor, why you will not let—

PROCTOR, *with a cry of his whole soul:* Because it is my name! Because I cannot have another in my life! Because I lie and sign myseif to lies! Because I am not worth the dust on the feet of them that hang! How may I live without my name? I have given you my soul; leave me my name!

DANFORTH, *pointing at the confession in Proctor's hand:* Is that document a lie? If it is a lie I will not accept it! What say you?

I will not deal in lies, Mister! *Proctor is motionless.* You will give me your honest confession in my hand, or I cannot keep you from the rope. *Proctor does not reply.* Which way do you go, Mister?

His breast heaving, his eyes staring, Proctor tears the paper and crumples it, and he is weeping in fury, but erect.

DANFORTH: Marshal!

PARRIS, *hysterically, as though the tearing paper were his life:* Proctor, Proctor!

HALE: Man, you will hang! You cannot!

PROCTOR, *his eyes full of tears:* I can. And there's your first marvel, that I can. You have made your magic now, for now I do think I see some shred of goodness in John Proctor. Not enough to weave a banner with, but white enough to keep it from such dogs. *Elizabeth, in a burst of terror, rushes to him and weeps against his hand.* Give them no tear! Tears pleasure them! Show honor now, show a stony heart and sink them with it! *He has lifted her, and kisses her now with great passion.*

REBECCA: Let you fear nothing! Another judgment waits us all!

DANFORTH: Hang them high over the town! Who weeps for these, weeps for corruption! *He sweeps out past them. Herrick starts to lead Rebecca, who almost collapses, but Proctor catches her, and she glances up at him apologetically.*

REBECCA: I've had no breakfast.

HERRICK: Come, man.

Herrick escorts them out, Hathorne and Cheever behind them. Elizabeth stands staring at the empty doorway.

PARRIS, *in deadly fear, to Elizabeth:* Go to him, Goody Proctor! There is yet time!

From outside a drumroll strikes the air. Parris is startled. Elizabeth jerks about toward the window.

PARRIS: Go to him! *He rushes out the door, as though to hold back his fate.* Proctor! Proctor!

Again, a short burst of drums.

HALE: Woman, plead with him! *He starts to rush out the door, and then goes back to her.* Woman! It is pride, it is vanity. *She avoids his eyes, and moves to the window. He drops to his knees.* Be his helper!—What profit him to bleed? Shall the dust praise him? Shall the worms declare his truth? Go to him, take his shame away!

ELIZABETH, *supporting herself against collapse, grips the bars of the window, and with a cry:* He have his goodness now. God forbid I take it from him!

The final drumroll crashes, then heightens violently. Hale weeps in frantic prayer, and the new sun is pouring in upon her face, and the drums rattle like bones in the morning air.

THE CURTAIN FALLS

ECHOES DOWN THE CORRIDOR

Not long after the fever died, Parris was voted from office, walked out on the highroad, and was never heard of again.

The legend has it that Abigail turned up later as a prostitute in Boston.

Twenty years after the last execution, the government awarded compensation to the victims still living, and to the families of the dead. However, it is evident that some people still were unwilling to admit their total guilt, and also that the factionalism was still alive, for some beneficiaries were actually not victims at all, but informers.

Elizabeth Proctor married again, four years after Proctor's death.

In solemn meeting, the congregation rescinded the excommunications—this in March 1712. But they did so upon orders of the government. The jury, however, wrote a statement praying forgiveness of all who had suffered.

Certain farms which had belonged to the victims were left to ruin, and for more than a century no one would buy them or live on them.

To all intents and purposes, the power of theocracy in Massachusetts was broken.

THE CRUCIBLE

A PLAY BY ARTHUR MILLER

STAGED BY JED HARRIS

CAST (*in order of appearance*)

REVEREND PARRIS	Fred Stewart
BETTY PARRIS	Janet Alexander
TITUBA	Jacqueline Andre
ABIGAIL WILLIAMS	Madeleine Sherwood
SUSANNA WALCOTT	Barbara Stanton
MRS. ANN PUTNAM	Jane Hoffman
THOMAS PUTNAM	Raymond Bramley
MERCY LEWIS	Dorothy Joliffe
MARY WARREN	Jennie Egan
JOHN PROCTOR	Arthur Kennedy
REBECCA NURSE	Jean Adair
GILES COREY	Joseph Sweeney
REVEREND JOHN HALE	E. G. Marshall
ELIZABETH PROCTOR	Beatrice Straight
FRANCIS NURSE	Graham Velsey
EZEKIEL CHEEVER	Don McHenry
MARSHAL HERRICK	George Mitchell
JUDGE HATHORNE	Philip Coolidge
DEPUTY GOVERNOR DANFORTH	Walter Hampden
SARAH GOOD	Adele Fortin
HOPKINS	Donald Marye

The settings were designed by Boris Aronson. The costumes were made and designed by Edith Lutyens.

Presented by Kermit Bloomgarden at the Martin Beck Theatre in New York on January 22, 1953.

APPENDIX

ACT TWO, SCENE 2

A wood. Night.

Proctor enters with lantern, glowing behind him, then halts, holding lantern raised. Abigail appears with a wrap over her nightgown, her hair down. A moment of questioning silence.

PROCTOR, *searching:* I must speak with you, Abigail. *She does not move, staring at him.* Will you sit?

ABIGAIL: How do you come?

PROCTOR: Friendly.

ABIGAIL, *glancing about:* I don't like the woods at night. Pray you, stand closer. *He comes closer to her.* I knew it must be you. When I heard the pebbles on the window, before I opened up my eyes I knew. *Sits on log.* I thought you would come a good time sooner.

PROCTOR: I had thought to come many times.

ABIGAIL: Why didn't you? I am so alone in the world now.

PROCTOR, *as a fact, not bitterly:* Are you! I've heard that people ride a hundred mile to see your face these days.

ABIGAIL: Aye, my face. Can you see my face?

PROCTOR, *holds lantern to her face:* Then you're troubled?

ABIGAIL: Have you come to mock me?

PROCTOR, *sets lantern on ground. Sits next to her:* No, no, but I hear only that you go to the tavern every night, and play shovel-board with the Deputy Governor, and they give you cider.

ABIGAIL: I have once or twice played the shovelboard. But I have no joy in it.

PROCTOR: This is a surprise, Abby. I'd thought to find you gayer than this. I'm told a troop of boys go step for step with you wherever you walk these days.

ABIGAIL: Aye, they do. But I have only lewd looks from the boys.

PROCTOR: And you like that not?

ABIGAIL: I cannot bear lewd looks no more, John. My spirit's changed entirely. I ought be given Godly looks when I suffer for them as I do.

PROCTOR: Oh? How do you suffer, Abby?

ABIGAIL, *pulls up dress:* Why, look at my leg. I'm holes all over from their damned needles and pins. *Touching her stomach:* The jab your wife gave me's not healed yet, y'know.

PROCTOR, *seeing her madness now:* Oh, it isn't.

ABIGAIL: I think sometimes she pricks it open again while I sleep.

PROCTOR: Ah?

ABIGAIL: And George Jacobs—*sliding up her sleeve*—he comes again and again and raps me with his stick—the same spot every night all this week. Look at the lump I have.

PROCTOR: Abby—George Jacobs is in the jail all this month.

ABIGAIL: Thank God he is, and bless the day he hangs and lets

me sleep in peace again! Oh, John, the world's so full of hypocrites! *Astonished, outraged:* They pray in jail! I'm told they all
pray in jail!

PROCTOR: They may not pray?

ABIGAIL: And torture me in my bed while sacred words are
comin' from their mouths? Oh, it will need God Himself to
cleanse this town properly!

PROCTOR: Abby—you mean to cry out still others?

ABIGAIL: If I live, if I am not murdered, I surely will, until the
last hypocrite is dead.

PROCTOR: Then there is no good?

ABIGAIL: Aye, there is one. *You* are good.

PROCTOR: Am I! How am I good?

ABIGAIL: Why, you taught me goodness, therefore you are good.
It were a fire you walked me through, and all my ignorance was
burned away. It were a fire, John, we lay in fire. And from that
night no woman dare call me wicked any more but I knew my
answer. I used to weep for my sins when the wind lifted up my
skirts; and blushed for shame because some old Rebecca called
me loose. And then you burned my ignorance away. As bare as
some December tree I saw them all—walking like saints to
church, running to feed the sick, and hypocrites in their hearts!
And God gave me strength to call them liars, and God made
men to listen to me, and by God I will scrub the world clean
for the love of Him! Oh, John, I will make you such a wife
when the world is white again! *She kisses his hand.* You will be
amazed to see me every day, a light of heaven in your house, a—
He rises, backs away amazed. Why are you cold?

PROCTOR: My wife goes to trial in the morning, Abigail.

ABIGAIL, *distantly:* Your wife?

PROCTOR: Surely you knew of it?

ABIGAIL: I do remember it now. How—how— Is she well?

PROCTOR: As well as she may be, thirty-six days in that place.

ABIGAIL: You said you came friendly.

PROCTOR: She will not be condemned, Abby.

ABIGAIL: You brought me from my bed to speak of her?

PROCTOR: I come to tell you, Abby, what I will do tomorrow in the court. I would not take you by surprise, but give you all good time to think on what to do to save yourself.

ABIGAIL: Save myself!

PROCTOR: If you do not free my wife tomorrow, I am set and bound to ruin you, Abby.

ABIGAIL, *her voice small—astonished:* How—ruin me?

PROCTOR: I have rocky proof in documents that you knew that poppet were none of my wife's; and that you yourself bade Mary Warren stab that needle into it.

ABIGAIL—*a wildness stirs in her, a child is standing here who is unutterably frustrated, denied her wish, but she is still grasping for her wits:* I bade Mary Warren—?

PROCTOR: You know what you do, you are not so mad!

ABIGAIL: Oh, hypocrites! Have you won him, too? John, why do you let them send you?

PROCTOR: I warn you, Abby!

ABIGAIL: They send you! They steal your honesty and—

PROCTOR: I have found my honesty!

ABIGAIL: No, this is your wife pleading, your sniveling, envious wife! This is Rebecca's voice, Martha Corey's voice. You were no hypocrite!

PROCTOR: I will prove you for the fraud you are!

ABIGAIL: And if they ask you why Abigail would ever do so murderous a deed, what will you tell them?

PROCTOR: I will tell them why.

ABIGAIL: What will you tell? You will confess to fornication? In the court?

PROCTOR: If you will have it so, so I will tell it! *She utters a disbelieving laugh.* I say I will! *She laughs louder, now with more assurance he will never do it. He shakes her roughly.* If you can still hear, hear this! Can you hear! *She is trembling, staring up at him as though he were out of his mind.* You will tell the court you are blind to spirits; you cannot see them any more, and you will never cry witchery again, or I will make you famous for the whore you are!

ABIGAIL, *grabs him:* Never in this world! I know you, John— you are this moment singing secret hallelujahs that your wife will hang!

PROCTOR, *throws her down:* You mad, you murderous bitch!

ABIGAIL: Oh, how hard it is when pretense falls! But it falls, it falls! *She wraps herself up as though to go.* You have done your duty by her. I hope it is your last hypocrisy. I pray you will come again with sweeter news for me. I know you will—now that your duty's done. Good night, John. *She is backing away, raising her hand in farewell.* Fear naught. I will save you tomorrow. *As she turns and goes:* From yourself I will save you. *She is gone. Proctor is left alone, amazed, in terror. Takes up his lantern and slowly exits.*

A NOTE ON THE TEXT

The preceding is the standard Viking Compass text of *The Crucible*, pagination unchanged. Aside from the scene in the Appendix, the text is essentially the one used in *Collected Plays*.

The extra scene was written after *The Crucible* opened on Broadway. Toward the end of the New York run (it closed July 11, 1953), before the play went on tour, Miller restaged the production and added the new scene. *Playbill* for the week beginning June 22 first lists it—as Act II, Scene 1. At that time, the present Act I was called Prologue and each of the other three acts carried a number one less than its present designation. Thus, the new scene was played as introductory to the present Act III. When the play was published in *Theatre Arts*, XXXVII (October 1953), 35-67, the scene became Act II, Scene 2, a designation used in the acting edition (New York: Dramatists Play Service, 1954). It has since been played both ways. To me, it seems obvious that it should introduce Act III, for a brief scene tacked on the end of Act II would milk away the dramatic force of Proctor's slow build to a commitment to fight the court and the rhetoric about "God's icy wind" with which he crowns his decision.

Miller wrote a second version of the insert scene for Laurence Olivier's production of the play at the Old Vic (1965), and "he [Olivier] went crazy about it." So Miller told a class at the University of Michigan. Then, despite his enthusiasm, Olivier dropped the scene. He explained to Miller:

You know really, you don't need it. It's nice when you read the play. You get an expanded view of it. But it destroyed that certain marching tempo that starts to get into that play to that place. There's a drumbeat underneath, which begins somewhere

—I don't know exactly where—but in a good production it starts to beat, and this scene stops the beat.

Ironically, although Olivier is probably right, the scene has existed until now only in the acted play. Here, the original version of the scene takes its place in the reading edition of the play—rightly in an Appendix, I think, since, whatever it adds to our understanding of Abigail, it is not an obligatory scene in the development of the play, either dramatically or thematically. The Miller-Olivier quotations are from the *Michigan Quarterly Review*, VI (Summer 1967), 182.

G. W.

EDITORIAL NOTE

In the critical section of this volume all footnotes are mine unless they carry the author's initials. Omissions, of course, are indicated by ellipses.

G. W.

II

CRITICISM AND ANALOGUES

Miller On *The Crucible*

MANY WRITERS: FEW PLAYS

It is impossible for anyone living in the midst of a cultural period to say with certainty why it is languishing in its produce and general vitality. This is especially true of the theatre, where we tend to compare our usually vapid present with "Chekhov's" period, or "Ibsen's," or our own previous decades, much to our disadvantage, forgetting that the giants usually stood alone in their time. Nevertheless, even optimists now confess that our theatre has struck a seemingly endless low by any standard. I cannot hope to try to explain the reasons for this, but certain clues keep recurring to me when I am thinking on the matter.

We can find no solace in the fact that there never have been more than a handful of first-class playwrights in any one country at any one time, for we have more than the usual number in America now, but few plays from them, and fewer still of any weight. A lizardic dormancy seems to be upon us; the creative mind seems to have lost its heat. Why?

From *The New York Times*, August 10, 1952, II, p. 1. Copyright 1952 by Arthur Miller. Although there is no mention of *The Crucible* in this essay, the play—at least, in an early form—would have been written by the time the piece appeared.

I think the answers will be found in the nature of the creative act. A good play is a good thought; a great play is a great thought. A great thought is a thrust outward, a daring act. Daring is of the essence. Its very nature is incompatible with an undue affection for moderation, respectability, even fairness and responsibleness. Those qualities are proper for the inside of the telephone company, not for creative art.

I may be wrong, but I sense that the playwrights have become more timid with experience and maturity, timid in ethical and social idea, theatrical method, and stylistic means. Because they are unproduced, no firm generalization can be made about the younger playwrights, but from my personal impressions of scripts sent me from time to time, as well as from talks I have had with a few groups of them, I have been struck and dismayed by the strangely high place they give to inoffensiveness.

I find them old without having been young. Like young executives, they seem proudest of their sensibleness—what they call being practical. Illusion is out; it is foolish. What illusion? The illusion that the writer can save the world. The fashion is that the world cannot be saved. Between the determinism of economics and the iron laws of psychiatrics they can only appear ridiculous, they think, by roaring out a credo, a cry of pain, a point of view. Perhaps they really have no point of view, or pain either. It is incomprehensible to me.

Recently a young Chilean director, who has put on more than thirty plays in his own country, and spent the past three years studying theatre on a fellowship in France, in Britain, and in two of our leading universities, told me this: "Your students and teachers seem to have no interest at all in the meanings of the ideas in the plays they study. Everything is technique. Your productions and physical apparatus are the best in the world, but among all the university people I came to know, as well as the professionals, scarcely any want to talk about the authors' ethical, moral, or philosophical intentions. They seem to see the theatre almost as an engineering project, the purpose being to study successful models of form in order, somehow, to reproduce them with other words."

All this means to me, if true, is that this generation is turning Japanese. The Japanese are said to admire infinite repetitions of time-hallowed stories, characters, and themes. It is the triumph of the practical in art. The most practical thing to do is to repeat what has been done and thought before. But the very liquor of our art has always been originality, uniqueness. The East is older. Perhaps this sterile lull is therefore the sign of our aging. Perhaps we are observing several seasons of hush and silence to mark the passage through of our youth. Our youth that was Shaw and Ibsen and O'Neill and all the great ones who kept turning and turning the central question of all great art—how may man govern himself so that he may live more humanly, more alive?

Japanism, so to speak, took over Hollywood long ago, and now the movie is ritual thinly veiled. The practical took command. The "showman" won. High finance took sterility by the hand, and together they rolled the product smooth, stripped off all its offensive edges, its individuality, and created the perfect circle—namely, zero.

I think the same grinding mill is at work in the theatre, but more deceptively because we have no big companies enforcing compliance to any stated rules. But we have an atmosphere of dread just the same, an unconsciously—or consciously—accepted party line, a sanctified complex of moods and attitudes, proper and improper. If nothing else comes of it, one thing surely has: it has made it dangerous to dare, and, worse still, impractical. I am not speaking merely of political thought. Journalists have recently made studies of college students now in school and have been struck by the absence among them of any ferment, either religious, political, literary, or whatever. Wealthy, powerful, envied all about, it seems the American people stand mute.

We always had with us the "showman," but we also had a group of rebels insisting on thrusting their private view of the world on others. Where are they? Or is everybody really happy now? Do Americans really believe they have solved the problems of living for all time? If not, where are the plays that reflect the soul-racking, deeply unseating questions that are being inwardly asked on the street, in the living room, on the subways?

Either the playwrights are deaf to them, which I cannot believe, or they are somehow shy of bringing them onto the stage. If the last is true we are unlikely to have even the "straight" theatre again, the melodramas, the farces, the "small" plays. It is hard to convince you of this, perhaps, but little thoughts feed off big thoughts; an exciting theatre cannot come without there being a ferment, a ferment in the colleges, in the press, in the air. For years now I seem to have heard not expressions of thought from people but a sort of oblong blur, a reflection in distance of the newspapers' opinions.

Is the knuckleheadedness of McCarthyism behind it all? The Congressional investigations of political unorthodoxy? Yes. But is that all? Can an artist be paralyzed except he be somewhat willing? You may pardon me for quoting from myself, but must one always be not merely liked but well liked? Is it not honorable to have powerful enemies? Guardedness, suspicion, aloof circumspection—these are the strongest traits I see around me, and what have they ever had to do with the creative act?

Is it quixotic to say that a time comes for an artist—and for all those who want and love theatre—when the world must be left behind? When, like some pilgrim, he must consult only his own heart and cleave to the truth it utters? For out of the hectoring of columnists, the compulsions of patriotic gangs, the suspicions of the honest and the corrupt alike, art never will and never has found soil.

I think of a night last week when a storm knocked out my

lights in the country, and as it was only nine o'clock it was unthinkable to go to bed. I sat a long time in the blacked-out living room, wide awake, a manuscript unfinished on the table. The idea of lying in bed with one's eyes open, one's brain alive, seemed improper, even degrading. And so, like some primitive man discovering the blessings of fire, I lit two candles and experimentally set them beside my papers. Lo! I could read and work again.

Let a storm come, even from God, and yet it leaves a choice with the man in the dark. He may sit eyeless, waiting for some unknown force to return him his light, or he may seek his private flame. But the choice, the choice is there. We cannot yet be tired. There is work to be done. This is no time to go to sleep.

INTRODUCTION TO
COLLECTED PLAYS

. . . If the reception of *All My Sons* and *Death of a Salesman* had made the world a friendly place for me, events of the early fifties quickly turned that warmth into an illusion. It was not only the rise of "McCarthyism" that moved me, but something which seemed much more weird and mysterious. It was the fact that a political, objective, knowledgeable campaign from the far Right was capable of creating not only

From *Collected Plays* by Arthur Miller (New York: Viking, 1957), pp. 39-45. Copyright © 1957 by Arthur Miller. All rights reserved. Published by The Viking Press, Inc. The complete Introduction (pp. 3-55) contains a general statement on playwriting and detailed comments on all the Miller plays from *All My Sons* through *A View from the Bridge*.

a terror, but a new subjective reality, a veritable mystique which was gradually assuming even a holy resonance. The wonder of it all struck me that so practical and picayune a cause, carried forward by such manifestly ridiculous men, should be capable of paralyzing thought itself, and worse, causing to billow up such persuasive clouds of "mysterious" feelings within people. It was as though the whole country had been born anew, without a memory even of certain elemental decencies which a year or two earlier no one would have imagined could be altered, let alone forgotten. Astounded, I watched men pass me by without a nod whom I had known rather well for years; and again, the astonishment was produced by my knowledge, which I could not give up, that the terror in these people was being knowingly planned and consciously engineered, and yet that all they knew was terror. That so interior and subjective an emotion could have been so manifestly created from without was a marvel to me. It underlies every word in *The Crucible.*

I wondered, at first, whether it must be that self-preservation and the need to hold on to opportunity, the thought of being exiled and "put out," was what the fear was feeding on, for there were people who had had only the remotest connections with the Left who were quite as terrified as those who had been closer. I knew of one man who had been summoned to the office of a network executive and, on explaining that he had had no Left connections at all, despite the then current attacks upon him, was told that this was precisely the trouble; "You have nothing to give them," he was told, meaning he had no confession to make, and so he was fired from his job and for more than a year could not recover the will to leave his house.

It seemed to me after a time that this, as well as other kinds of social compliance, is the result of the sense of guilt which individuals strive to conceal by complying. Generally it was a guilt, in this historic instance, resulting from their awareness that they were not as Rightist as people were supposed to be; that the tenor of public pronouncements was alien to them and that they must be somehow discoverable as enemies of the power overhead. There was a new religiosity in the air, not merely the kind expressed by the spurt in church construction and church attendance, but an official piety which my reading of American history could not reconcile with the free-wheeling iconoclasm of the country's past.[1] I saw forming a kind of interior mechanism of confession and forgiveness of sins which until now had not been rightly categorized as sins. New sins were being created monthly. It was very odd how quickly these were accepted into the new orthodoxy, quite as though they had been there since the beginning of time. Above all, above all horrors, I saw accepted the notion that conscience was no longer a private matter but one of state administration. I saw men handing conscience to other men and thanking other men for the opportunity of doing so.

I wished for a way to write a play that would be sharp, that would lift out of the morass of subjectivism the squirming, single, defined process which would show that the sin of public terror is that it divests man of conscience, of himself. It was a theme not unrelated to those that had invested the previous plays. In *The Crucible*, however, there was an attempt to move beyond the discovery and unveiling of the hero's guilt, a guilt that kills the personality. I had grown increasingly conscious of this theme in my past work, and aware too that it was no longer enough for me to build a play, as it were, upon the revelation of guilt, and to rely solely upon a fate which exacts payment from the culpable man. Now guilt appeared to me no longer the bedrock beneath which the probe could not penetrate. I saw it now as a

---

[1] See William Lee Miller, "Piety Along the Potomac," *The Reporter*, XI (August 17, 1954), 25-28, for a circumstantial account of the "new religiosity."

betrayer, as possibly the most real of our illusions, but nevertheless a quality of mind capable of being overthrown.

I had known of the Salem witch hunt for many years before "McCarthyism" had arrived, and it had always remained an inexplicable darkness to me. When I looked into it now, however, it was with the contemporary situation at my back, particularly the mystery of the handing over of conscience which seemed to me the central and informing fact of the time. One finds, I suppose, what one seeks. I doubt I should ever have tempted agony by actually writing a play on the subject had I not come upon a single fact. It was that Abigail Williams, the prime mover of the Salem hysteria, so far as the hysterical children were concerned, had a short time earlier been the house servant of the Proctors and now was crying out Elizabeth Proctor as a witch; but more—it was clear from the record that with entirely uncharacteristic fastidiousness she was refusing to include John Proctor, Elizabeth's husband, in her accusations despite the urgings of the prosecutors.[2] Why? I searched the records of the trials in the courthouse at Salem but in no other instance could I find such a careful avoidance of the implicating stutter, the murderous, ambivalent answer to the sharp questions of the prosecutors. Only here, in Proctor's case, was there so clear an attempt to differentiate between a wife's culpability and a husband's.

The testimony of Proctor himself is one of the least elaborate in the records, and Elizabeth is not one of the major cases either. There could have been numerous reasons for his having been ultimately apprehended and hanged which are nowhere to be found. After the play opened, several of his descendants wrote to me; and one of them believes that Proctor fell under suspicion because, according to family tradition, he had for years been an amateur inventor whose machines appeared

---

[2] As an example of finding what one seeks, compare this statement with "Abigail Williams *v.* John Proctor," the accusation reprinted, p. 372.

to some people as devilish in their ingenuity, and—again according to tradition—he had had to conceal them and work on them privately long before the witch hunt had started, for fear of censure if not worse. The explanation does not account for everything, but it does fall in with his evidently liberated cast of mind as revealed in the record; he was one of the few who not only refused to admit consorting with evil spirits, but who persisted in calling the entire business a ruse and a fake. Most, if not all, of the other victims were of their time in conceding the existence of the immemorial plot by the Devil to take over the visible world, their only reservation being that they happened not to have taken part in it themselves.

It was the fact that Abigail, their former servant, was their accuser, and her apparent desire to convict Elizabeth and save John, that made the play conceivable for me.

As in any such mass phenomenon, the number of characters of vital, if not decisive, importance is so great as to make the dramatic problem excessively difficult. For a time it seemed best to approach the town impressionistically, and, by a mosaic of seemingly disconnected scenes, gradually to form a context of cause and effect. This I believe I might well have done had it not been that the central impulse for writing at all was not the social but the interior psychological question, which was the question of that guilt residing in Salem which the hysteria merely unleashed but did not create. Consequently, the structure reflects that understanding, and it centers in John, Elizabeth, and Abigail.

In reading the record, which was taken down verbatim at the trial, I found one recurring note which had a growing effect upon my concept, not only of the phenomenon itself, but of our modern way of thinking about people, and especially of the treatment of evil in contemporary drama. Some critics have taken exception, for instance, to the unrelieved badness of the prosecution in my play. I understand how this is possible, and I plead no mitigation, but I was up against historical facts which were immutable. I do not think that either the record itself or the numerous commentaries upon it reveal any mitigation of the unrelieved, straightforward, and absolute dedication to evil displayed by the judges of these trials and the prosecutors. After days of study it became quite incredible how perfect they were in this respect. I recall, almost as in a dream, how Rebecca Nurse, a pious and universally respected woman of great age, was literally taken by force from her sickbed and ferociously cross-examined. No human weakness could be displayed without the prosecution's stabbing into it with greater fury. The most patent contradictions, almost laughable even in that day, were overridden with warnings not to repeat their mention. There was a sadism here that was breathtaking.

So much so, that I sought but could not at the time take hold of a concept of man which might really begin to account for such evil. For instance, it seems beyond doubt that members of the Putnam family consciously, coldly, and with malice aforethought conferred in private with some of the girls, and told them whom it was desirable to cry out upon next. There is and will always be in my mind the spectacle of the great minister and ideological authority behind the prosecution, Cotton Mather, galloping up to the scaffold to beat back a crowd of villagers so moved by the towering dignity of the victims as to want to free them.

It was not difficult to foresee the objections to such absolute evil in men; we are committed, after all, to the belief that it does not and cannot exist. Had I this play to write now, however, I might proceed on an altered concept. I should say that my own—and the critics'—unbelief in this depth of evil is concomitant with our unbelief in good, too. I should now examine this fact of evil as such. Instead, I sought to make Danforth, for instance, perceptible as a human being by showing him somewhat put off by Mary Warren's turnabout at the height of the trials, which caused no little confusion. In my play, Danforth seems about to conceive of the truth, and surely there is a disposition in him at least to listen to arguments that go counter to the line of the prosecution. There is no such swerving in the record, and I think now, almost four years after the writing of it, that I was wrong in mitigating the evil of this man and the judges he represents.[3] Instead, I would perfect his evil to its utmost and make an open issue, a thematic consideration of it in the play. I believe now, as I did not conceive then, that there are people dedicated to evil in the world; that without their perverse example we should not know the good. Evil is not a mistake but a fact in itself. I have never proceeded psychoanalytically in my thought, but neither have I been separated from that humane if not humanistic conception of man as being essentially innocent while the evil in him represents but a perversion of his frustrated love. I posit no metaphysical force of evil which totally possesses certain individuals, nor do I even deny that given infinite wisdom and patience and knowledge any human being can be saved from himself. I believe merely that, from whatever cause, a dedication to evil, not mistaking it for good, but knowing it as evil and loving it as evil, is possible in human beings who appear agreeable and normal. I think now that one of the hidden weaknesses of our whole approach to dramatic psychology is our inability to face this fact—to conceive, in effect, of Iago.

The Crucible is a "tough" play. My criticism of it now would be that it is not tough enough. I say this not merely

---

[3] Miller's choice of Danforth for this role perhaps stems from the fact that he signed the early arrest orders and presided at the examination of the Proctors. William Stoughton, the Lieutenant Governor of Massachusetts, who served as chief justice of the Special Court of Oyer and Terminer, which actually did the sentencing, comes closer to the figure Miller has in mind. See pp. 173-174 for a fuller statement by Miller on the Danforth character.

out of deference to the record of these trials, but out of a consideration for drama. We are so intent upon getting sympathy for our characters that the consequences of evil are being muddied by sentimentality under the guise of a temperate weighing of causes. The tranquillity of the bad man lies at the heart of not only moral philosophy but dramaturgy as well. But my central intention in this play was to one side of this idea, which was realized only as the play was in production. All I sought here was to take a step not only beyond the realization of guilt, but beyond the helpless victimization of the hero.

The society of Salem was "morally" vocal. People then avowed principles, sought to live by them and die by them. Issues of faith, conduct, society, pervaded their private lives in a conscious way. They needed but to disapprove to act. I was drawn to this subject because the historical moment seemed to give me the poetic right to create people of higher self-awareness than the contemporary scene affords. I had explored the subjective world in *Salesman* and I wanted now to move closer to a conscious hero.

The decidedly mixed reception to the play was not easily traceable, but I believe there are causes for it which are of moment to more than this play alone. I believe that the very moral awareness of the play and its characters—which are historically correct—was repulsive to the audience. For a variety of reasons I think that the Anglo-Saxon audience cannot believe the reality of characters who live by principles and know very much about their own characters and situations, and who say what they know. Our drama, for this among other reasons, is condemned, so to speak, to the emotions of subjectivism, which, as they approach knowledge and self-awareness, become less and less actual and real to us. In retrospect I think that my course in *The Crucible* should have been toward greater self-awareness and not, as my critics have implied, toward an enlarged and more pervasive subjectivism. The realistic form and style of the play would then have had to give way. What new form might have evolved I cannot now say, but certainly the passion of knowing is as powerful as the passion of feeling alone, and the writing of the play broached the question of that new form for me. . . .

BREWED IN *THE CRUCIBLE*

One afternoon last week I attended a rehearsal of the imminent Off Broadway production of *The Crucible*. For the first time in the five years since its opening on Broadway, I heard its dialogue, and the experience awakened not merely memories but the desire to fire a discussion among us of certain questions a play like this ought to have raised.

Notoriously, there is what is called a chemistry in the theatre, a fusion of play, performance, and audience temper which, if it does not take place, leaves the elements of an explosion cold and to one side of art. For the critics, this seems to be what happened with *The Crucible*. It was not condemned; it was set aside. A cold thing, mainly, it lay to one side of entertainment, to say nothing of art. In a word, I was told that I had not written another *Death of a Salesman*.

It is perhaps beyond my powers to make clear, but I had no desire to write another *Salesman*, and not because I lack love for that play but for some wider, less easily defined reasons

From *The New York Times*, March 9, 1958, II, p. 3. Copyright © 1958 by Arthur Miller. The Off Broadway revival which occasioned this article opened at the Martinique on March 11, 1958. Directed by Word Baker, the production ran for more than a year and closed on June 14, 1959, after 633 performances. The production used a narrator, called The Reader, to set the scenes and give the historical background of the play.

that have to do with this whole question of cold and heat, and, indeed, with the future of our drama altogether. It is the question of whether we—playwrights and audiences and critics—are to declare that we have reached the end, the last development of dramatic form. More specifically, the play designed to draw a tear; the play designed to "identify" the audience with its characters in the usual sense; the play that takes as its highest challenge the emotional relations of the family, for that, as it turns out, is what it comes to.

I was disappointed in the reaction to *The Crucible* not only for the obvious reasons but because no critic seemed to sense what I was after. In 1953 McCarthyism probably helped to make it appear that the play was bounded on all sides by its arraignment of the witch hunt. The political trajectory was so clear—a fact of which I am a little proud—that what to me were equally if not more important elements were totally ignored. The new production, appearing in a warmer climate, may, I hope, flower, and these inner petals may make their appropriate appearance.

What I say now may appear more technical than a writer has any business talking about in public. But I do not think it merely a question of technique to say that with all its excellences the kind of play we have come to accept without effort or question is standing at a dead end. What "moves" us is coming to be a narrower and narrower aesthetic fragment of life. I have shown, I think, that I am not unaware of psychology or immune to the fascinations of the neurotic hero, but I believe that it is no longer possible to contain the truth of the human situation so totally within a single man's guts as the bulk of our plays presuppose. The documentation of man's loneliness is not in itself and for itself ultimate wisdom, and the form this documentation inevitably assumes in playwriting is not the ultimate dramatic form.

I was drawn to write *The Crucible* not merely as a response to McCarthyism. It is not any more an attempt to cure witch hunts than *Salesman* is a plea for the improvement of conditions for traveling men, *All My Sons* a plea for better inspection of airplane parts, or *A View from the Bridge* an attack upon the Immigration Bureau. *The Crucible* is, internally, *Salesman*'s blood brother. It is examining the questions I was absorbed with before—the conflict between a man's raw deeds and his conception of himself; the question of whether conscience is in fact an organic part of the human being, and what happens when it is handed over not merely to the state or the mores of the time but to one's friend or wife.[1] The big difference, I think, is that *The Crucible* sought to include a higher degree of consciousness than the earlier plays.

I believe that the wider the awareness, the felt knowledge, evoked by a play, the higher it must stand as art. I think our drama is far behind our lives in this respect. There is a lot wrong with the twentieth century, but one thing is right with it—we are aware as no generation was before of the larger units that help make us and destroy us. The city, the nation, the world, and now the universe are never far beyond our most intimate sense of life. The vast majority of us know now—not merely as knowledge but as feeling, feeling capable of expression in art—that we are being formed, that our alternatives in life are not absolutely our own, as the romantic play inevitably must presuppose. But the response of our plays, of our dramatic form itself, is to faint, so to speak, before the intricacies of man's wider relationships and to define him further and redefine him as essentially alone in a world he never made.

The form, the shape, the meaning of *The Crucible* were all compounded out of the faith of those who were hanged. They were asked to be lonely and they refused. They were asked to deny their belief in a God of all men, not merely

---

[1] On this point, see the excerpt from *After the Fall*, pp. 174-175. In fact, see the whole play.

a god each individual could manipulate to his interests. They were asked to call a phantom real and to deny their touch with reality. It was not good to cast this play, to form it so that the psyche of the hero should emerge so "commonly" as to wipe out of mind the process itself, the spectacle of that faith and the knowing will which these people paid for with their lives.

The "heat" infusing this play is therefore of a different order from that which draws tears and the common identifications. And it was designed to be of a different order. In a sense, I felt, our situation had thrown us willy-nilly into a new classical period. Classical in the sense that the social scheme, as of old, had reached the point of rigidity where it had become implacable as a consciously known force working in us and upon us. Analytical psychology, when so intensely exploited as to reduce the world to the size of a man's abdomen and equate his fate with his neurosis, is a re-emergence of romanticism. It is inclined to deny all outer forces until man is only his complex. It presupposes an autonomy in the human character that, in a word, is false. A neurosis is not a fate but an effect. There is a higher wisdom, and if truly there is not, there is still no aesthetic point in repeating something so utterly known, or in doing better what has been done so well before.

For me *The Crucible* was a new beginning, the beginning of an attempt to embrace a wider field of vision, a field wide enough to contain the whole of our current awareness. It was not so much to move ahead of the audience but to catch up with what it commonly knows about the way things are and how they get that way. In a word, we commonly know so much more than our plays let on. When we can put together what we do know with what we feel, we shall find a new kind of theatre in our hands. *The Crucible* was written as it was in order to bring me, and the audience, closer to that theatre and what I imagine can be an art more ample than any of us has dared to strive for, the art of Man among men, Man amid his works.

[MORE ON DANFORTH]

. . . Danforth was indeed dedicated to securing the status quo against such as Proctor. But I am equally interested in his *function* in the drama, which is that of the rule-bearer, the man who always guards the boundaries which, if you insist on breaking through them, have the power to destroy you. His "evil" is more than personal, it is nearly mythical. He does more evil than he knows how to do; while merely following his nose he guards ignorance, he is man's limit. Sartre reduced him to an almost economic policeman.[1] He is thus unrecognizable to us because he lacks his real ideology, i.e., the ideology which believes that evil is good, that man must be preserved from knowledge. Sartre's Danforth does not see beyond the deception, ever. He too, like Proctor, should come to a realization. He must see that he has in fact practised deception, and then proceed to incorporate it in his "good" ideology. When I say I did not make him evil enough, it is that I did not clearly demarcate the point at which he knows what he has done, and profoundly accepts it as a good thing. This alone is evil. It is a counterpart to Proctor's ultimate realization that he cannot sell himself for his life. Hale

---

From Sheila Huftel, *Arthur Miller: The Burning Glass* (New York: Citadel, 1965), pp. 146-47. Copyright © 1965 by Sheila Huftel. Reprinted by permission of Citadel Press, Inc., New York. The paragraph is an untitled statement sent by Miller to Miss Huftel.

[1] Jean-Paul Sartre wrote the movie version of *The Crucible*. The excerpt, pp. 423-426, gives at least a hint of his Danforth.

goes the other way: on seeing the deception he rejects it as evil. One of the actual Salem judges drank himself to death after the hysteria was over. But only one. The others insisted they had done well.[2] In a word, Sartre's conception lacks moral dimension. It precludes a certain aspect of will. Also it is dramatically useless because his Danforth from beginning to end is the same. This serves only to reduce the importance of the whole story, for if it is not horrible enough to force Danforth to know that he must decide how to strengthen himself against what he has done, then he has done very little.

AFTER THE FALL

"Is the accuser always holy now?" asked John Proctor in Act Two of *The Crucible*. Reacting not to the Salem setting but to the presumed contemporary political analogy, some critics wondered, "Is the accuser always lying now?" When Miller returned to the accusation-confession

---

From Arthur Miller, *After the Fall* (New York: Viking Compass edition, 1968), pp. 32-37. Copyright © 1964 by Arthur Miller. All rights reserved. Published by The Viking Press, Inc. The play, directed by Elia Kazan, opened at the ANTA-Washington Square Theatre, January 23, 1964. It was the first production of the Lincoln Center Repertory Company, then run by Kazan and Robert Whitehead. The original hardcover edition of the play (New York: Viking, 1964) has an interesting variation on this scene, pp. 36-42.

[2] This is not quite true. Samuel Sewall, for instance, publicly acknowledged "the guilt contracted upon the opening of the late Commission of Oyer and Terminer" in a statement that he had read from the pulpit on January 14, 1697. It was Sewall who drew up the bill making that day a fast day, asking pardon for the errors committed during "the late tragedy raised among us."

situation ten years after *The Crucible*—in this scene from *After the Fall* —he suggested that motivations all around were more complicated than simple idealism, simple greed. *After the Fall* is essentially the story of Quentin, his attempt to define and accept his sense of guilt. Lou and Mickey are peripheral to his search, old friends whose relationship with him he must come to understand. Since Lou and Mickey are the central figures in this excerpt, it is not really characteristic of *Fall* as a whole. Some references here—the Listener, the tower, Holga—can only be understood by reading the complete play. The excerpt is here not as a sample of *After the Fall* but for what it suggests about *The Crucible*. Slide over the undefined references, concentrate on the Lou-Mickey quarrel, and read the scene in the context suggested by the critical essays that follow, particularly Eric Bentley's review of *The Crucible* (pp. 204-209) and Lee Baxandall's review of *After the Fall* (pp. 352-358).

MICKEY: Dear Lou; look at him down there, he never learned how to swim, always paddled like a dog. *Comes back.* I used to love that man. I still do. Quentin, I've been subpoenaed.

QUENTIN, *shocked*: Oh, God! The Committee?

MICKEY: Yes. I wish you'd have come into town when I called you. But it doesn't matter now.

QUENTIN: I had a feeling it was something like that. I guess I—I didn't want to know any more. I'm sorry, Mick. *To Listener*: Yes, not to see! To be innocent!

A long pause. They find it hard to look directly at each other.

MICKEY: I've been going through hell, Quent. It's strange—to have to examine what you stand for; not theoretically, but on a life-and-death basis. A lot of things don't stand up.

QUENTIN: I guess the main thing is not to be afraid.

MICKEY, *after a pause*: I don't think I am now.

A pause. Both sit staring ahead. Finally Mickey turns and looks at Quentin, who now faces him. Mickey tries to smile.

You may not be my friend any more.

QUENTIN, *trying to laugh it away—a terror rising in him*: Why?

MICKEY: I'm going to tell the truth.

Pause.

QUENTIN: How do you mean?

MICKEY: I'm—going to name names.

QUENTIN, *incredulously*: Why?

MICKEY: Because—I want to. Fifteen years, wherever I go, whatever I talk about, the feeling is always there that I'm deceiving people.

QUENTIN: But why couldn't you just tell about yourself?

Maggie enters, lies down on second platform.

MICKEY: They want the names, and they mean to destroy anyone who—

QUENTIN: I think it's a mistake, Mick. All this is going to pass, and I think you'll regret it. And anyway, Max has always talked against this kind of thing!

MICKEY: I've had it out with Max. I testify or I'll be voted out of the firm.

QUENTIN: I can't believe it! What about DeVries?

MICKEY: DeVries was there, and Burton, and most of the others. I wish you'd have seen their faces when I told them. Men I've worked with for thirteen years. Played tennis; intimate friends, you know? And as soon as I said, "I had been" —stones.

The tower lights.

QUENTIN, *to the Listener*: Everything is one thing! You see—
I don't know what we are to one another!

MICKEY: I only know one thing, Quent, I want to live a
straightforward, open life!

> *Lou enters in bathing trunks, instantly overjoyed at seeing
> Mickey. The tower goes dark.*

LOU: Mick! I *thought* I heard your voice! *Grabs his hand.* How
are you!

> *Lou and Mickey de-animate in an embrace. Holga appears
> with flowers on upper level.*

QUENTIN, *glancing up at Holga*: How do you dare make promises again? I have lived through all the promises, you see?

> *Holga exits.*

LOU, *resuming, moving downstage with Mickey*: Just the question of publishing my book, now. Elsie's afraid it will wake
up all the sleeping dogs again.

MICKEY: But don't you have to take that chance? I think a
man's got to take the rap, Lou, for what he's done, for what
he is. After all, it's your work.

LOU: I feel exactly that way! *Grabs his arm, including Quentin
in his feeling.* Golly, Mick! Why don't we get together as we
used to! I miss all that wonderful talk! Of course I know how
busy you are now, but—

MICKEY: Elsie coming up?

LOU: You want to see her? I could call down to the beach.
He starts off, but Mickey stops him.

MICKEY: Lou.

Lou, *sensing something odd*: Yes, Mick.

Quentin, *facing the sky*: Dear God.

Mickey: I've been subpoenaed.

Lou: No! *Mickey nods, looks at the ground. Lou grips his arm.* Oh, I'm terribly sorry, Mick. But can I say something—it might ease your mind; once you're in front of them it all gets remarkably simple!

Quentin: Oh dear God!

Lou: Everything kind of falls away excepting—one's self. One's truth.

Mickey, *after a slight pause*: I've already been in front of them, Lou. Two weeks ago.

Lou: Oh! Then what do they want with you again?

Mickey, *after a pause, with a fixed smile on his face*: I asked to be heard again.

Lou, *puzzled, open-eyed*: Why?

Mickey—*he carefully forms his thought*: Because I want to tell the truth.

Lou, *with the first rising of incredulous fear*: In—what sense? What do you mean?

Mickey: Lou, when I left the hearing room I didn't feel I had spoken. Something else had spoken, something automatic and inhuman. I asked myself, what am I protecting by refusing to answer? Lou, you must let me finish! You must. The Party? But I despise the Party, and have for many years. Just like you. Yet there is something, something that closes my throat when I think of telling names. What am I defending? It's a dream now, a dream of solidarity. But the fact is, I have no solidarity with the people I could name—excepting for you.

And not because we were Communists together, but because we were young together. Because we—when we talked it was like some brotherhood opposed to all the world's injustice. Therefore, in the name of that love, I ought to be true to myself now. And the truth, Lou, my truth, is that I think the Party *is* a conspiracy—let me finish. I think we *were* swindled; they took our lust for the right and used it for Russian purposes. And I don't think we can go on turning our backs on the truth simply because reactionaries are saying it. What I propose—is that we try to separate our love for one another from this political morass. And I've said nothing just now that we haven't told each other for the past five years.

LOU: Then—what's your proposal?

MICKEY: That we go back together. Come with me. And answer the questions.

LOU: Name—the names?

MICKEY: Yes. I've talked to all the others in the unit. They've agreed, excepting for Ward and Harry. They cursed me out, but I expected that.

LOU, *dazed*: Let me understand—you are asking my permission to name me?

   Pause.

You may not mention my name. *He begins physically shaking.* And if you do it, Mickey, you are selling me for your own prosperity. If you use my name I will be dismissed. You will ruin me. You will destroy my career.

MICKEY: Lou, I think I have a right to know exactly why you—

LOU: Because if everyone broke faith there would be no civilization! That is why that Committee is the face of the Philistine! And it astounds me that you can speak of truth and justice in relation to that gang of cheap publicity hounds! Not one syllable will they get from me! Not one word from my lips! No—your eleven-room apartment, your automobile, your money are not worth this.

MICKEY, *stiffened*: That's a lie! You can't reduce it all to money, Lou! *That* is false!

LOU, *turning on him*: There is only one truth here. You are terrified! They have bought your soul!

> *Elsie appears upstage, listening. Louise enters, watches.*

MICKEY, *angrily, but contained*: And yours? Lou! Is it all yours, your soul?

LOU, *beginning to show tears*: How dare you speak of my—

MICKEY, *quaking with anger*: You've got to take it if you're going to dish it out, don't you? Have you really earned this high moral tone—this perfect integrity? I happen to remember when you came back from your trip to Russia; and I remember who made you throw your first version into my fireplace!

LOU, *with a glance toward Elsie*: The idea!

MICKEY: I saw you burn a true book and write another that told lies! Because she demanded it, because she terrified you, because she has taken your soul!

LOU, *shaking his fist in the air*: I condemn you!

MICKEY: But from your conscience or from hers? Who is speaking to me, Lou?

LOU: You are a monster!

> *Lou bursts into tears, walks off toward Elsie; he meets her in the near distance; her face shows horror. At the front of stage Mickey turns and looks across the full width toward Quentin at the farthest edge of light, and . . .*

MICKEY, *reading Quentin's feelings*: I guess you'll want to get somebody else to go over your brief with you. *Pause.* Quent—

> *Quentin, indecisive, but not contradicting him, now turns to him.*

Good-by, Quentin.

QUENTIN, *in a dead tone*: Good-by, Mickey.

> *Mickey goes out.*

The Crucible
In Production:
Comments and Reviews

IN NEW YORK

HENRY HEWES

Henry Hewes, drama editor from 1952 to 1954 and drama critic
since 1954 for *Saturday Review,* has lectured on theatre at Sarah
Lawrence College and Columbia University. He edited the annual
Best Plays series from 1961 until 1964 and is the editor of *Famous
American Plays of the Forties.*

ARTHUR MILLER AND HOW HE
WENT TO THE DEVIL

On the strength of two plays that sank deep into the heart
of contemporary life, Arthur Miller has risen to the unchal-
lenged position of being one of this generation's two foremost
American dramatists, and there is no reason to doubt that he
will continue to write about everyday situations with equal
truth, equal power, and equal success. But, being something
of a nonconformist, Mr. Miller has chosen to turn away from

From *Saturday Review,* XXXVI (January 31, 1953), 24-26. Copyright
1953 The Saturday Review Associates, Inc.

the modern arena, where he is demonstrably at home, to try his hand at writing a historical play that involves some fairly remote events that happened during the Salem witchcraft trials of 1692.

Visited during a rehearsal break at the Martin Beck, the tall mantis-figured playwright seemed tired and watchful as he sat with his legs dangling over the orchestra seat in front of him. But serious and concerned as he was, he appeared surprisingly untroubled about the increase in complexity that goes with staging a twenty-two-character play set in another period, and putting into focus the tragedy of a whole society, not just the tragedy of an individual. "I've laid it out that way from the start," he said in a gently confident tone. "The first scene is purely an overture in which we emphasize the inability of these Puritans to cope with the strange sickness of the minister's little girl, and the resultant turn to accusations of witchcraft. The strict beliefs under which they all lived were doubly responsible. Their tenets were filled with witches and the Devil, and they gave them an authority-weighted reason for something they found hard otherwise to explain. In addition, the circle of children who made the accusations had grievances against the Puritan women they named, because these women had made their lives and the lives of their husbands cold and unpleasant. As Elizabeth Proctor, one of the accused wives, says:

It needs a cold wife to prompt lechery. I counted myself so plain, so poorly-made, no honest love could come to me! Suspicion kissed you when I did; I never knew how I should say my love. It were a cold house I kept. . . ."

The thirty-seven-year-old writer maintains, however, that this remorseless, unbending ideology of the Puritans had constructive uses in settling this country, as proved by the fact that the Massachusetts colony succeeded against heavy odds, while the non-ideological Virginia Colony failed despite an easier climate. "But, by 1692, the usefulness of the ideology had passed and it had become an orthodoxy which had to destroy the opposition or be itself destroyed. The tragedy of *The Crucible* is the everlasting conflict between people so fanatically wedded to this orthodoxy that they could not cope with the evidence of their senses."

Also necessary to establish in the first scene is the atmosphere of seventeenth-century Salem. "I use words like 'poppet' instead of 'doll,' and grammatical syntax like 'he have' instead of 'he has.' This will remind the audience that *The Crucible* is taking place in another time, but won't make it too difficult to understand, which it might if I used all the old language, with words like 'dafter' instead of 'daughter.' Also I have varied some of the facts. Actually, the girls were reported as dancing in the woods and practicing abominations. I have them dancing naked in the woods, which makes it easier for the audience to relate the Puritans' horror at such a thing to their own."

Mr. Miller has taken some other liberties with the historical facts, as he read them in the Salem courthouse and in a book written by Charles W. Upham in 1867. (Oddly enough, he is not familiar with Tennessee Williams' short story "The Yellow Bird," issued recently by Caedmon Records, which derives from the same incident.)[1]

For instance, from Abigail Williams, whose actual age was between eleven and fourteen, plus the evidence that she tried to have Goody Procter[2] killed by incantations, he manufactured

---

[1] Distantly derived. There is nothing terrifying about Williams' yellow bird. If you begin to feel trapped by all the ancient and modern horror in this volume, read his amusing story as a kind of thematic coffee break. It is in *One Arm and Other Stories* (New York: New Directions, 1954), pp. 199-211.

[2] Seventeenth-century spelling being a somewhat chancy operation, both "Proctor" and "Procter" appear in the trial documents. Upham, whom Hewes mentions above, settled on "Procter" in his book, which may explain Hewes's usage.

an eighteen-year-old wench who had seduced Goody Procter's husband. Likewise there is no specific evidence that Procter confessed and then recanted his confession as occurs in the play, although other accused persons did so. Says the author, "A playwright has no debt of literalness to history. Right now I couldn't tell you which details were taken from the records verbatim and which were invented. I think you can say that this play is as historically authentic as *Richard II*, which took place closer to Shakespeare's time than *The Crucible* did to ours."

After the overture of the first scene is over, the play more or less concentrates on the fate of one man, John Procter. "Any play is the story of how the birds came home to roost," says Miller.[3] "Procter acts and has to face the consequences of this action. In so doing he discovers who he is. He is a good man. Willy Loman in *Death of a Salesman* went through the same process, but, because he had lost Procter's sense of personal inviolability and had yielded completely to every pressure, he never found out who he was. That's what Procter means near the end of the play when he talks of his 'name.' He is really speaking about his identity, which he cannot surrender."

Another character who interests Miller is Reverend Hale, who initiates the witchcraft investigation. "Hale," he says, "is a man who permits a beloved ideology to overwhelm the evidence of his senses past the point when the evidence of his

---

[3] Playwrights, like everyone else, are given to favorite expressions. "The structure of a play is always the story of how the birds came home to roost," wrote Arthur Miller in "The Shadow of the Gods," *Harper's*, CCXVII (August 1958), 37. Most of the comments on the uses of history quoted or paraphrased by Hewes are variations on the notes later published with *The Crucible*, which may have been written by this time, and the "radical" label Miller hangs on *The Madwoman of Chaillot* a few paragraphs further on was to turn up later in the Introduction to *Collected Plays*, p. 37.

senses should have led him to question and revise his ideology. His tragic failure along with certain other honest leaders of that community was a lack of a sense of proportion."

While the dramatist is willing to talk about themes within his play, he doesn't pretend to know exactly what his play means. "I never know until at least a year after I've written it. A complex play can have many themes, but I don't sit down to write a play with a specific theme worked out in my mind. What I do have in my mind is a general sense of the quality I want it to have, much as you might try to present a picture of honesty or beauty by describing some honest or beautiful person you knew. Then I work on the script until it seems to have the aura of my original conception and at the same time I can see every moment of it as drama."

Although many people have seen Miller's previous plays as political or allegorical, the playwright is definite in his denial of any such simple intention. "I am not pressing a historical allegory here, and I have even eliminated certain striking similarities from *The Crucible* which may have started the audience to drawing such an allegory. For instance, the Salemites believed that the surrounding Indians, who had never been converted to Christianity, were in alliance with the witches, who were acting as a Fifth Column for them within the town. It was even thought that the outbreak of witchcraft was the last attack by the Devil, who was being pressed into the wilderness by the expanding colony. Some might have equated the Indians with Russians and the local witches with Communists. My intent and interest is wider and I think deeper than this. From my first acquaintance with the story I was struck hard by the breathtaking heroism of certain of the victims who displayed an almost frightening personal integrity. It seemed to me that the best part of this country was made of such stuff, and I had a strong desire to celebrate them and to raise them out of historic dust."

Mr. Miller believes the reason his plays are thought to be

so political is that the complete vacuousness of so many of our contemporary plays makes works of any substance seem political by comparison.

He points out that Giraudoux's *Madwoman of Chaillot* was a really radical play, but that because it was set in Paris people here did not take it as such. As far as he is concerned in his own plays, Miller prefers to consider the area of literature and the area of politics to be separate.

"Literature is a weapon, but not in the sense that Marxists, Fascists, and our own 'Americanists' believe. It is possible to read a royalist-Catholic writer and draw sustenance for a Leftwing position from him; it is possible to draw a conservative moral from an anti-conservative work. A work of art creates a complex world, and as the past hundred years have proved, the special 'truth' of one decade may turn out to be the reactionary falsehood of another. It is a poor weapon whose direction is so unstable as to serve one side at one moment and another side the next. The only sure and valid aim— speaking of art as a weapon—is the humanizing of man."

At this point we were interrupted by a deputation of actors who wanted the playwright to change a line or two in one of the scenes. Miller listened to them with a combination of Procter's sense of inviolability and the sense of proportion that Hale had lacked. Then he explained to the actors why this particular change should not be made.

"You know," he said after they had gone, "the most important thing for the playwright is to be able to make the right alterations during rehearsals. Each actor brings his own personality to his part and would—if you were not careful— tend to change the meaning of the play. The playwright must rewrite both in order to make the actor comfortable in the part and also to protect the meaning of the play from the intrusion of the actor's personal characteristics."

The Crucible is being directed by Jed Harris, who operates differently from most of the directors Miller is used to working with.[4] "Jed works from the outside in, which I think is best for this kind of large-canvas play. He is a very serious man, with superb taste and perception. Sometimes there'll be hours of rehearsal when I get worried because nothing seems to be getting accomplished. But then suddenly he'll work very quickly and closely with the actors, and do in half an hour what some directors would take days to do. Above all, he's a perfectionist."

Rehearsal was recommencing onstage, so I whispered a quick good-by and tiptoed my way out, leaving Arthur Miller with his sense of proportion and his inviolability to Jed Harris's inviolate world.

---

[4] Both Elia Kazan, who directed *All My Sons* and *Death of a Salesman*, and Robert Lewis, who directed Miller's adaptation of *An Enemy of the People*, began their directorial careers with the Group Theatre in the 1930s. There they worked with Lee Strasberg, whose emphasis—derived from Stanislavski by way of the American Laboratory Theatre—is on the psychological nature of the actor. Jed Harris, whom Strasberg has called "an enormous talent" (see *Strasberg at The Actors Studio*, New York: Viking, 1965, p. 29), is a more conventional Broadway director, in part because he has never worked within a community context such as that provided by the Group Theatre and the Actors Studio. The best way to get some sense of Harris (if not of his work on *The Crucible*) is to look at his book, *Watchman, What of the Night?* (New York: Doubleday, 1963), particularly at the "Epilogue," by Herman Shapiro. Miller was, of course, finally dissatisfied with Harris's direction, for he restaged the play himself when the new scene was added.

WALTER KERR

Walter Kerr was drama critic for *Commonweal* from 1950 to 1952 and for the *New York Herald Tribune* from 1951 to 1966, and has been drama critic for *The New York Times* since 1966. He is the author of *How Not to Write a Play*, *Criticism and Censorship*, *The Decline of Pleasure*, *The Theatre in Spite of Itself*, and *Tragedy and Comedy*, among other books. He won the George Jean Nathan Award for Drama Criticism (1963).

THE CRUCIBLE

Arthur Miller is a problem playwright, in both senses of the word. As a man of independent thought, he is profoundly, angrily concerned with the immediate issues of our society—with the irresponsible pressures which are being brought to bear on free men, with the self-seeking which blinds whole segments of our civilization to justice, with the evasions and dishonesties into which cowardly men are daily slipping. And to his fiery editorializing he brings shrewd theatrical gifts; he knows how to make a point plain, how to give it bite in the illustration, how to make its caustic and cauterizing language ring out on the stage.

He is also an artist groping toward something more poetic than simple, savage journalism. He has not only the professional crusader's zeal for humanity, but the imaginative writer's feeling for it—how it really behaves, how it moves about a room, how it looks in its foolish as well as in its noble attitudes—and in his best play, *Death of a Salesman*, he was able to rise above the sermon and touch the spirit of some simple people.

From the *New York Herald Tribune*, January 23, 1953, p. 12. Copyright 1953 by Walter Kerr.

In *The Crucible*, which opened at the Martin Beck last night, he seems to me to be taking a step backward into mechanical parable, into the sort of play which lives not in the warmth of humbly observed human souls but in the ideological heat of polemic.

Make no mistake about it: there is fire in what Mr. Miller has to say, and there is a good bit of sting in his manner of saying it. He has, for convenience's sake, set his troubling narrative in the Salem of 1692. For reasons of their own, a quartet of exhibitionistic young women are hurling accusations of witchcraft at eminently respectable members of a well-meaning, but not entirely clear-headed, society.

On the basis of hearsay—"guilt by association with the devil" might be the phrase for it—a whole community of innocents are brought to trial and condemned to be hanged. As Mr. Miller pursues his very clear contemporary parallel, there are all sorts of relevant thrusts: the folk who do the final damage are not the lunatic fringe but the gullible pillars of society; the courts bog down into travesty in order to comply with the popular mood; slander becomes the weapon of opportunists ("Is the accuser always holy now?"); freedom is possible at the price of naming one's associates in crime; even the upright man is eventually tormented into going along with the mob to secure his own way of life, his own family.

Much of this—not all—is an accurate reading of our own turbulent age, and there are many times at the Martin Beck when one's intellectual sympathies go out to Mr. Miller and to his apt symbols anguishing on the stage. But it is the intellect which goes out, not the heart.

For Salem, and the people who live, love, fear and die in it, are really only conveniences to Mr. Miller, props to his theme. He does not make them interesting in and for themselves, and you wind up analyzing them, checking their dilemmas against the latest headlines, rather than losing yourself in any rounded, deeply rewarding personalities. You stand back and think; you don't really share very much.

Under Jed Harris's firm and driving hand, a large and meticulously cast company performs expertly. Arthur Kennedy brings integrity and candor to a role that is not really much more than a banner for Mr. Miller's thought. But when he is shaking his head over the greediness of a minister and muttering, "It hurt my prayer, it hurt my prayer," or when he is laboriously naming the Ten Commandments and forgetting the one he has most recently broken, he invests a two-dimensional figure with great perception.

Beatrice Straight is a fine complement to him as the wife who has centered too much of her life on her husband's single infidelity, and Walter Hampden gives a beautifully varied, fiercely powerful performance as a wily judge who is jealous of his authority and bent on turning an official investigation to his own preconceived ends.

In lesser roles, Jean Adair is especially striking as an old woman of unquenchable honor, E. G. Marshall supplies a needed subtlety in the role of a man of God who must begin to doubt his own devils, Joseph Sweeney is rousing as a crusty villager with genuine common sense and Madeleine Sherwood finds a believable intensity for her venomous troublemaker.

Boris Aronson has designed four spare, clean settings which succeed in evoking that Salem which Mr. Miller has not been patient enough to create.

BROOKS ATKINSON

AT THE THEATRE

Arthur Miller has written another powerful play. *The Crucible*, it is called, and it opened at the Martin Beck last evening in an equally powerful performance. Riffling back the pages of American history, he has written the drama of the witch trials and hangings in Salem in 1692. Neither Mr. Miller nor his audiences are unaware of certain similarities between the perversions of justice then and today.

But Mr. Miller is not pleading a cause in dramatic form. For *The Crucible*, despite its current implications, is a self-contained play about a terrible period in American history. Silly accusations of witchcraft by some mischievous girls in Puritan dress gradually take possession of Salem. Before the play is over, good people of pious nature and responsible temper are condemning other good people to the gallows.

Having a sure instinct for dramatic form, Mr. Miller goes bluntly to essential situations. John Proctor and his wife, farm people, are the central characters of the play. At first the idea that Goodie Proctor is a witch is only an absurd rumor. But *The Crucible* carries the Proctors through the whole ordeal—first vague suspicion, then the arrest, the im-

From *The New York Times*, January 23, 1953, p. 15. © 1953 by The New York Times Company. Reprinted by permission.

placable, highly wrought trial in the church vestry, the final opportunity for John Proctor to save his neck by confessing to something he knows is a lie, and finally the baleful roll of the drums at the foot of the gallows.

Although *The Crucible* is a powerful drama, it stands second to *Death of a Salesman* as a work of art. Mr. Miller has had more trouble with this one, perhaps because he is too conscious of its implications. The literary style is cruder. The early motivation is muffled in the uproar of the opening scene, and the theme does not develop with the simple eloquence of *Death of a Salesman*.

It may be that Mr. Miller has tried to pack too much inside his drama, and that he has permitted himself to be concerned more with the technique of the witch hunt than with its humanity. For all its power generated on the surface, *The Crucible* is most moving in the simple, quiet scenes between John Proctor and his wife. By the standards of *Death of a Salesman*, there is too much excitement and not enough emotion in *The Crucible*.

As the director, Jed Harris has given it a driving performance in which the clashes are fierce and clamorous. Inside Boris Aronson's gaunt, pitiless sets of rude buildings, the acting is at a high pitch of bitterness, anger and fear. As the patriarchal deputy Governor, Walter Hampden gives one of his most vivid performances in which righteousness and ferocity are unctuously mated. Fred Stewart as a vindictive parson, E. G. Marshall as a parson who finally revels at the indiscriminate ruthlessness of the trial, Jean Adair as an aging woman of God, Madeleine Sherwood as a malicious town hussy, Joseph Sweeney as an old man who has the courage to fight the court, Philip Coolidge as a sanctimonious judge—all give able performances.

As John Proctor and his wife, Arthur Kennedy and Beatrice Straight have the most attractive roles in the drama and two or three opportunities to act them together in moments of tranquillity. They are superb—Mr. Kennedy clear and resolute, full of fire, searching his own mind; Miss Straight reserved, detached, above and beyond the contention. Like all the members of the cast, they are dressed in the chaste and lovely costumes Edith Lutyens has designed from old prints of early Massachusetts.

After the experience of *Death of a Salesman* we probably expect Mr. Miller to write a masterpiece every time. *The Crucible* is not of that stature and it lacks that universality. On a lower level of dramatic history with considerable pertinence for today, it is a powerful play and a genuine contribution to the season.

ARTHUR MILLER'S *THE CRUCIBLE* IN A NEW EDITION WITH SEVERAL NEW ACTORS AND ONE NEW SCENE

After an engagement of six months and the acquisition of a prize or two, Arthur Miller's *The Crucible* has come out in a new edition at the Martin Beck Theatre. Although the new edition is motivated by the necessity for economy during the hot months, the changes have improved Mr. Miller's drama. *The Crucible* has acquired a certain human warmth that it lacked amid the shrill excitements of the original version. The hearts of the characters are now closer to the surface than their nerves.

From *The New York Times*, July 2, 1953, p. 20. © 1953 by The New York Times Company. Reprinted by permission. See A Note on the Text, p. 153, for information on the revision of the play, and Appendix, p. 148, for the added scene.

The changes include a brief new scene between Abigail Williams and John Proctor that completely motivates their clash in the following scene laid in the courtroom. All the leading actors and many of the minor actors have been either transferred or replaced. By replacing the scenery with a black velour background, Boris Aronson has designed a fluid and dramatic production out of props and lighting. And Mr. Miller has personally redirected a good deal of the performance—giving it more variety and humanity than it had when it was new.

For nothing in the theatre is ever inevitable or final. There is always one more way of doing something that seemed sound originally. There are always values that a new approach discovers. Philip Coolidge does not duplicate the implacable righteousness of Walter Hampden's memorable performance of the deputy governor. But Mr. Coolidge's gentler approach loses none of the horrifying vindictiveness of the trial scene and puts the miscarriage of justice on a more normal level.

As the Proctor husband and wife, E. G. Marshall and Maureen Stapleton lack the sense of intellectual clarity that Arthur Kennedy and Beatrice Straight brought to the roles. But Mr. Marshall and Miss Stapleton indicate a rustic sincerity of character that makes the drama seem more homely or personal. Del Hughes is excellent as the liberal-minded Rev. John Hale, who is honestly seeking after the truth despite his personal complacence. As the deputy governor's satellites, Donald Marye and Don McHenry bring to the trial scene contrasting tones of remorselessness that drop some withering acid into that agonizing episode. Neil Harrison's detached characterization of Rebecca Nurse is a good one. From the original cast Madeleine Sherwood, Joseph Sweeney and Jenny Egan are still playing with fire and skill. By the quizzical shading in his acting Mr. Sweeney accounts for what little humor there is in this scorching drama.

Even in its new edition *The Crucible* does not seem to

this theatregoer like Mr. Miller's most eloquent drama. The prologue tries to pack too much information into a distracted first act. The last scene is a vacillating one; it gives the impression of changing points of view impulsively. Although Mr. Miller does not dwell specifically on the analogies between the Salem witch trials of 1692 and the hysterical bush-beating in search of subversives today, the analogies lurk in the background, and they are too inexact to be wholly persuasive. The overtones of a thesis play are the mediocre parts of *The Crucible*.

But as a drama about a man and woman whose devotion to each other is haunted by the memory of an infidelity, *The Crucible* shows a penetrating knowledge of people and is more moving now than it was originally. And the trial scene is a vivid piece of writing and acting. It dramatizes brilliantly the prosecutor's instinct for sacrificing truth to policy. This new edition of *The Crucible* considerably freshens the most genuine parts of the original production. The excitement is less metallic. The emotion is more profound.

WITCHCRAFT AND STAGECRAFT

The issue of civil liberty is too serious to be confused by its defenders as well as its enemies. Freedom is under menacing fire at home as well as abroad. But Arthur Miller, in his new play *The Crucible*, seems to us to have provided more confusion than defense.

Some may argue—as many of the drama critics did[1]—that this is just a play about Salem, Mass., in the time of the 1692 witch hunt. Having seen it ourselves, we dissent. It is inconceivable that Miller is unaware that the year is 1953 and that a play about Salem's witch hunt was inevitably bound to stir contemporary echoes.

The trouble is that the inferences are deceptive and, in an important sense, invalid. Whatever his original intention, Miller has pushed the people of Salem around in a loaded allegory which may shed some light on their time but ultimately succeeds in muddying our own.

The frenzied cruelty of Salem stemmed from superstition and fantasy: Lives were ruined and lost in the wild attempt

---

From the *New York Post*, February 1, 1953, p. 9M. Reprinted by permission of *New York Post*. © 1953, New York Post Corporation.

[1] Actually most of the reviewers recognized the contemporary analogy, but few of them examined its validity until the magazine critics got around to the play somewhat later. See the reviews by Shipley, Bentley, Warshow that follow. The *Post*'s own drama critic, Richard Watts, Jr., did little more than mention the connection between the play and the immediate political situation and then go on to praise Miller for working by implication. See *New York Theatre Critics' Reviews*, XIV (1953), 384.

to prove that witches were the root of all suffering. In Miller's script the labored implication is that modern political hysteria is similarly founded on totally irrational fear of nonexistent demons.

It would be nice if life were that simple.

Unhappily, the despotic threat that confronts modern society is real; the people who loved freedom in Czechoslovakia, China and other places now ruled by tyranny can testify to that. The threat is as real as it was when Nazism was over-running the world. International Communism is a disciplined, fanatic movement whose secret battalions have seized whole nations and enslaved millions of people. There *are* spies and saboteurs; there *are* accused agents who are guilty; the simple-minded in our time have too often been those who choose to believe that the gauleiters and the commissars are imaginary characters. The irony is that Miller's most fiery lines seem designed to caricature America's jitters rather than Prague's terror.[2]

In a matter of months the people of Salem banished the spectre of the witch and regained their own senses. But the problem of our age is how to resist the real and continuing peril of totalitarianism without destroying our freedoms in the process. It is how to combat authentic dangers without yielding to panic and hysteria. That is an infinitely more complicated problem than the cure of Salem's dementia.

In Miller's play many of his strained implications for the present would have been exploded if anyone had ridden across the stage of the Martin Beck on a broom, posing the trenchant

---

[2] The Communists took over Czechoslovakia in February 1948, re-placing the coalition government that had ruled since the end of World War II. A systematic repression began, ending with the Prague trials of November 1952, at which eleven men, after public confession, were con-demned to death. The immediate reference here is to those trials, which were widely accepted as a mockery of justice.

question: "What about Klaus Fuchs and Harry Gold?";[3] the whole onstage world of Salem would have collapsed.

In defending Joe McCarthy's crusade, his apologists tell us that truth and falsehood are inconsequential; all that matters, they say, is the alleged goal of "security." But there is an equal contempt for truth in a defense of free speech which pretends that the Soviet challenge is an elaborate hallucination of Western man, as fanciful as the madness that bedeviled Salem.

While we're on Broadway, we should like to add that a revival of a play written nineteen years ago seems to us to have far more authentic contemporary relevance. It is Lillian Hellman's *The Children's Hour*.[4] This is a moving story of the destruction wrought by a child-gossip and credulous elders. Today reckless slander usually takes political form; and the credulous are still with us. Seen in 1953 *The Children's Hour* is a wonderful indictment of those professional persecutors who would convict others without a trial, accept rumor as evidence and hold all defendants guilty until they prove themselves innocent.

---

[3] Klaus Fuchs, at one time chief of theoretical physics at the British atomic research center at Harwell, pled guilty to the charge that he had passed secrets to the Russians four times between 1943 and 1947. In March 1950 he was sentenced to fourteen years in prison. Later that year Harry Gold, who had served as courier between Fuchs and his Russian contact, pled guilty to an espionage charge and was sentenced by an American court to thirty years.

[4] The revival of *The Children's Hour*, produced by Kermit Bloomgarden, who also presented *The Crucible*, opened on December 18, 1952. Most of the reviewers welcomed the play but, aside from Brooks Atkinson in *The New York Times*, none of them made anything of the "contemporary relevance." See *New York Theatre Critics' Reviews*, XIII (1952), 151-53. The play closed on May 30, 1953, after 189 performances.

The impact of these techniques has been documented again in Oliver Pilat's Post series on the blacklist.[5] Miller's version of Salem has less meaning for us than Miss Hellman's timeless unpretentious comment on the eternal scandal-mongers.

---

[5] Pilat's six-part series appeared in the *Post* from January 26 to February 1, 1953, the last installment in the same issue as this editorial.

JOSEPH T. SHIPLEY

Joseph T. Shipley was drama critic for *The New Leader* from 1922 to 1962 and has taught at City College of New York, Brooklyn College, and Yeshiva College. He is author and translater of many books, among them *The Mentally Disturbed Teacher*, *Five Plays by Ibsen*, *Dictionary of World Literary Terms*, and *Playing with Words*.

ARTHUR MILLER'S NEW MELODRAMA
IS NOT WHAT IT SEEMS TO BE

Because these are troublous times, and because certain elements of society look upon the theatre as "a weapon in the class war," it seems wise to consider Arthur Miller's new play, *The Crucible*, from several points of view. His picture of the Salem witch hunts of 1692 may fitly be examined as a work of dramatic art, as a product of the author, and as a social document.

Let us try first to weigh *The Crucible* as dramatic art. It is, like the melodramas of Henri Bernstein fifty years ago, essentially a play of situation.[1] The author builds for the big

---

From *The New Leader*, XXXVI (February 9, 1953), 25-26. Copyright © 1953 The American Labor Conference on International Affairs, Inc. Reprinted with permission. I am using only the opening paragraphs. Later in the review, Shipley implies that Miller is motivated largely by venality, lists his credits as a fellow-traveler and ends by suggesting that the play would be a better analogy for iron-curtain than American justice (hence, the title). Since the latter point is implicit in several of the other selections in the volume, I have cut Shipley, but I urge anyone with a taste for his rhetoric—formed by the Socialist-Communist quarrels of the 1930s—to go back to the original.

[1] Bernstein (1876–1953) was a tremendously successful French playwright, celebrated for his skill in turning out highly stageworthy melodramas. For a time, among serious commentators on the theatre, he

scenes, and the characters are tugged about to make these more striking. Thus the strong John Proctor, who has before him as an example the steadfastness of his beloved wife, is nevertheless made to weaken, to "confess" to a lie—in order to give more theatrical effect to his final resolve to proclaim, and to die for, the truth. (There is no psychological similarity here to the turnabout of Bernard Shaw's St. Joan, whom the *Daily Worker* draws into its praise of Miller's play.)[2] Proctor will lie privately, but he refuses to sign so that his lie can be made public.

The one really neat turn of character comes during the questioning of Proctor's wife. After Proctor has assured the judge that his wife never lies, she falters and does lie to save her husband's reputation—not knowing that this very action brings on his ruin. She testifies that her husband is not a lecher and that Abigail—chief denouncer of the "witches"—was dismissed from her service only for incompetence—this after John has sworn that Abigail was his eager whore. A neat twist, dramatically effective, psychologically sound.

On the other hand, when basic soundness and immediate effectiveness conflict, Miller plumps for the box-office. The opening of the last act, for instance, presents two women who are being put out of their cell to make it a reception room for the deputy governor. No reason is given why the deputy governor could not have an office, if not a cell, of his own. If that last act opening is intended to provide a sort of emotional rest, like the Shakespearean comic interlude, it is as clumsy as the opening of the first act is confused.

There is great power in Miller's "big scene." In this, the

---

became the standard example for empty slickness on stage, but—despite his popularity early in the century—I doubt if Shipley's pejorative comparison would have meant much to his readers in 1953. Incidentally, Bernstein's name was Henry, not Henri; he had an American mother.

[2] See Henry Raymond in Bibliography. It was not only the *Daily Worker* reviewer who was reminded of the Shaw play. Richard Watts, Jr., in the *New York Post*, also made the comparison. A scene from the Shaw play, but not the one Shipley refers to, can be found, pp. 427-458.

Proctors' maid, who has withdrawn her accusation of witchcraft, is bullied by a hostile judge and badgered by her excited fellow witnesses until she recants her confession and cries "Witch! Witch!" to tear the Proctors down. The climactic growth of tension here is excellently managed.

But there is, unfortunately, a sense throughout that these movements are, after all, managed. The calculating craftsman, not the deeply moved creator, is at work. Take even such a detail as calling the first act a "Prologue."[3] There is nothing at all in it to justify separating it by that label from the rest of the play. It would be as logical to call the last act an "Epilogue." But the three-act play is the fashion of our time; a play in four acts might seem Ibsenian, dated. So *The Crucible* has a "Prologue and Three Acts." *It conforms.* This is trivial, no doubt, but it is a further indication that the play is not so much a creation of dramatic art as a concoction of the author's contriving mind. . . .

---

[3] See textual note, p. 153.

ERIC BENTLEY

Eric Bentley, drama critic for the *New Republic* from 1952 to 1956, was Brander Matthews Professor of Dramatic Literature at Columbia University until 1969, and is now writer-in-residence at Bennington College. Among his books are *The Playwright as Thinker*, *Bernard Shaw*, *In Search of Theater*, and *The Life of the Drama*. He is the editor of many play anthologies, including *The Modern Theatre* series, and the translator of twelve plays of Brecht and five of Pirandello. He won the George Jean Nathan Award for Drama Criticism (1966).

THE INNOCENCE OF ARTHUR MILLER

The theatre is provincial. Few events on Broadway have any importance whatsoever except to that small section of the community—neither an élite nor a cross section—that sees Broadway plays. A play by an Arthur Miller or a Tennessee Williams is an exception. Such a play is not only better than the majority; it belongs in the mainstream of our culture. Such an author has something to say about America that is worth discussing. In *The Crucible*, Mr. Miller says something that *has* to be discussed. Nor am I limiting my interest to the intellectual sphere. One sits before this play with anything but intellectual detachment. At a moment when we are all being "investigated," or imagining that we shall be, it is vastly disturbing to see indignant images of investigation on the other side of the footlights. Why, one wonders, aren't there

From Eric Bentley, *What Is Theatre? Incorporating "The Dramatic Event" and Other Reviews 1944–1967* (New York: Atheneum, 1968), pp. 62-65. Copyright © 1954 by Eric Bentley. Reprinted by permission of the author and Atheneum Publishers. The review, somewhat abridged, was first published under the title "Miller's Innocence" in *New Republic*, CXXVIII (February 16, 1953), 22-23.

dozens of plays each season offering such a critical account of the state of the nation—critical and *engagé*? The appearance of one such play by an author, like Mr. Miller, who is neither an infant, a fool, nor a swindler, is enough to bring tears to the eyes.

"Great stones they lay upon his chest until he plead aye or nay. They say he give them but two words. 'More weight,' he says, and died." Mr. Miller's material is magnificent for narrative, poetry, drama. The fact that we sense its magnificence suggests that either he or his actors have in part realized it, yet our moments of emotion only make us the more aware of half-hours of indifference or dissatisfaction. For this is a story not quite told, a drama not quite realized. Pygmalion has labored hard at his statue and it has not come to life. There is a terrible inertness about the play. The individual characters, like the individual lines, lack fluidity and grace. There is an O'Neill-like striving after a poetry and an eloquence which the author does not achieve. "From Aeschylus to Arthur Miller," say the textbooks. The world has made this author important before he has made himself great; perhaps the reversal of the natural order of things weighs heavily upon him. It would be all too easy, script in hand, to point to weak spots. The inadequacy of particular lines, and characters, is of less interest, however, than the mentality from which they come. It is the mentality of the unreconstructed liberal.

There has been some debate as to whether this story of seventeenth-century Salem "really" refers to our current "witch hunt" yet since no one is interested in anything *but* this reference, I pass on to the real point at issue, which is: the validity of the parallel. It is true in that people today are being persecuted on quite chimerical grounds. It is untrue in that communism is not, to put it mildly, merely a chimera. The word communism is used to cover, first, the politics of Marx, second, the politics of the Soviet Union, and, third, the activities of all liberals as they seem to illiberal illiterates.

Since Mr. Miller's argument bears only on the third use of the word, its scope is limited. Indeed, the analogy between "red-baiting" and witch hunting can seem complete only to communists, for only to them is the menace of communism as fictitious as the menace of witches. The non-communist will look for certain reservations and provisos. In *The Crucible*, there are none.

To accuse Mr. Miller of communism would of course be to fall into the trap of oversimplification which he himself has set. For all I know he may hate the Soviet state with all the ardor of Eisenhower. What I am maintaining is that his view of life is dictated by assumptions which liberals have to unlearn and which many liberals have rather publicly unlearned. Chief among these assumptions is that of general innocence. In Hebrew mythology, innocence was lost at the very beginning of things; in liberal, especially American liberal, folklore, it has not been lost yet; Arthur Miller is the playwright of American liberal folklore. It is as if the merely negative, and legal, definition of innocence were extended to the rest of life: you are innocent until proved guilty, you are innocent if you "didn't do it." Writers have a sort of double innocence: not only can they create innocent characters, they can also write from the viewpoint of innocence—we can speak today not only of the "omniscient" author but of the "guiltless" one.

Such indeed is the viewpoint of the dramatist of indignation, like Miss Hellman[1] or Mr. Miller. And it follows that

---

[1] Lillian Hellman. See note, p. 199 Bentley's review of the revival of *The Children's Hour* can be found in *What Is Theatre?* . . . (1968), pp. 49-52. In another essay written at about the same time, "The American Drama (1944–1954)," first published in *Avon Book of Modern Writing*, No. 2, ed. William Phillips and Philip Rahv (New York: Avon, 1954), pp. 269-86, Bentley continued his discussion of the "liberal" playwright, once again joining Miller and Miss Hellman. That essay is available in Eric Bentley, *The Theatre of Commitment* (New York: Atheneum, 1967), pp. 18-46.

their plays are melodrama—a conflict between the wholly
guilty and the wholly innocent. For a long time liberals were
afraid to criticize the mentality behind this melodrama because they feared association with the guilty ("harboring
reactionary sympathies"). But, though a more enlightened
view would enjoin association with the guilty in the admission of a common humanity, it does not ask us to underestimate the guilt or to refuse to see "who done it." The
guilty men are as black with guilt as Mr. Miller says—what
we must ask is whether the innocent are as white with innocence. The drama of indignation is melodramatic not so much
because it paints its villains too black as because it paints
its heroes too white. *Othello* is not a melodrama, because,
though its villain is wholly evil, its hero is not wholly virtuous. *The Crucible* is a melodrama because, though the hero
has weaknesses, he has no faults. His innocence is unreal because it is total. His author has equipped him with what we
might call Super-innocence, for the crime he is accused of
not only hasn't been committed by him, it isn't even a possibility: it is the fiction of traffic with the devil. It goes without
saying that the hero has all the minor accouterments of innocence too: he belongs to the right social class (yeoman farmer),
does the right kind of work (manual), and, somewhat contrary to historical probability, has the right philosophy (a dis-
tinct leaning towards skeptical empiricism) . . .

[The innocence of his author is known to us from life as
well as art. Elia Kazan made a public confession of having
been a communist and, while doing so, mentioned the names
of several of his former comrades. Mr. Miller then brought
out a play about an accused man who refuses to name comrades (who indeed dies rather than make a confession at all),
and of course decided to end his collaboration with the director
who did so much to make him famous. The play has been
directed by Jed Harris.

I think there is as much drama in this bit of history as

in any Salem witch hunt. The "guilty" director was rejected. An "innocent" one was chosen in his place. There are two stories in this. The first derives from the fact that the better fellow (assuming, for the purpose of argument, that Mr. Harris is the better fellow) is not always the better worker.]² The awkwardness I find in Mr. Miller's script is duplicated in Mr. Harris's directing. Mr. Kazan would have taken this script up like clay and remolded it. He would have struck fire from the individual actor, and he would have brought one actor into much livelier relationship with another. (Arthur Kennedy is not used up to half his full strength in this production; E. G. Marshall and Walter Hampden give fine per-

---

² The material in brackets was dropped from the original *New Republic* review. In "The American Drama (1944–1954)," Bentley wrote: "The production of the play was preceded by a quarrel between Mr. Miller and Elia Kazan. . . . But that one is not supposed to find any connection between that scene [Proctor's refusal to give names] and the Kazan incident I discovered when I tried to get some remarks on the subject into a liberal journal" (*The Theatre of Commitment*, p. 37). See also "On the Waterfront," Bentley's review of the Elia Kazan movie of that name and Miller's A *View from the Bridge* (in *What Is Theatre?* . . . (1968), pp. 258-61.) see note, p. 188. When Miller appeared before the House Un-American Activities Committee (see Bibliography), he denied ever calling Elia Kazan "a renegade intellectual" or "an informer" for having been a friendly witness before the HUAC. He explained that his break ("that word is not descriptive of my act") with the director was not necessarily a consequence of Kazan's testimony: "I am not at all certain that Mr. Kazan would have directed my next play in any case." When Richard Arens, the staff director of the committee, repeated his question about the Miller-Kazan split, the playwright insisted, "I stated earlier, sir, that I have never attacked Kazan. I will stand on that" (pp. 4677-78). Appearing before a directing class at the University of Michigan in February 1967, Miller answered a question about Kazan by sticking to how the director works. See *Michigan Quarterly Review*, VI (summer 1967), 181. Kazan testified on April 10, 1952; see United States House of Representatives, Committee on Un-American Activities, Communist Infiltration of Hollywood Motion-Picture Industry, Part 7, pp. 2407-14. There is no mention of Miller in Kazan's testimony so the celebrated quarrel, insofar as it existed, was based not on personal resentment but on abstract principle—an attitude toward testifying. See the excerpt from *After the Fall*, pp. 174-181.

formances but each in his own way, Mr. Hampden's way being a little too English, genteel and nineteenth century; the most successful performance, perhaps, is that of Beatrice Straight because here a certain rigidity belongs to the character and is in any case delicately checked by the performer's fine sensibility.) The second story is that of the interpenetration of good and evil. I am afraid that Mr. Miller needs a Kazan not merely at some superficial technical level. He needs not only the craftsmanship of a Kazan but also—his sense of guilt. Innocence is, for a mere human being, and especially for an artist, insufficient baggage. When we say that Mr. Kazan "added" to *Death of a Salesman*, we mean—if I am not saying more than I know—that he infused into this drama of social forces the pressure of what Freud called "the family romance," the pressure of guilt. *The Crucible* is *about* guilt yet nowhere in it is there any *sense* of guilt because the author and director have joined forces to dissociate themselves and their hero from evil. This is the theatre of two Dr. Jekylls. Mr. Miller and Mr. Kazan were Dr. Jekyll and Mr. Hyde.

ROBERT WARSHOW

Robert Warshow, a member of the staff of *Commentary* from 1946 until his death in 1955, wrote essays on film and American culture for *Commentary*, *Partisan Review*, and *American Mercury*, among other magazines.

THE LIBERAL CONSCIENCE
IN *THE CRUCIBLE*

One of the things that have been said of *The Crucible*, Arthur Miller's new play about the Salem witchcraft trials, is that we must not be misled by its obvious contemporary relevance: it is a drama of universal significance. This statement, which has usually a somewhat apologetic tone, seems to be made most often by those who do not fail to place great stress on the play's "timeliness." I believe it means something very different from what it appears to say, almost the contrary, in fact, and yet not quite the contrary either. It means: do not be misled by the play's historical theme into forgetting the main point, which is that "witch trials" are always with us, and especially today; but on the other hand do not hold Mr. Miller responsible either for the inadequacies of his presentation of the Salem trials or for the many undeniable and important differences between those trials and the "witch trials" that are going on now. It is quite true, nevertheless, that the play is, at least in one sense, of "universal significance."

From Robert Warshow, *The Immediate Experience* (New York: Doubleday, 1962), pp. 189-203. The article first appeared in *Commentary*, XV (March 1953), 265-71.

Only we must ask what this phrase has come to mean, and whether the quality it denotes is a virtue.

The Puritan tradition, the greatest and most persistent formulator of American simplifications, has itself always contained elements disturbingly resistant to ideological—or even simply rational—understanding. The great debate in American Calvinism over "good works" versus the total arbitrariness of the divine will was won, fortunately and no doubt inevitably, by those who held that an actively virtuous life must be at least the outward sign of "election." But this interpretation was entirely pragmatic; it was made only because it had to be made, because in the most literal sense one could not survive in a universe of absolute predestination. The central contradiction of Calvinism remained unresolved, and the awful confusions of the Puritan mind still embarrass our efforts to see the early history of New England as a clear stage in the progress of American enlightenment. Only Hawthorne among American writers has seriously tried to deal with these confusions as part of the "given" material of literature, taking the Puritans in their own terms as among the real possibilities of life, and the admiration we accord to his tense and brittle artistry is almost as distant as our admiration of the early New Englanders themselves; it is curious how rarely Hawthorne has been mentioned beside Melville and James even in recent explorations of the "anti-liberal" side of our literature.

The Salem witch trials represent how far the Puritans were ready to go in taking their doctrines seriously. Leaving aside the slavery question and what has flowed from it, those trials are perhaps the most disconcerting single episode in our history: the occurrence of the unthinkable on American soil, and in what our schools have rather successfully taught us to think of as the very "cradle of Americanism." Of Europe's witch trials, we have our opinion. But these witch trials are "ours"; where do they belong in the "tradition"?

For Americans, a problem of this sort demands to be resolved, and there have been two main ways of resolving it. The first is to regard the trials as a historical curiosity; a curiosity by definition requires no explanation. In this way the trials are placed among the "vagaries" of the Puritan mind and can even offer a kind of amusement, like the amusement we have surprisingly agreed to find in the so-called "rough justice" of the Western frontier in the last century. But the more usual and more deceptive way of dealing with the Salem trials has been to assimilate them to the history of progress in civil rights. This brings them into the world of politics, where, even if our minds are not always made up, at least we think we know what the issues are. Arthur Miller, I need hardly say, has adopted this latter view.

Inevitably, I suppose, we will find in history what we need to find. But in this particular "interpretation" of the facts there seems to be a special injustice. The Salem trials were not political and had nothing whatever to do with civil rights, unless it is a violation of civil rights to hang a murderer. Nor were the "witches" being "persecuted"—as the Puritans did persecute Quakers, for instance. The actual conduct of the trials, to be sure, was outrageous, but no more outrageous than the conduct of ordinary criminal trials in England at the time. In any case, it is a little absurd to make the whole matter rest on the question of fair trial: how can there be a "fair trial" for a crime which not only has not been committed, but is impossible? The Salem "witches" suffered something that may be worse than persecution: they were hanged because of a metaphysical error. And they chose to die—for all could have saved themselves by "confession"—not for a cause, not for "civil rights," not even to defeat the error that hanged them, but for their own credit on earth and in heaven: they would not say they were witches when they were not. They lived in a universe where each man was saved or damned by himself, and what happened to them was personal. Certainly their fate is not lacking in universal significance; it was a human fate. But its universality—if we must have the word —is of that true kind which begins and ends in a time and a place. One need not believe in witches, or even in God, to understand the events in Salem, but it is mere provinciality to ignore the fact that both those ideas had a reality for the people of Salem that they do not have for us.

The "universality" of Mr. Miller's play belongs neither to literature nor to history, but to that journalism of limp erudition which assumes that events are to be understood by referring them to categories, and which is therefore never at a loss for a comment. Just as in *Death of a Salesman* Mr. Miller sought to present "the American" by eliminating so far as possible the "non-essential" facts which might have made his protagonist a particular American, so in *The Crucible* he reveals at every turn his almost contemptuous lack of interest in the particularities—which is to say, the reality—of the Salem trials. The character and motives of all the actors in this drama are for him both simple and clear. The girls who raised the accusation of witchcraft were merely trying to cover up their own misbehavior. The Reverend Samuel Parris found in the investigation of witchcraft a convenient means of consolidating his shaky position in a parish that was murmuring against his "undemocratic" conduct of the church. The Reverend John Hale, a conscientious and troubled minister who, given the premises, must have represented something like the best that Puritan New England had to offer, and whose agonies of doubt might have been expected to call forth the highest talents of a serious playwright, appears in *The Crucible* as a kind of idiotic "liberal" scoutmaster, at first cheerfully confident of his ability to cope with the Devil's wiles and in the last act babbling hysterically in an almost comic contrast to the assured dignity of the main characters. Deputy Governor Danforth, presented as the virtual embodiment of early New England, never becomes more than a pompous, unimaginative politician of the better sort.

As for the victims themselves, the most significant fact is Miller's choice of John Proctor for his leading character: Proctor can be seen as one of the more "modern" figures in the trials, hardheaded, skeptical, a voice of common sense (he thought the accusing girls could be cured of their "spells" by a sound whipping); also, according to Mr. Miller, no great churchgoer. It is all too easy to make Proctor into the "common man"—and then, of course, we know where we are: Proctor wavers a good deal, fails to understand what is happening, wants only to be left alone with his wife and his farm, considers making a false confession, but in the end goes to his death for reasons that he finds a little hard to define but that are clearly good reasons—mainly, it seems, he does not want to implicate others. You will never learn from this John Proctor that Salem was a religious community, quite as ready to hang a Quaker as a witch. The saintly Rebecca Nurse is also there, to be sure, sketched in rapidly in the background, a quiet figure whose mere presence—there is little more of her than that—reminds us how far the dramatist has fallen short.

Nor has Mr. Miller hesitated to alter the facts to fit his constricted field of vision. Abigail Williams, one of the chief accusers in the trials, was about eleven years old in 1692; Miller makes her a young woman of eighteen or nineteen and invents an adulterous relation between her and John Proctor in order to motivate her denunciation of John and his wife Elizabeth. The point is not that this falsifies the facts of Proctor's life (though one remembers uneasily that he himself was willing to be hanged rather than confess to what was not true), but that it destroys the play, offering an easy theatrical motive that even in theatrical terms explains nothing, and deliberately casting away the element of religious and psychological complexity which gives the Salem trials their dramatic interest in the first place. In a similar way, Miller risks the whole point of *Death of a Salesman* by making his plot turn on the irrelevant discovery of Willy Loman's adultery. And in both plays the fact of adultery itself is slighted: it is brought in not as a human problem, but as a mere theatrical device, like the dropping of a letter; one cannot take an interest in Willy Loman's philandering, or believe in Abigail Williams's passion despite the barnyard analogies with which the playwright tries to make it "elemental."

Mr. Miller's steadfast, one might almost say selfless, refusal of complexity, the assured simplicity of his view of human behavior, may be the chief source of his ability to captivate the educated audience. He is an oddly depersonalized writer; one tries in vain to define his special quality, only to discover that it is perhaps not a quality at all, but something like a method, and even as a method strangely bare: his plays are as neatly put together and essentially as empty as that skeleton of a house which made *Death of a Salesman* so impressively confusing. He is the playwright of an audience that believes the frightening complexities of history and experience are to be met with a few ideas, and yet does not even possess these ideas any longer but can only point significantly at the place where they were last seen and where it is hoped they might still be found to exist. What this audience demands of its artists above all is an intelligent narrowness of mind and vision and a generalized tone of affirmation, offering not any particular insights or any particular truths, but simply the assurance that insight and truth as qualities, the things in themselves, reside somehow in the various signals by which the artist and the audience have learned to recognize each other. For indeed very little remains except this recognition; the marriage of the liberal theatre and the liberal audience has been for some time a marriage in name only, held together by habit and mutual interest, partly by sentimental memory, most of all by the fear of loneliness and the outside world; and yet the movements of love are still kept up—for the sake of the children, perhaps.

The hero of this audience is Clifford Odets. Among those who shouted "Bravo!" at the end of *The Crucible*—an exclamation, awkward on American lips, that is reserved for cultural achievements of the greatest importance—there must surely have been some who had stood up to shout "Strike!" at the end of *Waiting for Lefty*.[1] But it is hard to believe that a second Odets, if that were possible, or the old Odets restored to youth, would be greeted with such enthusiasm as Arthur Miller calls forth. Odets's talent was too rich—in my opinion the richest ever to appear in the American theatre —and his poetry and invention were constantly more important than what he conceived himself to be saying. In those days it didn't matter: the "message" at the end of the third act was so much taken for granted that there was room for Odets's exuberance, and he himself was never forced to learn how much his talent was superior to his "affirmations" (if he had learned, perhaps the talent might have survived the "affirmations"). Arthur Miller is the dramatist of a later time, when the "message" isn't there at all, but it has been agreed to pretend that it is. This pretense can be maintained only by the most rigid control, for there is no telling what small element of dramatic *élan* or simple reality may destroy the delicate rapport of a theatre and an audience that have not

---

[1] Odets was the most celebrated radical playwright of the 1930s; *Waiting for Lefty*, the play that launched his career, was first performed on January 5, 1935. It is an *agitprop* which ends with the audience and the actors joining to shout, "STRIKE, STRIKE, STRIKE!!!," an event which Harold Clurman, in *The Fervent Years* (New York: Hill and Wang, 1957, p. 139), has called "the birth cry of the thirties." For Warshow on Odets, see *The Immediate Experience*, pp. 55-67. For an extended look at Odets, see Gerald Weales, *Clifford Odets* (New York: Pegasus-Bobbs-Merrill, 1971).

yet acknowledged they have no more to say to each other. Arthur Miller is Odets without the poetry. Worst of all, one feels sometimes that he has suppressed the poetry deliberately, making himself by choice the anonymous dramatist of a fossilized audience. In *Death of a Salesman*, certainly, there were moments when reality seemed to force its way momentarily to the surface. And even at *The Crucible*—though here it was not Miller's suppressed talent that broke through, but the suppressed facts of the outside world—the thread that tied the audience to its dramatist must have been now and then under some strain: surely there were some in the audience to notice uneasily that these witch trials, with their quality of ritual and their insistent need for "confessions," were much more like the trial that had just ended in Prague[2] than like any trial that has lately taken place in the United States. So much the better, perhaps, for the play's "universal significance"; I don't suppose Mr. Miller would defend the Prague trial. And yet I cannot believe it was for this particular implication that anyone shouted "Bravo!"

For let us indeed not be misled. Mr. Miller has nothing to say about the Salem trials and makes only the flimsiest pretense that he has. *The Crucible* was written to say something about Alger Hiss and Owen Lattimore, Julius and Ethel Rosenberg, Senator McCarthy, the actors who have lost their jobs on radio and television, in short the whole complex that is spoken of, with a certain lowering of the voice, as the "present atmosphere."[3] And yet not to say anything about that either,

[2] See note, p. 198.

[3] Whittaker Chambers, a former Communist, charged that Alger Hiss, an official in the Department of State, passed confidential documents to the Russians. Hiss denied the charges and, after two trials, was convicted of perjury in January 1950. He was still in jail when *The Crucible* was produced. Both Chambers's own book, *Witness* (see pp. 410-414) and a second, enlarged edition of Alistair Cooke's 1950 study of the Hiss-Chambers case, *A Generation on Trial* (New York: Knopf),

but only to suggest that a great deal might be said, oh an infinitely great deal, if it were not that—what? Well, perhaps if it were not that the "present atmosphere" itself makes such plain speaking impossible. As it is, there is nothing for it but to write plays of "universal significance"—and, after all, that's what a serious dramatist is supposed to do anyway.

What, then, *is* Mr. Miller trying to say to us? It's hard to tell. In *The Crucible* innocent people are accused and convicted of witchcraft on the most absurd testimony—in fact, the testimony of those who themselves have meddled in witchcraft and are therefore doubly to be distrusted. Decent citizens who sign petitions attesting to the good character of

---

appeared in 1952, and Lord Jowitt's *The Strange Case of Alger Hiss* was to appear shortly after Warshow's article was first published—in England in May (London: Hodder and Stoughton) and in the United States in July (New York: Doubleday). Owen Lattimore, an expert on the Far East, was accused by Senator Joseph McCarthy (see pp. 406-409) of having been responsible for our losing China to the Communists (as if it were ours to lose), but was cleared of all charges by a subcommittee of the Senate Foreign Relations Committee. Lattimore's book, *Ordeal by Slander* (Boston: Atlantic-Little, Brown, 1950), is his account of that experience. He came up before the Senate Internal Security Committee in 1951 and, in December 1952, was indicted for perjury. So matters stood when Warshow wrote his article. The indictment was thrown out in May 1953; he was indicted again in 1954, but—after that too was dismissed by the court—the government dropped all perjury charges in 1955. In March 1951 the Rosenbergs were found guilty of conspiring to pass atomic secrets to Russia during World War II and sentenced to death. Warshow wrote his review while appeals were pending, at the height of the protest over the severity of the sentence. After their execution (June 19, 1953), Warshow wrote "The 'Idealism' of Julius and Ethel Rosenberg." See *The Immediate Experience*, pp. 69-81. To get some idea of the extent of blacklisting, see John Cogley, *Report on Blacklisting* (New York: The Fund for the Republic, 1956). All these did indeed form the "present atmosphere" in which the play was produced and the "liberal" audience responded to it, but it was an atmosphere that just as obviously produced the critiques of liberalism so fashionable at the time, of which the Bentley and Warshow reviews are good examples.

their accused friends and neighbors are thrown into prison as suspects. Anyone who tries to introduce into court the voice of reason is likely to be held in contempt. One of the accused refuses to plead and is pressed to death. No one is acquitted; the only way out for the accused is to make false confessions and themselves join the accusers. Seeing all this on the stage, we are free to reflect that something very like these trials has been going on in recent years in the United States. How much like? Mr. Miller does not say. But *very* like, allowing of course for some superficial differences: no one has been pressed to death in recent years, for instance. Still, people have lost their jobs for refusing to say under oath whether or not they are Communists. The essential pattern is the same, isn't it? And when we speak of "universal significance," we mean sticking to the essential pattern, don't we? Mr. Miller is under no obligation to tell us whether he thinks the trial of Alger Hiss, let us say, was a "witch trial"; he is writing about the Salem trials.

Or, again, the play reaches its climax with John and Elizabeth Proctor facing the problem of whether John should save himself from execution by making a false confession; he elects finally to accept death, for his tormentors will not be satisfied with his mere admission of guilt: he would be required to implicate others, thus betraying his innocent friends, and his confession would of course be used to justify the hanging of the other convicted witches in the face of growing community unrest. Now it is very hard to watch this scene without thinking of Julius and Ethel Rosenberg, who might also save their lives by confessing. Does Mr. Miller believe that the only confession possible for them would be a false one, implicating innocent people? Naturally, there is no way for him to let us know; perhaps he was not even thinking of the Rosenbergs at all. How can he be held responsible for what comes into my head while I watch his play? And if I think of the Rosen-

bergs and somebody else thinks of Alger Hiss, and still another thinks of the Prague trial, doesn't that simply prove all
over again that the play has universal significance?

One remembers also, as John Proctor wrestles with his conscience, that a former close associate of Mr. Miller's decided
some time ago, no doubt after serious and painful consideration, to tell the truth about his past membership in the Communist party, that he mentioned some others who had been in
the party with him, and that he then became known in certain theatrical circles as an "informer" and a "rat."[4] Is it possible that this is what Mr. Miller was thinking about when
he came to write his last scene? And is he trying to tell us
that no one who has been a member of the Communist party
should admit it? Or that if he does admit it he should not
implicate anyone else? Or that all such "confessions" may be
assumed to be false? If he were trying to tell us any of these
things, perhaps we might have some arguments to raise. But
of course he isn't; he's only writing about the Salem trials, and
who wants to maintain that John Proctor was guilty of
witchcraft?

But if Mr. Miller isn't saying anything about the Salem trials,
and can't be caught saying anything about anything else,
what did the audience think he was saying? That too is hard
to tell. A couple of the newspaper critics wrote about how
timely the play was, and then took it back in the Sunday edi-
tions, putting a little more weight on the "universal significance";[5] but perhaps they didn't quite take it back as much as

---

[4] See Eric Bentley on Elia Kazan and the accompanying note, p. 208.

[5] This is a doubtful statement. Both Brooks Atkinson and Walter F.
Kerr, given more space to work in, contemplated the use of Salem in
their Sunday pieces (see Bibliography). But despite the headline on
Kerr's piece ("*The Crucible* Retells Salem's Violent Story"), neither
critic ignored the contemporary relevance. Atkinson even considered the

they seemed to want to: the final verdict appeared to be merely that *The Crucible* is not so great a play as *Death of a Salesman*. As for the rest of the audience, it was clear that they felt themselves to be participating in an event of great meaning: that is what is meant by "Bravo!" Does "Bravo!" mean anything else? I think it means: we agree with Arthur Miller; he has set forth brilliantly and courageously what has been weighing on all our minds; at last someone has had the courage to answer Senator McCarthy.

I don't believe this audience was likely to ask itself what it was agreeing to. Enough that someone had said something, anything, to dispel for a couple of hours that undefined but very real sense of frustration which oppresses these "liberals"—who believe in their innermost being that salvation comes from saying something, and who yet find themselves somehow without anything very relevant to say. They tell themselves, of course, that Senator McCarthy has made it "impossible" to speak; but one can hardly believe they are satisfied with this explanation. Where are the heroic voices that will refuse to be stilled?

Well, last season there was *The Male Animal,* a play written twelve or thirteen years ago about a college professor who gets in trouble for reading one of Vanzetti's letters to his English composition class. In the audience at that play one felt also the sense of communal excitement; it was a little like a secret meeting of early Christians—or even, one might say, witches—where everything had an extra dimension of meaning experienced only by the communicants. And this year there has been a revival of *The Children's Hour,* a play of even more universal significance than *The Crucible* since it

witch-spy analogy in a way that could not have been uncongenial to Warshow. If there were other back-taking Sunday pieces, I have not found them.

doesn't have anything to do with any trials but just shows
how people can be hurt by having lies told about them. But
these were old plays, the voices of an older generation. It remained for Arthur Miller to write a new play that really
speaks out.[6]

What does he say when he speaks out?
Never mind. He speaks out.

One question remains to be asked. If Mr. Miller was unable
to write directly about what he apparently (one can only
guess) feels to be going on in American life today, why did
he choose the particular evasion of the Salem trials? After
all, violations of civil rights have been not infrequent in our
history, and the Salem trials have the disadvantage that they
must be distorted in order to be fitted into the framework of
civil rights in the first place. Why is it just the image of a
"witch trial" or a "witch hunt" that best expresses the sense
of oppression which weighs on Mr. Miller and those who feel
—I do not say think—as he does?

The answer, I would suppose, is precisely that those accused of witchcraft did *not* die for a cause or an idea, that

---

[6] *The Male Animal*, by James Thurber and Elliott Nugent, was revived
at the City Center on April 30, 1952. One of a number of revivals
put on by the New York City Theatre Company, it was to run for only
two weeks, but it was so enthusiastically received that John Golden
moved it to the Music Box Theatre for a commercial run. It played
317 performances, closing on January 13, 1953, shortly before *The
Crucible* opened. Bartolomeo Vanzetti and fellow anarchist Nicola Sacco
were convicted of murder and robbery in 1921, after a sensational trial
in which their politics seemed as much at issue as their presumed crime.
It was not until August 22, 1927, that they were finally executed. The
Sacco-Vanzetti case became one of the most celebrated instances of
doubtful American justice and—particularly among radicals and liberals
—the two men were widely accepted as martyrs. Their guilt or innocence
is still being argued as new books on the case keep coming out. For
the revival of *The Children's Hour*, see note, p. 199.

they represented nothing; they were totally innocent, accused of a crime that does not even exist, the arbitrary victims of a fantastic error. Sacco and Vanzetti, for instance, were able to interpret what was happening to them in a way that the Salem victims could not; they knew that they actually stood for certain ideas that were abhorrent to those who were sending them to death. But the men and women hanged in Salem were not upholding witchcraft against the true church; they were upholding their own personal integrity against an insanely mistaken community.

This offers us a revealing glimpse of the way the Communists and their fellow-travelers have come to regard themselves. The picture has a certain pathos. As it becomes increasingly difficult for any sane man of conscience to reconcile an adherence to the Communist party with any conceivable political principles, the Communist—who is still, let us remember, very much a man of conscience—must gradually divest his political allegiance of all actual content, until he stands bare to the now incomprehensible anger of his neighbors. What can they possibly have against him?—he knows quite well that he believes in nothing, certainly that he is no revolutionist; he is only a dissenter-in-general, a type of personality, a man frozen into an attitude.

From this comes the astonishing phenomenon of Communist innocence. It cannot be assumed that the guiltiest of Communist conspirators protesting his entire innocence may not have a certain belief in his own protest. If you say to a Communist that he is a Communist, he is likely to feel himself in the position of a man who has been accused on no evidence of a crime that he has actually committed. He knows that he happens to be a Communist. But he knows also that his opinions and behavior are only the opinions and behavior of a "liberal," a "dissenter." You are therefore accusing him of being a Communist because he is a liberal, because he is for peace and civil rights and everything good.

By some fantastic accident, your accusation happens to be true, but it is *essentially* false.

Consider, for example, how the controversy over the Hiss case reduced itself almost immediately to a question of personality, the "good" Hiss against the "bad" Chambers, with the disturbing evidence of handwriting and typewriters and automobiles somehow beside the point. Alger Hiss, for those who believe him innocent, wears his innocence on his face and his body, in his "essence," whereas Chambers by his own tortured behavior reveals himself as one of the damned. Hiss's innocence, in fact, exists on a plane entirely out of contact with whatever he may have done. Perhaps most of those who take Hiss's "side" believe that he actually did transmit secret documents to Chambers. But they believe also that this act was somehow transmuted into innocence by the inherent virtue of Alger Hiss's being.

In a similar way, there has grown up around figures like Whittaker Chambers, Elizabeth Bentley, and Louis Budenz the falsest of all false issues: the "question" of the ex-Communist. We are asked to consider, not whether these people are telling the truth, or whether their understanding of Communism is correct, but whether in their "essence" as ex-Communists they are not irredeemably given over to falsehood and confusion. (It must be said that some ex-Communists have themselves helped to raise this absurd "question" by depicting Communism as something beyond both error and immorality—a form of utter perdition.)

Or, finally, consider that most mystical element in the Communist propaganda about the Rosenberg case: the claim that Julius and Ethel Rosenberg are being "persecuted" because they have "fought for peace." Since the Rosenbergs had abstained entirely from all political activity of any sort for a number of years before their arrest, it follows that the only thing they could have been doing which a Communist might interpret as "fighting for peace" must have been spying for the Soviet Union; but their being "persecuted" rests precisely on the claim that they are innocent of spying. The main element here, of course, is deliberate falsification. But it must be understood that for most partisans of the Rosenbergs such a falsification raises no problem; all lies and inconsistencies disappear in the enveloping cloud of the unspoken "essential" truth: the Rosenbergs are innocent *because* they are accused; they are innocent, one might say, by definition.

In however inchoate a fashion, those who sat thrilled in the dark theatre watching *The Crucible* were celebrating a tradition and a community. No longer could they find any meaning in the cry of "Strike!" or "Revolt!" as they had done in their younger and more "primitive" age; let it be only "Bravo!"—a cry of celebration with no particular content. The important thing was that for a short time they could experience together the sense of their own being, their close community of right-mindedness in the orthodoxy of "dissent." Outside, there waited all kinds of agonizing and concrete problems: were the Rosenbergs actually guilty? was Stalin actually going to persecute the Jews? But in the theatre they could know, immediately and confidently, their own innate and inalienable rightness.

The Salem trials are in fact more relevant than Arthur Miller can have suspected. For this community of "dissent," inexorably stripped of all principle and all specific belief, has retreated at last into a kind of extreme Calvinism of its own where political truth ceases to have any real connection with politics but becomes a property of the soul. Apart from all belief and all action, these people are "right" in themselves, and no longer need to prove themselves in the world of experience; the Revolution—or "liberalism," or "dissent"—has entered into them as the grace of God was once conceived to have entered into the "elect," and, like the grace of God, it is given irrevocably. Just as Alger Hiss bears witness to virtue even in his refusal to admit the very act wherein his "virtue" must reside if it resides anywhere, so these bear witness to "dissent" and "progress" in their mere existence.

For the Puritans themselves, the doctrine of absolute election was finally intolerable, and it cannot be believed that this new community of the elect finds its position comfortable. But it has yet to discover that its discomfort, like its "election," comes from within.

HAROLD HOBSON

Harold Hobson, drama critic for *The Sunday Times* (London)
since 1947, is the author of *The Theatre Hour* and *Ralph Richard-
son*, among other books, and is the editor of *International Theatre
Annual*.

FAIR PLAY

Mr. Arthur Miller's play about witch hunting in seventeenth-
century Massachusetts keeps one eye steadily fixed on the
present anti-Communist investigations in the United States;
and it gives a rather better case to Senator McCarthy than
might have been supposed from the reports that have reached
us from the other side of the Atlantic, or than could have
been expected from a writer of Mr. Miller's Leftist convictions.
This is an important fact which for dramatic, not political,
reasons seems to me entirely in the play's favour.

What Acton said was the duty of the historian is no less
that of the dramatist: to be fair to the other side. Is this a
truism? If so, it is one often neglected. Thucydides was as fair
to the Spartans as to the Athenians, Anouilh can see Cauchon's point of view as well as Joan's, but Macaulay was as
unjust to the Tories as he was to the University of Oxford,

From *The Sunday Times* (London), November 14, 1954, p. 11. The
first English production of *The Crucible*, directed by Warren Jenkins,
opened at the Theatre Royal, Bristol, November 9, 1954. In general,
it was less well received than Hobson's review suggests. The play was
first done in London by George Devine at the Royal Court, April 9,
1956; in 1965 it was revived at the National Theatre under Laurence
Olivier's direction.

or as Gibbon was to the early Christians; and Mr. Charles Morgan in *The Burning Glass*, when he makes his conspirator a melodramatic villain, metaphorically calling for green limelight, is as vulnerable artistically as Mr. Ewen MacColl, who, in *Uranium 235*, remembers the pact between Chamberlain and Hitler but conveniently forgets that of Molotov and Ribbentrop.[1]

Mr. Miller has not this selective memory, nor does he allow his personal convictions to interfere with the dramatist's responsibility for presenting every one of his characters with understanding and sympathy. He shows that the witch hunting of bygone Salem generated hysteria, terror, cruelty, and injustice; that it degraded the nature of those taking part in it; that it brought ruin and death to the innocent. He protests against the brutality and stupidity with which evil was persecuted, but he does not claim either that the evil did not exist, or that, existing, it was good.

In other words, he postulates the reality of the conspiracy. When the Reverend Samuel Parris suspects that his niece and her friends have made woodland nocturnal trips and danced naked in the moonlight, and invoked the devil, he is right in his fears; these things have taken place. Nor are they merely the foolish activities of unbalanced girls; they are the setting for an attack upon the state, the state of matrimony and domestic happiness. One of the witches, Abigail Williams, is genuinely plotting to overthrow that particular part of the American way of life which is represented by the family of

---

[1] Of the plays Hobson refers to, only Charles Morgan's *The Burning Glass* had recently been done in London, opening at the Apollo Theatre on February 18, 1954. Ewan (not Ewen) MacColl's *Uranium 235* was first performed on May 12, 1952. Jean Anouilh's *L'Alouette*, first performed in Paris on October 14, 1953, had not yet become *The Lark*, but Christopher Fry's adaptation would open in London on May 11, 1955. As for the references to the historians—Lord Acton, Thucydides, Macaulay, Gibbon—I will let you search them out yourself.

Elizabeth Proctor and her husband, John. She is determined to secure the condemnation and hanging of Mrs. Proctor, and deliberately works upon the Massachusetts judges so as to inflame their superstition and alarm.

But Mr. Miller goes farther than to admit that there is some basis for the investigation. He represents the chief of the persecutors as a man honestly desiring to do right and to seek justice, and even—in what to many people will seem an excess of generosity—he shows us the investigations as though they were indeed conducted according to the form of law. His Deputy-Governor Danforth, played by Mr. John Kidd with pedantic integrity, is genuinely concerned to see justice done.

The Crucible therefore is a fair play; it is also an exciting one. The scene in the courtroom in which, before the horrified eyes of the gullible and frightened judges, Abigail and her friends claim that they can feel the presence of the devil like a rushing, mighty wind is magnificently theatrical; and it is played by Miss Pat Sandys with assured diabolism; for all her frail appearance, Miss Sandys here looks as though she might well have trafficked with unmentionable things.

Not all the players are as good as Miss Sandys. But Mr. Michael Allinson excellently catches the anguish of a man whose situation and profession force him to see guilt where no guilt is; Mr. Peter Wylde has small opportunity to do more than to give to Judge Hathorne a look of concentrated fanaticism; yet the little chance he is given he takes with certainty.

The two principals are Miss Rosemary Harris and Mr. Edgar Wreford as Elizabeth and John Proctor. Mr. Wreford, trying to rescue his wife, makes appropriate gestures of sadness, bewilderment and revolt, but never seems to hit on the tone or the movement that pierces the heart. About Miss Harris I am in a difficulty; I am sure that she is, on her day, a good actress; but her present performance is so lifeless, so maudlin, so devitalisedly self-righteous that she altogether falsifies the values of the play, and almost makes one wish that the enterprising Abigail will get Elizabeth hanged quickly, and then turn to work worthier of her mettle.

HERBERT BLAU

Herbert Blau, co-founder and producer of the San Francisco
Actors' Workshop, is now Academic Vice-President and Dean of
the Theatre School at the California Institute of the Arts. From
1965 until 1967 he was co-director of the Lincoln Center Repertory
Company. He is the author of *The Impossible Theater: A Manifesto*
and two plays, *Telegraph Hill* and *A Gift of Fury*.

COUNTERFORCE I: THE SOCIAL DRAMA

. . . It was another play by Miller, striving to achieve this
image in a rather conventional form, that had the most
resounding influence on our developing audience. Even to this

From Herbert Blau, *The Impossible Theater* (New York: Macmillan,
1964), pp. 188-92. Copyright © 1964 Herbert Blau. Reprinted by permission of The Macmillan Company. The Actor's Workshop, which
Blau and Jules Irving ran in San Francisco from 1952 until 1965, when
they came to New York to take over the repertory theatre at Lincoln
Center, first put on *The Crucible* at the Elgin Street Theatre on December 3, 1954, with Robert Ross directing. When the company, in a
burst of upward mobility, moved downtown on April 15, 1955, it was
a revised production of *The Crucible*, directed by Blau, with which they
opened at the Marine's Memorial Theatre. Irving played John Proctor.
The play was revived, under Irving's direction, in 1959. This essay is
hardly a director's account of what and how. It is a production seen
almost ten years after the event by a director whose theatrical concerns
had led him in directions alien to the intentions of *The Crucible* and
whose ruminative habits would, in any case, have forced him to circle
the play like a cat teasing a mouse. Between production and comment
came, too, Miller's own second thoughts on the play, in the Introduction
to the *Collected Plays*, which Blau quotes freely. The "image" in the
first sentence of the excerpt is Miller's man in society and the "another"
is there because Blau has been talking about *Death of a Salesman*. The
title, which may seem somewhat grand for these remarks on *The
Crucible*, is that of the chapter from which the selection is taken, for
which it is very appropriate.

day, a revival of *The Crucible* will take up slack at the box office. Whatever that may be a sign of, in our theatre there was no doubt the reign of McCarthy had a lot to do with its initial success. Miller, however, has tried to minimize the immediate parallel: "It was not only the rise of 'McCarthyism' that moved me, but something which seemed more weird and mysterious. It was the fact that a political, objective, knowledgeable campaign from the far Right was capable of creating not only a terror, but a new subjective reality, a veritable mystique which was gradually assuming even a holy resonance."

The mystique was resonating into an even more subtle shape than Miller had imagined. But while it lacked the terrifying impartiality of greater drama, *The Crucible* had nevertheless the vehemence of good social protest. The play was unevenly cast, put into rehearsal in haste (lest somebody take advantage of the release of rights before we did), the director was replaced after about three weeks, but the actors, upon whom the drama makes no special demands, played it with fervor and conviction if not subtlety. And in our program notes we stressed the McCarthy parallel, speaking of guilt by association and Ordeal by Slander.[1]

The production made us a lot of liberal friends. They are all, all honorable men, but while I have signed the same petitions, that friendship in the theatre has always been a little unsettling and subsequent plays have borne out my feeling that if we have the same politics, we do not always have it for the same reasons. While the power of mass psychosis is one of the strongest elements in the play, there is a melodrama in the fervency that always made me uncomfortable. When I brought it up, it made others uncomfortable. But I think it behooves us to understand both the appeal and limitations of this forceful drama—one of those which seems

---

[1] A reference to Owen Lattimore. See note, p. 218.

effective so long as it is even middlingly well played, and despite its fate on Broadway.

The Puritan community, as Hawthorne knew in *The Scarlet Letter*, is the ideal setting for a realistic narrative of allegorical dimensions. As Miller puts it, drawing on the annals of the Salem trials: "To write a realistic play of that world was already to write in a style beyond contemporary realism." And there is a powerful admonition beyond that in Proctor's final refusal to be *used*. Like Miller before the congressional committee, he will not lend his name to the naming of names.[2] On this level the play has authority, and it serves as an exemplum. Several critics have pointed out that the analogy between witches and Communists is a weak one, for while we believe in retrospect there were no witches, we know in fact there were some Communists, and a few of them were dangerous. (If Miller were another kind of dramatist, he might claim there *were* witches, but we shall come to that in a moment.) Yet as a generalization, the play's argument is worthy; as a warning against "the handing over of conscience," it is urgent; and to the extent his own public life has required it Miller has shown the courage of his convictions beyond most men—and hence has some right to call for it. One might still wish he were more inventive in form, but in a period where the borders between art and anarchy are ill-defined, we might apply the caution stated in II Corinthians: "All things are lawful, but not all things edify." It is no small thing to say *The Crucible* is an edifying drama.

What the play does not render, however, is what Miller claims for it and what is deeply brooding in the Puritan setting: "the interior psychological question," the harrowing descent of mass hallucination into the life of the individual,

---

[2] Miller's own refusal came in 1956, after he had written John Proctor's; the wording of this sentence might suggest otherwise. See Bibliography for the hearings.

where value is deranged, no reason is right, and every man drives his bargain with the sinister. One sees this in *The Brothers Karamazov*, which Miller invokes as that "great book of wonder," and more relevantly in *The Possessed*, where political evil is the reptilian shadow of indecipherable sin. For Proctor, a sin is *arranged*, so that his guilt might have cause. All we can say is: that is not the way it is. For Miller, a psychosis is no more than a psychosis, with clear motive and rational geography. The symptoms are fully describable. His love of wonder is deflated by his desire "to write rationally" and to put a judgmental finger on "the full loathesomeness of . . . anti-social action." The desire is admirable, but the danger is to locate it in advance. Studying Dostoyevsky, Miller had resolved to "let wonder rise up like a mist, a gas, a vapor from the gradual and remorseless crush of factual and psychological conflict." But while that is a good description of the source of wonder in Dostoyevsky, Miller is restive in the mist, which in Dostoyevsky is thickened to nightmare by every wincing judgment and every laceration of meaning, writhing in the imminence of wrong.

By contrast, we know only too well what *The Crucible* means, nor were the issues really ever in doubt. Wanting to write a drama "that would lift out of the morass of subjectivism the squirming, single, defined process" by which public terror unmans us, Miller fills in the record with the adultery of John Proctor and Abigail Williams. He thus provides the rationalist's missing link to the mystery of the crying out. The adultery brings the drama back toward the "subjectivism" Miller was trying to avoid, but its real subjective life remains shallow. Taking up charges of coldness, he says he had never written more passionately and blames the American theatre—actors, directors, audience, and critics—for being trained "to take to heart anything that does not prick the mind and to suspect everything that does not supinely reassure."

About the American theatre, I think this is exactly so.

But my own reservations have to do with the fact that, while moral instruction may be a legitimate ambition of the drama, the play *does* reassure—and it is the *mind* which rebels finally against its formulas while the emotions may be overwhelmed by its force. A play is privileged to reconstruct history for its own purposes; but here we have a play which pretends to describe in realistic terms a community instinctively bent on devotion to God. The Puritans were readers of signs, and the signs, in daily behavior, were evidences of God's will. Hawthorne's novel retains the impermeable quality of that experience by accepting completely the terms of the divine or demonic game. It is yours to choose whose game it really is, according to his strategy of alternative possibilities. But Miller's play makes the choices for you, and its hero does not stand —as one approving critic has said—"foursquare in his own time and place." The records do show that he considered the inquisition a fraud; but though he is bound to the community as a farmer, he does not, in Miller's play, take to heart "all the complex tensions of the Salem community," for he responds to things like an eighteenth-century rationalist with little stake in established doctrine. Truer to time and place is the Reverend Hale, who knew "the devil is precise" and saw him in the godly, in himself. He is certainly the more dramatic figure in being compelled to disavow what by instinct and conditioning he has come to believe. Hale resembles Captain Vere in Melville's *Billy Budd*, where the drama is truly divested of "subjectivism" by characters who are, by *allegiance* to retarded doctrine, impaled upon the cross of choice.

One can also see in Melville's Claggart the kind of character that Miller now wishes he had portrayed in Danforth: evil embodied to the utmost, a man so dedicated to evil that by his nature we might know good. Melville saw that to create such a character he would have to stretch his skepticism toward the ancient doctrine of "depravity according to nature," which alone could explain a Claggart or an Iago. He does this by a strategy of insinuation. He suggests to us that there was once such a doctrine, in which intelligent modern men, of course, can hardly believe. The story virtually drives us back to the "superstition," as Kafka virtually restores Original Sin. (I should add that Melville does this in the prose style of the novelette, which could not always be compensated for in the admirable dramatization by Coxe and Chapman.)[3] Doing so, he takes us back through time, justifying as far as form can reach the eternal intimations of Billy's rosy-dawned execution; a scene which is almost enough to make you believe, with the sailors, that a chip of the dockyard boom "was a piece of the Cross."

Almost. Having proposed to us a possibility just over the edge of reason, Melville writes an ironic coda in which he leaves us to take our own risks of interpretation. Miller, for all his moral conviction and belief in free choice, leaves us none. A master of conventional dramaturgy, with all the skills of building and pacing, he drives past the turbid aspect of social hypnosis to the predetermined heroism of Proctor. Perception yields to sensation and the choice of classical tragedy to its wish-fulfillment. (It is curious that Billy, *typed* down to his stammer, is a more inscrutable character than anyone in Miller's play.) The final irony is that John Proctor, dramatic hero of the populist mind, might even be applauded by members of the congressional committee that cited Miller for contempt. It is no accident, too, that in temperament and general conduct Proctor resembles our true culture hero, John Glenn, who would be perfectly cast for the role if the astronauts were to start a little theatre. One may not have the courage to be a Proctor at the final drumroll, nor a Glenn at the countdown, but no one doubts they are worthy of imitation.

---

[3] Louis O. Coxe and Robert Chapman, whose *Billy Budd* opened in New York on February 10, 1951.

This absence of doubt reduced the import of *The Crucible* for those who thought about it, while increasing the impact for those who didn't. You do a play for its virtues, and one devious aspect of the art of theatre lies in concealing the faults. Actually, my belief is that if you know what's not there, you can deal more powerfully with what is. Little of what I have said, however, came up during rehearsals of *The Crucible* (which was not so much conceived as put on), but rather in critiques and discussions of plays done later. Whatever its weaknesses, the production was hard-driving in keeping with the play's rhythm, and performance by performance the actors rose to overwhelming approval. Because we would be doing better productions which would not be so approved, it was important to keep our heads. And, indeed, I think this attitude has made it more possible for our actors to sustain their belief through more subtle plays that have not been so vigorously applauded.

At the time we produced *The Crucible*, Miller was already the most powerful rational voice in the American theatre. Questioning the play later, I wanted the company to understand that to criticize him was to take his ideas seriously, and to begin to give some shape to our own. The people we often had to question most were those with whom we seemed to agree. Because we were all vulnerable to easy judgments and that depth psychology of the surface which is so inherent in American drama (and acting), it was necessary to see why *The Crucible* was not really the "tough" play that Miller claimed; I mean dramatically tough, tough in soul, driving below its partisanship to a judgment of anti-social action from which, as in Dostoyevsky, none of us could feel exempt. I wouldn't have asked the questions if Miller didn't prompt them with his reflections on Social Drama and the tragic form. But compare the action of Proctor to that of the tragic figures of any age—Macbeth, or Brittanicus, or Raskolnikov: can you approve or disapprove of their action? Can you make the choice of imitating them? Or avoid it? *The Crucible* may confirm what we like to think we believe, but it is not, as Miller says, intimidating to an "Anglo-Saxon audience" (or actors), nor does it really shock us into recognizing that we don't believe what we say we do. Beyond that, the profoundest dramas shake up our beliefs, rock our world; in *The Crucible*, our principles are neither jeopardized nor extended, however much we may fail to live by them anyhow.

As for the inquisitors, Miller wants us to see evil naked and unmitigated. I am prepared to believe it exists (I am certain it exists), and I won't even ask where it comes from. But—to be truer than tough—if you want absolute evil, you've got to think more about witches. Miller wants the Puritan community without Puritan premises or Puritan intuitions (which is one reason why, when he appropriates the language, his own suffers in comparison). His liberalism is the kind that, really believing we have outlived the past, thinks it is there to be used. The past just doesn't lie around like that. And one of these days the American theatre is really going to have to come to terms with American history.

Axiom for liberals: no play is deeper than its witches.

MARCEL AYMÉ

Marcel Aymé wrote *Clérambard* and *Les Oiseaux de la Lune*, among other plays, and he has written more than ten novels. He wrote screenplays for Hollywood based on several of his own works, and adapted American dramas for French film as well.

I WANT TO BE HANGED
LIKE A WITCH

Before having the experience, I used to think that the work of the adapter should consist, once and for all, of transcribing a foreign author's play into honest French, capable as far as possible of reaching across the footlights. Not that I didn't know that theatrical truth is far from being universal (I knew it well enough so that it never crossed my mind to try to control the foreign adaptations of my own plays). But, as theatre is a somewhat imprecise art, I always imagined that slight twists of expression would be enough in transforming dramatic reality from one continent to another. I understood my error when I began my work on Arthur Miller's *The Crucible* (become *Les Sorcières de Salem*). From the start I ran into a theatrical situation dangerous to the adapter, one

---

From *Arts*, December 15–21, 1954, pp. 1, 3. Translated by Gerald Weales. *Les Sorcières de Salem*, directed by Raymond Rouleau, opened at the Théâtre Sarah Bernhardt on December 16, 1954. Somewhat earlier, the Belgian National Theatre had performed *The Crucible* in a translation by Herman Closson, *La Chasse aux Sorcières*. The Aymé translation (Paris: Grasset, 1955) is also available in Arthur Miller, *Théâtre* (Paris: Robert Laffont, 1959), pp. 371–534.

which was evident at first reading without yet alarming me as much as it should have. Let me recapitulate briefly.

In 1690,[1] an American farmer, a husband and father, after deflowering a sixteen-year-old servant, churlishly breaks with her on orders from his wife, who pitches his mistress out the door. The little victim applies herself to the puerile practices of witchcraft in the hope that her lover will come back to her, even if it costs his wife her life. In the first act we are present at the lovers' first brief meeting after seven months of separation. She proclaims her love; he doesn't listen to anything, solemnly affirms his regret, and warns the girl he has seduced that she will soon be the disgrace of the village. Now, for the working-out of the plot and meaning of the play, it is necessary that audience sympathy go immediately to the farmer on that occasion.

No doubt it is possible in Arthur Miller's work: the sympathy of the American spectator belongs to the seducer. The reasons for that preference, though inadmissible for a Frenchman, are still weighty ones. Rugged pioneer of an earlier era, one of those resolute New England plowmen who carry in their Puritan round heads the shining promises of the age of skyscrapers and the atom bomb, the farmer is an indisputable hero from the outset. He has only to step on a Broadway stage. It's as if he were wrapped in the Star-Spangled Banner, and the public, its heart swollen with tenderness and pride, eats him up. In the presence of this eminent forefather, the girl who has given herself to him with so much passion is nothing more than a little slut come to sully the glorious

---

[1] 1692, of course. That Selz also says 1690 (p. 243) suggests that, at some point the date may have been used in the French version of the play, but it is correctly 1692 in Aymé's published translation. Not that a year or two makes that much difference to Aymé; later in the sentence he knocks a year off Abigail's age, presumably to give piquancy to his version of Miller's plot. In any case, Miller started the whole thing by changing the age of the historical Abigail.

dawn of the U.S.A. Worse, she is the odious image of sin. Indeed, at no time in the play does the Puritan take account of his responsibility toward her. Pursued by remorse for having committed adultery, he shows no regrets regarding his gravest shortcoming, that of having led astray a little soul who had been entrusted to him. It certainly isn't the Broadway playgoer who will reproach him for it. In the eyes of the American of today, a Puritan family in Massachusetts in 1690 is one of those good Biblical families in which the master of the house exercises prudent thrift in conjugal patience by screwing the servant girls with God's permission.

In France, it must be said, the Bible is not much read. Then again, an American peasant doesn't excite extraordinary feeling in the heart of the Parisian public, and the fact that he lives in 1690 in no way gives him a halo. This Puritan petticoat-rumpler who dreams only of restoring peace in his household and his chance for paradise can't fail to look bad to us, and our sympathy quite naturally will go first to the seduced girl—an orphan, into the bargain, I forgot to say. It seemed to me necessary to bring the pair of lovers back into balance, that is, to blacken the victim and give her a Machiavellianism that she does not have in the Arthur Miller play, in which, in order to save her life and in the sway of group hysteria, she is led to unleash a witch hunt. I wanted to give her full consciousness of the evil in her. Doubtless, in doing that, I greatly falsified the author, and I sincerely regret it. Nevertheless, I am far from having taken all the liberties with his text that seemed desirable to me, but that is another story, the moral of which I have already drawn for my own use—I want to be hanged like a common witch if I ever do an adaptation again.[2]

---

[2] Unhanged, Aymé adapted Miller's *A View from the Bridge* in 1958.

JEAN SELZ

Jean Selz, who is best known for his writings on art, was theatre critic for *France Observateur* from 1958 to 1960 and has written both theatre and art criticism for *Les Lettres Nouvelles* since 1953. His books include *Odilon Redon, XIXth Century Drawings and Watercolors,* and *Modern Sculpture.*

RAYMOND ROULEAU AMONG
THE WITCHES

When Judge Hathorne, in the third act of *Les Sorcières de Salem,* rose to address the tribunal which, with the serenity of good servants of God, sent to the gallows all those on whom sat the accusation of trafficking with the Devil, a voice burst from the auditorium of the Théâtre Sarah Bernhardt, that of a spectator in the balcony carried away by his anger, shouting "Shut up, you cur." If one knows that the action of the play is set in a small American village in the seventeenth century, one is astonished at the power with which a theatrical fiction in performance can involve the soul of the audience. Such cries from the heart are rare today. Not because people have less heart, but because the theatre calls up fewer cries. They prove that to create a connection between stage and auditorium it is not necessary to unite them by steps, to cut down the curtain, or to convert to theatre-in-the-round. The evening was also an unconscious homage to the actors of a performance of which the dramatic tension is such that it can keep an audience in its grip and upset for three hours. For this, the work of three men was needed: a genuine play-

From *Les Lettres Nouvelles*, année 3 (March 1955), 422-26. Translated by Gerald Weales.

wright, the American Arthur Miller; an excellent adapter, Marcel Aymé; and a great director, Raymond Rouleau.

In writing *Les Sorcières de Salem*, of which the original title is *The Crucible*, Arthur Miller relied on an authentic witch trial which took place in 1690[1] in New England and which is like innumerable trials France experienced at the time of the Inquisition (at least, judging by the accounts that have been preserved, the trial documents, for the most part, having mysteriously disappeared from our archives). From the pretended dealings in witchcraft with which Abigail Williams, a young girl of Salem, amused herself one day, to the death sentence of the farmer John Proctor, a scorching wind of fanatic madness blew on the little Puritan village, spreading its terror like a scourge and engulfing in its frenzy of purification—through death, that is—dozens of innocent souls. Yet the one who escaped punishment, Abigail, is not innocent. But her crime, invisible to the eyes of the judges, for whom faith had replaced psychology (wasn't Marcel Aymé tempted to call the play *Other People's Souls?*) is not to have trafficked with the Devil but, with truly diabolic determination, to have brought about the ruin of a woman whom she cannot forgive for being married to the one she loves. Around that theme, stupidity, self-interest, hypocrisy, falsehood, intolerance, and fear move to delineate the interlacings of a labyrinth in which judges and accused plunge more and more deeply, powerless to escape.

The construction of the play introduces the notable device of retracing the movement of the dramatic line in the succession of sets: first a room in the house of Reverend Parris, where, through the high window, a clear ray of sun still penetrates; then Proctor's house, invaded by twilight and anxiety; then the closed, well-guarded courtroom; finally the dark vault where the condemned are held. The severity and the

---

[1] See note, p. 240.

inevitability with which we are dragged, as if through the chambers of a nightmare, toward a space more and more sealed in and distressing and toward the blind alley of a conflict where everyone gets lost in the vertigo of his own conscience, make the theatrical dialectic of Arthur Miller rest on a logic at once ineluctable and hopeless. Hopeless for the heroes of the drama, if not for frightened mankind, whom the inhabitants of Salem represent, since before the curtain falls we sense that men more just than their justices will not let the unleashed forces of revolt be appeased.[2]

The work of Arthur Miller, in which conflicts of very different kinds are intermixed and in which contrasting characters strike against one another, shows itself rich in meaning. But we certainly should not have followed with so much emotion each conflict in its twistings and each character in his inner being (Abigail, the liar, in her pride; Reverend Parris in his selfish designs) had the play not been brought to its clear fulfillment—the clear fulfillment of its intelligence—by a director whose lucidity and energy seem to have controlled with astonishing precision not only the gestures of the characters but the movement of their thoughts. In saying that, I do not intend to underestimate the value and the personal effort of the actors, but it is very obvious that the continuity of that kind of inner current which binds the characters together and the modulations employed in the intensity of that current depend on the acuity of the director's view and his willingness to impose it. It is that which permits us to follow, step by step, through all their changes, certain ideas insinuatively latent in the action of the play.

Let us examine, for instance, one of the underlying themes of the play—the most important, in my opinion—one which could be labeled "the avatars of truth." We see truth—at

---

[2] See Jean-Paul Sartre's comment on the play and the excerpt from his screenplay, pp. 421-426.

first forceful and sure of itself—get enmeshed in the ways of uncertainty, falter and grow pale and transform itself little by little into a mean and sorry thing, vulnerable and luckless, stripped of every means of making itself known, incapable of finding a place where it will not be uneasy. It moves through the whole play, then, like a wandering ghost, like an erring spirit who tries to become flesh and whom everyone refuses to accept. And when it finally succeeds in finding asylum and protection in the conscience of a girl—little Mary Warren— those impostors who call themselves judges pounce on that conscience with the eagerness of doctors on a foolish person who has taken poison, determined to make him spit it up. The scene in which Mary Warren begins to feel that truth could be, in effect, a poison and in which we are witnesses (one would like to beg her not to weaken, not to retract) to that dimming of her conscience and to that collapse of her will which forces truth to become once more the invisible heroine of *Les Sorcières de Salem,* is one of the most pathetic scenes in the play. Now, if all that is made palpable and upsetting to us, if we come to see and to be fascinated by this "invisible heroine" and at moments ourselves come to doubt the reality of her existence (we, too, are very close to seeing the Devil appear), it is thanks to the authoritative reach that Raymond Rouleau has given to the art of directing.

The hold that he exercises on the playing of the actors can be seen in striking fashion in the fact that we see twenty-seven performers play with equal rightness on the stage of the Théâtre Sarah Bernhardt. Little used to such cohesion, we remain dumfounded at it. The theatrical inexperience of Simone Signoret and of Yves Montand risked being made worse by the reputation they have made in films and in popular music. In becoming a star, one acquires a taste for sparkling. But no. They were revealed as two good performers who gave to Elizabeth and John Proctor the dignity, the simplicity of peasants, and the kind of toughness with which, despite their distress, they bear the weight of crushing injustice. In the part of Abigail, at once childish and treacherous, Nicole Courcel has caught the ambiguous face and with remarkably dramatic sobriety and intensity has expressed the inhuman character, passing from icy cruelty to hysterical frenzy. In the role of Mary Warren, naïve and troubled, torn between her conscience and her fear, Francette Vernillat shows herself impressively true. One could thus highlight the qualities which fixed our attention for each name in the cast, from Pierre Mondy, Robert Moor, Jean d'Yd, Brigitte Barbier, to little Christiane Ferez (who, with her long skirts and her long hair, makes one think of the little girls so strangely photographed by Lewis Carroll).[3]

In the style and the colors (limited to ochers, browns, black, and white) Lila de Nobili brought to the costumes, and in the sets of *Les Sorcières de Salem* are found again that rigor of design and that austerity that one admires in the still-life painters of the seventeenth century and in portraitists such as Camille de Vos.[4] The costumes of the women, so simple in silhouette and so marvelously complicated in the play of pleats, seem, by a mixture of modest heaviness and gracefulness, to reflect the very character of those who wear them. They help give the movements on stage—so studied in their detail—their harmony and beauty. Thus one is held for a long time by the beauty of group movement in the third act, in which the league of little girls is revealed to us in all its hellish grandeur; after having feigned fright at an apparition, they let their malice explode in a roundelay which this time one really could believe was caused by witches. Everything here is unexpected, seems spontaneous, has the air of

---

[3] Mondy played John Hale; Moor, Francis Nurse; d'Yd, Giles Corey; Barbier, Mercy Lewis; Ferez, Betty Parris.

[4] I assume that he has in mind Cornelis de Vos, the seventeenth-century Flemish painter, but there were a number of painting Voses, none of them named Camille.

inspired disorder. Under scrutiny, the intention always remains unforced.

The great importance which Raymond Rouleau attaches to all the nuances of stage business is useful not only to satisfy our aesthetic demands; it also has the effect of considerably reinforcing our interest in the theme of the play. Tediousness on stage is often due to the fact that what we have to hear is almost lost in what we have to see. Our eyes get bored, and the boredom of the eyes is a bad example for the ears. If, on the contrary, we are captured by the connections that are established and continually renewed among the actor's expression, his business, what he says, the way he says it, and all the inanimate things which suddenly take on life around him, the attention with which we follow the dialogue feeds our appetite for observation and we listen to it all the more passionately as we devour the stage with our eyes. It is thus that fiction succeeds in ousting the real and getting hold of us, just as it got hold of that self-forgetting spectator, absorbing him—with his cry, his dream, his whole emotional being—into the magnetic play of *Les Sorcières de Salem*.

The Crucible
IN RETROSPECT:
ESSAYS ON THE PLAY

DAVID LEVIN

David Levin has taught English and American studies at Stanford Unviersity since 1952. He is the author of *History as Romantic Art* and the editor of *What Happened in Salem?* He is also the general editor of Harbrace Sourcebooks.

SALEM WITCHCRAFT IN RECENT
FICTION AND DRAMA

In the last six years American publishers have issued one history, an anthology of trial documents, two novels, and two plays about the Salem witchcraft trials. The subject is especially

From *The New England Quarterly*, XXVIII (December 1955), 537-42. Copyright *The New England Quarterly*, 1955. Reprinted with permission of the author and *The New England Quarterly*. I have cut away that part of the essay (pp. 542-46) in which Levin considered Lyon Phelps's play about Martha Corey, *The Gospel Witch* (Cambridge: Harvard University Press, 1955), and the two novels, Shirley Barker's *Peace, My Daughters* (New York: Crown, 1949) and Esther Forbes's *A Mirror for Witches* (Boston: Houghton Mifflin, 1954); since Levin makes occasional direct comparisons with the Miller play in his discussion of these works, you may interesting today because of a few parallels to McCarthyism and because of our interest in abnormal psychology, which has drawn some writers to study the adolescent girls whose fits and accusations led twenty people to the gallows. Since the Salem episode has become a symbol of the bigot's tyranny—a symbol so completely accepted that a prominent Washington correspondent of *The New York Times* and a comic-strip writer for the San Francisco *Chronicle* can both refer, without being corrected, to the witches whom Cotton Mather burned in Salem—the four recent novels and plays raise some interesting questions about the aims and techniques of historical fiction and drama.

None of these books is merely a story set against the background of the period; three of them concentrate on real historical characters, and all four pretend to portray history, give or take a few facts. All try to explain the outbreak of accusations and the curious testimony against the defendants. All but one begin with the first accusations and end with the last executions. All have something to say of the connection between Puritan theology and the injustice done at Salem.

Arthur Miller makes the most ambitious historical claims, and for that reason among others his play *The Crucible* deserves a more thorough discussion than I have space for here. Although confessing, perhaps patronizingly, that his play is not history in the "academic historian's" sense, he declares that it reveals "the essential nature of one of the strangest and most awful episodes in human history." *The Crucible*, although it set few records on Broadway, has been steadily popular elsewhere. Produced simultaneously by amateur theatre

---

want to consult the original essay. The Forbes novel, published first in 1928, is not about the Salem trials; it is, however, one of the most rewarding fictional treatments of witchcraft in New England, obliquely attacking the phenomenon through a presumably naïve narrator. For fans of the Reverend Parris, I recommend Chapter 6 of Miss Barker's novel, in which she has him sign the Devil's Book. The chapter title: "To the Glory of God."

groups in San Francisco and San Mateo, California, it attracted such large audiences over a period of several months last year that the San Francisco company turned professional and continued for some time to produce the same play as its first professional offering.[1] In France, too, the play has been popular. Besides Mr. Miller's dramatic skill, there are several reasons for this popularity.

The subject, of course, is adaptable to the stage, and Arthur Miller has taken advantage of its dramatic opportunities. One could transcribe verbatim the examination of any of a dozen defendants, and if played with moderate skill the scene would amuse, anger, and terrify an audience. The magistrates' persistent cross-examination, the afflicted girls' screams and fits (which Mr. Miller certainly underplays), the defendant's helplessness in the face of what seems to us a ludicrously closed logical system (*Examiner:* Why do you hurt these girls? *Defendant:* I don't. *Judge:* If you don't, who does?), the appearance of her "specter" on the beam or in the magistrate's lap at the very time when she is declaring her innocence, her evasive answers, her contradictions, and her collapse into confession—these are almost unbearable to watch.

The Crucible dramatizes brilliantly the dilemma of an innocent man who must confess falsely if he wants to live and who finally gains the courage to insist on his innocence—and hang. To increase the impact of this final choice, Mr. Miller has filled his play with ironies. John Proctor, the fated hero, has been guilty of adultery but is too proud to confess or entirely to repent. In order to save his wife from execution by showing that her leading accuser is "a whore," he has at last brought himself to confess his adultery before the Deputy Governor of Massachusetts Bay; but his wife, who "has never told a lie" and who has punished him severely for his infidelity, now lies to protect his name. Denying that he had

---

[1] The Actor's Workshop. See Herbert Blau, pp. 231-238.

been unfaithful, she convinces the court that he has lied to save her life. In the end, Proctor, reconciled with his wife and determined to live, can have his freedom if he will confess to witchcraft, a crime he has not committed.

This battery of ironies is directed against the basic objective of the play: absolute morality. In the twentieth century as well as the seventeenth, Mr. Miller insists in his preface, this construction of human pride makes devils of the opponents of orthodoxy and destroys individual freedom. Using the Salem episode to show that it also blinds people to truth, he has his characters turn the truth upside down. At the beginning of the play, the Reverend John Hale announces fatuously that he can distinguish precisely between diabolical and merely sinful actions; in the last act the remorseful Hale is trying desperately to persuade innocent convicts to confess falsely in order to avoid execution. The orthodox court, moreover, will not believe that Abigail Willams, who has falsely confessed to witchcraft, falsely denied adultery, and falsely cried out upon "witches," is "a whore"; but it is convinced that Proctor, who has told the truth about both his adultery and his innocence of witchcraft, is a witch.

What Mr. Miller considers the essential nature of the episode appears quite clearly in his play. The helplessness of an innocent defendant, the court's insistence on leaping to dubious conclusions, the jeopardy of any ordinary person who presumes to question the court's methods, the heroism of a defendant who cleaves to truth at the cost of his life, the ease with which vengeful motives can be served by a government's attempt to fight the Devil, and the disastrous aid which a self-serving confession gives injustice by encouraging the court's belief in the genuineness of the conspiracy—all this makes the play almost oppressively instructive, especially when one is watching rather than reading it. When one remembers the "invisible" nature of the crimes charged, the use of confessed conspirators against defendants who refuse to confess, the punishment of those only who insist on their innocence, then the analogy to McCarthyism seems quite valid.

But Mr. Miller's pedagogical intention leads him into historical and, I believe, aesthetic error. Representative of the historical distortion is his decision to have the Deputy Governor declare the court in session in a waiting room in order to force a petitioner to implicate an innocent man or be held in contempt of court. Obviously suggested by the techniques of Senator McCarthy, this action is unfair to the Puritan Judge. And it is only the least of a number of such libels. In the Salem of 1692 there were indictments and juries; in *The Crucible* there are none. Mr. Miller's audience sees in detail the small mind and grandiose vanity of Samuel Parris, the selfish motives of the afflicted girls, the greed of Thomas Putnam; but it does not learn that a doubtful judge left the court after the first verdict, that there was a recess of nearly three weeks during which the government anxiously sought procedural advice from the colony's leading ministers, or that the ministers' "Return," though equivocal, hit squarely on the very logical fallacies in the court's procedure which *The Crucible* so clearly reveals. In 1692 there was a three-month delay between the first accusations and the first trial. Each defendant was examined first, later indicted, and then tried. In *The Crucible* the first "witch" is condemned to death just eight days after the first accusations, when only fourteen people are in jail. Whatever its eventual justice, a government which adheres to trial by jury and delays three months while 150 people are in jail is quite different from a government which allows four judges to condemn a woman to death within a week of her accusation.

Since Mr. Miller calls his play an attack on black-or-white thinking, it is unfortunate that the play itself aligns a group of heroes against a group of villains. In his "Note on Historical Accuracy," Mr. Miller remarks scrupulously that he has changed the age of Abigail Williams from eleven to seventeen in order to make her eligible for adultery. But this apparently minor change alters the entire historical situation. For Mr. Miller's Abigail is a vicious wench who not only exploits her chance to supplant Elizabeth Proctor when the time comes, nor only maintains a tyrannical discipline among the afflicted girls, but also sets the entire cycle of accusations in motion for selfish reasons. Although Mr. Miller's preface to the book suggests other psychological and historical reasons for the "delusion" and even admits that there were some witches in Salem Village, his portrayal of Parris, Abigail, and the Putnams tells his theatre audience that a vain minister, a vicious girl, and an arrogant landgrabber deliberately encouraged judicial murder and that a declining "theocracy" supported the scheme in order to remain in power. One might fairly infer from the play itself that if Abigail had never lain with Proctor nobody would have been executed.

There can be no doubt that "vengeance" was, as Mr. Miller's Proctor says, "walking Salem," but it is equally certain that many honest people were confused and terrified. Underplaying this kind of evidence, Mr. Miller consistently develops historically documented selfish motives and logical errors to grotesque extremes. Every character who confesses in *The Crucible* does so only to save his skin. Every accuser is motivated by envy or vengeance, or is prompted by some other selfishly motivated person. And the sole example of ordinary trial procedure is an examination in which the judges condemn a woman because they regard her inability to recite her commandments as "hard proof" of her guilt.

The skeptical defendant's plight is naturally moving, but making the "witch hunters" convincing is not so simple a task. Mr. Miller fails to do them justice, and this failure not only violates the "essential nature" of the episode but weakens the impact of his lesson on the audience. The witch hunters of *The Crucible* are so foolish, their logic so extremely burlesqued, their motives so baldly temporal, that one may easily underestimate the terrible implications of their mistakes. Stupid or vicious men's errors can be appalling; but the lesson would be even more appalling if one realized that intelligent men, who tried to be fair and saw the dangers in some of their methods, reached the same conclusions and enforced the same penalties.

The central fault is Mr. Miller's failure to present an intelligent minister who recognizes at once the obvious questions which troubled real Puritan ministers from the time the court was appointed. Cocksure in the first act and morally befuddled in the last, Mr. Miller's John Hale is in both these attitudes a sorry representative of the Puritan ministry. "Specter evidence," the major issue of 1692, is neither mentioned nor debated in *The Crucible*. Preferring to use Hale as a caricature of orthodoxy in his first act, Mr. Miller does not answer the question which a dramatist might devote his skills to answering: What made a minister who saw the dangers, who wanted to protect the innocent and convict the guilty, side with the court?

Even though the dramatist must oversimplify history, the fact that dramatic exposition may be tedious does not excuse *The Crucible*'s inadequacies; Mr. Miller finds plenty of time for exposition in the first act and in the later speeches of Hale and the Deputy Governor. The fault lies in Mr. Miller's understanding of the period; its consequences damage his play as "essential" history, as moral instruction, and as art. . . .

PENELOPE CURTIS

Penelope Curtis holds the position of Lockie Fellow in Creative Writing and Australian Literature at the University of Melbourne, Australia. She has published articles on Chaucer, Pope, and Yeats, and is presently completing a book on Chaucer.

THE CRUCIBLE

The most interesting feature of *The Crucible* is that it is so impressively a play about evil forces, despite the fact that it *seems* to be a play discrediting belief in such forces. In this, it may not be the work Miller wanted to write, yet it is, in my judgment, his only great one, and for similar reasons: as if the instinctive dramatist in him had responded to the unusual nature of his material and urged him beyond his ordinary limits. But whatever the creative process, the achievement is striking, and I am struck most of all by the way, in the Court scenes, the communication of hysteria from one person to another creates a dramatic illusion of a quasi-impersonal force, more powerful and more malignant than its individual agents.

These scenes are probably the finest, though they arise most convincingly (I won't say "naturally") from earlier developments. Two features, in particular, suggest a double insight into the "forces" they dramatize: the fact that they *are* "Court" scenes, so that what we see is not just "mass" but institutionalized hysteria; and, second, the fact that while the girls seem genuinely beside themselves, the outcome of their actions looks so very calculated. It can easily be objected that Abigail, unlike Mary, is perfectly in control of herself all the

From *The Critical Review*, No. 8 (1965), 45-58. © Penelope Curtis 1965.

time; yet the actual stage-impression is somewhat different. Extraordinary opportunist as she is, her personality by itself does not seem adequate to that strange dual impression of incalculable factors in a situation mysteriously beyond control, and an outcome at once monstrous and precise. A *possessed community*: that is what the staging inevitably suggests to me, for all the calm rationality of Miller's notes. I do not know any other play which makes quite this startling use of theatre.

At the same time, however, there are other closely related factors that are equally important: I mean the extraordinarily close-knit nature of the Salem community, and the quasi-poetic compression of language in this play. In fact so closely are these related to one another, and to the staging of the Court scenes, that in putting forward my view of the whole action, I will need to move continuously between them.

Although other plays by Miller are more overtly based on Greek models, *The Crucible* is the only one in which a whole community is directly, and tragically, implicated; it is, I realize, an almost impossible achievement for plays with a modern setting (hence the comparative futility of "modernizing" Greek models at all, whether the dramatist is Anouilh or O'Neill or Miller himself),[1] but it is a tremendous strength in *The Crucible*; it bears directly on the dramatizing of forces. At the same time, the language is much more flexible, more compelling, than in the other plays; there is an altogether more adventurous play of metaphor. Miller is usually too inclined, for reasons of necessity, to confine himself within a comparatively inexpressive colloquial idiom. Here, because the idiom is unfamiliar, he is freer to heighten it; and he gives its homely, Biblical turn of phrase a kind of biting metaphoric fanciful-

---

[1] Miss Curtis is presumably referring to Jean Anouilh's *Antigone*, Eugene O'Neill's *Mourning Becomes Electra*, and Miller's *A View from the Bridge*, although the latter is not the same kind of Greek-model modernization.

ness. The result is that if he cannot create his themes *in* the language, as Shakespeare does, he can do the next best thing: use his language to suggest and support them.

By "community" I mean, of course, something very much more than common social factors of the kind we see in, say, A *View from the Bridge*: area, class, occupation, certain habits of life, a few slang words, and the simple code that a man must not "snitch." In so far as these represent the life of a community, that life is an impoverished one. But in any case, only individuals are *directly* implicated in what happens to Eddie. In this respect, *The Crucible* is closer in spirit to Sophoclean drama; for the fate of the Salem people actually depends, to a lesser or greater extent, on the choices of individual men. There's more diversity in *The Crucible* than, say, in *Oedipus Rex*, a wider range of individual choices (it covers Hale *and* Abigail *and* Putnam, as well as Proctor) but the principle is similar. And the fate of the community involves more than the physical life or death of its members: there is a metaphysic at stake, and a way of life; the reputation of a people which becomes, by extension, an image of human possibilities. As with the Greek *polis*, every aspect of life was involved in the whole; but Salem being the kind of theocracy it was, the pressure of involvement was greater to an unnatural degree. It is interesting to see at what point, in each case, community life becomes significant. In both plays, drama occurs at the meeting point of divine and secular law: in a personal ruler in the one, and the religious courts in the other. In *Oedipus Rex*, however, there was a second figure of authority in the prophet Teiresias; but in Salem there was, in the crucial period, no court of appeal. Hence there were greater possibilities of moral disaster *in the community itself*.

Clearly when John Proctor speaks about his "name," it has a much denser meaning than when Eddie speaks of his. The Salem community was so closely knit that there was constant difficulty in distinguishing salvation from personal integrity, reputation, prestige, factional power, and selfish pride. The language of the play reveals a shifting preoccupation with all of these, in such a way as to suggest how the nature of the drama arises from the nature of the community.

As Miller points out, the two crucial factors in their lives were the land and their religion. So powerfully did these unite them that he was able to give his characters an expressive, wide-ranging idiom that draws continuously on both sources. Their speech has the saltiness, the physicality, of a life lived close to the soil and the waste; it is enriched, too, by a literary influence that has likewise been assimilated into daily life: the Bible, partly mediated by a seventeenth-century sermon convention. From both, it draws a quality of passion. Take, for instance, an early speech of Proctor's:

Learn charity, woman. I have gone tiptoe in this house all seven month since she is gone. I have not moved from there to there without I think to please you, and still an everlasting funeral marches round your heart. . . .

The phrasing is harsh ("without I think . . ."), but very physically suggestive, and its suggestiveness is suddenly embodied in that piece of highly individual rhetoric: "still an everlasting funeral marches round your heart." The emotion is Proctor's own; the tone of righteous fury comes from the pulpit tradition.

Or take this much later speech of Elizabeth's to him:

I have read my heart this three month, John. I have sins of my own to count. It needs a cold wife to prompt lechery.

The rhetoric of this is less obviously individual. The language comes more directly from the common ethic ("read my heart," "sins," "lechery") yet the cadences are quite movingly her own: "this three month, John," "a cold wife," and again we find an instinctively physical quality in the language—as in that word "prompt." Miller has not merely borrowed an idiom; he has given it considerable range, using it to distinguish different voices, different qualities of emotion, as well as to suggest the common sources of their lives. Proctor's speech is impressive, and certainly felt, but it has an element of bombast by comparison with the later one by Elizabeth. And the greater sincerity of her statement reflects, quite directly, the spiritual maturing they have both experienced in the course of the play.

Since the difference is crucial for his achievement, it is worth looking at a passage from *A View from the Bridge* on a similar theme.

BEATRICE: I'm tellin' you. . . . That's why I was so happy you were going to go out and get work, you wouldn't be here so much, you'd be a little more independent. I mean it. It's wonderful for a whole family to love each other, but you're a grown woman and you're in the same house with a grown man. So you'll act different now, heh?
CATHERINE: Yeah, I will. I'll remember.
BEATRICE: Because it ain't only up to him, Katie, you understand? I told him the same thing already. . . .
CATHERINE, *quickly*: What?
BEATRICE: That he should let you go. But, you see, if only I tell him, he thinks I'm just bawlin' him out, or maybe I'm jealous or somethin', you know?

This is idiomatic speech too, but it is almost completely non-metaphoric. Not only that, but it has very little physical suggestiveness. The conceptual range is so familiar ("happy," "independent," "whole family," "grown woman," "act different," "jealous or somethin'") that we scarcely notice how abstract it is. It is the language of near-cliché, which works in little flat statements and pauses. The characters are almost inarticulate; and though the feelings are there, in a simple form, their significance is not. To be fair to the play, its chorus, Alfieri, is *more* articulate, and his speech does occasionally have metaphoric force:

I remember him now as he walked through my doorway. His eyes were like tunnels; my first thought was that he had committed a crime. But soon I saw it was only a passion that had moved into his body, like a stranger.

Yet what Alfieri is doing is conferring on the hero a significance —and it is very short-lived—that he would otherwise lack. There is something tending to condescension in such a conception of the chorus, just as there is a tendency to the sob in the throat in a language of halts and pauses. Miller represses this second tendency fairly well, but a little sob goes a long way. Alfieri, on the other hand, sometimes sounds quite false, as in his summing up of the action at the end.

By comparison, the characters in *The Crucible* are not just more articulate, but much more fully revealed to us through their metaphoric habits, and not only more fully revealed, but tougher-minded too. They have to be. Nobody in Salem is likely to bother with other people's little breaks and pauses; if a man has something to say, he has to *say* it, and forcibly. In doing so, he touches on a range of sensations and passions which give density to his meaning. Consider, for instance, this fairly ordinary exchange between the Reverend Parris and his niece.

PARRIS, *studies her, then nods, half convinced*: Abigail, I have fought here three long years to bend these stiff-necked people to me, and now, just now when some good respect is rising for me in the parish, you compromise my very character. I have given you a home, child, I have put clothes upon your back—now give me upright answer. Your name in the town—it is entirely white, is it not?
ABIGAIL, *with an edge of resentment*: Why, I am sure it is, sir. There be no blush about my name.
PARRIS, *to the point*: Abigail, is there any other cause than you have told me, for your being discharged from Goody Proctor's service? I have heard it said, and I tell you as I heard it, that

she comes so rarely to church this year for she will not sit so close to something soiled. What signified that remark?

ABIGAIL: She hates me, uncle, she must, for I would not be her slave. It's a bitter woman, a lying, cold, sniveling woman, and I will not work for such a woman!

PARRIS: She may be. And yet it has troubled me that you are now seven month out of their house, and in all this time no other family has ever called for your service.

ABIGAIL: They want slaves, not such as I. Let them send to Barbados for that. I will not black my face for any of them!

The language is not just compressed; it has a muscularity which enforces the meaning. "I have fought here three long years to bend these stiff-necked people to me": Parris is "stiff-necked," too—it comes out in his harsh, determined, fearful speech, together with the resistance offered by "these people." There is a lively play of half-metaphor that suggests several things at once about his preoccupations, and those of the community. What is obstinacy in others is "upright" in himself and his own; and we can sense, in the blend of ugliness and resonance in his language, just how far he is typical of the others, and how far his feelings are extreme ones.

The play of what I have called "half-metaphor" is the staple of the dialogue, and helps immensely to suggest the implications of what this or that character says so tersely. "There be no blush about my name," says Abigail, when she is asked if it is "entirely white." Both she and Elizabeth Proctor understand the idea of a "white" name, but Abigail sees the impediment to it in terms of her own hot blood, in terms of personal humiliation. Goody Proctor uses a different expression: "She will not sit so close to something soiled." There is just as much feeling, just as much physicality; but *she* sees the impediment in terms of a moral pollution that deprives the sinner of human status: "*something* soiled." These half-developed metaphors are continually used to suggest (though not, in the

Shakespearian sense, to create) the themes of the play; and
while one should not pause too long over the associations—if
one tries to bring the implications of "blush," "something
soiled," and "I will not black my face" into too direct a relationship, the dialogue will start to fall apart—the language
seems to me to avoid all dangers of quaintness or artificiality:
not only in its cadences, but in the muscular way it keeps
the Salem preoccupations and prejudices alive in our minds.

². . . Our very first stage-impression is of a child lying on a
bed, who, though immovably asleep, cries at the name of the
Lord, attempts to fly, and so on. And while there are all sorts
of possible explanations, familiar psychological ones, the play
does not in fact give them. Only Rebecca Nurse is able to
declare that there is no witchcraft here, that "she'll wake when
she tires of it." But Goody Nurse herself carries such an impressive burden of innocence, of positive goodness, that it is
hard to say that she is simply giving a rational explanation.
One feels that when she enters and sits by the child ("who
gradually quiets") she is opposing herself, the quality of being
she brings with her, to whatever it is that is upsetting the adults
and keeping the child in an unnatural condition. When she
says, "A child's spirit is like a child, you can never catch it
by running after it; you must stand still, and, *for love*, it will
soon itself come back" (my italics), she herself names a
motive which can also be, and in her own case is, a force.
The effect of her entry is subtly to engage us in a situation
which, however unreal it seems at first, is seen progressively
as more complex and disturbing. With the uncovering of the
practices of "witchcraft" (and these are unmistakable: naked
dancing, frogs, drinking blood, and conjuring of spirits), at
least two foci of human malice are discovered, one of them

---

² I have cut a passage in which Miss Curtis seemed to be talking about
what the play was not.

is a middle-aged woman. And as more people gather, other, less readily identifiable, warnings are sounded, as in the Putnam-Proctor exchange: "I am sick of meetings; cannot the man turn his head without he have a meeting?" "He may turn his head, but not to Hell"; or again, in Rebecca Nurse's sanity, "There is prodigious danger in the seeking of loose spirits. I fear it, I fear it. Let us rather blame ourselves . . ." But before the Courts are instituted, malice and accusation have insignificant power. There is the promise of worse to come, in the way Abigail's private acts of bullying lead into the semi-public scene where Tituba is accused and "forgiven"—a small drama prefiguring the larger one. But where her social equals are concerned, Proctor's usual toughness and forthrightness are quite equal to threats made out of court. What these rumours and preliminary disturbances do accomplish is to expose the weaknesses in the community and its various members, through which the forces of evil will later act.

Evil with a capital "E" comes into power only when the community gives it institutional status; when in the words of Danforth, "the entire contention of the State in these trials is that the voice of Heaven is speaking through the children"; when the community surrenders the sacred power over life and death to the hands of a corrupt judge and a group of hysterical or malicious girls. And Evil with a capital "E" can be rendered on stage only by the metaphoric quality of the speeches (as in *Macbeth*), or as here when the fever of malice can be visibly transmitted from one person to another in public. For this is what happens in the Court scenes.

It may need to be said that three of the four acts are in some direct sense "Court scenes"; so fully does the Courts' authority penetrate the life of the community we are shown. Act II shows these courts in action, but at a domestic remove, marking a stage in, and a deflection of, their progress towards dominance. Already there are outbreaks of malice and hysteria *in authority*, and a throbbing tension, towards the end, between Mary Warren's weeping "I cannot, I cannot," and Proctor's final speech,

Now Hell and Heaven grapple on our backs, and all our old pretense is ripped away. . . . It is a providence, and no great change; we are only what we always were, but naked now. Aye, naked! And the wind, God's icy wind, will blow!

Proctor himself exults in the approaching conflict, with its promise of purgation; and even if there is something faltering about his rhetoric, the speech brings the metaphysical implications into the open. But it is not until the following act that these are fully dramatized; for, though the conflict is remarkably drawn out—and stubborn—on both sides, the play's real horror, and its greatest drama, comes in Act III, culminating in the crying out. The first thing that strikes us, in the clear dialogue of voices offstage, is the strange and hopeless logic of the proceedings.

MARTHA COREY'S VOICE: I am innocent to a witch. I know not what a witch is.
HATHORNE'S VOICE: How do you know, then, that you are not a witch?
MARTHA COREY'S VOICE: If I were, I would know it.
HATHORNE'S VOICE: Why do you hurt these children?
MARTHA COREY'S VOICE: I do not hurt them. I scorn it!—

and so on. The voices, disembodied as they are, outline the more than logical impossibility. It's an impasse at which innocence is trapped, unable to make contact with its judges; a mysterious situation in which the rhetorical appeal of "these children" overbears that mere factual innocence which has no symbol.

But if the procedure is relentless, it's by no means predictable. For one thing, there's a considerable range of personalities and claims, a powerful, if choked, resistance. For another, there is the peculiarly rhetorical nature of the evidence, and the extraordinary dynamism latent in large gatherings of people. Mary cannot faint at will; her crime is not really her own, so her powers are not at her own disposal. Her inability to faint marks the impossibility of disproving the evidence by facts. But in any case, it was never really that kind of evidence: it is the evidence of *personal testimony*. And as such, it can be "disproved" only by a more forceful testimony, by a more persuasive force of personal conviction. Hence the procedure is that of men *declaring* their evidence, proving their case by the force of their sincerity. And when "sincerity" becomes the criterion for a communal judgment, one finds released into the situation all the power of mixed or false motives, all the force of the human need to be justified. When I say one finds this power "released," I mean that the dialogue pulsates with it, every speech is filled with the ring of this or that man's conviction. The excitement, the sense of crisis, communicates itself over a whole variety of rhetorical certainties, from Danforth's, "I tell you straight, Mister—I have seen marvels in this court. I have seen people choked before my eyes by spirits; I have seen them stuck by pins and slashed by daggers," to Giles's "helpless sobs" . . . " 'I have broke charity with the woman, I have broke charity with her.' " Such a conflict can be won only by the side which adapts itself to, and makes use of, this condition of excitement, of rhetorical excess. And yet it is precisely such excess that Proctor sets himself against. He cannot convince, because he cannot fully abandon himself to his own rhetoric. He is at once too controlled and too little calculating.

It is obvious that the nature of the court, and hence of its evidence, lends itself very directly to a stage convention. My second point is even more closely connected with the staging: that where one tense scene dissolves, it leaves a gap which can be filled by an even greater tension; or to put it another way, a state of excitement can be generated among a gathering of people which is quite out of proportion to the individual emotions, and which, like fire, can leap incalculable distances.

This is a basic principle of drama (being, among other things, a matter of timing), and it has come to be a truism of mass psychology; but I do not know any other play which makes quite such conscious and electrifying use of it or which allows the principle to appropriate quite such implications in a moral struggle. The crucial scene begins when Elizabeth is called in, and ends with Mary Warren's capitulation. . . .[3]

The pacing is careful, not rushed. The dialogue retains its qualities of irony, even of humour ("Envy is a deadly sin, Mary") and sane protest; yet even these are made to serve, by delaying and heightening, a quite different total effect. After the tension and the waiting, Elizabeth's brave lie comes *dramatically* as a kind of moral collapse, leaving a vacuum which is therefore able to be filled by Abby, and the force that sweeps through her and the others is overpowering. Even the stage directions become permeated with it (*"Danforth, himself engaged and entered by Abigail"*); and by the time the girls are fully under the influence of Abigail, or of that power which she temporarily represents, we too look up expecting to see the yellow bird in the rafters. But if we do so, it is not that we are momentarily convinced by her lies, and look towards the rafters for Mary Warren's naughty spirit; it is not that kind of optical, or moral, delusion. It is because we feel the presence of a malevolent power so great it might easily reveal itself as a terrible yellow bird. And the malevolence shows in the ugly effect the girls' screaming has on Mary, with her own prolonged scream, her finger pointing, and her "Abby, Abby, I'll never hurt you more!"

If the climax of the play lies in this conflict, and the triumph of evil, the play as a whole is in some kind of tragic "mode,"

---

[3] I have cut a long quotation, unnecessary since you can consult the scene, pp. 112-119.

with Proctor as hero—which makes for a certain imbalance. There is a process, however shadowy and incomplete, from the fierce drama culminating in Act III to a simpler, more nearly self-righteous, "Proctor-tragedy"; and this process can be traced in the movements of the subplot. For the Proctor-Proctor-Williams triangle, like Proctor himself, is given somewhat different emphasis from the rest of the play—a more modern emphasis. While the private drama parallels the wider, more important conflict in the community, the terms of the choice are differently experienced. There is a tension between the kind of exchange we hear between Proctor and Abigail, in their first scene together, where we find not merely physical awareness, but, I think, some passion ("I have a sense for heat, John, and yours has drawn me to my window . . ."), and the growing relationship between Elizabeth and John, which is passionate in another way. *They* share a passionate desire for trust and wholeness, for a mutual growth in self-knowledge, which is brought (despite doubts and reticences) to an apotheosis in Elizabeth's speech: "I have read my heart this three month, John. I have sins of my own to count. It needs a cold wife to prompt lechery. . . ." The crucial difference between this sexual conflict and the larger, more metaphysical one, is that here Abby, in her simple human aspect, has some value: inferior to Elizabeth's in that she is not capable of growth, but nevertheless showing a fierce sense of deprivation which merits, at the least, our sympathy. Both women use the name "John" with a love that is almost visible.

So long as the sexual triangle qualifies and deepens the main drama, well and good; but there comes a time when it may threaten to supersede it. Abby, as a member of the triangle, is nothing—or rather, she acts powerfully on circumstances, but as a figure of interest she is soon forgotten. On the other hand our growing involvement in the relationship between John and Elizabeth may warn us of a change of emphasis. It is not simply that the play wanders from the Aristotelian ideal, by making so much depend on something incalculable, almost a trick. After all, it never really followed the Aristotelian pattern; tricks, unexpectedness, decisions of the moment, are essential to the drama in Act III. It is rather that, as Proctor's dilemma comes to the fore its representative nature seems less and less clear. Elizabeth's lie—the true pivot of the play— is felt dramatically as a failure and a miscalculation; but not because it was morally wrong. For the first time, the drama and the moral issues seem to diverge. In so far as Rebecca Nurse and her friends represent the polarized "good" (and up till now they have done so), the question put to Elizabeth represents, at this point, an absolute moral test; if she should tell the truth, both Proctor's freedom and some kind of communal regeneration would be likely to follow. But in the excitement of the moment we think only of Proctor. The dramatic emphasis invites us to hope, not that Elizabeth should make the morally uncompromising decision, but that her husband should be spared decision altogether. It is odd to find this weakness at the high point of the play, yet I would maintain it is there. Certainly the collapse after her lie allows for the full force of the "crying out"; but by the time the question of absolute decision is revived, the play has partly changed its character, and Proctor is noticeably a less representative figure. There is a shift of attention, effected here, but felt more fully later, from the struggle of forces in a community to a private tension of feeling.

The moment when Elizabeth lies and condemns Proctor marks a further shift of attention: from John's relationship with his wife to his relationship with himself. From this point the stress falls more and more, not on his representative dilemma, suffering, a choice, though these remain in view, but rather on his representative personality. And it is here that Miller almost falters. Proctor is unlike his usual, carefully objectified, "little men" heroes, and he is a much more satis-factory full-scale hero than the crass mouthpiece of *After the Fall*; the trouble lies, perhaps, in Proctor's being so very un-objectionable to twentieth-century prejudices and taste. He has all the sceptical virtues, together with a guilty conscience and an upright heart, and in creating him Miller comes closest to writing the play he seems to have intended. Certainly, for the first three acts, Proctor is satisfactorily handled as one strong member in a complex drama; as independent "chooser" he is adequately related to that polarization of "good" and "evil" characters which Richard Watts finds too simple,[4] but which is in my opinion crucial to the *seen* metaphysical con-flict. Towards the end, though, Proctor seems to be imagina-tively detached from the other Salem "accused," even from the accusers, in a way which is partly a distraction. There are moments when he speaks out of context, as a man faced with an archetypal, but *abstract*, dilemma. "Because it is my name!" he cries. "Because I cannot have another in my life . . .."; and again, "I can. And there's your first marvel, that I can. You have made your magic now, for now I do think I see some shred of goodness in John Proctor." These are moving statements. They *are* related to the moral life of the com-munity, and they will affect the other innocent accused; they are infused with metaphysical concepts; and there is a force of conviction which partly goes to meet the previous displays of hysteria, meet something of the expectations raised by "God's icy wind will blow." And yet, here as nowhere else, John Proctor's "name" and his "goodness" seem to come forward from their context and take on a more familiar twentieth-century meaning—or, perhaps, a generalized, simplified mean-ing—but by way of a recognizably modern device. The words

---

[4] In his introduction to the Bantam edition of the play (see Bibli-ography), an essay that Miss Curtis quotes in the deleted passages.

"magic" and "marvel" seem to have inverted commas around them. Indeed, it is only under pressure of the final scenes that we fully realize he does not believe in "heaven" in the way his friends do. It is to some extent a different choice for him and for them.

It is not hard to see why Miller has concentrated on Proctor somewhat to the exclusion of Rebecca Nurse and her kind. Rebecca is, or seems to be, unshakable and thus hard to understand. If she feels any private agony, it would be most difficult to represent; she is at once so transparent and so reserved. Only a great poet could deal directly with her inner experience. And the focus must change; since I do not think "goodness' can, like the hysteria of the Court scenes, be dramatized as an almost tangible force, transforming a community before our eyes. The shift of attention is by no means absolute, and in any case it is only in part a weakness, only in part a narrowing of dramatic interest. It is also a renewal, an intensification, of concern. Nevertheless, since the focus *is* so directly on Proctor at the end, since Miller offers in him an image of a hero which is partly drawn from Greek models, it may be worth comparing it with another: that of Sophocles in *Oepidus Rex*. The two plays already show a resemblance, in the way they visualize the role of a suffering community. But since Proctor's own suffering is mainly that of indecision, it has its limit. By contrast with *Oedipus, The Crucible* ends on a note of powerful, but comparatively shallow, exultancy. Proctor and Oedipus choose the difficult and, despite each one's stubbornness, the selfless path; but Proctor, having done so, can exult in his own psychological freedom, his newly clear conscience. Oedipus cannot. What is so terrible and so profound about *his* end is that there are no compensations: right action only brings him increase of shame and self-loathing.

The difference is, of course, partly one of the metaphysic involved, which raises questions that cannot be proposed or answered here, and partly also a difference of achievement. But

Oedipus Rex is one of the greatest plays ever written. *The Crucible* is certainly a very fine one; and its Court scenes make an extraordinary discovery about the potentialities of the stage. It too seems to me a great play.

STEPHEN FENDER

Stephen Fender teaches English at the University of Edinburgh and is the author of Shakespeare's *"A Midsummer Night's Dream."*

PRECISION AND PSEUDO PRECISION IN *THE CRUCIBLE*

I

Writing almost four years after *The Crucible* was first performed, Arthur Miller seemed uncertain how to describe the ethics of the society he had tried to reproduce in the play. He notes, for example, that the Puritans' "religious belief did nothing to temper [their] cruelty" but instead "served to raise this swirling and ludicrous mysticism to a level of high moral debate. . . . It is no mean irony," Miller continues, "that the theocratic persecution should seek out the most religious people for its victims." [1]

On the other hand—and in the same essay—Miller claims that he chose Salem for the play's setting because it provided people "of higher self-awareness than the contemporary scene affords," so that by opposing the articulate John Proctor to an equally articulate society he could dramatize his theme of the danger of "handing over of conscience to another."

But Miller's audience did not always appear to understand the theme, and the play's reception was mixed. The author has his own idea of what went wrong:

From *Journal of American Studies*, I (April 1967), 87-89. Reprinted by permission of Cambridge University Press.

[1] This and the other Miller quotations that follow are from the Introduction to *Collected Plays*, pp. 161-169.

I believe that the very moral awareness of the play and its characters—which are historically correct—was repulsive to the audience. For a variety of reasons I think that the Anglo-Saxon audience cannot believe the reality of characters who live by principles and know very much about their own characters and situations, and who say what they know.

Most Miller scholars have more or less accepted his account of the play as the story of John Proctor at odds with a monolithic society. Albert Hunt, for example, writes that the play "comments on modern fragmentation by withdrawing to the vantage point of a community which is whole and self-aware."[2] In an extremely interesting article on Miller, John Prudhoe interprets Proctor's stance against Salem as the "most 'modern' moment in *The Crucible*" because in it the hero works out his own solution "unaided by comfortable slogans, the weight of opinion of those around him or a coherently worked-out philosophy." Proctor's thought is free of the traditional beliefs of Salem and of the "surprisingly articulate" speech in which the town expresses its values. Proctor's plea for his "name" at the end of the play "is the cry of a man who has rejected the world in which he lives and hence can no longer use the language of that world."[3]

This essay attempts to support Prudhoe's reading of *The Crucible* as a dramatic contest of language, but to question the assumption that he shares with Miller himself and with other critics of Miller that the Puritans in the play have a consistent moral outlook. Indeed, if one examines the language, both of real Puritans and of the characters in *The Crucible*, it becomes clear that it is the speech of a society totally without moral referents. Salem confronts Proctor not with a monolithic ethic (however misguided) but with the total absence of any ethic. The townspeople are certain of

---

[2] See p. 328.
[3] *English Studies*, 43 (1962), 430. [S.F.]

their moral standards only on the level of abstraction; on the
level of the facts of human behaviour they share no criteria
for judgement, and it is this lack which makes them victims
—as well as protagonists—of the witch hunt. Their language
reflects this complete disjunction between their theory and
the facts of human action. Proctor finally demolishes their
phony language and painfully reconstructs a halting, but honest
way of speaking in which words are once again related to their
lexis. But the effect of this achievement is not to break away
from the ethic of Salem; rather it is to construct the first consistent moral system in the play, a system in which fact and
theory can at last coalesce. Proctor serves himself by recovering
his "name"; he serves Salem by giving it a viable language.

II

In the Introduction to the *Collected Plays* Miller writes
that what struck him most forcefully when he examined the
records of the Salem trials was the "absolute dedication to
evil displayed by the judges." What is more obvious to the
audience of *The Crucible* is the extent to which Miller—
always sensitive to the spoken word—has picked up and transmitted the language of these verbatim reports, and not only
the language but the entire Puritan "system" of ethics which
that language embodies.

The ethics of a society as nearly theocratic as that of the
American Puritans owed much to the society's doctrine of
salvation. American Puritans called themselves "Covenanters"
and thought of themselves as having achieved a compromise
between the Calvinist theory of predestination and the
Arminian stress on works as efficacious for salvation. Calvinism
taught that before the Creation a certain, immutable number
of men were elected to salvation and the rest left to eternal
damnation. Because nothing in the subsequent lives of men
could affect their predetermined fate, good works were in-

efficacious to salvation. The obvious practical application was that no one need bother about his conduct; though behaviour might or might not be an indication of one's predetermined state, it had no formal effect on it.

Covenantal theology tried to soften this demoralizing theory by developing the doctrine of the two Covenants. God was said to have offered man two Covenants: the first, the Covenant of Works, made with Adam, offered everlasting life in return for obedience to the Laws; after Adam had broken this agreement and his sin had been imputed to all mankind, God in his mercy offered another Covenant, first to Abraham, then through Moses to the Israelites, finally through Christ to Christians. This Covenant of Grace offered life in return for a more passive obedience: faith in, and imitation of God. Man must still keep the law to the best of his ability, but, by the new Covenant of Grace, he will be judged by the spirit, not by the letter, of the law.[4] It is doubtful, however, whether the doctrine of the Covenants really altered much the basic tenets—and the practical effects—of the notion of predestination. Works might be interpreted as efficacious for salvation, but still only if they proceeded from a state of grace. Man's role was passive; once he had been involved in the Covenant of Grace, he could perform works fruitful to his salvation, but God withheld or extended the initial, "triggering" grace at his pleasure. There could be no question of a man "earning" grace by his works.

---

[4] The doctrine was first popularized by William Perkins, Fellow of Christ's College, Cambridge, from 1584 to 1594; by his student, the Calvinist moral theologian William Ames; and by John Preston, the brilliant Fellow of Queen's College and later Master of Emmanuel. The works of all three men were widely read and admired in New England. One of the clearest of the early and basic statements of the Covenantal doctrine of salvation is Preston's *The New Covenant or the Saints Portion* (London, 1629), a collection of sermons edited by Richard Sibbes and John Davenport. [S.F.]

This, then, was predestination all over again.[5] The Puritan theologian John Preston writes: "*All men are divided into these two rankes, either they are good or bad, either they are polluted or cleane, either they are such as sacrifice or such as sacrifice not:* There is no middle sort of men in the world; . . ."[6]
How can one tell if he is among the elect?

First; *the tree must be good*, as you have it in *Math.* 7. 16. 17. that is, a man then is said to be a good man, when there is good sap in him . . . when there are some supernaturall graces wrought in him. . . . Secondly; consider whether thou *bring forth good fruit*, that is, not onely whether thou doest good actions, but whether they flow from thee, whether they grow in thine heart as naturally, as fruit growes on the tree, that flowes from the sap within . . . and the meaning of the *holy Ghost* is therefore to show, that then a man is good, when his heart is fitted to good workes, when he knowes how to go about them, whereas another bungles them, and knowes not how to doe them . . .[7]

Preston's stress on man's passivity is unmistakable. Man is capable of efficacious works only after he has been touched by God's grace; they must flow "naturally" from him; he cannot begin the process himself. But how is a man to know if his works—by any objective test "good"—really and essentially proceed from a state of grace? The Westminster Con-

---

[5] For a fuller discussion of the extent to which Covenantal theology modified the Calvinist doctrine of salvation, see Perry Miller, *The New England Mind* (New York: 1939). Professor Miller argues that the modification was considerable: ". . . by conceiving of grace as a readiness of God to join in covenant with any man who will not resist Him, the theory declared in effect that God has taken the initiative, that man can have only himself to blame if he does not accede to the divine proposal" (p. 395). For reasons given above and later in the paper, I should like to suggest that, essentially, or at least practically, the Covenantal Puritans retained the doctrine of the inefficacy of works. [S.F.]

[6] Preston, Vol. III, p. 23. [S.F.]

[7] Preston, Vol. III, pp. 26-28. [S.F.]

fession, the articles of faith for the American Covenanters as
well as for the Scottish Presbyterians, is even more uncompromising in refusing to answer the question:

Good works are only such as God hath commanded in his holy
word, and not such as, without the warrant thereof, are devised
by men out of blind zeal, and upon any pretence of good intention [ch. xvi, i]. Works done by unregenerate men, although,
for the matter of them, they may be things which God commands,
and of good use both to themselves and others; yet, because they
proceed not from an heart purified by faith; nor are done in a
right manner, according to the word; nor to a right end, the glory
of God; they are therefore sinful, and cannot please God, or make
a man meet to receive grace from God [ch. xvi, vii].

It is possible to make too little of the Covenantal theo-
logians' attempt to compromise with Calvinism; after all,
though they confused Calvinism's brutal logic, they also made
it more human and, if one may say so, more Christian. Nevertheless, the central doctrine of predestination was left intact.
Works are no longer exclusively inefficacious; now some good
works are more equal than others. But we are still denied
objective criteria for determining which is which. This fact,
combined with the notion that, as Preston says, all men are
"good or bad" and "there is no middle sort of men in the
world" is the theory behind perhaps the biggest single effect
of the Reformation on practical morality. For better or worse,
as two American critics have noted, Puritan predestination
breaks down the whole structure of Aristotelian–Scholastic
ethics, sweeping away any idea of *degrees* of good and evil.
H. W. Schneider makes this point in *The Puritan Mind*:[8]

No one can live long in a Holy Commonwealth without becoming
sensitive, irritable, losing his sense of values and ultimately his
balance. All acts are either acts of God or of the Devil; all issues
are matters of religious faith; all conflicts are holy wars . . . no mat-

---

[8] San Francisco (1930), pp. 51-52. [S.F.]

ter how harmless a fool might be, he was intolerable if he did not fit into the Covenant of Grace; no matter how slight an offence might be, it was a sin against Almighty God and hence infinite.

And Yvor Winters applies this point to another literary re-creation of American Puritan society, *The Scarlet Letter*:

Objective evidence . . . took the place of inner assurance, and the behaviour of the individual took on symbolic value. That is, any sin was evidence of damnation; or, in other words, any sin represented all sin. When Hester Prynne committed adultery, she committed an act as purely representative of complete corruption as the act of Faustus in signing a contract with Satan. This view of the matter is certainly not Catholic and is little short of appalling.[9]

The Roman Catholic doctrine of salvation was and is a rational system, depending on man's free will to do good and evil—actively and consciously. Sins are either venial or mortal. Everywhere the idea of degree prevails; the sinner can neutralize his transgressions by greater or smaller acts of penance, depending on the degree of sin committed. One spends a greater or lesser time in purgatory, according to one's degree of perfection. The practical psychological effect of this system is that by it man is taught to deal with his acts severally, to analyse the details of his behaviour and experience one by one and to weigh one against the other. On the other hand, the Calvinists, and even the Covenantal Puritans, were taught to think of their behaviour (and the behaviour of their neighbours) as evidence only, not as conscious acts causing salvation or damnation. As evidence of total salvation or total damnation, their several acts were unimportant in themselves; there was less stress on evaluating each act and more on merely identifying it as evidence of grace or damnation.

---

[9] "Maule's Curse," in *In Defense of Reason* (Denver, 1947), p. 159. [S.F.]

In the light of these ideas, it is interesting to read, for example, through "Concerning an History of some *Criminals* executed in *New England* for Capital Crimes . . . ," originally written by "one of the *New English Ministers* . . . in hopes that the horrible sight would cause that worst Enemy to fly before it," and reprinted in Cotton Mather's history of New England.[10] Mather includes the accounts of the trials and the confessions of the convicted in an appendix to his chapter ". . . Discoveries and Demonstrations of the Divine Providence in Remarkable Mercies and Judgements on Many Particular Persons . . . of *New England* . . . ," remarking that, in the account of executed criminals, "the *remarkable judgements of God* were wonderfully Exemplify'd" (book IV, p. 37). This statement itself is important. The sins of the criminals (in these cases, their crimes, though the distinction between sin and crime is rather vague in Puritan New England) are not acts leading to their damnation; they are evidence of divine judgement already determined.

The various accounts are written in such a way as to support the construction Mather puts on them. What is particularly interesting is the nature of the criminals' confessions, the way in which they deal with their experience, and the writer's remarks on their behaviour. For instance, James Morgan was a "passionate fellow" who "swore he would run a Spit into a man's Bowels" and ". . . was as good as his word" (book VI, p. 40). He was hanged in Boston in 1686. His confession recounts a number of his sins:

I have been a great Sinner, guilty of Sabbath-breaking, of Lying, and of uncleanness; but there are especially two Sins whereby I have offended the Great God; one is that Sin of Drunkenness, which has caused me to commit many other Sins; for when in Drink, I have been often guilty of Cursing and Swearing, and

---

[10] *Magnalia Christi Americana* (London, 1702), book VI, pp. 37-49. Subsequent references in the text. [S.F.]

Quarrelling, and striking others. But the Sin which lies most heavy upon my Conscience, is that I have despised the word of God, and many a time refused to hear it preached [book VI, p. 40].

It is too harsh, perhaps, to expect a man about to be hanged to analyse his behaviour with any great precision, but one cannot help noticing the curious confusion of values by which drunkenness and refusing to hear the word of God become major sins and murder is not mentioned. Later in his confession, when he does deal with the act that brought him to the gallows, Morgan treats it not as a sin, but as a crime, of civil importance only:

I own the Sentence which the Honour'd Court has pass'd upon me, to be Exceeding Just; inasmuch as (though I had no former Grudge and Malice against the man whom I have kill'd, yet) my Passion at the time of the Fact, was so outragious as that it hurried me on to the doing of that which makes me now justly proceeded against as a Murderer [ibid].

And even here he (or whoever is helping him formulate his confession) speaks as though he were the passive agent in the act of murder. What counts is not the act itself (even the name of "murder" is carefully circumvented by the periphrastic "that which makes me now justly proceeded against as a Murderer"), but some "cause proportionate" which the murderer is powerless to resist: drunkenness and "Passion." One recalls Preston insisting that good works must flow from within "as the fruit growes on the tree." Presumably this applies also to "bad" works; either way the need for human responsibility seems to be diminished.

It is worth looking at one more excerpt from this grisly catalogue, a sermon preached at the hanging in 1698 of a "miserable Young Woman" who had murdered her illegitimate child. The minister makes only a passing reference to her "crime" and, surprisingly, to her adultery: "Thus the *God*, whose Eyes are like a Flame of Fire, is now casting her into a Bed of burning Tribulation: and, ah, Lord, where wilt thou cast those that have committed Adultery with her, except they repent!" (book vi, p. 48). The minister is really interested, for the most part, in her other sins:

Since her Imprisonment, she hath declared, that she believes, God hath left her unto this undoing Wickedness, partly for her staying so prophanely at home, sometimes on *Lords Days*, when she should have been hearing the Word of Christ, and much more for her not minding that Word, when she heard it.

And she has confessed, That she was much given to Rash Wishes, in her mad passions, particularly using often that ill Form of speaking, *I'll be hang'd*, if a thing be not thus or so; and, *I'll be hang'd*, if I do not this or that: Which Evil now, to see it, coming upon her, it amazes her! But this *Chief Sin* of which this *Chief of Sinners* now cries out, is, her undutiful Carriage towards her Parents. Her Language and her Carriage towards her Parents, was indeed such that they hardly durst speak to her; but when they durst, they often told her, It would come to this [book vi, p. 49].

Every aspect of this nasty document is important—the gallows humour, the language, the preacher's total confusion of values. In this strange system ignoring the Sabbath and insulting one's parents become as serious as adultery and murder. The girl's parents could see—where we cannot—that she was unregenerate and thus capable of *anything*. They knew it would come to this because she had been "undutiful" at home. They knew that unless she finally showed evidence of being among the saved (through confessing and repenting) she was surely among the damned. One piece of evidence was as good as another.

III

Orwell said that if a politician wished to control a democratic country he had to begin by controlling its language —that, to put it simply, a man who wanted to persuade people to do things they didn't want to do might profitably begin by calling those things by different names.[11] Advertising, too, depends on distorting the conventional meanings of words, or even on coining deliberately imprecise phrases. Patent medicines are said to cure "tired blood" or "night starvation" because these terms are imprecise enough to include a wide spectrum of ailments and thus promote a wide sale. Jonson anticipated this trick when he made Volpone, as mountebank, advertise his elixir as a specific for *tremor-cordia* and retired nerves.

But, as any literary critic knows, language can be distorted less consciously and less maliciously by people who are merely uncertain of their attitude towards whatever they are using words to describe. It seems likely that the vague and ultimately meaningless language which the preacher brings to bear on the "miserable Young Woman's" sin ("Tribulation," "Wickedness," "prophanely," "Rash Wishes") results from his own uncertainty about the comparative value of various human acts. This uncertainty may also account for the dubious taste of the passage, since what we call "bad taste" is nothing more than a dislocation between a fact and the level of language used to describe that fact.

So, far from having a "higher self-awareness," as Miller thought, the American Puritans were undecided about how much importance to give to specific human acts: good works may or may not proceed from a state of grace; all that was certain was that nothing was what it seemed; the concrete fact had no assured validity. But what Miller has caught so successfully, despite his theory, is the peculiar way in which the Puritans spoke whenever they talked about sin. One can say even more than that: Miller has, in fact, made the fullest dramatic use of the language, using its peculiarities to limit

---

[11] "Politics and the English Language," *Horizon* (April 1946), pp. 252-65. [S.F.]

the characters speaking it and even making it part of the play's subject.

The language plays its part, for example, in establishing the rather complex ironic structure in the scene in which the Reverend Hale first appears. Betty is lying ill, and Parris, secretly fearing that she might be affected by witchcraft, has called in an expert in detecting it. The situation itself is ironic; it is a measure of his own confusion about Betty that Parris must call in an expert with weighty volumes under his arms to tell him what to think about his daughter's exhaustion and shock. The audience also suspects that Parris depends on Hale's authority as a compensation for being unable to deal with Abigail. Another aspect of the irony is that the audience knows the expert's opinion will change nothing; the Putnams and the other townspeople—even Parris himself—have now convinced themselves that witchcraft is to blame. Finally, of course, the audience has already been given enough evidence—in the hasty conference between Abigail, Betty, and Mary Warren and in Abigail's plea to Proctor—that Hale's knowledge of witchcraft is irrelevant to the situation.

In the light of all this confusion, it is interesting to examine in some detail Hale's first extended speech:

PUTNAM: She cannot bear to hear the Lord's name, Mr. Hale; that's a sure sign of witchcraft afloat.
HALE, *holding up his hands:* No, no. Now let me instruct you. We cannot look to superstition in this. The Devil is precise; the marks of his presence are definite as stone, and I must tell you all that I shall not proceed unless you are prepared to believe me if I should find no bruise of hell upon her.

We miss the point if we see this scene as the opposition of the frightened, confused townspeople on the one hand, to the sane, certain, rational expert on the other. Hale's precision is pseudo precision: the speech is ironic because the audience knows that Hale's distinction between "superstition" and real witchcraft is less clear than he supposes. His simile to illustrate the Devil's precision supports this reading: "definite as stone"; it looks precise, possibly because it is a "hard" image, but stone is actually an imprecise image for "definite" because stone seldom appears clearly differentiated from other material, either in nature or in artifact.

Hale's pseudo precision is established beyond doubt a few lines further on in the scene:

HALE, *with a tasty love of intellectual pursuit:* Here is all the invisible world, caught, defined, and calculated. In these books the Devil stands stripped of all his brute disguises. Here are all your familiar spirits—your incubi and succubi; your witches that go by land, by air, and by sea; your wizards of the night and of the day. Have no fear now—we shall find him out if he has come among us, and I mean to crush him utterly if he has shown his face!

At first sight this list—with its division of material into various categories—has all the exactness of the encyclopaedia, but at second sight we are not convinced that the categories are well chosen. (Why, for example, should witches be arranged according to how they travel?) A modern audience is uncertain about what all the terms mean (just what is the difference between incubi and succubi?).

The audience familiar with Jonson may experience a tinge of *déjà vu* at this point. What we are hearing is a kind of conflation of *Volpone* and *The Alchemist,* Tribulation Wholesome acting the mountebank. In fact, the speech is a wild flight of jargon, quite unrelated to the situation with which Hale has been asked to deal, and if the audience has held out any hope for Hale's ability to recall the community to sanity, they must abandon that hope at this point. It is quite obvious that Hale, in his unique way, is divorced from reality. The others see evidence of witchcraft in the illness of a hysterical girl, and the witch hunt will express their repressed envy, libido, and land lust. Hale, too, sees witchcraft behind the events in Salem. He will use the witch hunt to express his manic expertise.

What makes Hale so vulnerable to the witch hunt is not—as with the other townspeople—his repressed emotions, but his love of abstraction. Hale, like any other educated Puritan, discounts the obvious. The concrete fact is not to be trusted. Thus at his first entrance, he recognizes Rebecca Nurse without having been introduced to her because she looks "as such a good soul should." But later, when he begins to apply his theories to the problem of Salem, he tells the Proctors "it is possible" that Rebecca is a witch. Proctor answers: "But it's hard to think so pious a woman be secretly a Devil's bitch after seventy year of such good prayer." "Aye," replies Hale, "but the Devil is a wily one, you cannot deny it." His search for the form behind the shadow finally leads him to an almost comical reversal of cause and effect:

I cannot think God be provoked so grandly by such a petty cause. The jails are packed—our greatest judges sit in Salem now—and hangin's promised. Man, we must look to cause proportionate. Was there murder done, perhaps, and never brought to light? Abomination? Some secret blasphemy that stinks to heaven? Think on cause, man, and let you help me to discover it.

When the facts become unimportant (and in this case the fact is Hale's "petty cause"—Abigail's alleged jealousy of Elizabeth Proctor), the choice of words becomes unimportant also: "abomination" and "secret blasphemy" mean little to us because Hale himself is unsure of what he means by them.

Danforth, too, has his pseudo precision:

. . . you must understand, sir, that a person is either with this court or he must be counted against it, there be no road between. This is a sharp time, now, a precise time—we no longer live in the dusky afternoon when evil mixed itself with good and befuddled the world. Now, by God's grace, the shining sun is up, and them that fear not light will surely praise it. I hope you will be one of those.

This reminds us of Hale's catalogue of witches, of John Preston's statement that ". . . *all men are divided into these two rankes, either they are good or bad*"; Miller has made good ironic use of the Puritan habit of constructing false disjunctions. Danforth's formulation looks precise, but misses the point because it establishes a false criterion of guilt (whether the accused approves of the court). So not only is it untrue to say that one is either with the court or "must be counted against it"; it is irrelevant. The trial has now reached its final stage in its retreat from the realities of the situation: it began unrealistically enough by examining the causes for the presence of something which had yet to be proved; then it began to take account of the wrong evidence, to listen to the wrong people; finally it becomes completely self-enclosed, and self-justifying, asking not whether the accused is guilty of being a witch but whether he or she supports the court.

In its withdrawal from reality the court takes advantage of the semantic uncertainty of the Salem townspeople, and, in so doing, makes them even more uncertain. Act Three opens with the sounds of Hathorne examining Martha Corey offstage:

HATHORNE'S VOICE: Now, Martha Corey, there is abundant evidence in our hands to show that you have given yourself to the reading of fortunes. Do you deny it?
MARTHA COREY'S VOICE: I am innocent to a witch. I know not what a witch is.
HATHORNE'S VOICE: How do you know, then, that you are not a witch?

Later, when even Hale begins to doubt the wisdom of the court, he tells Danforth: "We cannot blink it more. There is a prodigious fear of this court in the country—" And Danforth answers: "Then there is a prodigious guilt in the country." Terms are now quite rootless; the syntax suggests that "gear" and "guilt" are interchangeable.

How can the honest man combat this utter confusion of language and of the values which language transmits? One solution is simply to reject the slippery terminology and revert to a more primitive way of speaking:

DANFORTH, *turning to Giles:* Mr. Putnam states your charge is a lie. What say you to that?
GILES, *furious, his fists clenched:* A fart on Thomas Putnam, that is what I say to that!

This is one of the funniest moments in the play because it is true *discordia concors.* The audience senses the discrepancy (to say the least) between Giles's level of speech and the rhetoric of the court, but it also appreciates the desperate need to break away from the court's dubious terminology.

John Proctor's attack on the court's language is more serious, and more complex. He first meets it straightforwardly, trying to reverse the distorted meanings of the words it uses, or at least to restore the proper words to their proper places. When Cheever visits his house to tell him Elizabeth has been accused, Proctor says: "Is the accuser always holy now? Were they born this morning as clean as God's fingers? I'll tell you what's walking Salem—vengeance is walking Salem. We are what we always were in Salem but now the little crazy children are jangling the keys of the kingdom, and common vengeance writes the law!" Although Proctor is talking here to Cheever, he is also trying to put right a false formulation that Hale has made earlier in the scene, a characteristically imprecise use of a concrete image as an abstraction: "the Devil is alive in Salem." Proctor is trying to reassert the authority of the proper word. "We are what we always were"; only the words to describe us have changed.

But Proctor, of course, has his own guilt. Already he has been unable to say the word "adultery" when asked to recite the commandments. Finally when he faces his guilt—and tries to make the community accept it—in court, his formulation is painfully inarticulate: "It is a whore!" The statement contrasts powerfully with the smooth, meaningless language of his wife's accusers. At the end of the scene, when even his painful confession has failed to move them, he indicts them in *their* language, as though as a last resort he is trying to turn their own weapons upon them: "A fire, a fire is burning! I hear the boot of Lucifer, I see his filthy face! And it is my face, and yours, Danforth!"

Even if Miller's stage direction didn't call for Proctor to "laugh insanely" at this point, we could not accept this as the right solution; turnabout may be fair play, but in choosing to use their language against them, Proctor cannot escape its imprecisions. There is, after all, some distinction between him and Danforth, and, in the terms of this play, this difference can only be asserted by a total rejection of Danforth's language. This rejection comes—by implication, at least—when Proctor makes his genuine sacrifice at the end of the play, when he reclaims his "name": "Because it is my name! Because I cannot have another in my life! Because I am not worth the dust on the feet of them that hang! How may I live without my name? I have given you my soul; leave me my name." It is as though in regaining his name he finally ends the confusion about names which has been the town's sickness.

Proctor must indeed cast off the terminology of Salem. But what he is rejecting is not a monolithic system, not a "coherently worked-out philosophy." Salem speech is "articulate" in only a very limited sense of the word; "voluble" or "smooth" would apply more aptly. One needs to make this point because our response to the play is more complex than it would be if Proctor were a modern existential hero working out his own solution in opposition to the conventions of society. Salem has no conventions. Its evil is not positive. Its ethics are not wrong; they are nonexistent. What makes the progress of the witch hunt so terrifying for the audience is the realization that the trial has no programme. If Proctor and the others were being tested—and found wanting—according to a wrong-headed but consistent set of values, our reaction to the play would be quite different. What terrifies us is that we never know from what direction the next attack will come, and we are struck more by what Miller, in his Introduction to the *Collected Plays*, calls "the swirling and ludicrous mysticism [elevated] to a level of high moral debate" of the characters than we are by their "moral awareness." John Proctor acts not as a rebel but as the restorer of what the audience take to be normal human values. What Miller actually achieved in *The Crucible* is far more important than what he apparently feels guilty for not having achieved.

The Crucible
IN RETROSPECT:
ESSAYS ON THE PLAYWRIGHT

WILLIAM WIEGAND

William Wiegand has taught English at San Francisco State College since 1962 and is the author of *The Treatment Man*, among other books.

ARTHUR MILLER

AND THE MAN WHO KNOWS

A little over a year ago, *Holiday Magazine* gave Arthur Miller, author of *Death of a Salesman*, a chance to go home again.[1] They assigned him to write as part of their series on American colleges the story of the University of Michigan, as it was Then when Miller was a student there, and as it is Now. Miller stayed in Ann Arbor for about a week, gathering material, then returned to New York and wrote the article, a highly sensitive and keenly nostalgic piece about how things had

From *The Western Review*, XXI (Winter 1957), 85-102. Reprinted by permission of William Wiegand and *The Western Review*.
[1] Arthur Miller, "University of Michigan," *Holiday*, XIV (December 1953), 68-70, 128-43.

changed at Michigan, mostly about how impersonal they had become, and how, for some reason, the students were no longer making themselves felt. It was the "hanging around the lamp post" that Miller missed; it was the failure of the student to experience that sense of being alive, that unique feeling of participation which Miller cherished in his own memories of college life.

The reaction of university officials to Miller's article was not cordial. Most of them were either hurt by it, or dismissed it as one alumnus official did who remarked that "perhaps the university has not changed as much as Arthur Miller has." This may have been a consoling idea, but it was a diagnosis that was controverted by the evidence. The amazing thing was quite the opposite: Arthur Miller, far from having changed "so much," had not changed at all. He still believed in 1934-to-1938 with a passion that was undeniable. Nor was it so much a passion for the shadowy romance of anybody's college days, as it was a passion for the Values students held then (the capital "V" is Miller's). These Values were what made the difference, not specifically what was believed in those tarnished days, but the fact that anything was believed at all. The excitement of belief is what is gone, Miller says, and its absence portends, in his words, "a tragedy in the making."

As a man and a playwright who is deeply conscious of "tragedy" and whose voice has become of some importance on the stage today, the point of view implicitly suggested here raises some interesting questions about what Miller is. It offers a new suggestion perhaps that his work has been at least partly misunderstood, and this is important because *Death of a Salesman*, if not his other works too, has had an impact not only on critics but on popular audiences as well. Already, despite some controversial opinion about it, *Salesman* has been allowed the standing of a young classic. But where did it come from? "Classics" do not appear by means of magical processes; they come from somewhere and are obliged to be going some place.

By definition, "classic" means "of or pertaining to a coherent system."

My feeling is that the foundations and ramifications of *Salesman* have not been properly understood on the level of anything like a system but have been worked out only in the obvious terms of a "tradition." Because of this, *Salesman* is left a mere *fait accompli*. It casts no shadow forward; it has only *been*, and this is sometimes fatal to classics. Provoked by the *Holiday* article, I would like to find this "system" by trying to factor *Salesman* out on the basis of something more alive than, say, Ibsenian realism or the disillusionment of the Thirties; more specifically, on the basis of the long and going career of Arthur Miller himself.

In writing *Salesman*, Miller, first of all, accomplished something significant to the drama anthologists: he had tidied up a seventy-five-year cycle in the theatre. Titles like *From Ghosts to Death of a Salesman*, as John Gassner's latest collection is called,[2] mean to suggest more, I think, than a simple bracketing of a group of recent plays. Gassner, in fact, has shown that Miller has taken the theatre back to Ibsen while at the same time assimilating most of the major technical influences that have arisen since that time. Moreover, the ghosts of paternal sin that trouble Oswald Alving are very much the same as those that plague Biff Loman, but Miller makes the whole cycle glitter by showing off the enriched post-Ibsen heritage in projecting them. "Here [in *Salesman*]" Gassner writes, ". . . the expressionistic and realistic styles exist in a fused state."

In the process of describing the cycle, the epicycle—the literary history of Arthur Miller—has, however, been largely

---

[2] The subtitle of Gassner's *A Treasury of the Theatre* (New York: Simon and Schuster, 1950) was *From Henrik Ibsen to Arthur Miller*, although *Ghosts* and *Salesman* were the first and last plays in the collection. Revised in 1960, the collection got a new subtitle: *From Henrik Ibsen to Eugene Ionesco*. Time catches up with generalizations, as well as with playwrights. Not that Wiegand loses his original point.

ignored. The reason for this is implied almost in passing, again by Gassner: "[Miller] had been working steadily toward excellence and had already distinguished himself with much thoughtful writing in his thirty-three years." In other words, if a *Death of a Salesman* was going to be written at that moment, what more natural, he seems to say, than that it should come from this seasoned professional, this winner of a Critics' Circle Award, this published novelist, this keen social conscience who was never associated with the "private sensibility" drama most of his fellow playwrights were producing? The same lack of real interest in Miller was shared by the play's less friendly critics, who levied various reasonable, but impersonal complaints. Some dwelt, for example, on Willy Loman's failure as a tragic hero (a contention denied by some of the play's supporters). Others thought that the dialogue was "bad poetry." Eric Bentley said that the play was "vague" with a "blurring of outlines."[3]

So, in general, *Salesman* was treated like a new baby whose arrival is not completely expected but is totally appropriate just the same because it is the product of an ideal marriage between a healthy, if nondescript, playwright and a dramatic tradition that has proved beautifully fertile after all. This fertility preoccupied most of the offspring's strongest admirers. Those less impressed carped about the shape of Baby's fingernails perhaps, but showed no great interest as to what it was in Miller's genes that made them that way. Father was only Father, too much respected maybe, but also too much taken for granted. The reason for restoring Miller's parental rights, thus, is not that he has been resentful of the dandling wayfarers' attentions to his progeny, but that it has become almost impossible by now to determine how much of the play is Miller, how much is that of the "can-a-little-man-be-a-tragic-hero?" scholar, and how much

---

[3] For Bentley's opinion of the play, see *In Search of Theater* (New York: Knopf, 1953), pp. 84-87.

belongs to that almost legendary businessman who weeps in the orchestra because Willy Loman reminds him so much either of his Uncle George or of his own secret self. With the perspective of five more years and the advantage of an additional play during that period, it should be possible to find specific characteristics of Miller—"Miller traditions," as it were—which may or may not be congruent with the social and dramatic traditions with which he is usually identified.

In order to do this, first of all it is perhaps necessary to dispose quickly of some of the prevalent popular opinions of what Miller is. The most common of these was recently reasserted when the State Department refused to allow Miller a passport to visit Europe last May, evidently on the grounds that his record suggested that he might be lured into making anti-American-way-of-life statements abroad. The fellow-traveler stigma is nothing new for him. *Life* magazine helped wish it on him a few years back when they ran his name in an impromptu list of suspicious intellectuals.[4] Whatever extra-literary factors may have operated in the diplomatic decision, Miller's work itself, it is clear, has not been Marxist for over ten years; I do not see that this is anything but obvious, unless, of course, one falls prey to the current confusion whereby peripheral criticism of The System is equated with "being a Red." Miller has, in fact, more often than not in his commentaries bent over backward to be above politics, claiming to be interested strictly in the "moral dilemma" of our society.

But if he has himself shied away from doctrinaire interpretations of his plays, this has not stopped other people, some nominally Miller's friends, from attempting to define his ideology and from occasionally feeling insulted by the cloudiness of it. *The Crucible*, for example, was criticized by Robert

---

[4] "Red Visitors Cause Rumpus," *Life*, XXVI (April 4, 1949), 39-43. The famous collection of *Life*-labeled "Dupes and Fellow Travelers," Miller among them, fills a two-page (42-43) spread.

Warshow in *Commentary* magazine for waging a totally inadequate attack on McCarthyism,[5] a purpose the liberal wing
necessarily presumed Miller did or should have had in writing
the play. Warshow was at least an antidote to fuzzy-minded
myopics like columnist Ed Sullivan, who inquired after *The
Crucible*, why Miller hadn't rather written a play that praised
our colonial heritage.

For the most part, then, it was only long after *Salesman*
had become an institution that the vested-interest experts got
concerned about the errors in Miller's ways. Generally, their
disapproval was a whimsical as it was predisposed. However,
without shaking off the spell of both the overzealous liberal
"friends" on one hand and the Comintern mentalities in Washington on the other, it would be difficult to look at Miller's
touchy early plays and see them as anything more than adolescent symptoms of his dislike of The System. The plays are part
of his artistic development, however, and seem fruitful, I think,
because they contain the seeds of an important nonpolitical
premise in Miller's work—an idea which lay dormant after he
left college only to reach full bloom later in the plays that have
been written since the war. I will discuss this idea shortly.

II

Let us look first at the early work: two full-length plays which
Miller wrote as an undergraduate at the University of Michigan.
Both won awards in the University Avery Hopwood Contests,
respectively, in 1936 and 1937. Both also were cast strictly in
the Marxist mold of the Thirties.[6]

The earlier, *Honors at Dawn*, deals with an obtuse young
proletarian named Max Zabriskie who is blacklisted by the
capitalists after participating, rather unwittingly, in an abortive

---

[5] See pp. 210-226.
[6] These plays exist only in manuscript; copies are at the University of
Michigan. A typescript of *They Too Arise* is in the New York Public
Library.

strike at the plant where he has worked. Once out of The System, he elects to go to college, the seat of integrity and idealism. His brother, a much better student than he, is already there, and unknown to Max is subsidized by the university to spy on campus radicals. When Max learns of his brother's perfidy and the even greater corruption of the university, his illusions about college are dispelled. Max leaves and works himself back into the union movement, where with sound social conscience he participates in a real strike. The play climaxes with the hero beaten up, but with a sure sense that he has found "at dawn" the "honors" he was seeking at the university before he learned of their false foundation.

Miller's other Hopwood play, *No Villain*, was later revised and expanded into a drama called *They Too Arise*, which won a national WPA award in 1938. This play revolves around the family of a middle-class garment manufacturer in New York and takes place during one of the labor crises in the industry. Abe Simon, the father, is determined to cross the picket lines to make deliveries which will save his small and shaky business. His older son, Ben, is his right bower, schooled in the family traditions but cynical about carrying them out. Arnie, the younger son, home from college for the summer, is called a Communist by his father and wears the title proudly. Arnie will not scab for his father against the strikers.

It becomes clear at last that only the big manufacturers will survive the strike. Ben, however, is offered a cheap out when given an opportunity to marry the daughter of one of the bigger enterprisers. Arnie's influence is too persuasive, though. Ben rejects the marriage, the business folds, the old grandfather symbolically dies. With the two boys joined, it seems that Abe and his wife have little choice but to convert too. As the play ends, they are getting used to the idea, much as the Gordons did in Clifford Odets's *Paradise Lost*.[7]

---

[7] For Odets, see note, p. 216.

All this was before 1940. Out of school only a few years when the war broke out, Miller was immediately enlisted as a propaganda writer of sorts, much of his output being absorbed by radio and in sponsored one-act plays like *That They May Live*, a work dedicated to urging its audience to turn in OPA price-ceiling violators. Margaret Mayorga, who includes this play in one of her annual collections, reports that in production the in-the-script interruption of the stage action by a man planted in the audience on several occasions almost started a riot. This indicated at least that Miller had a certain capacity to stir live audiences, although it must be presumed that this particular uprising occurred out of simple irritation with a loudmouth rather than any kind of *Waiting for Lefty* indignation against black market offenders.

In any case, Miller suddenly found himself on one hand writing social messages for money and on the other hand, on his own, for the stage he was writing a play with virtually no dialectic significance at all. This work, which reached Broadway in 1944, was called *The Man Who Had All the Luck*. It reads like part Willa Cather and part Sigmund Freud, involving in its plot a young gasoline-station operator who experiences such a series of good breaks that eventually he can't stand it any more. He finally succeeds in cooking up a situation that financially destroys him. His homespun wife, however, recognizes that his guilt feelings over his success must be alleviated somehow and cheerfully accepts the disaster, which unfortunately has little real impact since it is only financial.

The play ran less than a week on Broadway, the Cather elements turning out perhaps too bland, the Freud too thick (although Miller blames a bad production). He was at any rate a produced playwright on Broadway. Oddly enough, however, his major work (at this point) had not only no tinge of Marxism; it hardly had a point of view. For a young man like Miller, who was apparently interested in much more than mere craft, this was unusual. One might speculate whether or not he was still nursing a dialectic that had to remain dormant for the duration of the emergency.

By this time, however, the war was beginning to cast up specters more disturbing than price violators. Miller received an assignment from Hollywood to prepare himself for writing the screenplay of *The Story of G. I. Joe*, the film version of Ernie Pyle's stories. A 4-F himself, Miller accepted the task enthusiastically. If the Marxists had long known what society was like, they had no ready answers for what war was like, and on his own he meant to find out.

The result of his tour of Army camps and war-casualty hospitals is reported in a book Miller wrote after he finished his film scenario. This work, *Situation Normal*, bridges the crucial gap, I think, between Miller of the early discipline and Miller of the later one. The book ends this way:

. . . you are over New York harbor now. In the plane the Navy flier buttons his jacket, fixes his tie, runs a comb through his hair, sets his battle ribbons straight. He stares, summing up his appointments for the day, the people to call, the important girl. He feels for his money, is assured. He counts the days ahead and mentally apportions a certain amount of cash to each, knowing, however, that he will soon forget how much he allowed himself to spend and will probably be broke in four days regardless of calculations. We land and he descends the steps to the ground and hurries into the airport building. He secludes himself in the phone booth and begins to pick up his life. Mother answers and is waiting for him. The girl picks up the phone at the very first ring and a party is being organized. Already odors of woman assail him and the sound of certain kinds of evening gowns. Hearing her voice he is filled with a dull longing for something from her, something he wishes he could sense between her words and among the various pitches in her voice. And he cannot find it there. One minute she is filled with pity for him, the next pride. He suffers for her and for his inability to know what it really is he wants her to feel. He recalls how easy it was to talk to the guys in the squadron, how simple to communicate without talking at all. She asks him how it was and he says it was pretty bad in the beginning but it got all right later on and suddenly he is very tired. Sad, strangely. He makes the date and hangs up. What the hell does he want her to do, know what it was like out there? How could she when she wasn't there? Maybe it's something she ought to want. Wanting him back, being glad he is back . . . it's like everything they had been doing out there added up to one thing—that he had gotten back at last and could go dancing and see his mother. . . . His mother kisses him, walks him into the house where he smells the food. He washes in the old bathroom, finds a razor he has forgotten about and starts to shave. For an instant, the curious notion strikes him that it will be good to get out of here again, it will be good to be going back. Exactly why, he doesn't know, but good it will be. Good to be going in one direction with the other guys. Good to have certain things mutually understood again. He goes downstairs and mother talks and he watches her. It is growing strange. He has found her with nothing more than joy at his returning. He wonders again what on earth he would have these people feel. God knows he doesn't want her calling him her hero. The heroes aren't coming home to mother any more. But they did change something by going out there, didn't they? Or did they? The newspaper on the chair looks up at him. "In the next war the probability is that the rocket bomb . . ." The next war. Well now, as easy as that. When are they going to start figuring out this war? His mother questions. Between mouthfuls he answers his mother. "Well, in the beginning," he mutters, "it was pretty bad. But after a while . . . it was all right." Oh, hell, let it go at that. It doesn't matter anyway.

Does it?

This final "does it?" this apparently rhetorical question, is what Miller has been trying to answer ever since. He has endeavored to show that the failure of people to communicate with one another does matter, of course. It mattered to some extent even in the very early plays. But after *Situation Normal*, the idea became crucial: certain men know certain truths; people suffer and sometimes die because these truths fail to be communicated. Consequently, his Navy flier quiet and puzzled, always the square peg in the round hole, has since descended from the clouds in the alter egos of Chris Keller in *All My Sons*, Biff Loman in *Death of a Salesman*, and John Proctor in *The Crucible*, all of whom found their supernal, ineffable awareness to be tragically incommunicable when they reached the earth below.

The repetition of the same situation and especially of the same characters is, I think, the kind of thing Bentley was talking about when he speaks of "the blurring of outlines." Biff Loman is an undelineated sensitive man, stamped from the international archetype, likewise Chris and Proctor; all three of these roles can be and incidentally were played on Broadway by the same archetypically sensitive actor, Arthur Kennedy. More specifically, in terms of the Navy flier, each of these characters may be described as a Man Who Knows (a term, by the way, that Miller himself first used to designate one of the *dramatis personae* in the one-act play mentioned above). Inevitably in Miller's plays, the Man Who Knows is the character with whom the major share of the audience's sympathy lies (not to be confused with pity, the emotion necessarily felt toward Willy Loman), and is the one who has the soundest suspicion that something is wrong with the society around him. Unfortunately, however, he can do nothing to forestall the imminent tragedy.

Chris, Biff, and Proctor, of course, have still other similarities. All three express themselves in forceful colloquial dialogue, much as Odets's heroes do. Unlike Odets's men, however, the passion with which they speak does not conceal any personal fight with the devil inside. All of these Men seem to have been born right-thinking; even Proctor's dalliance with his young tormentress never seems particularly evil of him, but is merely a necessary thread of the plot. And Biff Loman's stealing is kleptomania, hence no breach of the Ten Commandments. What the Man Who Knows knows is what is true, what should be. Beyond his inborn wisdom, he is an innocent and helpless tool.

To complete the pattern in these three works are characters foiling the Man Who Knows, each of whom may be described as the Man Who Learns. These characters are wrong-thinking at the beginning, mostly because of pride, but they learn something by the end. Joe Keller, who manufactures defective airplane engines and kills twenty-one pilots, hears that his own son has committed suicide because of the disgrace, forcing him to accept the fact that they were, as he says, "all my sons." Because of his early misapprehension, Joe must kill himself too. Willy Loman never comes to a complete awareness of his mistake; that is the major impact and irony of *Death of a Salesman*. Still, even if there is no capacity to act on or talk about it, there is a Learning in *Salesman*, a Learning that gets through to the audience and to Willy too: the dream is a sham and there can be no possibility of his surviving to test it further. Both Keller and Willy hence become victims, perhaps because they learn too late.

The pattern is varied slightly in *The Crucible*. The Man Who Learns here is the Reverend Hale, but unlike the earlier two plays, it is not he who suffers the death in the third act. But Hale takes the play over so completely from the victim, Proctor (who after all only Knows and is static), that the latter's martyrdom seems almost a sentimental afterthought. "I denounce these proceedings," Hale says at the curtain of the second last scene, but the tide of majority stupidity has already engulfed them. He is too late too, and this is his tragedy.

What is Miller's verdict on these people who learn so slowly and painfully? Well, as Uncle Charlie says at Willy Loman's funeral, "No one dast blame this man." No one dast blame any of them—Keller, Willy, Hale. But it is sad, Miller says, sad that the few who comprehend the truth from the first were powerless to communicate it so that it could be understood in time.

Miller's moral lesson ends in every case the same way. The false faith leads to martyrdom. In *All My Sons*, this faith is that "the world ends at the building line." In *Salesman*, it is, of course, that material success is everything, and in *The Crucible*, the error is that witches exist and cast evil spells. In each case, a prevalent misapprehension sets the machine in motion. Whatever the nature of the false faith, someone must be marytred in the trial. This dramatic pattern is familiar, of course, in Greek tragedy.

Miller's three latest plays, in other words, aspire to more than what has been called "social drama." Note, for example, that the strong motif of retribution does not appear in his "optimistic" Marxist plays, where false faiths in the university and in the business were respectively undermined without more than bloodying the hero a little. Similarly, there is, of course, no "Greek" expiation in the play Miller adapted for a New York production in 1951—Ibsen's *Enemy of the People*. The Man Who Knows in this work is entirely capable of communicating his truth even though people don't like it. Ibsen makes his point by showing Doctor Stockmann ostracized in his community. He does not need to award him martyrdom as a kind of consolation prize.

Of *Enemy of the People*, Miller writes in the preface to his adaptation the following:

. . . I believed this play could be alive for us because its central theme is, in my opinion, the central theme of our social life today. Simply, it is the question of whether the democratic guarantees protecting political minorities ought to be set aside in time of crises. More personally, it is the question of whether one's vision of the truth ought to be a source of guilt at a time when the mass of men condemn it as a dangerous and devilish lie. . . .

Here again, in making a judgment on what is important, on what indeed is "*the* central theme of our social life today," he focuses on a problem specifically involving individual martyrdom. Also, in choosing quickly to treat the "question" of minority rights on an oblique personal level, he sees immediately what he wants to see in the play: a "source of guilt" or sin, even in Knowing, although there is no evidence that Stockmann feels anything of the kind. Miller reads a classic sin-and-retribution theme into the play.

According to Miller, what makes Ibsen a giant is not the boldness of his themes (which are of course no longer bold), but it is rather the eternal truth of his situations. Elsewhere in his preface, Miller says:

. . . I had a private wish to demonstrate that Ibsen is really pertinent today, that he is not "old-fashioned" and implicitly, that those who condemn him are themselves misleading our theatre and our playwrights into a blind alley of senseless sensibility, triviality, and the inevitable waste of our dramatic talents; for it has become the fashion of plays to reduce the "thickness" of life to a fragile facsimile, to avoid portraying the complexities of life, the contradictions of character, the fascinating interplay of cause and effect that have long been part of the novel.

In working toward objectives like these in his own plays, Miller's point of view on the theatre implicitly becomes directly opposite to those of playwrights like John Van Druten, for example. Van Druten has written: "The theatre is ephemeral and plays are a perishable commodity. . . . [Still] I see no reason for being ashamed of one's part in it, nor for avoiding the effort to do one's best at it."[8]

Where Van Druten is "unashamed" but resigned, Miller is militant and determined that certain values are deathless. He glimpses them in Ibsen, and, as I have noted, pursues them even more hotly down old Hellenic corridors when he says, as Plato might have: "I don't see how you can write anything

---

[8] See John Van Druten, *Playwright at Work* (New York: Harper, 1953), pp. 7-8.

decent without using the question of right and wrong as the basis." And when he writes an *All My Sons*, which fits the dramatic specifications offered by Aristotle right down to recognition and peripety.

III

The consequences of Miller's adoption of classic moral values are complicated. Obviously, appropriating Sophocles' religion does not make one Sophocles, even if we ignore the large issue of respective lyric capacities. The question of how the values have been embraced and revealed remains. Miller's "expression," in other words, must stand up as drama. It must bear criticism. To this end, but in fear of interposing any rigidly abstract standards, either ancient or modern, I would like to make a few purely comparative judgments of Miller's plays, as drama, against those of two playwrights who have worked approximately in his milieu: again Ibsen and Odets. This comparison is only partially fair to Miller since we have, of course, a longer span of work by which to judge the other two dramatists.

The congruities between *An Enemy of the People* and *The Crucible* I have already partially noted. Both are stories of men who have, in Miller's words, a "vision of the truth [which is] condemned by the mass of men as a dangerous and devilish lie." If the likenesses are evident, there are also these important differences between the plays: Ibsen's hero, Stockmann, invites his own disaster by freely publishing the report on the pollution of the waters, which will destroy the economy of his village. He does this without compunction and with a cavalier kind of thoughtlessness. Miller's Proctor, on the other hand, is almost a casual victim of his village. His "sin" with the girl, which Miller tries to insist on, lies outside the immediate public concern and has no bearing on his fate. He appears, innocent, at the witch trials in order to defend his wife, herself unjustly branded. In time, Proctor finds himself accused too and eventually convicted. Offered an opportunity to confess and save his life, he refuses, preferring the martyr's death instead. Thus he dies gratuitously, bravely perhaps, but rather like the soldier on the battlefield who will not turn and run despite the fact he finds himself in a world he never made.

Stockmann has entered the battle in full tilt. His opponents have no choice but to defend themselves; the danger to them is apparent, and undoubtedly more real to us, in dramatic terms, than Salem's witches. The "villains" in *Enemy of the People* are not victims of a mere temporary, even if recurring, social delusion. They have power, but so does Stockmann. He is never reduced, as is Proctor, to go begging to his opponents for wisdom and justice. Unlike Proctor, he has a chance to win on his own terms. And, at the end, with rocks crashing through the window, he says: "We must live through this." He continues to make plans although he is well aware "there'll be a long night before it's day." The light of this "day" is what Miller never allows for, except as it may be seen in the gaudy fire that burns his martyr. He ends with the roll of drums and the suffering of a sad, but somewhat cheap, injustice. The curbstone "justice" that Stockmann gets, base as it is, seems in some proportion to his injury to the community. Aesthetically, this ending has much better conscience than the ending of *The Crucible*.

Miller's sentimentality, at least in this area, may possibly be due to the fact that he is too glib an ideologist. It is so easy for him to fit the raw material into the "lesson" that there are no rough edges. Everything is schematized and smooth as glass. He writes, for instance, among much other prefatory and interpolative commentary in the published version of *The Crucible*, this:

In the countries of the Communist ideology, all resistance of any import is linked to the totally malign capitalist succubi and in America any man who is not reactionary in his view is open to the charge of alliance with the Red hell. Political opposition thereby is given an inhumane overlay which then justifies the abrogation of all normally applied customs of civilized intercourse. . . .

While this sort of interlinear display is forgivable self-indulgence, it does invite suspicion that the cart is pulling the horse, or that everything in the play is too tightly yoked to its elaborately explicated intentions.

Even further in the direction of didacticism is Miller's decision in his adaptation of *Enemy of the People* to edit out certain speeches of Stockmann which, according to Miller, "have been taken to mean Ibsen was a Fascist." He devotes a short section of his preface to considering this matter, then finally says:

I have taken the justification for *removing those examples which no longer prove the theme* [italics mine]—examples I believe Ibsen would have removed were he alive today—the line in the original manuscript that reads: "There is no established truth[9] that can remain true for more than seventeen, eighteen, at most twenty years. . . ." The man who wrote A *Doll's House*, the clarion call for the equality of women, cannot be equated with a fascist. . . .

John Gassner, among others, has pointed out in detail how Ibsen is "one of the most deceptive of dramatists," how his inherent contradiction is a large part of his dramatic strength. To Miller, however, Ibsen was a man who occasionally wrote "tendentious speeches spoken into the blue" and had to be revised in order "to prove the theme."

This artistic nearsightedness in Miller is perhaps magnified when we compare him with Clifford Odets, a thesis dramatist who is roughly contemporary with Miller. The relationship between these two writers is a close one. Rather than saying, however, that Odets, who came first, was an influence on Miller, it is probably more accurate to say they were both influenced

---

[9] Miller apparently distinguishes between "established" or pragmatic truth, and absolute truth. [W.W.]

by similar backgrounds and similar economic experiences. Both began by writing Jewish family plays with strong Marxist themes. Later, the more strident leftism was sacrificed along with the ethnic settings. Both, though, continued to work with middle-class characters.

Miller repeats with astonishing frequency dramatic situations that Odets used first. In *Awake and Sing*, for example, an old man commits an "accident"-suicide in a futile effort to supply the scion of the family with much-needed insurance money. This is exactly the climax of *Death of a Salesman*. In *Paradise Lost*, Odets's favorite among his own plays, the personal history of Ben Gordon wholly anticipates that of Biff Loman. Ben's boyhood victory in a Madison Square Garden track meet parallels Biff's moment of glory in the Ebbets Field football game. Ben has medals and a statue of himself in the living room; his young bride says adoringly: "My Ben can be anything he wants," much as Biff Loman's mother says: "He could be a —anything in that suit!" Ben, like Biff, is unable to live up to his high-school prestige, experiences a complete self-contempt, and winds up a petty gunman much as Biff does a thief.

The rougher similarities between the work of the two men are beyond count; *Golden Boy* and *Rocket to the Moon* both have echoes in *Salesman*, for instance, and *Till The Day I Die* treats the same problem that *The Crucible* does. It is, however, the differences between their respective treatments rather than the similarities which suggest the particular nature of Miller's selectivity and emphasis. In the situations mentioned above, for example, Odets practically throws away Jacob Berger's suicide in *Awake and Sing*. To him this is matter for the second act and not the third. Dying is incidental to the living that is going on. No funeral eulogies are spoken for old Jacob but this does not mitigate the fact that it is a brave thing he has done rather than simply a terribly pathetic thing. Odets is thus able later to close the play with an unsentimental affirmation of the life-force, an entirely appropriate ending.

In *Paradise Lost,* for the second-act curtain, Ben Gordon expires offstage in a rain of police bullets. But somehow Odets has saved this from simple pathos, too. Ben's fall never holds more than part of the stage and yet his flashy finish is no less a one than he has a right to. Because he is a man, he has traded confidences, cynically enough only with the person who is cuckolding him; he does not, like Biff Loman, weep self-reproach on the shoulders of his mother and father.

Both *Awake and Sing* and *Paradise Lost* are of Odets's Marxist period. These plays, however, survive despite the outdatedness of their particular message. The reason for this must be that Odets was either too slipshod a Communist, too artful a dramatist, or, more likely, both. Today the speeches fit the play like period furniture on the set—they would not really be missed if removed; at the same time they add something to the place and time and spirit of the occasion. But certainly it is unlikely that the plays could be produced in Moscow today since they never fulfill the political responsibility they invite. They are too Chekhovian.

Such evasion of "responsibility" Miller is incapable of. His primary dedication is to "prove the theme." The result is that Odets's plays, with their characters and individual scenes that transcend the gestalt, are often less than the sum of their parts; and, conversely, Miller's may seem more. But in Miller's case, we may ask: how large are the parts? His characters too often are flat and humorless. He shows no love for them and very little respect, except here and there the kind a schoolboy might hold for George Washington, and then not Washington the man but Washington the symbol. His people are passionate but bloodless. Where in Miller, for example, is there anybody with the heart of Moody in *Golden Boy,* Moe in *Awake and Sing,* or Prince in *Rocket to the Moon,* all superficially selfish characters?

To these same people, Miller seems able to offer only pity. "A man is a jellyfish," he has a character say in *The Man Who*

Had All the Luck, "and a jellyfish can't swim no matter how he tries; it's the tide that pushes him every time. So just keep feeding and enjoy the water till you're thrown up on the beach." Although this particular character is a cynic, it is remarkable how often Miller reverts to comparisons of men with beasts of land or sea, particularly helpless ones. The best he will allow for human beings is a basically negative metaphor: "A man is not a piece of fruit," as Willy Loman says. Yet he is only animate enough to feel pain and to resist being peeled.

Miller sees no particular charm or other possibilities in the weaknesses of his characters. Their ineffectuality leaves them simply an object of pity or, vaguely, an inspiration for moral regeneration. They are examples, even sermons, because they sermonize. "Attention must be paid to such a man," Linda Loman says when she knows the tide is pushing Willy up on the beach. Joe Keller's wife shares Linda's undefined need for some sort of acknowledgment of the terrible situation. After Joe's crime has been confessed, Kate asks her son, "What more can we be [than 'sorry']?" Chris says, "You can be better." And even much earlier, Esther Simon in *They Too Arise* speaks the weary final curtain line: "Yeh, we gotta learn; a lotta things we gotta learn." People are so hopelessly far away from grasping simple truths, Miller says, they have no right to bid for anything but pity at the moment.

The only major characters not defeated in their own terms and more or less from the outset are Proctor, and, in the novel *Focus,* Newman. Proctor is engulfed just the same. Newman, the timid personnel executive, arrives at a sort of bogus victory by ceasing at the end of the book to deny he is a Jew after being mistaken for one and abused because of it up until that point. This is doubly ironic because Newman has been somewhat anti-Semitic himself. Unfortunately, however, his acceptance of the Jewish identity that has been thrust upon him occurs while he is making a complaint in a police station; again society's brutality is too much for him to handle by himself.

Like many of Miller's characters, he only wants to be let alone, but denied this, he wears the martyr's badge proudly, the Man Who Learns, in effect, how to adapt himself to what is perhaps the most ancient heritage of martyrdom in existence. Finding this role, he loses his fear. He learns late, like Willy Loman, Joe Keller, and the Reverend Hale, that he had been contaminated by the poison in the social sea. The realization may be relieving to the jellyfish, but will, of course, have no effect on the tidal waters.

Partly aware of this "relief," there have been recent efforts by some who, while attacking the drama of "senseless sensibility," have tried to build up a case for "tragedy of the common man." Longing for the tragical catharsis has become a shibboleth to modern critics, and those most friendly to the contemporary stage seem determined to fit certain modern plays into the classic formulae. Without much poking and prodding, Miller fits— if only, they seem to say, we can accept the protagonist as sufficiently symbolic of the society as classic royalty was. This is the nub of the problem.

A better question, it would seem to me, in the light of any close examination of Miller's characters, is not whether they are broad enough symbols but whether they are deep enough men. Is their power perhaps *merely* symbolic? Is Willy Loman a cross that Miller is shaking at us, its basic impact lying somewhere outside the play, in the house where Uncle George lives, for instance? Certainly Uncle George is no less real and no more mythic than Sacco and Vanzetti were, for instance, when liberal sentiment engendered by their conviction magnified Maxwell Anderson's *Winterset* into "tragedy" for a time, largely because it drew a recognizable parallel with a real situation fraught with social implication.[10] Unwittingly or not, *The Crucible* does the same thing with the McCarthy bogey.

The danger of harvesting these extra-play dividends is obvi-

---

[10] For Sacco and Vanzetti, see note, p. 222.

ous: in most cases, the symbol stifles any chance the individual character might have if left on his own. We are deluded by the symbol's mystic tribal sanction. We are lulled by a myth. In certain ways, it might even be contended that Miller's ritual pilgrimages in the coach of Human Truth lead only to a brave mirage quite as insubstantial as that sought by commercial writers who hitch up to the resplendent locomotive called The American Dream in order that all the passengers may feel familiar and easy in the club car.

It is ironic perhaps to associate a writer as "moral" and Knowing as Miller with this kind of fallacy, and yet, like them, he is fundamentally reliant on response to ritual beliefs. His problem, consequently, is one which even the old minstrels had: how to make the singing of a legend seem fresh and pure and convincing. Right now, rather than being a tragedian, Arthur Miller is like the man who comes to a funeral and tells many traditional stories about the deceased, except you get the feeling he was anticipating the occasion of the epitaph even while he was witnessing the events.

In summary, Miller has been writing for the last ten years what might be called modern-dress versions of classical martyrdoms. While the beginning of his success as a dramatist was coincident with his discovery of a particular pattern for accomplishing this adaptation, the germ of it lay in his very early work as well. Although these works superficially called for political action, they indicated his instincts and interests were more deeply "tragic," if we accept the word with all its moral connotations. In *Situation Normal*, for instance, he expresses grievance with the producers of *The Story of G. I. Joe* when they revised his screenplay. "About three of them [soldiers] were going to die at first," Miller writes. "Then we cut it down to two, and finally I think only one died dead, the others ending up with wounds. It is very hard to kill a good character in Hollywood because the public seems to prefer pictures in which nobody dies. . . ."

The discovery of the uncommunicated-truth pattern was a discipline for this kind of Lost Generation disillusionment. Miller afterwards no longer had to guess "about three" deaths were sufficient for his tragical purposes. He simply made a religion of absolute, but non-sectarian, truth, martyrs for which were to be drawn from the ranks of men who knew this truth but could not communicate it and men who did not know it at the start but came to learn it.

It is not unlikely that this "truth" represented some kind of substitute for the Marxist "truth" which had fortified Miller's early career and answered all the questions of life. After he abandoned it, he probably felt for a time something like his Navy flier who realized in the limbo that the central principle of existence was lacking. The flier thinks: it would "be good to be going back. Exactly why, he doesn't know, but good it will be. Good to be going in one direction with the other guys. Good to have certain things mutually understood again." Vague things, to be sure, and a vague direction. But something.

It is no discredit to Miller that he needed a direction, nor no credit to Odets, for instance, that he did not. Ten years older than Miller, Odets had not grown up with the depression, with the sharp early sense of group identity that the whole "anti" movement offered. Miller, younger, perhaps more impressionable, was genuinely moved by the opportunities for martyrdom that are relished by hard-minded youth. Odets, on the other hand, was, as Harold Clurman's book on the Group Theatre[11] indicates, more egocentric, more the *Naturkind* of the Twenties. He put on Marxism like a coat and took it off again as easily. But for Miller the loss of the old feeling is a tragedy. If there is at Michigan no communication among students and between students and faculty; if the ideals are lost in some old book or on some professor's muted tongue; if everything is really changed; then it is unbearably sad. He says, it may be, of course, that he

---

[11] *The Fervent Years* (New York: Hill and Wang, 1957).

does not know where to look any more. But truth and beauty were here somewhere. Their passing is a cause for genuine sorrow. This nostalgic sorrow is the emotional link with the Thirties Miller has never been able to cut.

Which brings us to the present and a look ahead to Miller's shortly expected next play,[12] eagerly awaited in New York for reasons others have accurately expressed. Reasons like: Miller is always timely, he is not afraid of large emotions, he has a great gift for structure and dramatic development; if his techniques are largely traditional, he is aware of and has made impressive use of more experimental methods. He is "fresh" and poetic, with none of what has been called "the mystique of O'Neill and . . . the formality and generalized rhetoric of Anderson; [his work] never leaves the actual world! it does not cultivate naïveté; and it takes a responsible view of life in our society . . ."[13] Clurman, Odets's old director, has also spoken of Miller's "humanistic jurisprudence."

All this, however, to be worthwhile, ought to be channeled past certain facts apparent about the writer: one, he does not give much to human goodness, intelligence, or charm; social vice inevitably defeats them. Two, a few men are in touch with truth and they suffer most because reality is so bad in comparison. Three, dying is the loudest proof of having lived.

Hence, this eclectic social consciousness of Arthur Miller is levered from hardly more than a single fulcrum of superstition: that the men who know are destined to be trampled upon, yet to arrive at this "knowing" is a man's only chance of saving his soul. Here I must argue with the Clurman opinion quoted above. Miller's superstition is not so "humanistic"; it belongs

---

[12] The play was A *View from the Bridge*. Although Wiegand's article was not printed until 1957, it was apparently written before the New York opening of *View* in 1955.

[13] The words are John Gassner's, from his introduction to *Death of a Salesman* in the anthology Wiegand cited earlier. There, too, Wiegand found the Clurman quotation (*Treasury*, 1960 ed., pp. 1060-62).

more to a mysticism which, unlike O'Neill's, minimizes the essential life-force of the little man, and which, in past eras, has often been a portent of monolithic and reactionary societies. This may be the shadow that *Death of a Salesman* is casting forward, and which makes the play unwittingly timely in a decade when they say that both God and the Kremlin are growing in strength every day. Standing against them and their temper in our time, the "fragile facsimiles" made by Miller's contemporaries, sadly enough, seem fragile indeed.

RICHARD H. ROVERE

Richard H. Rovere, staff writer for *The New Yorker* since 1944, is the author of *Affairs of State: The Eisenhower Years, Senator Joe McCarthy, The American Establishment,* and *The Goldwater Caper,* among other books.

ARTHUR MILLER'S CONSCIENCE

"I will protect my sense of myself," Arthur Miller told the House Committee on Un-American Activities when he refused to identify some writers who had once been Communists.[1] "I could not use the name of another person and bring trouble on him." The refusal brought Miller a conviction for contempt of Congress from a judge who found his motives "commendable" but his action legally indefensible.

A writer's sense of himself is to be projected as well as protected. It becomes, through publication and production, a rather public affair. For this and other reasons, it is fitting that what Miller saw as the testing of his integrity—the challenge to his sense of himself—was a question involving not himself but others. Of himself, he had talked freely, not to say garrulously. He chatted, almost gaily, about his views in the thirties, his views in the forties, his views in the fifties, about Ezra Pound and Elia Kazan and other notables, about the Smith Act and Congressional investigations and all manner of things. When he was asked why he wrote "so morbidly, so sadly," he responded patiently and courteously, rather as if it were the

---

From *New Republic*, CXXXVI (June 17, 1957), 13-15. © 1957 by Richard Rovere. From his volume *The American Establishment and Other Reports, Opinions and Speculations,* (New York: Harcourt Brace and World, 1962), pp. 276-284. Reprinted by permission of Harcourt, Brace Jovanovich, Inc.
[1] See Bibliography.

"question period" following a paid lecture to a ladies' club. His self-esteem was offended only when he was asked to identify others.

Thus, one might say, it was really a social or political ethic that he was defending, while of his sense of himself he gave freely. In legal terms, this might be a quibble, for there is no reason why a man should not have a right to his own definition of self-respect. In a literary sense, it is not a quibble, for Miller is a writer of a particular sort, and it was in character for him to see things this way. He is, basically, a political, or "socially conscious" writer. He is a distinguished survivor of the thirties, and his values derive mostly from that decade. He is not much of a hand at exploring or exploiting his own consciousness. He is not inward. He writes at times with what may be a matchless power in the American theatre today, but not with a style of his own, and those who see his plays can leave them with little or no sense of the author as a character. He is not, in fact, much concerned with individuality of any sort. This is not an adverse judgment; it is a distinction, or an attempt at one. What interests Miller and what he can often convey with force is the crushing impact of society upon its members. His human beings are always on the anvil, awaiting the hammer, and the act that landed him in his present trouble was an attempt to shield two or three of them from the blow. (It was, of course, a symbolic act, a gesture, for Miller knew very well that the committee knew all about the men he was asked to identify. He could not really shield; he could only assert the shielding principle.) What he was protecting was, in any case, a self-esteem that rested upon a social rule or principle or ethic.

One could almost say that Miller's sense of himself is the principle that holds "informing" to be the ultimate in human wickedness. It is certainly a recurrent theme in his writing. In *The Crucible*, his play about the Salem witchcraft trials, his own case is so strikingly paralleled as to lend color—though doubtless not truth—to the view that his performance in Washington was a case of life paying art the sincere flattery of imitation. To save his life, John Proctor, the hero, makes a compromise with the truth. He confesses, falsely, to having trafficked with Satan. "Did you see the Devil?" the prosecutor asks hims. "I did," Proctor says. He recognizes the character of his act, but this affects him little. "Good, then—it is evil, and I do it," he says to his wife, who is shocked. He has reasoned that a few more years on earth are worth his betrayal of his sense of himself. (It is not to be concluded that Proctor's concession to the mad conformity of the time parallels Miller's testimony, for Proctor had never in fact seen the Devil, whereas Miller had in fact seen Communists.) The prosecutor will not let him off with mere self-incrimination. He wants names; the names of those Proctor has seen with the Devil. Proctor refuses; does not balk at a self-serving lie, but a self-serving lie that involves others will not cross his lips. "I speak my own sins," he says, either metaphorically or hypocritically, since the sins in question are a fiction. "I cannot judge another. I have no tongue for it." He is hanged, a martyr.

In his latest play, *A View from the Bridge*, Miller returns to the theme, this time with immense wrath. He holds that conscience—indeed humanity itself—is put to the final test when a man is asked to "inform." Eddie, a longshoreman in the grip of a terrible passion for his teen-age niece, receives generous amounts of love and sympathy from those around him until his monstrous desire goads him into tipping off the Immigration officers to the illegal presence in his home of a pair of aliens. His lust for the child has had dreadful consequences for the girl herself, for the youth she wishes to marry, and for Eddie's wife. It has destroyed Eddie's sense of himself and made a brute of him. Yet up to the moment he "informs" he gets the therapy of affection and understanding from those he has hurt the most. But once he turns in the aliens, he is lost; he crosses the last threshold of iniquity. "In the garbage can he belongs," his wife says. "Nobody is gonna talk to him again if he lives to a hundred."

A *View from the Bridge* is not a very lucid play, and it may be that in it Miller, for all of his wrath, takes a somewhat less simple view of the problem of the informer than he does in *The Crucible*. There is a closing scene in which he appears to be saying that even this terrible transgression may be understood and dealt with in terms other than those employed by Murder, Incorporated. I think, though, that the basic principle for which Miller speaks is far commoner in Eddie's and our world than it could have been in John Proctor's. The morality that supports it is post-Darwinian. It is more available to those not bound by the Christian view of the soul's in-finite preciousness or of the body as a temple than it could have been to pre-Darwinian society. Today, in most Western countries, ethics derive mainly from society and almost all values are social. What we do to and with ourselves is thought to be our own affair and thus not, in most circumstances, a matter that involves morality at all. People will be found to say that suicide, for a man or woman with few obligations to others, should not be judged harshly, while the old sanctions on murder remain. Masochism is in one moral category, sadism in another. Masturbation receives a tolerance that fornication does not quite receive. A man's person and his "sense of him-self" are disposable assets, provided he chooses to see them that way; sin is only possible when we involve others. Thus, Arthur Miller's John Proctor was a modern man when, after lying about his relations with the Devil, he said, "God in heaven, what is John Proctor, what is John Proctor? I think it is honest, I think so. I am no saint." It is doubtful if anyone in the seventeenth century could have spoken that way. The real John Proctor surely thought he had an immortal soul, and if he had used the word "honest" at all, it would not have been in the sophisticated way in which Miller had him use it. He might have weakened sufficiently to lie about himself and the Devil, but he would surely not have said it was "honest" to do so or reasoned that it didn't really matter because he was only a speck of dust. He was speaking for the social ethic which is Arthur Miller's—and he resisted just where Miller did, at "informing."

It is, I think, useful to look rather closely at Miller's social ethic and at what he has been saying about the problems of conscience, for circumstances have conspired to make him the leading symbol of the militant, risk-taking conscience in this period. I do not wish to quarrel with the whole of his morality, for much of it I share—as do, I suppose, most people who have not found it possible to accept any of the revealed religions. Moreover, I believe, as Judge McLaughlin did, that the action Miller took before the committee was a courageous one.[2] Nevertheless, I think that behind the action and behind Miller's defense of it there is a certain amount of moral and political confusion. If I am right, then we ought to set about examining it, lest conscience and political morality come to be seen entirely in terms of "naming names"—a simplification which the House Un-American Activities Committee seems eager to foist upon us and which Miller, too, evidently accepts.

A healthy conscience, Miller seems to be saying, can stand anything but "informing." On the one hand, this seems a meager view of conscience. On the other, it makes little political sense and not a great deal of moral sense. Not all "informing" is bad, and not all of it is despised by the people who invariably speak of it as despicable. The question of guilt is

---

[2] Charles F. McLaughlin of United States District Court, Washington, D.C. Rovere's assumption about McLaughlin's opinion of Miller's courage is presumably based on the judge's statement: "However commendable may be regarded the motive of the defendant in refusing to disclose the identity or the official position of another with whom he was in association, lest said disclosure might bring trouble on him, that motive and that refusal have been removed from this court's consideration" (quoted in *The New York Times*, June 1, 1957, p.8).

relevant. My wife and I, for example, instruct our children not to tattle on one another. I am fairly certain, though, that if either of us saw a hit-and-run driver knock over a child or even a dog, we would, if we could, take down the man's license number and turn him in to the police. Even in the case of children, we have found it necessary to modify the rule so that we may be quickly advised if anyone is in serious danger of hurting himself or another. (The social principle again.) Proctor, I think, was not stating a fact when he said, "I cannot judge another"—nor was Miller when he said substantially the same thing. For the decision not to inform involves judging others. "They think to go like saints," Proctor said of those he claimed he could not judge, and Miller must have had something of the sort in mind about the writers he refused to discuss. He reasoned, no doubt, that their impulses were noble and that they had sought to do good in the world. We refuse to inform, I believe, either when we decide that those whose names we are asked to reveal are guilty of no wrong or when we perceive that what they have done is no worse than what we ourselves have often done. Wherever their offenses are clearly worse—as in the case of a hit-and-run driver or a spy or a thief—we drop the ban.

If the position taken by Miller were in all cases right, then it would seem wise to supplement the Fifth Amendment with one holding that no man could be required to incriminate another. If this were done, the whole machinery of law enforcement would collapse; it would be simply impossible to determine the facts about a crime. Of course, Congressional committees are not courts, and it might be held that such a rule would be useful in their proceedings. It would be useful only if we wished to destroy the investigative power. For we live, after all, in a community, in the midst of other people, and all of our problems—certainly all of those with which Congress has a legitimate concern—involve others. It is rarely possible to conduct a serious inquiry of any sort without talking about other people and without running the risk of saying something that would hurt them. We can honor the conscience that says, "I speak my own sins. I cannot judge another," but those of us who accept any principle of social organization and certainly those of us who believe that our present social order, whatever changes it may stand in need of, is worth preserving cannot make a universal principle of refusing to inform. If any agency of the community is authorized to undertake a serious investigation of any of our common problems, then the identities of others—*names* —are of great importance. What would be the point of investigating, say, industrial espionage if the labor spies subpoenaed refused to identify their employers? What would be the point of investigating the Dixon-Yates contract[3] if it were impossible to learn the identity of the businessmen and government officials involved?

The joker, the source of much present confusion, lies in the matter of *seriousness*. Miller and his attorneys have argued that the names of the writers Miller had known were not relevant to the legislation on passports the Committee was supposed to be studying. This would certainly seem to be the case, and one may regret that Judge McLaughlin did not accept this argument and acquit Miller on the strength of it. Nevertheless, the argument really fudges the central issue, which is that the Committee wasn't really investigating passport abuses at all when it called Miller before it. It was only pretending to do so. The rambling talk of its members with

---

[3] A contract having to do with the building of a power plant to supply electricity to the Atomic Energy Commission, presumably to reduce pressure on TVA facilities. The charges against the operation ranged from simple old-fashiond business corruption to an attempt to destroy public power in this country. The scandal became so noisome that President Eisenhower canceled the contract on July 11, 1955. The men who gave their names to the contract were Edgar H. Dixon, then president of Middle South Utilities of New York, and Eugene A. Yates, then board chairman of the Southern Company.

Miller was basically frivolous, and the Un-American Activities Committee has almost always lacked seriousness. In this case, as Mary McCarthy has pointed out,[4] the most that it wanted from Miller was to have him agree to its procedure of testing the good faith of witnesses by their willingness to produce names. It was on this that Miller was morally justified in his refusal.

Still, Miller's principle, the social ethic he was defending, cannot be made a universal rule or a political right. For it is one thing to say in the *New Republic* that a committee is frivolous or mischievous and another to assert before the law that such a judgment gives a witness the right to stand mute without being held in contempt. As matters stand today, Miller was plainly in contempt. At one point in *The Crucible*, John Proctor is called upon to justify his failure to attend the church of the Reverend Mr. Parris and to have his children baptized by that divine. He replies that he disapproves of the clergyman. "I see no light of God in that man," he says. "That is not for you to decide," he is told. "The man is ordained, therefore the light of God is in him." And this, of course, is the way the world is. In a free society, any one of us may arrive at and freely express a judgment about the competence of duly constituted authority. But in an orderly society, no one of us can expect the protection of the law whenever we decide that a particular authority is unworthy of our cooperation. We may stand by the decision, and we may seek the law's protection, but we cannot expect it as a matter of right. There are many courses of action that may have a sanction in morality and none whatever in law.

Yet the law is intended to be, among other things, a codification of morality, and we cannot be pleased with the thought that a man should be penalized for an act of conscience—even when his conscience may seem not as fully

---

4 See Bibliography.

informed by reason as it ought to be. In a much more serious matter, war, we excuse from participation those who say their consciences will permit them no part in it. One of the reasons the order of American society seems worth preserving is that it allows, on the whole, a free play to the individual's moral judgments. In recent years, Congressional committees have posed the largest single threat to this freedom. The issues have often been confused by the bad faith of witnesses on the one hand and committee members on the other. Still and all, the problem is a real one, as the Miller case shows. If there is not sufficient latitude for conscience in the law, then there ought to be. It would be unrealistic, I think, simply to permit anyone who chooses to withhold whatever information he chooses. The Fifth Amendment seems to go as far as is generally justified in this direction. Changes in committee procedures have often been urged, but it is doubtful if much clarification of a problem such as this can be written into rules and by-laws. The problem is essentially one of discretion and measurement; it is, in other words, the most difficult sort of problem and one of the kind that has, customarily, been dealt with by the establishment of broad and morally informed judicial doctrines. It is surely to be hoped that in the several cases, including Arthur Miller's, now in one stage or another of review, the courts will find a way of setting forth a realistic and workable charter for the modern conscience

ALBERT HUNT

Albert Hunt, an English schoolmaster, reviewed plays for *Encore* and other British magazines.

REALISM AND INTELLIGENCE:
SOME NOTES ON ARTHUR MILLER

When Arthur Miller's *The Crucible* was produced at the Royal Court four years ago—and, more recently, when it was revived on television—it was described by many critics as an anti-McCarthy tract.[1] The image of a small town caught up in the communal insanity of a witch hunt was, of course, a conscious reflection of the madness which swept through American society in the early fifties, and it was Miller's personal contact with this madness which brought the story of Salem alive for him in a new way. But it is misleading to think of *The Crucible* as being no more than a liberal tract. Several years after the fall of McCarthy, *The Crucible* remains a cogent and powerful statement about the destructive tensions of our own world. It is an intellectual affirmation made in directly passionate terms. And it is, in both conception and treatment, an important example of realist art.

Like most critical terms, the word realism is often used very loosely. Miller himself, in the preface to his *Collected Plays*[2] writes of it mainly as a style, or a technique. "Realism,"

From *Encore*, VII (May–June 1960), 12-17, 41.

[1] The Royal Court production, directed by George Devine, opened on April 9, 1956. The television production, directed by Henry Kaplan, was broadcast by Independent Television on November 3, 1959. Sean Connery was English TV's John Proctor, Susannah York, Abigail.

[2] See pp. 161-169.

he concludes, "is neither more nor less an artifice . . . than any other form. It is merely more familiar in this age. If it is used as a covering of safety against the evaluation of life it must be overthrown. . . ." This is clearly true of any technique. "Genius," wrote Balzac, "consists in throwing light on every situation by words, and not in muffling the personages in phrases which might apply to anything." The charge of muffling can be levelled both at the flat, contrived exchanges which pass for realistic dialogue in Maugham and Rattigan,[3] and at the soft cocoon of words in which Christopher Fry wraps *his* witch hunt in *The Lady's Not for Burning*.

But realism is, I believe, much more than a technique, although it leads to a number of technical problems. Perhaps the best definition is Eric Bentley's: "the candid presentation of the natural world. An increasing closeness to objective facts; special techniques for their reproduction; an empirical outlook —these are realism."[4] It is this empirical outlook which, more than anything else, forms the basis of realism. Realism is distorted when, instead of reacting to his experience of reality, the artist imposes his own simplified formula on reality. This is what Rattigan does. He has a set of counters representing human emotions which he arranges in the right pattern to produce the mechanical response. The surface trappings of realism are there, but the stuff of life—the complex struggle between external reality and the writer's creative intelligence —is missing. Even when such a play deals with an urgent theme, the result is, in the end, trivial.

There is, however, the other side to the equation. For realism is not simply the accurate recording of objective facts. The tape-recorder, left haphazardly in the corner of a room,

---

[3] Somerset Maugham, of course, and Terence Rattigan. A good example of Rattigan's "realism" is *Separate Tables* (1958).

[4] "Realism embraces all writing in which the natural world is candidly presented," wrote Eric Bentley in *The Playwright as Thinker* (Cleveland: Meridian Books, 1955), p. 3.

does not produce significant theatre, and the move from draw-ing-room to sweaty bed-sitter is, in itself, valuable only in so far as it represents a more open approach to experience. The danger is that we shall confuse reality with the Salford slum. Realism demands not only an empirical outlook, but a shaping intelligence, a capacity to evaluate life by an imaginative scrutiny of the processes of living. The writer must react to experience; but he must transform that experience into a mean-ingful statement. Arthur Miller is important because he offers us the spectacle of a powerful mind struggling to come to artistic terms with the complex reality of modern society. He is not always successful—but he never "settles for half."

The Crucible, written in 1952, is the third of Miller's major plays. It comes after *All My Sons* and *Death of a Salesman*, but before the disturbing, and yet somehow unsatisfactory, *A View from the Bridge*. For Miller, the central problem of our society is one of consciousness, the inability to connect personal and social values. In *All My Sons*, Miller achieves this connection by showing the developing consciousness of Joe Keller. The social consequences of his actions are brought home to him by the collapse of his personal life, so that when, at the end of the play, he says, "Sure, he was my son. But I think to him they were all my sons. And I guess they were, I guess they were," the naturalistic language has an intensity of feeling which makes it do far more work than the words themselves suggest. "The fiat for intense language is intensity of action," Miller has written. Here the language is simple, but the situation is so intense that the simplicity is explosive. It is interesting to compare the end of *All My Sons* with the last scene in *Roots*. Arnold Wesker is the only one of our new realists who seems to me to be working on the same level as Miller and the theme of *Roots* is the awakening of Beatie's consciousness. For most of the play, she is repeating a lifeless formula, but in this final scene, Ronnie's values be-come her own personal experience. Yet, moving though this scene is, it is not entirely convincing. Beatie's discovery is like a religious conversion, and is the result of one traumatic shock she receives nearly at the end of the play. Joe Keller's awakening, on the other hand, is the last stage of a relentlessly developing situation. It is as if a broken mirror is slowly pieced together, so that at last he sees the full, horrifying image of himself as he really is. Beatie's language is more lyrical, more intense, but it is Joe Keller who becomes more deeply articulate.

The form of *All My Sons* is that of the well-made naturalistic play, and the family relationships are rooted in a world of concrete experience. In his second play, *Death of a Salesman*, Miller abandons surface naturalism, and turns towards his own form of expressionism. Keller has the past gradually forced upon him; for Willy Loman, past and present co-exist in his head. But the balance between real experience and Miller's shaping intelligence is not always kept, so that Loman is not completely realised as a person (as Raymond Williams has pointed out, it is the Salesman rather than Willy who remains the dominating image).[5] The woman in the hotel bedroom, for example, is one of the crucial figures in the breakdown of Willy's life—but Miller has never imagined her as a human being deserving attention, and she remains a stock symbol, so that the whole of Willy's relationship with her is conducted on a purely formula level. Again, Uncle Ben is simply a success symbol, the bodiless extension of Willy's subjective mind. On the other hand, in the scenes in which Willy's false consciousness—and the false consciousness it has produced in his own sons—leads him to a failure of concrete relationships with people who really exist around him, the play is intensely and immediately alive (the weaknesses and

---

[5] See Raymond Williams, "The Realism of Arthur Miller," *Critical Quarterly*, I (Summer 1959), pp. 140-49. Hunt's ideas of realism owe something to the Williams article.

strengths of the play are there together in the scene where Willy's sons, who have invited him out to dinner, desert him for a couple of tarts). *Death of a Salesman* is a powerful but uneven play, which reveals a certain amount of unresolved conflict between concept and form.

In *A View from the Bridge*, Miller takes a character who never becomes fully articulate. The crisis which suddenly unveils Eddie's incestuous and homosexual desires, is never, within the framework of the story, fully understood by Eddie himself. He knows only that he has lost something, his "name" —and for this he finally sacrifices himself. To present this character, Miller uses a device "to separate openly, and without concealment, the action of the . . . play from its generalised significance." He introduces the "engaged narrator" in the person of Eddie's lawyer. "Something perversely pure calls me from his memory," says Alquieri[6] in his closing speech, "not purely good, but himself purely, for he allowed himself to be wholly known." But it is Miller's fear that Eddie has *not* "allowed himself to be wholly known," which leads him to set a commentator between the audience and the action. In this play, Miller faces the central problem of modern realism—the difficulty of giving meaning to a fragment of modern life without violating the unique quality of that life. *The Crucible* comments on modern fragmentation by withdrawing to the vantage point of a community which is whole and self-aware.

The Crucible tells the story of the Salem witch hunt. When the play opens, a group of young girls, including the Minister Parris's own daughter, have been conjuring spirits in the forest. Two of them are in a hypnotic trance. A religious expert in witchcraft is called in ("Now let me instruct you. We cannot look to superstition in this. The Devil is precise"), and soon the girls, in a state of revivalist enthusiasm, are calling out

[6] Alfieri.

the names of people they have seen with the Devil. A court is set up. At first only the riff-raff are named, but gradually the circle widens as social feuds become entangled with personal emotions, and presently Elizabeth Proctor, a cold, harsh Puritan, is framed by one of the girls (Abigail), whom she has dismissed from her service after finding her in adultery with her husband, John Proctor. Proctor, supported by a tough old individualist, Giles Corey, takes it on himself to oppose the court. He persuades one of the girls, Mary Warren, to confess that it is all a fraud, and by admitting his adultery with Abigail, tries to discredit her as a witness. But Elizabeth, called in to confirm his testimony, lies for the only time in her life, and Mary is once again contaminated by hysteria. After this, Proctor himself is condemned. The last act deals with the struggle of his conscience. To escape the gallows, he has only to confess that he is in league with the Devil. Is not life, he reasons, like Brecht's Galileo, worth a compromise? "Let Rebecca go like a saint; for me it is a fraud!" But, finally, he tears up his confession. "You have made your magic now, for now I do think I see some shred of goodness in John Proctor. Not enough to weave a banner with, but white enough to keep it from such dogs."

A summary can do no justice to the richness and complexity of the play. Sartre's film version, which turned it into a projection of the class struggle, kept some of the power, but lost the depth of the original.[7] For Miller sees this community, not as an abstraction, but as a totality. Compare, for instance, Anouilh's *Antigone*. Anouilh uses the Greek legend simply as a peg for contemporary ideas. Creon and Antigone are modern creatures, abstracted from any real social context. They play out their tragedy in a vacuum; nobody is concerned, nobody is involved. Cut off from its social roots, Antigone's choice amounts to a Romantic death-wish (in the original

---

[7] For Sartre film, see pp. 423-426.

Sophocles, the tragedy is alive with the real issue of obedience to the law).

John Proctor stands four-square in his own time and place. This is not to say that his story is historically accurate. It is one of the fallacies of our pseudo-realism that historical accuracy is the same as reality (*Sink the Bismarck*[8] is the latest example). But Proctor is real because he stands at the heart of all the complex tensions of the Salem community. He is totally involved as a human being: socially, as a farmer in a farming community who, against his will, is caught up in the town's factions; intellectually, because his mind rejects the insanity of the witch hunt; emotionally, because he is linked with that insanity through his adultery with Abigail; morally, because this adultery is not just a sin against the community, but a sin against his own conscience, so that his death becomes, more than a pointlessly heroic gesture, a rediscovery of his own goodness.

To achieve this sense of reality, Miller uses a heightened naturalism. Perhaps this is what he has in mind when he writes, "To write a realistic play of that world was already to write in a style beyond contemporary realism." But within this closed world, action follows action, crisis follows crisis with a natural logic. The language is formal, but its formality is rooted in human speech patterns and it expresses precisely at every step what Miller intends it to express. As in *All My Sons*, some of the most powerful statements are made in the simplest language. "But, woman," cries Hale to Elizabeth, "you do believe there are witches in . . ." and she replies, "If you think that I am one, then I say there are none." It is a passionate, but basically simple statement. Giles Corey, with stones on his chest, says, "More weight." And Elizabeth provides the play's final comment, as Proctor goes to the gallows:

---

[8] This film, made in England by Twentieth Century-Fox, was released in both England and the United State in February 1960.

"He have his goodness now. God forbid I take it from him!" There is a purity about the language which gives it great tragic power.

The most immediately powerful scene in the play is the one in which Mary Warren tries to expose the fraud. Again, everything that happens is realistic, but it is a realism which takes into account the fact that delusions too are real to those who hold them, and can change a given reality. As Mary testifies, the other girls fix their eyes on the ceiling. Mary has become a bird trying to possess them. Presently, she *does* possess them. Everything she says is repeated, horrifyingly, in chorus by the girls, until Mary's own mind is broken down, and she herself is screaming at the ceiling. As Proctor repeats, "Mary, tell the Governor," she turns on him and shrieks, "You're the Devil's man!" Reason and intelligence are powerless before this outburst of human darkness. Proctor penetrates to the heart of our own, human situation when he declares, "I hear the boot of Lucifer, I see his filthy face! And it is my face and yours, Danforth! We will burn, we will burn together!" Like Joe Keller's "they're all my sons," this is not just an abstract argument. It is a real and personal truth, forced out of concrete, human experience.

Proctor comments on our own situation, not by aping our ideas, but by *being*: the comment is all the more immediate because of Miller's intense and lucid concentration on the past. And it is this objective concentration which makes *The Crucible* a work in the realist tradition—and suggests that Miller's own conception of realism is much too narrow.

For Miller's realism is something much more fundamental than "an artifice." It is the essence of his vision, and his experiments in form have been attempts to purify that vision. Faced with the shallowness of a Rattigan, many critics have come to the conclusion that realism itself is played out, and that the only way forward is through some self-conscious formal experiment. For Eliot, the solution was a return to verse drama, but his only real success was *Murder in the Cathedral,* in which the liturgical material was naturally linked with the verse form. For Brecht, epic drama provided the answer, and certainly opened up new possibilities. But a wholesale application of Brecht's theories, divorced from his vision, can only lead back to a fresh formalism.

"Neither poetry nor liberation," writes Miller, "can come merely from a rearrangement of the lights, or from leaving the skeletons of the flats exposed instead of covered by painted cloths; nor can it come merely from the masking of the human face or the transformation of speech into rhythmic verse, or from the expunging of common details of life's apparencies. A new poem on the stage is a new concept of relationships between the one and the many and the many and history, and to create it requires greater attention, not less, to the inexorable, common, pervasive conditions of existence in this time and this hour."

Miller's importance lies in the quality of his attention. To make people feel is, as John Osborne sees it, the basic problem confronting the British theatre. Our audiences, like Archie Rice, are "dead behind these eyes."[9] But if the success of *Look Back in Anger* proves that feeling *is* possible in our theatre, the failure of *Paul Slickey* suggests that feeling itself is not enough. The feeling is there in *Paul Slickey,* but it is unorganised and ends in impotence. In Miller, the feeling is directed by a ruthless intelligence, and it is this intelligence, pressing on the "conditions of existence in this time and this hour," which makes him a major figure in contemporary theatre.

---

[9] Rice is the protagonist of Osborne's *The Entertainer* and the words are his own (New York: Criterion Books, 1958, p. 72). *The World of Paul Slickey,* which opened in London on May 5, 1959, was the most recent Osborne play when Hunt wrote his article.

GERALD WEALES

ARTHUR MILLER:
MAN AND HIS IMAGE

He's got his stance, he's got his pace, he's got his control down to a pinpoint. He's almost original sometimes. When it comes to throwin' a ball, he's all there.
—Augie Belfast in *The Man Who Had All the Luck*

Arthur Miller is one of those playwrights, like Thornton Wilder, whose reputation rests on a handful of plays. The quality of that reputation changes from year to year, from critic to critic, but now, five years after the production of his most recent play (the revision of *A View from the Bridge*), it is generally conceded, even by those who persist in not admiring his work, that Miller is one of the two playwrights of the post-war American theatre who deserve any consideration as major dramatists. Tennessee Williams is the other.

There are many ways of approaching Miller's work. In the late forties, after *All My Sons* and *Death of a Salesman*, popular reviewers tended to embrace him enthusiastically, while consciously intellectual critics, displaying the carefulness of their kind, hoped that in explaining him they might explain him away. For a time, his plays were lost in discussions of the author's politics, past and present, or were buried beneath the pointless academic quibble about whether or not they are true tragedies. Miller's own defensiveness on these two points helped

From *American Drama Since World War II* by Gerald Weales (New York: Harcourt, Brace & World, 1962), pp. 3-17. Copyright © 1962 by Gerald Weales. Reprinted by permission of Harcourt, Brace Jovanovich, Inc.

feed the controversy. In the last few years, however, with no new Miller play to stir up opinion, his work has begun to be considered outside the immediate context that produced it.

Even so, there is no single handle by which to grasp his works. Because each of his four chief plays is built on a family situation—*Sons* and *Salesman* on the father-son conflict, *The Crucible* and *View* on the triangle—the plays can be treated as domestic dramas. Because they obviously criticize or comment upon the structure of society, they may be considered conventional social plays; still, as Eric Bentley has pointed out,[1] noting the chief motivating force in most of the plots, they are as much sexual as social dramas. There are probably enough biographical reflections in the plays to send the psychological critic in search of personal analogies; Maurice Zolotow, for instance, interrupts the psycho-anecdotage of *Marilyn Monroe* long enough to point out that both *Crucible* and *View* deal with marital problems caused by the attraction of an older man to a younger woman and to suggest that they stem from the fact that the author could not get Miss Monroe out of his mind between his first meeting with her in 1950 and his marriage to her in 1956.

Any of these approaches, even Zolotow's, may manage to say something valid about Miller's plays. To me, however, the most profitable way of looking at his work is through his heroes and through the concern of each, however inarticulate, with his identity—his *name*, as both John Proctor and Eddie Carbone call it. Perhaps the simplest way to get at what Miller is doing in these plays is to force a path through the confounding prose of his general comments on contemporary drama and on the kind of play he hopes he has written. Although his opinions on the nature of drama are scattered through interviews, introduc-

---

[1] Eric Bentley, "Theatre," *New Republic*, CXXXIII (December 19, 1955), 22. This (pp. 21-22) is his review of *A View from the Bridge*.

tions, and occasional articles for *The New York Times,* the bulk
of his theoretical writing is contained in four essays: "On Social
Plays," printed as an introduction to A *View from the Bridge*
(1955); "The Family in Modern Drama," originally a lecture
given at Harvard (*Atlantic Monthly,* April 1956); Introduction
to the *Collected Plays* (1957); "The Shadows of the Gods"
(*Harper's,* August 1958). Although each of these essays has a
particular job to do, a recurring idea about the possibilities of
modern drama seeps through the ponderousness of all of them,
climbs over the barriers of Miller's Germanic fondness for definition and redefinition. For Miller, the serious playwright writes
social drama, but that genre, for him, is not simply "an arraignment of society's evils." Just as he refuses to accept the standard
definition of the social play, a product of the thirties, so too he
rejects the drama which he sees as most representative of contemporary American theatre, the play in which the characters
retreat into self-preoccupation and give little hint that there is a
society outside themselves. The true social drama, the "Whole
Drama," as he calls it, must recognize that man has both a
subjective and an objective existence, that he belongs not only
to himself and his family, but to the world beyond.

Since Miller's plays were written before these essays were, it
is probably safe to assume that the theorizing is *ex post facto*
in more ways than one, and that his general conclusions about
the drama are based, in part, on what he thinks he has done
as a playwright; his ready use of *Salesman* as an example
strengthens such an assumption. I have no trouble accepting his
belief that the best of drama has always dealt with man in both
a personal and a social context, but his generalizations are most
useful as approaches to his own work. His plays are family-
centered, obviously, because our drama the last few years has
been uncomfortable in any context larger than the family; his
heroes, however, are more than failed husbands and fathers
because he has recognized that the most impressive family plays,

from *Oedipus* through *Hamlet* to *Ghosts,* have modified the concept of the family and of the individual under the pressure of society.

Each of his heroes is involved, in one way or another, in a struggle that results from his acceptance or rejection of an image that is the product of his society's values and prejudices, whether that society is as small as Eddie Carbone's neighborhood or as wide as the contemporary America that helped form Willy Loman. Miller's work has followed such a pattern from the beginning. Even Ben, the hero of *They Too Arise,* a now happily forgotten prizewinner from the mid-thirties, has to decide whether he is to be the man that his middle-class, small-businessman father expects or the comrade that his radical brother demands; the play ends, of course, in leftist affirmation, but the conflict has been in terms of opposed images, both of which are assumed to have validity for Ben. The hero of *The Man Who Had All the Luck* (1944), Miller's first produced play, accepts the town's view of him as a man who has succeeded through luck not ability; he assumes that all luck must turn and, in his obsession, almost brings disaster on his head until his wife convinces him that he should reject the town's rationalizing bromide and accept the principle that man makes his own luck. In his novel *Focus* (1945), a fantasy-tract, his anti-Semitic hero finally accepts the label that his neighbors force on him; he admits that he is a Jew. Most of Miller's short stories reflect the same kind of preoccupation with the self that someone else expects the hero to be; in one of his most recent stories, "I Don't Need You Any More" (*Esquire,* December 1959), the five-year-old hero's idea of himself is formed on half-understood perceptions picked up from his parents and the adult world they live in, the only society that he recognizes outside himself. The lament and the longing implicit in Martin's thought—"If only he *looked* like his father and his brother!"—is a small echo of the bewilderment that haunts all the Miller heroes who do the right things and come to the wrong ends.

In *All My Sons* (1947), Miller's first successful play, Joe Keller, who is admittedly a good husband and a good father, fails to be the good man, the good citizen that his son Chris demands. "I'm his father and he's my son, and if there's something bigger than that I'll put a bullet in my head!" Chris makes clear that, for him, there is something bigger than the family, and Joe commits suicide. Much more interesting than the unmasking and punishment of Joe's crime (he shipped out cracked cylinder heads during the war and let his partner take the blame and go to jail) is Joe as a peculiarly American product. He is a self-made man, a successful businessman "with the imprint of the machine-shop worker and boss still upon him." There is nothing ruthless about Joe, no hint of the robber baron in his make-up; his ambitions are small—a comfortable home for his family, a successful business to pass on to his sons —but he is not completely fastidious in achieving his goals. Not only has he accepted the American myth of the primacy of the family, his final excuse for all his actions, but he has adopted as a working instrument the familiar attitude that there is a difference between morality and business ethics. Not that he could ever phrase it that way. "I'm in business, a man is in business . . ." he begins his explanation, his plea for understanding, and moves on to that dimly lit area where the other man's culpability is his forgiveness.

When Miller at last moves in on Joe, brings Chris and discovery to destroy him, there is no longer any possibility of choice. His fault, according to Miller and Chris, is that he does not recognize any allegiance to society at large; his world, as he mistakenly says of that of his dead son Larry, "had a forty-foot front, it ended at the building line." Joe's shortness of vision, however, is a product of his society. Even Chris shares his goals: "If I have to grub for money all day long at least at evening I want it beautiful. I want a family, I want some kids, I want to build something I can give myself to." The neighbors, in the figure of Sue, respect Joe's methods: "They give him credit for being smart." At the end of the play, finally confronted with another alternative ("But I think to him they were all my sons"), Joe Keller, in killing himself, destroys the image that he has accepted.

There is a disturbing patness about *All My Sons*, an exemplary working out of the conflict that is as didactic as Chris's more extended speeches. With *Death of a Salesman* (1949), Miller escapes into richness. The ambiguity that occasionally touches the characters in the earlier play, that makes the supposedly admirable idealist son sound at times like a hanging judge, suffuses the playwright's second success, his finest play. It might be possible to reduce the play to some kind of formula, to suggest that Biff's end-of-the-play declaration, "I know who I am, Kid," is a positive statement, a finger pointing in some verifiable direction, a refutation of all the beliefs to which Willy clings and for which he dies. Miller suggests, in his Introduction to the *Collected Plays*, that Biff does embody an "opposing system" to the "law of success" which presumably kills Willy, but there are almost as many contradictions in Miller's Introduction as there are in his play. Since the last scene, the "Requiem," is full of irony—Charley's romantic eulogy of the Salesman, Linda's failure to understand ("I made the last payment on the house today. . . . We're free and clear"), Happy's determination to follow in his father's failed footsteps—there is no reason to assume that some of the irony does not rub off on Biff. We have been with the lying Lomans so long, have seen them hedge their bets and hide their losses in scene after self-deluding scene, that it is at least forgivable if we respect Willy's integrity as a character (if not as a man) and suspect that Biff is still his son. The play, after all, ends with the funeral; there is no sequel.

When we meet Willy Loman, he, like Joe Keller, is past the

point of choice, but his play tells us that there are at least three
will-o'-the-wisp ideals—father figures, all—that Willy might
have chosen to follow. The first is his own father, the inventor,
the flute maker, the worker-with-his-hands, who walked away
one day and left the family to shift for itself. His is the flute
melody that opens the play, "small and fine, telling of grass and
trees and the horizon." From what we hear of him, he was a
man who did not make his fortune because he did not know
that a fortune was a thing worth making and, if his desertion
of his family means anything, he needed the world's good
opinion as little as he needed its idea of conventional success.
The chances of Willy's going the way of his father are as dead
as the frontier, of course; so when the flute appears in the play
it is no more than a suggestion of a very vague might-have-been.
Nor is the second possible choice, that embodied in the figure
of Ben, a likely one for Willy; it is difficult to imagine him
among the business buccaneers. For that reason, perhaps, Miller
has chosen to make a comic caricature of Ben: "Why, boys,
when I was seventeen I walked into the jungle, and when I was
twenty-one I walked out. And by God I was rich." Ben, with
his assurance, his ruthlessness ("Never fight fair with a stranger,
boy"), his connections in Africa and Alaska, looms a little larger
than life in Willy's mind, half cartoon, half romance. There is
romance enough—liberally laced with sentiment—in the ideal
that Willy does choose, Dave Singleman, the old salesman who,
at eighty-four, could, through the strength of his personality,
sit in a hotel room and command buyers. Willy admires Singleman for dying "the death of a salesman, in his green velvet
slippers in the smoker of the New York, New Haven and
Hartford," without ever recognizing that there is more than one
way to kill a salesman.

Willy can no more be Dave Singleman than he can be his
father or his brother Ben. From the conflicting success images
that wander through his troubled brain comes Willy's double
ambition—to be rich and to be loved. As he tells Ben, "the

wonder of this country [is] that a man can end with diamonds here on the basis of being liked!" From Andrew Carnegie, then, to Dale Carnegie. Willy's faith in the magic of "personal attractiveness" as a way to success carries him beyond cause and effect to necessity; he assumes that success falls inevitably to the man with the right smile, the best line, the most charm, the man who is not only liked, but well liked. He has completely embraced the American myth, born of the advertisers, that promises us love and a fortune as soon as we clear up our pimples, stop underarm perspiration, learn to play the piano; for this reason, the brand names that turn up in Willy's speeches are more than narrow realism. He regularly confuses labels with reality. In his last scene with Biff, Willy cries out, "I am not a dime a dozen! I am Willy Loman, and you are Biff Loman!" The strength and the pathos of that cry lie in the fact that Willy still thinks that the names should mean something; it is effective within the play because we have heard him imply that a punching bag is good because "It's got Gene Tunney's signature on it," and that a city can be summed up in a slogan—"Big clock city, the famous Waterbury clock."

The distance between the actual Willy and Willy as image is so great when the play opens that he can no longer lie to himself with conviction; what the play gives us is the final disintegration of a man who has never even approached his idea of what by rights he ought to have been. His ideal may have been the old salesman in his green velvet slippers, but his model is that mythic figure, the traveling salesman of the dirty joke. Willy tries to be a kidder, a caution, a laugh-a-minute; he shares his culture's conviction that personality is a matter of mannerism and in the sharing develops a style that is compounded of falseness, the mock assurance of what Happy calls "the old humor, the old confidence." His act, however, is as much for himself as it is for his customers. The play shows quite clearly that from the beginning of his career Willy has lied about the size of his sales, the warmth of his reception, the number of his friends. It is true that he occasionally doubts himself, assumes that he is too noisy and undignified, that he is not handsome enough ("I'm fat. I'm very—foolish to look at"), but usually he rationalizes his failure. His continuing self-delusion and his occasional self-awareness serve the same purpose; they keep him from questioning the assumptions that lie beneath his failure and his pretense of success. By the time we get to him, his struggle to hold on to his dream (if not for himself, then for his sons) has become so intense that all control is gone; past and present are one to him, and so are fact and fiction. A suggestion becomes a project completed; a possibility becomes a dream fulfilled. When Biff tries to give him peace by making him realize, and accept the realization, that he is a failure and a mediocrity and see that it makes no difference, Willy hears only what he wants to hear. He takes Biff's tears not only as an evidence of love, which they are, but as a kind of testimonial, an assurance that Willy's way has been the right one all along. Once again secure in his dream ("that boy is going to be magnificent"), he goes to his suicide's death, convinced that, with the insurance money, Biff will be—to use Willy's favorite nouns—a hero, a prince.

Joe Keller and Willy Loman find ready-made societal images to attach themselves to and both become victims of the attachment. Society is not nearly so passive in Miller's next play, *The Crucible* (1953). Salem tries to force John Proctor to accept a particular image of himself, but he chooses to die. Although there are occasional voices in the earlier plays (the neighbors in *All My Sons*, the bartender in *Death of a Salesman*) who speak for society, Miller operates for the most part on the assumption that his audience knows and shares the ideas that work on the Kellers and the Lomans. He cannot be that certain in *The Crucible*. Whether we are to accept his Salem as historical or as an analogy for the United States in the early fifties, Miller needs to create a mood of mass hysteria in which guilt and confession become public virtues. For this reason, Proctor is not so intensively on stage as the protagonists of the earlier plays are; the playwright has to work up a setting for him, has to give his attention to the accusers, the court, the town.

Now that Joe McCarthy is dead and Roy Cohn is running Lionel trains,[2] it has become customary to consider *The Crucible* outside the context in which it was written. Since the play is not simply a tract, there is good sense in that attitude; whatever value the play comes to have will be intrinsic. Still, there is something to be learned about John Proctor from Arthur Miller's opinions at the time the play was written. About six months after the play was produced, the *Nation* (July 3, 1954) published Miller's "A Modest Proposal for Pacification of the Public Temper," a not very successful attempt at Swiftian satire. What the piece does do is make quite clear that Miller believed that the America of that moment, like the Salem of his play, was going in for a kind of group therapy that demanded each man's *mea culpa*. It would be simple enough to dissect Miller's use of Salem and to show, as so many critics have, that the Massachusetts witch hunts are not analogous to the postwar Communist hunts, but such an exercise is finally beside the point. The important thing is that Miller found Salem both relevant and dramatically useful. A resurrection of the political situation at this time is valuable only because it is quite obvious that Miller's involvement with that situation dictated his treatment of the material. I am not thinking of the villainous Danforth, the ambitious Parris, the greedy Putnam, the envious Abigail, each of whom uses the cryings-out to his own advantage, although Miller was plainly intent on questioning the sincerity of accusers and investigators in general. It is John Proctor who shows most clearly Miller's attitude. His hero

---

[2] McCarthy died in 1957. In October 1959, Cohn and a group of associates, with money borrowed in Hong Kong and Panama, gained control of the Lionel Corporation, of which Lionel Toys was a subsidiary. Cohn did not become chief executive until March 1962; no longer in control, he resigned as director in November 1963.

might have been another Willy Loman, another Joe Keller, an accepter not a defier of society, and his play would have had just as much—perhaps more—propaganda value. There is such a character in the play—the Reverend John Hale, the witch expert, who breaks under the strain of the trials—and one can make a good case for Hale as the protagonist of *The Crucible*. Although Hale is a much more interesting character than Proctor, it is Proctor's play and here Miller has produced, as he has not in his earlier plays, a romantic hero. It seems likely that Miller's opposition to the investigations and particularly to the form they took, the ritual naming of names, made him want a conventional hero, not, as usual, a victim-hero. When he appeared before the House Committee on Un-American Activities in June 1956, there was dignity in his refusal to give names, in his willingness to describe his past without apologizing for it, in his simple, "I accept my life." Ironically, not even Elizabeth's "He have his goodness now" can make Proctor's dignity convincing. The simplicity of the real situation is impossible on stage. Miller's need to push Proctor to his heroic end causes him to bring to *The Crucible* too many of the trappings of the standard romantic play; the plot turns on that moment in court when Elizabeth, who has never lied before, lies out of love of her husband and condemns him by that act. This is a sentimental mechanism almost as outrageous as the hidden-letter trick in the last act of *All My Sons*. There is excitement enough in the scene to hold an audience, but the attention that such a device demands is quite different from that required by John Proctor's struggle of conscience.

Although Proctor is never completely successful as a character, Miller makes a real effort to convince us that he is more than the blunt, not so bright good man he appears to be; and once again Miller works in terms of societal concepts. The Proctor who appears in the novelistic notes that Miller has sprinkled through the text of the published play is not quite the Proctor of the play itself; but there are similarities. We are to assume that Proctor is a solid man, but an independent one, not a man to fit lightly into anyone else's mold. When we meet him, however, he is suffering under a burden of guilt—intensified by his belief that Elizabeth is continually judging him. Miller makes it clear that in sleeping with Abigail Williams, Proctor has become "a sinner not only against the moral fashion of the time, but against his own vision of decent conduct." In Act III, when he admits in open court that he is a lecher, he says, "A man will not cast away his good name." When he is finally faced with the choice of death or confession (that he consorted with the Devil), his guilt as an adulterer becomes confused with his innocence as a witch; one sin against society comes to look like another, or so he rationalizes. In the last act, however, Elizabeth in effect absolves him of the sin of adultery, gives him back the name he lost in court, and clears the way for him to reject the false confession and to give his life: "How may I live without my name?"[3]

Eddie Carbone in *A View from the Bridge* (1955; revised 1956) also dies crying out for his name, but when he asks Marco to "gimme my name" he is asking for a lie that will let him live and, failing that, for death. Eddie is unusual among the Miller heroes in that he accepts the rules and prejudices of his society, an Italian neighborhood in Brooklyn, and dies because he violates them. Early in the play, Eddie warns Catherine to be closemouthed about the illegal immigrants (the "submarines") who are coming to live with them; he tells her with approbation about the brutal punishment meted out to an informer. By the end of the play, the "passion that had moved

---

[3] Miller's use of "name" in *The Crucible* is more complicated and more interesting than my discussion above suggests. Abigail is also worried about her "name" in the first scene with her uncle, a conventional usage (reputation) that contrasts with Proctor's final use of the word. Consider, too, the implications of the emphasis on signing in the light of all the Devil's book talk, particularly Mary Warren's hysterical lie in Act III, "He come at me by night and every day to sign, to sign, to—"

into his body, like a stranger," as Alfieri calls it, so possesses Eddie that to rid himself of the presence of Rodolpho he is willing to commit an act that he abhors as much as his society does. Miller's own comments on the play and the lines that he gives to Alfieri, a cross between the Greek chorus and Mary Worth, indicate that he sees Eddie in the grip of a force that is almost impersonal in its inevitability, its terribleness, "the awesomeness of a passion which . . . despite even its destruction of the moral beliefs of the individual, proceeds to magnify its power over him until it destroys him." The action in *View* seems to me somewhat more complicated than the clean line Miller suggests; its hero is more than a leaf blown along on winds out of ancient Calabria. Eddie chooses to become an informer; his choice is so hedged with rationalization—his convincing himself that Rodolpho is homosexual, that he is marrying Catherine for citizenship papers—that he is never conscious of his motivation. He comes closer and closer to putting a label on his incestuous love for Catherine (although technically she is his niece, functionally she is his daughter) and his homosexual attraction to Rodolpho (how pathetically he goes round and round to keep from saying *queer*). By comparison, informing is a simpler breach of code, one that has justification in the world outside the neighborhood. It is almost as though he takes on the name *informer* to keep from wearing some name that is still more terrible to him, only to discover that he cannot live under the lesser label either.

"It is not enough any more to know that one is at the mercy of social pressures," Miller writes in "On Social Plays"; "it is necessary to understand that such a sealed fate cannot be accepted." Each of his four heroes is caught in a trap compounded of social and psychological forces and each one is destroyed. Miller is concerned that their deaths not be dismissed as insignificant, the crushing of little men by big forces. His description of Eddie Carbone expresses his opinion of all his heroes: "he possesses or exemplifies the wondrous and humane fact that he too can be driven to what in the last analysis is a sacrifice of himself for his conception, however misguided, of right, dignity, and justice."

Playwrights, however, have always been better at telling men how to die than how to live. A dramatist in opposition is always more comfortable than one in affirmation. When Miller chooses to be a social critic, in the old-fashioned sense, it is apparent what he is against. Although he disavows any blanket attack on capitalism, both *Salesman* and *Sons* contain explicit criticism of a business-oriented society in which corruption, selfishness, indifference, are the norms. The political and governmental targets are obvious enough in *Crucible*; in *View* there is an implicit condemnation of a social system that turns men into submarines. Back in the childhood of his career as a playwright, the days of *They Too Arise*, Miller might have been able to conceive of some kind of political action as a cure for such societal wrongs, but it has become increasingly clear that his concern is with personal morality, the individual's relation to a society in which the virtuous goals (Joe Keller's sense of family, Willy Loman's idea of success) are almost as suspect as the vicious methods. When there is a concrete situation, a problem like that of Joe Keller's cylinder heads, Miller has no difficulty; who in the audience is going to suggest that Keller was right in sending them out? It is with those other alternatives—the ones embedded in generalizations—that the trouble arises.

Biff can say, at the end of *Death of a Salesman*, "He had the wrong dreams," but we have seen enough of Willy to know that for this man there is probably no right dream. Still, Biff suggests that there is: "There's more of him in that front stoop than in all the sales he ever made." And Charley seems to agree: "He was a happy man with a batch of cement." The play is filled with references to Willy's pride in working with his hands, his desire for a garden. This theme that so pervades *Salesman* is hit glancingly in some of the other plays, in John

Proctor's obvious love for his farm and in Eddie Carbone's
pleasure in working a shipload of coffee. Smell, touch, taste, the
physical contact between a man and his work, a man and the
thing created—this is at least part of the alternative. It is a
sentimental possibility, a compounding of two quasi-literary
myths—the thirties' insistence on the dignity of labor coupled
with the older back-to-nature idea. Reduced to its simplest, it
is the respectable commonplace that a man is happiest doing
work that he likes.

The rest of the "right dream" is not so concrete. It has to do
with the relation of one man to another (a man to society,
Miller might say), but it can only be defined in terms of the
great words, the words that we use on state occasions. The
fascination of Miller's plays is that he knows so well the way
a society edits the meaning of the grand abstractions and forces
(or entices) men to embrace them. Implicit in his work, however, is the possibility of a society that might not lead the
Willys of this world astray. In *Situation Normal*, a volume of
reportage that grew out of his army-camp research for the movie
The Story of G.I. Joe, Miller insists that the main purpose of
the book is to find the Belief (he uses the capital letter) that is
sending men into war. When he finds it ("And that Belief says,
simply, that we believe all men are equal"), it is traditional and
it is honorable, but it is as amorphous as Chris Keller's *brotherhood*. Chris embodies the idea that a good society will follow
when men choose not to live only for themselves. Vague as this
idea is, it does represent a kind of commitment; Miller's characters, however, can effectively express or represent that commitment only in terms of opposition.

In Miller's most recent work, *The Misfits* (1961), both in the
movie and the cinema novel (as his publisher calls it), there
has been a change of attitude. It can be seen most clearly in two
ideas that have preoccupied Miller the last few years: one is his
assumption that in our society the hero is reduced to the misfit;
the other is the chief dramatic cliché of the fifties, faith in the

curative powers of love. To understand this change clearly, one must go back to *Death of a Salesman*, begin with Biff, who is, after all, the prototype of the Miller misfit. Uncomfortable in Willy's competitive world, Biff goes west, becomes an outdoors bum—like Gay, Guido, and Perce in *The Misfits*. Although *Salesman* is too ambiguous, too good a play to allow Biff to wear a single label, it implies at least that there is something positive in Biff's choice. Certainly, as late as 1955, in the novelistic notes he added to the Bantam edition of the play, Miller was to describe Happy as "less heroically cast" than Biff, a phrase that suggests that Biff is somehow heroic. The same year, however, in "On Social Plays," Miller shook his head sadly over the state of the hero, said that "our common sense reduces him to the size of a complainer, a misfit." *Salesman* suggests reasons for this reduction in size in Biff's case; he is "lost," to use a cliché that Miller shares with Linda Loman, the queen of the bromides, but the implication is that he is incapacitated by his sense of guilt at having rejected his father and his father's dream. Although there are suggestions of psychological dislocation in the story version of "The Misfits" (*Esquire*, October 1957), it is primarily the story of three men who have no place in the world of job, home, and family. "Well, it's better than wages," says Gay of their pathetic roundup of wild horses, and Perce answers, "Hell, yes. Anything's better than wages." Using the roundup as plot, the story insists that, even though the West might once have been big enough for a man or horse to be proud and free, the mustang has become dogfood and the mustanging hero, a dogfood-hunting bum. In this form, "The Misfits" is a kind of twilight of the gods, and it has the dignity and sadness that such a theme demands.

In the later versions, the movie and the novel, the regret turns to therapy. Although Miller has often criticized the sentimentality of contemporary drama, his commitment to the generalized good seems finally to have forced him to embrace the last decade's faith in love as an anodyne. In the Introduction to

Collected Plays, published the year that "The Misfits" first
appeared, Miller says that in *Salesman* he wanted to set up
"an opposing system which, so to speak, is in a race for Willy's
faith, and it is the system of love which is the opposite of the
law of success." There is no such thing in the play. Biff obviously loves Willy as much as he hates him, but this fact hardly
constitutes a system; nor is it presented as a possible opposite
to Willy's desire for success. Miller is simply trying to read back
into the earlier play a concept of love that comes too late to
save Willy, but just in time to destroy the hero-misfit. The
movie and the novel pick up the psychological hints of the
story, develop them at great length and indicate that these men
are not misfits in the grand tradition of Daniel Boone and Kit
Carson; they are would-be conformists looking for a home. At
the end of the movie, Perce is going back to wages, to the
mother and ranch he lost when she remarried after the death
of his father. Guido is still crying out in anger, but there is more
frustration than principle in his cries. It is with Gay that the
sentimentality is most obvious. As he and Roslyn drive off at
the end of *The Misfits,* after he has released the wild horse and
with it any claim he has to independence, she says, "How do
you find your way back in the dark?" He answers, "Just head
for that big star straight on. The highway's under it; take us
right home." It has been suggested that this end is as ironic as
the Requiem of *Salesman,* but there is too much evidence
against such an interpretation: Miller's remarks about love and
Biff, the sudsiness that pervades the prose and the characters
in the novel, the clichés (John Huston's as well as Miller's)
that fill the movie.

It is too early to tell whether *The Misfits* is an anomaly or an
indication, whether—when and if he returns to the theatre—
Miller will again concern himself with society and its effects on
men or, like so many of his contemporaries, crawl into the
personal solution to public problems. Whatever happens, it is
necessary to say that Miller's early work for the theatre has

earned him an important place in American drama. The faults
of his plays are obvious enough. *All My Sons*, for all its neat-
ness, tends to go to pieces in the last act when the recognition
of Joe's guilt no longer comes from the interaction of characters,
but from the gratuitous introduction of Larry's letter. In *Death
of a Salesman*, peripheral characters such as Howard and Bernard are completely unbelievable and Miller has not saved
them, as he has Ben, by turning them into obvious caricatures.
There are distressing structural faults in *The Crucible*, violations
of the realistic surface of the play, such as the unlikely scene in
Act I in which Proctor and Abigail are left alone in the sick
girl's bedroom. Nor was it such a good idea for Miller to attempt, in that play, to suggest the language of the period; the
lines are as awkward and as stagily false as those in John
Drinkwater's *Oliver Cromwell*. The pretentiousness of Alfieri's
speeches in *A View from the Bridge*, the conscious attempt to
make an analogy between Red Hook and Calabria, reduces the
impact of Eddie Carbone's story; any connection between Eddie
and the passion-ridden heroes of old should have been made
implicitly.

   Miller's virtues, however, outweigh these faults. The theme
that recurs in all his plays—the relationship between a man's
identity and the image that society demands of him—is a major
one; in one way or another it has been the concern of most
serious playwrights. A big theme is not enough, of course; Miller
has the ability to invest it with emotion. He is sometimes sentimental, sometimes romantic about both his characters and their
situations; but sentiment and romance, if they can command
an audience without drowning it, are not necessarily vices. Even
in *A Memory of Two Mondays*, in which he peoples his stage
with stereotypes, he manages, in the end, to make Bert's departure touching. The test of the good commercial playwright is
the immediate reaction of an audience; the test of the good
playwright is how well his plays hold up under continuing observation. Each time I go back to *All My Sons*, to *The Crucible*,

to *A View from the Bridge,* the faults become more ominous, but in each of these plays there are still scenes that work as effectively as they did when I first saw the play. *Death of a Salesman* is something else again. It does not merely hold its own, it grows with each rereading. Those people who go in for good-better-best labels—I am not one of them—would be wise, when they draw up their list of American plays, to put *Death of a Salesman* very near the top.

LEE BAXANDALL

Lee Baxandell is a critic with a strong Leftist orientation. He has translated Bertolt Brecht's *Mother* and Peter Weiss's *Song of the Lusitanian Bogey*, and has assembled a bibliography, *Marxism and Aesthetics*.

ARTHUR MILLER:
STILL THE INNOCENT

Arthur Miller has failed spectacularly with his first play in nine years. *After the Fall* is rhetorical as language, insufficiently imagined as characters in action, and defective in its basic aesthetic and moral structure.

Centering upon a lawyer, Quentin, who finds he has little wish or ability to pick up the pieces of a shattered life following various amatory and political disillusionments, Miller has written a scarcely metamorphosed allegory of his own crisis. It seems that Miller cannot shake his imagination loose from the shattered data of a career that eludes and obsesses him. The consequence is, on one hand, that the self-analysis of the *raisonneur* Quentin grows obtuse, prolix, and interminable. On the other hand, accordingly, the drama of several characters in action is rendered negligible. There is a sustained passage in the second act when Miller gets down to cases about his relationship with Marilyn Monroe. Here he lets a brilliant actress, Barbara Loden, remain on stage long enough to develop a

---

From *Encore*, XI (May–June 1964), 16-19. This review should be read in conjunction with the excerpt from *After the Fall*, pp. 174-181, and the comments on Kazan and Miller in Bentley (p. 207) and Warshow (p. 220).

character that leaps into life. Otherwise, the actors run in and they run out, while the garrulous monologue is left to provide as it may for cohesion and development.

In works like *All My Sons* and *Death of a Salesman,* Miller drew successfully upon personal experience. That is to say, living characters were created throughout, and we cared little about their prototypes in Miller's experience. By comparison, there will be much that doesn't tie up for the spectator of *After the Fall,* if he is ignorant of who on the stage equals who off the stage. He had better see the equivalence of Maggie with Marilyn Monroe; of Louise with Miller's first wife; of Holga with Miller's third wife; of the lawyer Mickey with Elia Kazan, Miller's director. The more extraneous facts the spectator holds at his command, the more he will be able to make the relational connections that Miller should have and didn't; the more he will be able to puzzle out what the evidence on stage may have signified *really,* in Miller's life.

One can almost sense the passion of conviction evanesce from Miller's language, while his thought settles elephantinely upon the ocean shoals of ineptitude. Commentary is superfluous, when the playwright's purple effusions are at hand for quotation:—"What the hell is moral—and who am I to ask it?" . . . "Who can be innocent again on this mountain of skulls?" . . . "Is it that I'm looking for some simple-minded constancy, that never is and never was?" . . . "What burning cities taught her, and the death of love taught me—that we are very *dangerous!*"

As Quentin says of his past: ". . . it's like swallowing a lump of earth."

But it also dawns upon the spectator, as Quentin alternately thinks aloud to the audience and takes his part in enacting scenes from the past, that the author himself might have been a lawyer, not an experienced dramatist; for—despite much talk of guilt, or perhaps because of the burden of guilt—Miller falls recurrently into special pleading on Quentin's behalf. A dramatist cannot so proceed. He is the impartial judge of all his characters, and must deal equally with them.

Yet Miller has his reasons for so earnestly haranguing himself and us. He is trying to get something across, to himself as well as to us; and attention, attention must be paid. He wants to say that he has transcended the illusions he clung to in an earlier day; he has fallen from innocence, and now accepts the guilt he incurred because of his innocence. All these protestations notwithstanding, the truth is that Miller never has written before such credulous or such cramped nonsense as fills *After the Fall*. Finding a small truth, Miller has lost the large world. He learned, over the last decade, that truth and morality are specific and unique in individual application, difficult to come by and to live by, and that each person is alone responsible in the final analysis for the humane conduct of his life. Well and good; in the meanwhile, Miller has entirely forgotten that the individual's truth and morality exist only in a structured historical context; and when the context is left out of account, not a great deal of truth and morality can remain.

We arrive now at the heart of the play's structural defects. These are aesthetic and moral, inseparably; for a flawed human perspective must necessarily lead to a flawed artistic perspective, so long as the representation of human beings is in view. Miller sets forth two "faiths" that failed him; one per act. Socialism is the first; Quentin says, "We only turned left because it seemed the truth was there." If Quentin never quite gets around to saying what disillusioned him with the Left, the Kazan figure, Mickey, is less reticent. Nor does Quentin contradict Mickey when he sputters: "They took our lust for the right and used it for Russian purposes."

In the next act the "faith" Miller sees through at last is Marilyn, and "the lie of limitless love." This was the more difficult illusion to lose, Miller suggests; since the infinite adoration that he sought in her, and formerly had received from his parents, was an emotional crutch during the difficult days of McCarthyism.

Where then does Arthur Miller come out? What is the message that Quentin brings to a groping humanity? We look around, and see that Quentin has led us straight into the sterile desert of an ultra-personalist scepticism, relativism, and individualism.

"We are all separate people," Quentin confidently announces. "I tried not to be . . . but that's how it is." One would have thought that the separateness of individuals was an evident point, to be acknowledged and used as the touchstone of departure. No doubt it has been that, for less sentimental persons; to Miller it seems the latest discovery. At last a consciously separate person, he turns this new stability (like the previous ones) into an article of faith; less adequate, and more constricting and imaginatively debilitating, however, than its forerunners. In his eviscerated passion for the personalist truth, Miller seems wholly to have lost the knack for attachments outside himself. Balanced and impersonal aesthetic structures are hardly to be erected on such a perspective.

Let us see how the flaw creeps in, first in respect to the political thread. Although Miller is at great pains to express his loss of confidence in socialism, he incorporates no examples of purposeful socialist activity. Thus we turn by default to his treatment of the *retreat from* socialism. That does get mention, if only in the discussion whether Mickey will give names to the investigators, and if he does what Quentin and we are to think of it. (The question of whether a man will stick to his "inner convictions" has alone interested Miller, in plays where he has included a "progressive" figure: *An Enemy of the People* (adapted from Ibsen), *The Crucible, After the Fall*. The actual process of social change has not attracted him.) Thus the question of keeping faith with one's convictions and one's own past does afford a marginal socialist issue in this first act. But to our utter astonishment, we note that the theme of the man who "stools" on his friends—Kazan—is left dangling and unresolved! Miller throws dust in our eyes. At play's end he has another subpoenaed figure leap under a subway train.

Audience attention is diverted; some spectators may accept the suicide as a tie-up of the political thread. But of course it is not. The tie-up exists; but whether or not it is made will, as we earlier said, depend on the spectator's *extrinsic* knowledge. To comprehend why Miller drops the Kazan theme, clumsily undermining the entire play's structure, one must know that Kazan *did* give names, Miller denounced him publicly, later they were reconciled, and now Kazan is director of this very play.

Once the extrinsic connections have been made, Quentin's pronouncements on personal morality reflect with a new light back upon Miller's politics. We must ourselves hook up Miller's general ethics with the mishandled Kazan theme; Miller evidently hadn't the guts to, although the application hardly can be in doubt. Says Quentin to Maggie: never "come between another and his truth." What can such an injunction mean, when applied to stool-pigeons, undemocratic politicians and tyrants, if not an ostrich or a hands-off policy? Moans Quentin, "always in your own blood-covered name you turn your back"; what are we to see in this phrase, if not the rationale of Miller's conciliation to Kazan—and, more generally, to political fatuousness and irrelevance?

This is convenient truth that Miller has come to in his new sobriety. It permits him to work with moral Calibans. It interests him in atonement, while productive truths go neglected, and he withdraws from social accountability. Among the more important truths now lost on Miller is the bankruptcy of live-and-let-live ethics so long as this world is ruled by force and hunger. Miller seems instinctively to sense this; when he does send Quentin and Holga on a visit to a concentration camp, he has Quentin make the facile analogy of his love troubles to the world's Hitler troubles, earlier quoted. But he doesn't try to make anything more of the death-camp bit than this exotic presumption to comparison.

Even in love, however, Miller's freshly inadequate perspective flaws the dramatic structure. To his first wife he is grossly unfair; she comes off as a scapegoat and an unconvincing character. Holga too, the wife of the future, is a juiceless abstraction. Some homosexuals have protested with much right that Miller exhibits less sympathetic understanding of female characters than do often-criticised homosexual playwrights. The long Maggie sequence has life in it, although the tasteless *voyeur* aspect reminds one that more agony than invention went into these scenes; moreover, even here intrudes that complacent special pleading. Thus it is true that Miller has Maggie score Quentin's egotism; but it remains undocumented, in structural theatrical terms, since Miller offers in evidence only Quentin's talk of guilt and his passivity.

Miller behaved at the height of the McCarthy period with greater courage than did many of his companions in peril; and his play *The Crucible* was, all things considered, an admirable counterstroke. However, when we think back to that work, we shall see that while its hero, John Proctor, did stand up for his beliefs and die in their name, he did this essentially as an individualist and a sentimentalist. Miller might have let Proctor live; he wanted him to die, and to refuse all possible alternatives, in one stroke depriving the social scene and the Proctor family of his contribution and leadership. Others might consider how to live. Proctor had to savour his integrity—no matter how restrictive the perimeter he might draw about it. The perimeter of that integrity, as *After the Fall* shows, has now drawn tight as a suicide's noose.

One more obituary notice has been handed us out of the twin plagues of McCarthyism and distant Stalinism. Writ long and crudely in the victim's own hand, *After the Fall* has to be reckoned a symptom but no summation.

Contexts of *The Crucible:*
HISTORICAL

A NOTE ON WITCHCRAFT

Out of these is shaped us the true idea of a witch,—an old, weather-beaten crone, having her chin and her knees meeting for age, walking like a bow, leaning on a staff; hollow-eyed, untoothed, furrowed on her face, having her limbs trembling with the palsy, going mumbling in the streets; one that hath forgotten her Paternoster, and yet hath a shrewd tongue to call a drab a drab. If she hath learned of an old wife, in a chimney-end, Pax, Max, Fax, for a spell, or can say Sir John Grantham's curse for the miller's eels, "All ye that have stolen the miller's eels, Laudate dominum de cœlis: and all they that have consented thereto, Benedicamus domino:" why then, beware! look about you, my neighbors. If any of you have a sheep sick of the giddies, or a hog of the mumps, or a horse of the staggers, or a knavish boy of the school, or an idle girl of the wheel, or a young drab of the sullens, and hath not fat enough for her porridge, or butter enough for her bread, and she hath a little help of the epilepsy or cramp, to teach her to roll her eyes, wry her mouth, gnash her teeth, startle with her body, hold her arms and hands stiff, &c.; and then, when an old Mother Nobs hath by chance called her an idle young housewife, or bid the Devil scratch her, then no doubt but Mother Nobs is the witch, and the young girl is owl blasted, &c. They that have their brains baited and their fancies distempered with the imaginations and apprehensions of witches, conjurers, and fairies, and all that lymphatic chimera, I find to be marshalled in one of these five ranks: children, fools, women, cowards, sick or black melancholic discomposed wits.

—Samuel Harsnett, 1599.

The lines are from *A Discovery of the Fraudulent Practises of John Darrel, Bacheler of Artes.* . . . In 1597 and 1598, Harsnett, then Archbishop of York, was on a commission that condemned Darrel for pretending to exorcise devils; the book, which showed how witch-finders played on popular prejudices, was a justification of the commission findings. I took it from Charles W. Upham's *Salem Witchcraft* (New York: Ungar, 1959, Volume I, pp. 369-70), which explains the modernized spelling and punctuation. Upham, whose classic study of Salem was first published in 1867, used the quotation to prove that there were men who treated demonology as a superstition a century before the outbreak at Salem. I reprint it here because it contains phrases that recall lines in *The Crucible* and displays a general assumption about the crying out of witches that would not be alien to Arthur Miller. Besides, I simply like the paragraph.

I am not at all certain that it is a compliment to Miller, but it would not be surprising if a reader began with *The Crucible* and ended up to his earlobes in Salem witches. That is what happened to me while I was putting this volume together. For that reason, I offer a few hints. Crochety old Upham is fascinating, but the sheer detail of his massive two volumes may defeat you before you get started. I suggest two more lively books: Marion L. Starkey, *The Devil in Massachusetts* (New York: Knopf, 1950) and Chadwick Hansen, *Witchcraft at Salem* (New York: Braziller, 1969). Miss Starkey, whose view of Salem is very like Miller's, was cited by a number of the play's reviewers. Hansen takes quite another tack. His is really a defense of the Massachusetts establishment, a dismissal of the old assumptions that greed and malice were loose in Salem. Unfortunately, and perhaps unwittingly, an ugly tone mars the book. One finishes it with the impression that it may have been all right to hang Sarah Good since she was sharp-tongued ("may not be deserving of sympathy"—p. 218) and that somehow there is less guilt in hanging Rebecca Nurse than in slandering Cotton Mather, as Hansen assumes historians, following Robert Calef, have always done. One of the best things on Mather and the Salem trials is "The Judgment of the Witches," in Perry Miller, *The New England Mind: From Colony to Province* (Cambridge: Harvard University Press, 1953), pp. 191-208. For Mather himself and the other contemporary commentators, including the ones excerpted in this volume, the best source is George Lincoln Burr, *Narratives of the Witchcraft*

Cases, 1648–1706 (New York: Scribner, 1914). As to general books on witchcraft, two of the best are Margaret Murray, *The God of the Witches* (New York: Oxford, 1952) and Charles Williams, *Witchcraft* (London: Faber & Faber, 1941). The latter is available in paperback from Meridian Books.

Of course, if you do not become witch-bitten, if you are interested in Salem only in relation to *The Crucible*, the documents that follow will be all that you want or need.

RECORDS OF SALEM WITCHCRAFT

Examination of Sarah Good.

The examination of Sarah Good before the worshipfull Assts John Harthorn Jonathan Curran

(H.) Sarah Good what evil Spirit have you familiarity with

(S. G.) None

(H.) Have you made contracte with the devil

   Good answered no.

(H.) Why doe you hurt these children

(g) I doe not hurt them. I scorn it.

(H) Who doe you imploy then to doe it.

From *Records of Salem Witchcraft from the Original Documents*, ed. W. Elliot Woodward (Roxbury, Mass.: privately printed, 1864), Vol. I, pp. 17-19, 44-48, 55-56, 63-66, 82-87, 128-32. I have retained the spelling and punctuation as Woodward gave them, but I have reordered the selections so that they are now chronological. Since this is a book on *The Crucible*, I see no point in identifying the names that Miller did not use; if you are curious, the 1959 Upham has a good index. Miss Starkey (p. 302) comments favorably on Woodward's accuracy. His two volumes, however, do not exhaust the Salem documents; the best source for them is a transcription made in 1938 by the WPA, but this exists only in a typescript (3 volumes) on file in the Court House in Salem.

(g) I imploy no body

(H) What creature do you imploy then.

(g) no creature but I am falsely accused.

(H) why did you go away muttering from Mr Parris his house.

(g) I did not mutter but I thanked him for what he gave my child.

(H) have you made no contract with the devil.

(g) no.

(H) desired the children all of them to look upon her and see if this were the person that had hurt them and so they all did looke upon her, and said this was one of the persons that did torment them—presently they were all tormented.

(H) Sarah Good do you not see now what you have done, why doe you not tell us the truth, why doe you thus torment these poor children

(g) I doe not torment them.

(H) who do you imploy then.

(g) I imploy nobody I scorn it.

(H) how came they thus tormented

(g) what doe I know you bring others here and now you charge me with it

(H) why who was it.

(g) I doe not know but it was some you brought into the meeting house with you.

(H) wee brought you into the meeting house.

(g) but you brought in two more.

(H) who was it then that tormented the children.

(g) it was osburn.

(H) what is it you say when you go muttering away from persons houses

(g) if I must tell I will tell.

(H) doe tell us then

(g) if I must tell, I will tell, it is the commandments. I may say my commandments I hope.

(H.) what commandment is it.

(g) if I must tell I will tell, it is a psalm.

(H) what psalm.

(g) after a long time shee muttered over some part of a psalm.

(H) who doe you serve

(g) I serve God

(H) what God doe you serve.

(g) the God that made heaven and earth. though shee was not willing to mention the word God. her answers were in a very wicked spitfull manner. reflecting and retorting against the authority with base and abussive words and many lies shee was taken in it was here said that her husband had said that he was afraid that she either was a witch or would be one very quickly. the worsh. Mr. Harthon asked him his reason why he said so of her, whether he had ever seen any thing by her, he answered no, not in this nature, but it was her bad carriage to him, and indeed said he I may say with tears that shee is an enemy to all good.

Salem Village March the 1ˢᵗ 169¼

Written by Ezekiell Chevers

Salem Village March th 1ˢᵗ 169¼[1]

Examination of Titiba Indian.

The examination of Titibe.

(H) Titibe whan evil spirit have you familiarity with.

(T) none.

(H) why do you hurt these children.

(T) I do not hurt them.

---

[1] According to the Old Style calendar still in use in England at this time, the legal year began on March 25. Thus, this date, which was March 1, 1692, as we now count, was technically March 1, 1691. The double designation 169¼ was often employed, reflecting both legal and popular usage.

(H) who is it then.

(T) the devil for ought I know.

(H) Did you never see the devil.

(T) The devil came to me and bid me serve him.

(H) Who have you seen.

(T) Four women sometimes hurt the children.

(H) Who were they.

(T) Goode Osburn and Sarah Good and I doe not know who the other were. Sarah Good and Osburne would have me hurt the children but I would not she further saith there was a tale[2] man of Boston that she did see.

(H) when did you see them.

(T) Last night at Boston.

(H) what did they say to you.

　　　they said hurt the children

(H) and did you hurt them

(T) no there is 4 women and one man they hurt the children and they lay all upon me and they tell me if I will not hurt the children they will hurt me.

(H) but did you not hurt them

(T) yes, but I will hurt them no more.

(H) are you not sorry you did hurt them.

(T) yes.

(H) and why then doe you hurt them.

(T) they say hurt children or wee will doe worse to you.

(H) what have you seen.

　　　an man come to me and say serve me.

(H) what service.

(T) hurt the children and last night there was an appear-

---

[2] Tall. Presumably in the old sense, meaning "excellent," "fine," "comely." At least, when the "tal man" in black clothes she mentions at the end of her examination finally was named, it was George Burroughs, once pastor in Salem, apparently a stocky man, not "tall" as the word is now used.

ance that said kill the children and if I would no go on hurting the children they would do worse to me.

(H) what is this appearance you see.

(T) Sometimes it is like a hog and sometimes like a great dog, this appearance shee saith shee did see 4 times.

(H) what did it say to you

(T) it ʃ the black dog said serve me but I said I am afraid he said if I did not he would doe worse to me.

(H) what did you say to it.

(T) I will serve you no longer. then he said he would hurt me and then he looked like a man and threatens to hurt me, shee said that this man had a yellow bird that kept with him and he told me he had more pretty things that he would give me if I would serve him.

(H) what were these pretty things.

(T) he did not show me them.

(H) what also have you seen

(T) two rats, a red rat and a black rat.

(H) what did they say to you.

(T) they said serve me.

(H) when did you see them.

(T) last night and they said serve me, but I said I would not

(H) what service.

(T) shee said hurt the children.

(H) did you not pinch Elizabeth Hubbard this morning

(T) the man brought her to me and made me pinch her

(H) why did you goe to Thomas Putnams last night and hurt his child.

(T) they pull and hall me and make me goe

(H) and what would have you doe.

Kill her with a knif.

Left. Fuller and others said at this time when the child saw these persons and was tormented by them that she did complayn of a knife, that they would have her cut her head off with a knife.

(H) how did you go

(T) we ride upon stickes and are there presently.

(H) doe you goe through the trees or over them.

(T) we see nothing but are there presently.

[H] why did you not tell your master.

[T] I was afraid they said they would cut of my head 'if I told.

[H] would you not have hurt others if you cold.

[T] They said they would hurt others but they could not

[H] what attendants hath Sarah Good.

[T] a yellow bird and shee would have given me one

[H] what meate did she give it

[T] it did suck her between her fingers.

[H] did not you hurt Mr Currins child

[T] goode good and goode Osburn told that they did hurt Mr Currens child and would have had me hurt him two, but I did not.

[H] what hath Sarah Osburn.

[T] yellow dog, shee had a thing with a head like a woman with 2 legges, and wings. Abigail Williams that lives with her Uncle Parris said that she did see the same creature, and it turned into the shape of Goode Osburn.

[H] what else have you seen with Osburn.

[T] another thing, hairy it goes upright like a man it hath only 2 leggs.

[H] did you not see Sarah Good upon Elizabeth Hubbard, last Saterday.

[T] I did see her set a wolfe upon her to afflict her, the persons with this maid did say that she did complain of a wolfe.

T. shee further saith that shee saw a cat with good at another time.

[H] What clothes doth the man go in

[T] he goes in black clouthes a tal man with white hair I thinke

[H] How doth the woman go

[T] in a white whood and a black whood with a top knot

[H] doe you see who it is that torments these children now.

[T] yes it is Goode Good, shee hurts them in her own shape

[H] and who is it that hurts them now.

[T] I am blind now. I cannot see.

Salem Village   Written by Ezekiell Cheevers.

March the 1st 169½   Salem Village March 1st 169½

Giles Corey v. Martha Corey.

The evidence of Giles Choree testifieth and saith y^t last Satturday in the Evening Sitting by the fire my wife asked me to go to bed. I told I would go to prayer and when I went to prayer I could not utter my desires w^h any sense, not open my mouth to speake, my wife did perceive itt and came towards me and said she was coming to me. After this in a little space I did according TO MY MEASURE attend the duty.

Sometime last weake I fitcht an ox well out of the woods about noone and he lay ng down in the yard. I went to raise him to yoake him, but he could not rise but dragd his HINDER PARTS as if he had been hipt shott, butt after did rise. I had a catt sometimes last weeke strangly taken on the suddain, and did make me think she would have died presently my wife bid me knock her in the head butt I did not and since SHE IS WELL.

Another time going to duties I was interrupted for a space butt AFTERWARD I was helpt according to my poore measure. My wife hath ben wont to sett up after I went to bed and I have perceived her to kneel down on the harth as if she were at prayer but heard nothing.

May 24th 169½.

Examination of Rebecca Nurse.

The Examiination of Rebeckah Nurse at Salem Village 24. Mar. 169½,

Mͬ Harthorn. Wat do you say (speaking to one afflicted) have you seen this woman hurt you.

yes, she beat me this morning.

Abigail. have you been hurt by this woman?

Yes.

Ann Putnam in a grevous fit cryed out that she hurt her.

Goody Nurse: here are two: An: Putnam the child and Abigail Williams, complains of your hurting them What do you say to it

N. I can say before my Eternal Father I am innocent and God will clear my innocency

Here is never a one in the Assembly but desires it. but if you be Guilty Pray God discover you.

Then Hen: Kenney rose up to speak.

Goodm, Kenney what do you say,

Then he entered his complaint and farther said that since this Nurse came into the house he was seized twise with an amas'd condition.

Here are not only these but here is yᵉ wife of Mr Tho Putnam who accuseth you by creditable information and that both of tempting her to iniguity and of greatly hurting her.

N. I am innocent and clear, and have not been able to get out of doors these 8. or 9. daeys.

Mr. Putnam give in what you have to say.

Then Mr Edward Putman gave in his relate.

Is this true Goody Nurse.

I never afflicted no child no never in my life.

You see these accuse you. is it true.

No.

Are you an innocent person ralating to this witchcraft

Here Tho: Putmans wife cryed out Did you not bring the Black man with you, did you not bid me tempt Cod and dye. How oft have you eat and drunk your own damnation What do you say to them

Oh Lord, help me, and spread out her hands and the afflicted were greevously vexed

Do you see what a solemn condition these are in? when your hands are loose the persons are afflicted

Then Mary Walcot, (who often heretofore said she had seen her but never could say or did say that she either bit or pincht her, or hurt her) and also Elis Hubbard. under the like circumstances both openly accused her of hurting them.

Here are then 2 grown persons now accuse you what say you? Do not you see these afflicted persons, and hear them accuse you

The Lord knows: I have not hurt them: I am an innocent person

It is very awfull for all to see these agonies and you an old professor, thisscharged with contracting with the devil by the effects of it, and yet to see you stand with dry eyes when there are so many whet.

You do not know my heart.

You would do well if you are Guilty to confess give Glory to God.

I am as clear as the child unborn.

What uncertainty there may be in apparitions I know not yet this with me strikes hard upon you, that you are at this very present, charged with familiar spirits this is your bodily person they speak to: they say now they see these familiar spirits come to your bodily person, now what do you say to that.

I have none. Sir.

If you have confest. and give Glory to God I pray God clear you, if you be innocent, and if you be Guilty discover you And therefore give me an upright answer: have you any familiarity with these spirits?

No I have none but with God alone.

How came you sick for there is an odd discourse of that in the mouths of many.

I am sick at my stomach.

Have you no wounds.

I have not but old age.

You do Know whether you are Guilty and have familiarity with the devil, and now when you are here present, to see such a thing as these testify a black man whispering in your ear and birds about you, what do you say to it.

It is all false. I am clear.

Possibly you may apprehend you are no witch but have you not been led aside by temptations that way.

I have not.

What a sad thing it is that a church member here and now another of Salem, should be thus accused and charged

Mr⁸ Pope fell into a grievous fit and cryed out a sad thing sure enough. And then many more fell into lamentable fits.

Tell us, have not you had visible appearances more than what is common in nature?

I have none nor never had in my life.

Do you think these suffer voluntary or involuntary.

I cannot tell.

That is strange every one can judge.

I must be silent

They accuse you of hurting them, and if you think it is not univellingly but by designe, you must look vpon them as murderers.

I cannot tell what to think of it.

Afterwards when this was somewhat insisted on she said: I do not think so: she did not understand aright what was said.

Well then give an answer now do you think these suffer against their wills or not.

I do not think these suffer against their wills.

Why did you never visit these afflicted persons.

Because I was afraid I should have fits too.

Note Upon the motion of her body fits followed upon the complainants, abundantly and very frequently.

Is it not an unaccountable case that when you are examined these persons are afflicted?

I have got no body to look to but God.

Again vpon stirring her hands the afflicted persons. were seized with violent fits of torture.

Do you beleive these afflicted persons are bewitcht.

I do think they are.

When this witchcraft came vpon the stage there was no suspicion of Tituba (Mr Parris's Indian woman) she professt much love to that child Betty Parris, but it was her apparition did the mischief, and why should not you also be guilty for your apparition doth hurt also.

Would you have me bely myself.

she held her neck on one side, and accordingly so were the afflicted taken.

Then authority requiring it, Sam: Parris read what he had in Characters taken from Mr Tho: Putmans wife in her fitts.

What do you think of this.

I cannot help it, the Devil may appear in my shape.

This a true account of the sume of hir examination but by reason of great noyses, by the afflicted and many speakers, many things are pretermitted memorandum

Nurse held her neck on one side and Eliz Hubbard. (one of the sufferers) had her neck set in that posture whereupon another patient Abigail Williams, cryed out, set up Goody Nursis head, the maid's neck will be broke. and when some set up Nurse's head. Aaron Wey. observed yt Betty Hubbards was immediately righted.

Salem Village March. 24th. 169¼.

The Revert mr Samuell Parris being desired to take in urighting ye examination of Rebeckah Nurse hath retured itt as aforesaid.

Vpon hearing the afores'd and seeing what wee then did see together with ye charge of the persons then present wee committed Rebekah Nurse ye wife of ffrans Nurse of Salem

village vnto theire Majes^{ts} Goale in salem as p amittimus[3]
then given out. in order to farther Examination

JOHN HATHORNE ⎱ Assist
JONATHAN CORWIN ⎰

Abigail Williams v. John Proctor.

1692. Apr. 4. *Abig Williams*. complained of Goodm. *Proctor*
and cryed out w^t are you come to, are you come to you can
pinch as well as your wife and more to that purpose.

6. At night she complained of Goodm Proctor again, and
beat upon her breast and cryed he pinched her.

The like I hear at Tho: Putmans house.[4]

12. Day. when the marshall was sent up to enquire of
John Proctor and the others, and I was writing some what
there of as above I met with nothing but interruptions by
reason of fits vpon John Indian and Abigail, and Mary Wolcott
happening to come in just before, they one and another cryed
out there is Goodm: Proctor very often, and Abigail said
there is Goodm: Proctor in the magistrates lap. at the same
time Mary Wolcott was sitting by a knitting, we askt her if
she saw Goodm: Proctor, [for Abigail was immediately seized
with a fit] but she was deaf and dumb, yet still a knitting.
then Mary recovered herselfe and confirmed what Abigail had
said that Goodm Proctor she saw in the magistrates lap, Then
John cryed out to the Dog under the table to come away for
Goodm Proctor was upon his back; then he cryed out of
Goody Cloyce, O you old witch, and fell immediately into
a violent fitt that 3 men and the marshall could not without
exceeding difficulty hold him. In which fit Mary Walcot that
was knitting and well composed, said there was Goodm. Proc-

---

[3] *Per mittimus.*

[4] A remark of Miss Starkey's (p. 84) suggests that the "I" of this
entry is Reverend Parris. Certainly Parris did "take in urighting," as the
Nurse document above puts it, many of the examinations.

tor and his wife and Goody Cloyse helping of him, but so great were the interruptions of John and Abigail by fits while we were observing these things to notify them, that we were fain to send them both away that I might have liberty to write this without disturbance, Mary Walcot abiding composed and knitting whilst I was writing and the two other sent away, yet by and by whilest I was writing Mary Walcot said there Goody Cloyse has pincht me now

Note Mary Walcot never saw Proctor nor his wife till last night coming from the examination at Salem and then she saw Goody Proctor behind her brother Jonathan all the way from the widow Gidneys to Phillips, where Jonathan made a little stay, But this day and time I have been writing this, she saw them many times.

Note Just now as soon as I had made an end of reading this to the Marshall, Mary W***** immediately cryed O yonder is Good: Proctor and his wife and Goody Nurse and Goody Korey and G**** Cloyse and Goods child and then said O Goodm: Proctor is going to choake me and immediately she was choake^t.

Munday 11th 111 ditto. Lut. Nath: Ingersoll declared y^t John Proctor tould Joseph Pope, y^t if hee hade John Indian in his Custody hee would svone beat ye devell out of him, an so said severall others.

Examination of Mary Warren.

Mary Warrens Examination May 12th. 1692.[5]

Q. Whether you did not know y^t itt was ye Devills book when you signed.

A I did nott know itt then but I know itt now to be sure itt was ye Devills book, in ye first place to be sure I did sett

---

[5] There were several examinations of Mary Warren as she vacillated between her loyalty to Proctor and her place among the accusers. This was the final one.

my hand to ye devills book: I have considered of it since you
were here last and itt was yᵉ devills book yᵗ my Master Proctor
brought to me and he tould me if I would sett my hand to
yᵗ book I should beleuve and I did sett my hand to itt but
yᵗ wᵗʰ I did itt was done with my finger. he brought yᵉ book
and tould me if I would take ye book and touch itt that I
should be well and I thought then yᵗ itt was yᵉ Devills book.

Q. Was there nott your consent to hurt yᵉ children when
you were hurt?

A. Noe Sir. but when I was afflicted my master Proctor
was in yᵉ Roome and said if yᵘ are afflicted I wish yᵉ were
more afflicted and you and all: I said Master what makes
you say so. He answered, because yᵘ goe to bring out Innocent persons, I tould him yᵗ that could not bee. and whether
yᵉ Devill took advantage att yᵗ I know not to afflict yᵐ and
one night talking about yᵐ I said I did nott care though yᵉ
were tormented if ye charged me

Q Did you euer see any poppetts?

An. Yes once I saw one made of cloth in Mistris proctor's
hand

Q whoe was itt like, or whch of ye Children was itt for?

An I cannott tell, whether for Ann Putnam or Abigail
Williams for one of yᵐ itt was I am sure, itt was in my
mistris's hand.

Q What did you stick into yᵉ poppitt?

An I did stick in a pin about ye neck of itt as itt was in
proctors hand

Q How many more did you see afterwards?

An I doe nott remember yᵗ euer I saw any more, yes I
remember one and yᵗ Goody parker brought a poppitt unto me
of Mercy Lewis and she gave me another and I stook itt some
where about yᵉ wasts and she appeared once more to me in
ye prison and shee said to me what are you gott here? and
she tould me yᵗ she was comeing here hirself. I had another
person yᵗ appeared to me, itt was Goody Pudeator and said

she was coming to see me there. itt was in apparition and she brought me a poppitt itt was like to Mary Walcott and itt was a piece of stick y^t she brought me to stich into itt. and somewhere about hir armes I stook itt in.

Q Where did she bring itt to you?

An vp att Proctors. Goody Proctor towld me she had bin a witch these 12 years and more; and pudeator tould me y^t she had done damage and tould me y^t she had hurt James Coyes child taking it out of ye mothers hand.

Q whoe brought ye last to you?

An. my mistris and when she brought itt, she brought itt in hir owne person and hir husband with his owne hands brought me ye book to Signe and he brought me an Image wch looked yellow and I believe itt was for Abigail Williams being like hir and I putt a thing like a thorne into itt this was done by his bodily person after I had signed. the night after I had sighned ye book while she was thus confessing Parker appeared and bitt her extremely on hir armes as she affirmed unto us.

Q Whoe have you seen more?

An Nurse and Cloys and Goods child after I had sighned

Q What sayd y^y to you?.

An They sayd y^t I should never tell of them nor any thing about y^m and I have seen Goody Good hirself.

Q Was that true of Giles Cory yt you saw him y^t he afflicted you the other day.?

An Yes. I have seen him often and he hurts me very much and Goody Oliver hath appeared to me and afflicted me and brought the Book to tempt me and I have seen Goody Cory. the first night I was taken I saw as I thought ye Apperition of Goody Cory and catched att itt as I thought and caught my master in my lap thoo I did not see my master in the place att ye time, upon wch my master said itt is noe body, but I itt is my shaddow y^t you see, but my master was nott before me y^t I could desarne but Catching at ye apperition y^t looked like Goody Cory I caught hold of my master and pulled him downe into my lap; upon wch he said I see there is noe heed to any of your talkings, for you are all possesst with ye Devill for itt is nothing but my shape; I have seen Goody Cory att my masters house in person, and she tould me y^t I should be condemned for a witch as well as she cry out and bring out all.

Q was this before you had sighned?

An Yes before I had my fitts

Q Now tell ye truth about ye Mountebank what writeing was y^t.

An I do not know. I asked hir what itt was about but she would not tell mee saying she had promised nott to lett any body see itt.

Q Well, but whoe did you see more?

An I dont know any more

Q How long hath your Mas^{tr} and Mistris bin witches?

An I dont know they never tould me. . . .[6]

Return of Searching Committee v. John Proctor and John Willard.

We whose names vnder written haueing searched ye bodyes of John Proctor sen^r and John Willard now in ye Goale and doe not find anything to farther suspect them.

Dated June 2. 1692.

N Roudel ap^{re}testis	J. Barton Chyrg^e
John Rogers.	John Gyles.
Joshua Rea Junr.	William Hyne.
John Cooke.	Ezekel Cheever.

The morning after ye examination of Goody Nurse Sam Sibley met John Proctor about Mr Phillips was called to said Sibley as he was going to sd Phillips and askt how ye folks did at the village. He answered he heard they were very bad

---

[6] I have dropped the rest of this document since it deals with persons other than those who figure in the play.

last night, but he had heard nothing this morning. Proctor replyed he was going to fetch home his jade, he left her there last night and had rather given 40 c[7] than let her come up, sd Tibley askt why he talkt so. Proctor replyed if thay were let alone sr. we should all be devills and witches quickly they should rather be had to the whipping post, but he would fetch his jade home and thust[8] the Devil out of her and more to the like purpose crying hang them, hang them. And also added that when she was first taken with fits he kept her close to the wheile[9] and thrdtend to thresh her, and then she had no more fits till the next day he was gone forth and then she must have her fits again forsooth &c.

Jurat in Curia.

Proctor ownes he meant Mary Warren.

Attest.   ST. SEWALL. Cler.

---

[7] David Levin tentatively suggests "crowns." *What Happened In Salem?* (New York: Harcourt, Brace & World, 1960), p. 59.

[8] Thrash.

[9] Presumably her spinning wheel.

DEODAT LAWSON

A BRIEF AND TRUE NARRATIVE

Of some Remarkable Passages Relating to sundry
Persons Afflicted by Witchcraft, at Salem Village Which
happened from the Nineteenth of March, to the
Fifth of April, 1692.

In the beginning of the Evening, I went to give Mr. P. a
visit. When I was there, his Kins-woman, Abigail Williams,
(about 12 years of age,) had a grievous fit; she was at first
hurryed with Violence to and fro in the room, (though Mrs.
Ingersol endeavoured to hold her,) sometimes makeing as if
she would fly, stretching up her arms as high as she could,
and crying "Whish, Whish, Whish!" several times; Presently
after she said there was Goodw. N. and said, "Do you not
see her? Why there she stands!" And the said Goodw. N.
offered her The Book, but she was resolved she would not

First printed Boston, 1692. Lawson had been pastor in Salem Village
from 1684 to 1688. He came back during the witchcraft troubles and
delivered a sermon, "Christ's Fidelity the Only Shield against Satan's
Malignity," on March 24, 1692. Since the sermon was in effect a
defense of the proceedings, Upham (Vol. II, pp. 76-77) assumed that
his appearance was part of a malicious plot to keep the witches' pot
abrewing. Long after the event, in a published version of the sermon
(London, 1704), he said that he came back out of concern for his
"Christian Friends and former Acquaintance" and to investigate the
testimony that Lawson's wife and daughter had been killed by one of
the accused through witchcraft. The excerpted paragraph describes the
evening of March 19; Mr. P. is Parris, of course, and Goodw. N.,
Rebecca Nurse.

take it, saying Often, "I wont, I wont, I wont, take it, I do
not know what Book it is: I am sure it is none of Gods Book,
it is the Divels Book, for ought I know." After that, she run
to the Fire, and begun to throw Fire Brands, about the house;
and run against the Back, as if she would run up Chimney,
and, as they said, she had attempted to go into the Fire in
other Fits.

ROBERT CALEF

MORE WONDERS OF THE
INVISIBLE WORLD:
Or, The Wonders of the
Invisible World, Display'd in Five Parts.

John Procter and his Wife being in Prison, the Sheriff
came to his House and seized all the Goods, Provisions, and
Cattle that he could come at, and sold some of the Cattle at
half price, and killed others, and put them up for the West-
Indies; threw out the Beer out of a Barrel, and carried away

First published, London, 1700. Calef was a Boston merchant, allied
with those men—such as William Brattle of Cambridge (see his famous
letter, Burr, pp. 165-90)—who opposed the Salem proceedings. Calef's
book was written by 1697 and was a direct attack on Cotton Mather,
whose *The Wonders of the Invisible World* (Boston, 1693), using
carefully selected cases, was a defense of the trials and executions. It was
presumably Mather's influence that kept Calef's book from being published in New England. Part V deals with the Salem trial, and it is
from that section that the following excerpts come.

the Barrel; emptied a Pot of Broath, and took away the Pot, and left nothing in the House for the support of the Children: No part of the said Goods are known to be returned. Procter earnestly requested Mr. Noyes to pray with and for him, but it was wholly denied, because he would not own himself to be a Witch.

During his Imprisonment he sent the following Letter, in behalf of himself and others.

Salem-Prison, July 23, 1692.

Mr. Mather, Mr. Allen,
Mr. Moody, Mr. Willard, and
Mr. Bailey.[1]
Reverend Gentlemen.

The innocency of our Case with the Enmity of our Accusers and our Judges, and Jury, whom nothing but our Innocent Blood will serve their turn, having Condemned us already before our Tryals, being so much incensed and engaged against us by the Devil, makes us bold to Beg and Implore your Favourable Assistance of this our Humble Petition to his Excellency, That if it be possible our Innocent Blood may be spared, which undoubtedly otherwise will be shed, if the Lord doth not mercifully step in. The Magistrates, Ministers, Jewries,[2] and all the People in general, being so much inraged and incensed against us by the Delusion of the Devil, which we can term no other, by reason we know in our own Consciences, we are all Innocent Persons. Here are five Persons who have lately confessed themselves to be Witches, and do accuse some of us, of being along with them at a Sacrament, since we were committed into close Prison, which we know to be Lies. Two of the 5 are (Carriers Sons)[3] Young-

---

[1] These were Massachusetts clergymen with a reputation for doubt or caution toward the whole Salem proceedings. The Mather is Increase, Cotton's father.

[2] Juries.

[3] Richard and Andrew, the sons of Martha Carrier of Andover. She was hanged with John Proctor on August 19, 1692.

men, who would not confess any thing till they tyed them Neck and Heels till the Blood was ready to come out of their Noses, and 'tis credibly believed and reported this was the occasion of making them confess that they never did, by reason they said one had been a Witch a Month, and another five Weeks, and that their Mother had made them so, who has been confined here this nine Weeks. My son William Procter, when he was examin'd, because he would not confess that he was Guilty, when he was Innocent, they tyed him Neck and Heels till the Blood gushed out at his Nose, and would have kept him so 24 Hours, if one more Merciful than the rest, had not taken pity on him, and caused him to be unbound. These actions are very like the Popish Cruelties. They have already undone us in our Estates, and that will not serve their turns, without our Innocent Bloods. If it cannot be granted that we can have our Trials at Boston, we humbly beg that you would endeavour to have these Magistrates changed, and others in their rooms, begging also and beseeching you would be pleased to be here, if not all, some of you at our Trials, hoping thereby you may be the means of saving the shedding our Innocent Bloods, desiring your Prayers to the Lord in our behalf, we rest your Poor Afflicted Servants,

JOHN PROCTER, etc.

He pleaded very hard at Execution, for a little respite of time, saying that he was not fit to Die; but it was not granted.

. . .

Giles Cory pleaded not Guilty to his Indictment, but would not put himself upon Tryal by the Jury (they having cleared none upon Tryal) and knowing there would be the same Witnesses against him, rather chose to undergo what Death they would put him to. In pressing his Tongue being prest out of his Mouth, the Sheriff with his Cane forced it in again, when he was dying. He was the first in New-England, that was ever prest to Death.

. . .

If Baalam became a Sorcerer by Sacrifizing and Praying
to the true God against his visible people;[4] Then he that shall
pray that the afflicted (by their Spectral Sight) may accuse
some other Person (whereby their reputations and lives may
be indangered) such will justly deserve the Name of a Sorcerer.
If any Person pretends to know more then can be known
by humane means, and professeth at the same time that they
have it from the Black-Man, *i.e.* the Devil, and shall from
hence give Testimony against the Lives of others, they are
manifestly such as have a familiar Spirit; and if any, knowing
them to have their Information from the Black-Man, shall be
inquisitive of them for their Testimony against others, they
therein are dealing with such as have a Familiar-Spirit.

And if these shall pretend to see the dead by their Spectral Sight, and others shall be inquisitive of them, and receive
their Answers what it is the dead say, and who it is they accuse, both the one and the other are by Scripture Guilty of
Necromancy.

These are all of them crimes as easily proved as any whatsoever, and that by such proof as the Law of God requires, so
that it is no Unintelligible Law.

But if the Iniquity of the times be such, that these Criminals not only Escape Indemnified, but are Incouraged in
their Wickedness, and made use of to take away the Lives of
others, this is worse than a making the Law of God Vain, it
being a rendring of it dangerous, against the Lives of Innocents, and without all hopes of better, so long as these Bloody
Principles remain.

As long as Christians do Esteem the Law of God to be
Imperfect, as not describing that crime that it requires to be
Punish'd by Death;

As long as men suffer themselves to be Poison'd in their

---

[4] For Balaam, see Numbers, 22-24.

Education, and be grounded in a False Belief by the Books of the Heathen;

As long as the Devil shall be believed to have a Natural Power, to Act above and against a course of Nature;

As long as the Witches shall be believed to have a Power to Commission him;

As long as the Devils Testimony, by the pretended afflicted, shall be received as more valid to Condemn, than their Plea of Not Guilty to acquit;

As long as the Accused shall have their Lives and Liberties confirmed and restored to them, upon their Confessing themselves Guilty;

As long as the Accused shall be forc't to undergo Hardships and Torments for their not Confessing;

As long as Tets for the Devil to Suck are searched for upon the Bodies of the accused, as a token of guilt;

As long as the Lords Prayer shall be profaned, by being made a Test, who are culpable;

As long as Witchcraft, Sorcery, Familiar Spirits, and Necromancy, shall be improved to discover who are Witches, etc.,

So long it may be expected that Innocents will suffer as Witches.

So long God will be Daily dishonoured, And so long his Judgments must be expected to be continued.

Finis.

JOHN HALE

A MODEST ENQUIRY INTO THE NATURE OF WITCHCRAFT,

and How Persons Guilty of that Crime may be Convicted: And the means used for their Discovery Discussed, both Negatively and Affirmatively, according to Scripture and Experience.

Here was generally acknowledged to be an error (at least on the one hand) but the Querie is, Wherein?

[A.] 1. I have heard it said, That the Presidents[1] in England were not so exactly followed, because in those there had been previous quarrels and threatnings of the Afflicted by those that were Condemned for Witchcraft; but here, say they, not so. To which I answer.

1. In many of these cases there had been antecedent personal quarrels, and so occasions of revenge; for some of those Condemned, had been suspected by their Neighbours several years, because after quarrelling with their Neighbours, evils

---

First published, Boston, 1702. As we know from the play, Hale was pastor at Beverly—had been since 1665. He was closely involved in the prosecutions. According to Calef, he changed his views after his wife was accused in October 1692; that was a little late, since the last group of "witches" had been hanged in September. In his book, which was written by 1698 but not published until after his death (1700), Hale lamented the errors in the Salem proceedings, but he was unwilling to dismiss the Devil and his witches, choosing rather to warn against extremes. What follows is Hale's Chapter IV.

[1] Precedents.

had befallen those Neighbours. As may be seen in the Printed Tryals of S. M. and B. B.[2] and others: See *Wonders of the Invisible World*, Page 105 to 137.[3] And there were other like Cases not Printed.

2. Several confessors acknowledged they engaged in the quarrels of other their confederates to afflict persons. As one Timothy Swan suffered great things by Witchcrafts, as he supposed and testifyed. And several of the confessors said they did so torment him for the sake of one of their partners who had some offence offer'd her by the said Swan. And others owned they did the like in the behalf of some of their confederates.

3. There were others that confessed their fellowship in these works of darkness, was to destroy the Church of God (as is above in part rehearsed) which is a greater piece of revenge then to be avenged upon one particular person.

[A.] 2. It may be queried then, How doth it appear that there was a going too far in this affair.

1. By the numbers of the persons accused which at length increased to about an hundred and it cannot be imagined that in a place of so much knowledge, so many in so small a compass of Land should so abominably leap into the Devils lap at once.

2. The quality of several of the accused was such as did bespeak better things, and things that accompany salvation. Persons whose blameless and holy lives before did testify for them. Persons that had taken great pains to bring up their Children in the nurture and admonition of the Lord: Such as we had Charity for, as for our own Souls: and Charity is a Christian duty commended to us. 1 Cor. 13 Chapt., Col. 3. 14, and in many other Scriptures.

---

[2] Susannah Martin and Bridget Bishop.

[3] In Burr, pp. 223-36. I have unblushingly borrowed from Burr in the notes to the selections from Lawson, Calef, and Hale.

3. The number of the afflicted by Satan dayly increased, till about Fifty persons were thus vexed by the Devil. This gave just ground to suspect some mistake, which gave advantage to the accuser of the Brethren[4] to make a breach upon us.

4. It was considerable that Nineteen were Executed, and all denied the Crime to the Death, and some of them were knowing persons, and had before this been accounted blameless livers. And it is not to be imagined, but that if all had been guilty, some would have had so much tenderness as to seek Mercy for their Souls in the way of Confession and sorrow for such a Sin. And as for the condemned confessors at the Bar (they being reprieved) we had no experience whether they would stand to their Self-condemning confessions, when they came to dye.

5. When this prosecution ceased, the Lord so chained up Satan, that the afflicted grew presently well. The accused are generally quiet, and for five years since, we have no such molestations by them.

6. It sways much with me that I have since heard and read of the like mistakes in other places. As in Suffolk in England about the year 1645 was such a prosecution, until they saw that unless they put a stop it would bring all into blood and confusion. The like hath been in France, till 900 were put to Death, And in some other places the like; So that N. England is not the only place circumvented by the wiles of the wicked and wisely Serpent in this kind. . . .

If there were an Error in the proceedings in other places,[5] and in N. England, it must be in the principles proceeded upon in prosecuting the suspected, or in the misapplication of the principles made use of. Now as to the case at Salem, I con-

---

[4] Satan. See Revelation, 12:10.
[5] I cut two paragraphs citing examples of erroneous "proceedings in other places."

ceive it proceeded from some mistaken principles made use of; for the evincing whereof, I shall instance some principles made use of here, and in other Countrys also, which I find defended by learned Authors writing upon that Subject.

. . .

Contexts of *The Crucible*: CONTEMPORARY

ALDOUS HUXLEY

Aldous Huxley's works include *Brave New World, Eyeless in Gaza, After Many a Summer Dies the Swan,* and *Time Must Have a Stop.* His forty-fifth and last book, *Literature and Science,* combines his preoccupation with the occult and his interest in science. He died in 1963.

THE DEVILS OF LOUDUN

. . . From all this it must be evident that if, as the Roman Church maintained, ESP phenomena and PK effects[1] are the hallmark of diabolic possession (or, alternatively, are extraor-

From Aldous Huxley, *The Devils of Loudun* (New York: Harper, 1952), pp. 186-90. Huxley's book is a psychological, social, and political study of the strange events that took place in Loudun in 1634, in which the presumed possession of the nuns of Saint Ursula's Convent, led by their prioress, Sister Jeanne des Anges, brought about the death of Urbain Grandier, the vicar of St. Peter's Church, Loudun, a priest

[1] Extrasensory perception and psychokinesis.

dinary graces), then the Ursulines of Loudun were merely hysterics who had fallen into the hands, not of the fiend, not of the living God, but of a crew of exorcists, all superstitious, all hungry for publicity, and some deliberately dishonest and consciously malevolent.

In the absence of any evidence for ESP or PK, the exorcists and their supporters were compelled to fall back on even less convincing arguments. The nuns, they asserted, must be possessed by devils; for how, otherwise, could one account for the shamelessness of their actions, the smut and irreligion of their conversation? "In what school of rakes and atheists," asks Father Tranquille, "have they learned to spew forth such blasphemies and obscenities?" And with a touch almost of boastfulness, de Nion assures us that the good sisters "made use of expressions so filthy as to shame the most debauched of men, while their acts, both in exposing themselves and in inviting lewd behavior from those present, would have astounded the inhabitants of the lowest brothel in the country."[2] As for their

---

whose life and opinions managed to offend a great many conventional men. John Whiting tried not too successfully to make a play—*The Devils* (1961)—out of Huxley's impressive book. An interesting film on the Loudun incident was made in Poland in 1960 by director Jerczy Kawalerowicz; it was released in this country as *Mother Joan of the Angels*. The excerpt here may be useful in thinking about the effects on the afflicted girls in Salem of their public performances and of the expectations of audience and officials alike.

[2] When Sister Claire was ordered by the exorcist (as a test for ESP) to obey an order, secretly whispered by one of the spectators to another, she went into convulsions and rolled on the floor "*relevant jupes et chemises, montrant ses parties les plus secrètes, sans honte, et se servant de mots lascifs. Ses gestes devinrent si grossiers que les témoins se cachainent la figure. Elle répétait, en s' . . . des mains, Venez donc, foutez-moi.*" On another occasion this same Claire de Sazilly, *se trouva si fort tentée de coucher avec son grand ami, qu'elle disait être Grandier, qu'un jour s'étant approchée pour recevoir la Sainte Communion, elle se leva soudain et monta dans sa chambre, où ayant été suivie par quelque'une des Sœurs, elle fut vue avec un Crucifix dans la main, dont elle se préparait. . . . L'honnêteté,* (adds Aubin) *ne permet pas d'écrire les ordures de cet endroit.* [A.H.]

oaths and blasphemies—these were "so unheard of that they could not have suggested themselves to a merely human mind."

How touchingly ingenuous this is! Alas, there is no horror which cannot suggest itself to human minds. "We know what we are," says Ophelia, "but we know not what we may be." Practically all of us are capable of practically anything. And this is true even of persons who have been brought up in the practice of the most austere morality. What is called "induction" is not confined to the lower levels of the brain and nervous system. It also takes place in the cortex, and is the physical basis of that ambivalence of sentiment which is so striking a feature of man's psychological life.[3] Every positive begets its corresponding negative. The sight of something red is followed by a green afterimage. The opposing muscle groups involved in any action automatically bring one another into play. And on a higher level we find such things as a hatred that accompanies love, a derision begotten by respect and awe. In a word, the inductive process is ubiquitously active. Sister Jane and her fellow nuns had had religion and chastity drummed into them from childhood. By induction, these lessons had called into existence, within the brain and its associated mind, a psychophysical center, from which there emanated contradictory lessons in irreligion and obscenity. (Every collection of spiritual letters abounds in references to those frightful temptations against the faith and against chastity, to which the seekers after perfection are peculiarly subject. Good directors point out that such temptations are normal and almost inevitable features of the spiritual life and must not be permitted to cause undue distress.)[4] At ordinary times

---

[3] See above [the Harper edition], p. 157 ff., and Ischlondsky, *Brain and Behaviour* (London, 1949). [A.H.]

[4] In a letter dated January 26, 1923, Dom John Chapman writes as follows: "In the 17th-18th centuries most pious souls seem to have gone through a period in which they felt sure that God had reprobated them. . . . This doesn't seem to happen nowadays. But the *corresponding*

these negative thoughts and feelings were repressed or, if they rose into consciousness, were by an effort of will denied any outlet in speech or action. Weakened by psychosomatic disease, made frantic by her indulgence in forbidden and unrealizable phantasies, the Prioress lost all power to control these undesirable results of the inductive process. Hysterical behavior is infectious, and her example was followed by the other nuns. Soon the whole convent was throwing fits, blaspheming and talking smut. For the sake of a publicity which was thought to be good for their respective Orders and the Church at large, or with the deliberate intention of using the nuns as instruments for the destruction of Grandier, the exorcists did everything in their power to foster and increase the scandal. The nuns were forced to perform their antics in public, were encouraged to blaspheme for distinguished visitors and to tickle the groundlings with displays of extravagant immodesty. We have already seen that, at the beginning of her malady, the Prioress did not believe herself to be possessed. It was only after her confessor and the other exorcists had repeatedly assured her that she was full of devils that Sister Jane came at last to be convinced that she was a demoniac and that her business, henceforth, was to behave as such. And the same was true of some at least of the other nuns. From a pamphlet published in 1634 we learn that Sister Agnes had frequently remarked, during exorcism, that she was not possessed, but that the friars had said she was and had constrained her to undergo exorcism. And "on the preceding twenty-sixth of June, the exorcist having by mistake let fall some burning sulphur on Sister Claire's lip, the poor girl burst into tears, saying

---

trial of our contemporaries seems to be the *feeling of not having any faith*; not temptation against any particular article (usually), but a mere feeling that religion is not true. . . . The only remedy is to *despise* the whole thing and pay no attention to it except (of course) to assure our Lord that one is ready to suffer from it as long as He wishes, which seems an absurd paradox to say to a Person one doesn't believe in." [A.H.]

that, "Since she had been told she was possessed, she was ready to believe it, but that she did not on that account deserve to be treated in this way.'" The work begun spontaneously by hysteria was completed by the suggestions of Mignon, Barré, Tranquille and the rest. All this was clearly understood at the time. "Granted that there is no cheat in the matter," wrote the author of the anonymous pamphlet cited above, "does it follow that the nuns are possessed? May it not be that, in their folly and mistaken imagination, they believe themselves to be possessed, when in fact they are not?" This, continues our author, can happen to nuns in three ways. First, as a result of fasts, watchings and meditations on hell and Satan. Second, in consequence of some remark made by their confessor—something which makes them think they are being tempted by devils. "And thirdly, the confessor, seeing them act strangely, may imagine in his ignorance that they are possessed or bewitched, and may afterward persuade them of the fact by the influence he exercises over their minds." In the present case the mistaken belief in possession was due to the third of these causes. Like the mercurial and antimonial poisonings of earlier days, like the sulfa poisoning and serum-fevers of the present, the Loudun epidemic was an "iatrogenic disease," produced and fostered by the very physicians who were supposed to be restoring the patients to health. The guilt of the exorcists seems the more enormous when we remember that their proceedings were in direct violation of the rules laid down by the Church. According to these rules, exorcisms were to be performed in private, the demons were not to be allowed to express their opinions, they were never to be believed, they were consistently to be treated with contempt. At Loudun, the nuns were exhibited to enormous crowds, their demons were encouraged to hold forth on every subject from sex to transubstantiation, their statements were accepted as gospel truth and they were treated as distinguished visitors from the next world, whose utterances had the authority almost of the Bible. If they blasphemed and talked bawdy—well, that was just their pretty way. And anyhow bawdry and blasphemy were box office. The faithful fairly lapped them up and came back, in their thousands, for more.

Supernatural blasphemy, more than human bawdry—and if these were not sufficient proofs of diabolic possession, what about the nuns' contortions? what about their exploits in the acrobatic field? Levitation had quickly been ruled out; but if the good sisters never rose into the air, they at least performed the most amazing feats on the floor. Sometimes, says de Nion, "they passed the left foot over the shoulder to the cheek. They also passed their feet over the head, until the big toes touched the nose. Others again were able to stretch their legs so far to the left and right that they sat on the ground, without any space being visible between their bodies and the floor. One, the Mother Superior, stretched her legs to such an extraordinary extent that, from toe to toe, the distance was seven feet, though she herself was but four feet high." Reading such accounts of the nuns' performances, one is forced to the conclusion that, as well as *naturaliter Christiana*, the feminine soul is *naturaliter Drum-Majoretta*. So far as the Eternal Feminine is concerned, a taste for acrobacy and exhibitionism would seem to be built in, only awaiting a favorable opportunity to manifest itself in handsprings and back somersaults. In the case of cloistered contemplatives, such opportunities are not of frequent occurrence. It look seven devils and Canon Mignon to create the circumstances in which, at long last, it became possible for Sister Jane to do the splits.

That the nuns found a deep satisfaction in their gymnastics is proved by de Nion's statement that, though for months at a stretch they were "tortured by the devils twice a day," their health in no way suffered. On the contrary, "those who were somewhat delicate seemed healthier than before the possession."

The latent drum majorettes, the cabaret dancers *in posse* had been permitted to come to the surface and, for the first time, these poor girls without a vocation for prayer were truly happy. . . .

HENRY STEELE COMMAGER

Henry Steele Commager, Professor of History at Columbia University from 1939 to 1956, and at Amherst College since 1956, is the author of more than thirty books, among them *Nature and Problems of History, The Great Proclamation, The Great Declaration,* and *The American Mind.*

WHO IS LOYAL TO AMERICA?

On 6 May 1947 a Russian-born girl, Mrs. Shura Lewis, gave a talk to the students of the Western High School of Washington, D.C. She talked about Russia—its school system, its public-health program, the position of women, of the aged, of the workers, the farmers, and the professional classes—and compared, superficially and uncritically, some American and Russian social institutions. The most careful examination of the speech—happily reprinted for us in the *Congressional Record*—does not disclose a single disparagement of anything American unless it is a quasi-humorous reference to the cost of having a baby and of dental treatment in this country. Mrs. Lewis said nothing that had not been said at least a thousand times, in speeches, in newspapers, magazines, and books. She said nothing that any normal person could find objectionable.

Her speech, however, created a sensation. A few students

From Henry Steele Commager, *Freedom, Loyalty, Dissent* (New York: Oxford, 1954), pp. 135-55. Copyright 1954 by Oxford University Press, Inc. Reprinted by permission. Originally published in *Harper's,* CXCV (September, 1947), 193-99. In his Preface to the book, dated February 1954, Commager wrote, "The theme, alas more relevant today than it was even in 1947, when the first of these essays was written, is the necessity of freedom in a society such as the American . . ." (p. vii).

walked out on it. Others improvised placards proclaiming their devotion to Americanism. Indignant mothers telephoned their protests. Newspapers took a strong stand against the outrage. Congress, rarely concerned for the political or economic welfare of the citizens of the capital city, reacted sharply when its intellectual welfare was at stake. Congressmen Rankin and Dirksen thundered and lightninged; the District of Columbia Committee went into a huddle; there were demands for house-cleaning in the whole school system, which was obviously shot through and through with communism.

All this might be ignored, for we have learned not to expect either intelligence or understanding of Americanism from this element in our Congress. More ominous was the reaction of the educators entrusted with the high responsibility of guiding and guarding the intellectual welfare of our boys and girls. Did they stand up for intellectual freedom? Did they insist that high-school children have the right and the duty to learn about other countries? Did they protest that students are to be trusted to use intelligence and common sense? Did they affirm that the Americanism of their students is staunch enough to resist propaganda? Did they perform even the elementary task, expected of educators above all, of analyzing the much criticized speech?

Not at all. The District Superintendent of Schools, Dr. Hobart Corning, hastened to agree with the animadversions of Representatives Rankin and Dirksen. The whole thing was, he confessed, "a very unfortunate occurrence," and had "shocked the whole school system." What Mrs. Lewis said, he added gratuitously, was "repugnant to all who are working with youth in the Washington schools," and "the entire affair contrary to the philosophy of education under which we operate." Mr. Danowsky, the hapless principal of the Western High School, was "the most shocked and regretful of all." The District of Columbia Committee would be happy to know that, though he was innocent in the matter, he had been properly reprimanded!

It is the reaction of the educators that makes this episode more than a tempest in a teapot. We expect hysteria from Mr. Rankin and some newspapers; we are shocked when we see educators, timid before criticism and confused about first principles, betray their trust. And we wonder what can be that "philosophy of education" which believes that young people can be trained to the duties of citizenship by wrapping their minds in cotton-wool.

Merely by talking about Russia Mrs. Lewis was thought to be attacking Americanism. It is indicative of the seriousness of the situation that during this same week the House found it necessary to take time out from the discussion of the labor bill, the tax bill, the International Trade Organization, and the world famine to meet assaults upon Americanism from a new quarter. This time it was the artists who were undermining the American system, and members of the House spent some hours passing around reproductions of the paintings which the State Department had sent abroad as part of its program for advertising American culture. We need not pause over the exquisite humor which Congressmen displayed in their comments on modern art: weary statesmen must have their fun. But we may profitably remark the major criticism which was directed against this unfortunate collection of paintings. What was wrong with these paintings, it shortly appeared, was that they were un-American. "No American drew those crazy pictures," said Mr. Rankin—who ought to know. The copious files of the Committee on Un-American Activities were levied upon to prove that of the forty-five artists represented "no less than twenty were definitely New Deal in various shades of Communism." The damning facts are specified for each of the pernicious twenty; we can content ourselves with the first of them, Ben-Zion. What is the evidence here? "Ben-Zion was one of the signers of a letter sent to President Roosevelt by the United American Artists which urged help to the USSR and Britain after Hitler attacked Russia." He was, in short, a fellow-traveler of Churchill and Roosevelt.

The same day that Mr. Dirksen was denouncing the Washington school authorities for allowing students to hear about Russia ("In Russia," Mrs. Lewis said, "equal right is granted to each nationality. There is no discrimination. Nobody says, you are a Negro, you are a Jew"), Representative Williams of Mississippi rose to denounce the *Survey-Graphic* magazine and to add further to our understanding of Americanism. The *Survey-Graphic*, he said, "contained 129 pages of outrageously vile and nauseating anti-Southern, anti-Christian, un-American, and pro-Communist tripe, ostensibly directed toward the elimination of the custom of racial segregation in the South." It was written by "meddling un-American purveyors of hate and indecency."

All in all, a busy week for the House.[1] Yet those who make a practice of reading their *Record* will agree that it was a typical week. For increasingly Congress is concerned with the eradication of disloyalty and the defense of Americanism, and scarcely a day passes that some Congressman does not treat us to exhortations and admonitions, impassioned appeals and eloquent declamations, similar to those inspired by Mrs. Lewis,

---

[1] A long week. The attack on Ben-Zion by Fred E. Busbey (Rep., Ill.) took place on May 13, 1947. The distress of John Bell Williams (Dem., Miss.) over the *Survey Graphic* and the dismay of Everett M. Dirksen (Rep., Ill.) and John Rankin (Dem., Miss.) over Mrs. Lewis's speech were voiced on May 20, 1947. If you want to see how restrained Commager is, consult the days in question in *Congressional Record*, Vol. 93, Part 4. Dirksen, as Chairman of the House Committee that governs the District of Columbia, protecting *his* schools, introduced the Lewis speech into the *Record*; it can be found in the volume cited, pp. 5535-37. It was apparently the issue of *Survey Graphic* for January 1947 that so upset Williams; it was devoted entirely to a study of segregation.

Mr. Ben-Zion, and the editors of the *Survey-Graphic*. And scarcely a day passes that the outlines of the new loyalty and the new Americanism are not etched more sharply in public policy.

And this is what is significant—the emergence of new patterns of Americanism and of loyalty, patterns radically different from those which have long been traditional. It is not only the Congress that is busy designing the new patterns. They are outlined in President Truman's Loyalty Order of March 1947; in similar orders formulated by the New York City Council and by state and local authorities throughout the country; in the programs of the Daughters of the American Revolution, the American Legion, and similar patriotic organizations; in the editorials of the Hearst and the Mc-Cormick-Patterson papers;[2] and in an elaborate series of advertisements sponsored by large corporations and business organizations. In the making is a revival of the Red hysteria of the early 1920s, one of the shabbiest chapters in the history of American democracy; and more than a revival, for the new crusade is designed not merely to frustrate communism but to formulate a positive definition of Americanism, and a positive concept of loyalty.

What is the new loyalty? It is, above all, conformity. It is the uncritical and unquestioning acceptance of America as it is—the political institutions, the social relationships, the economic practices. It rejects inquiry into the race question or socialized medicine, or public housing, or into the wisdom or validity of our foreign policy. It regards as particularly heinous any challenge to what is called "the system of private enterprise," identifying that system with Americanism. It abandons

---

[2] The New York City papers in William Randolph Hearst's chain were the *Journal-American* and the *Mirror*. Colonel Robert McCormick ran the Chicago *Tribune*, and his cousin, Joseph Patterson, the New York *Daily News*.

evolution, repudiates the once popular concept of progress, and regards America as a finished product, perfect and complete.

It is, it must be added, easily satisfied. For it wants not intellectual conviction or spiritual conquest but mere outward conformity. In matters of loyalty it takes the word for the deed, the gesture for the principle. It is content with the flag salute, and does not pause to consider the warning of our Supreme Court that "a person gets from a symbol the meaning he puts into it, and what is one man's comfort and inspiration is another's jest and scorn." It is satisfied with membership in respectable organizations and, as it assumes that every member of a liberal organization is a Communist, concludes that every member of a conservative one is a true American. It has not yet learned that not everyone who saith Lord, Lord, shall enter into the kingdom of Heaven. It is designed neither to discover real disloyalty nor to foster true loyalty.

What is wrong with this new concept of loyalty? What, fundamentally, is wrong with the pusillanimous retreat of the Washington educators, the antics of Washington legislators, the outcries of alarm from the American Legion, the vulgar appeals of business corporations? It is not merely that these things are offensive. It is rather that they are wrong—morally, socially, and politically.

The concept of loyalty as conformity is a false one. It is narrow and restrictive, denies freedom of thought and of conscience, and is irremediably stained by private and selfish considerations. "Enlightened loyalty," wrote Josiah Royce, who made loyalty the very core of his philosophy,

means harm to no man's loyalty. It is at war only with disloyalty, and its warfare, unless necessity constrains, is only a spiritual warfare. It does not foster class hatreds; it knows of nothing reasonable about race prejudices; and it regards all races of men as one in their need of loyalty. It ignores mutual misunderstandings. It loves its own wherever upon earth its own, namely loyalty itself, is to be found.

Justice, charity, wisdom, spirituality, he added, were all definable in terms of loyalty, and we may properly ask which of these qualities our contemporary champions of loyalty display.

Above all, loyalty must be to something larger than oneself, untainted by private purposes or selfish ends. But what are we to say of the attempts by the NAM and by individual corporations to identify loyalty with the system of private enterprise? Is it not as if officeholders should attempt to identify loyalty with their own party, their own political careers? Do not those corporations which pay for full-page advertisements associating Americanism with the competitive system expect, ultimately, to profit from that association? Do not those organizations that deplore, in the name of patriotism, the extension of government operation of hydro-electric power expect to profit from their campaign?

Certainly it is a gross perversion not only of the concept of loyalty but of the concept of Americanism to identify it with a particular economic system. This precise question, interestingly enough, came before the Supreme Court in the Schneiderman case of 1943—and it was Wendell Willkie who was counsel for Schneiderman. Said the Court:

Throughout our history many sincere people whose attachment to the general Constitutional scheme cannot be doubted have, for various and even divergent reasons, urged differing degrees of governmental ownership and control of natural resources, basic means of production, and banks and the media of exchange, either with or without compensation. And something once regarded as a species of private property was abolished without compensating the owners when the institution of slavery was forbidden. Can it be said that the author of the Emancipation Proclamation and the supporters of the Thirteenth Amendment were not attached to the Constitution?

There is, it should be added, a further danger in the willful identification of Americanism with a particular body of economic practices. Some economists have predicted for the future an economic crash similar to that of 1929. If Americanism is equated with competitive capitalism, what happens to it if competitive capitalism comes a cropper? If loyalty and private enterprise are inextricably associated, what is to preserve loyalty if private enterprise fails? Those who associate Americanism with a particular program of economic practices have a grave responsibility, for if their program should fall into disrepute, they expose Americanism itself to disrepute.

The effort to equate loyalty with conformity is misguided because it assumes that there is a fixed content to loyalty and that this can be determined and defined. But loyalty is a principle, and eludes definition except in its own terms. It is devotion to the best interests of the commonwealth, and may require hostility to the particular policies which the government pursues, the particular practices which the economy undertakes, the particular institutions which society maintains. "If there is any fixed star in our Constitutional constellation," said the Supreme Court in the Barnette flag-salute case, "it is that no official, high or petty, can prescribe what shall be orthodox in politics, nationalism, religion, or other matters of opinion, or force citizens to confess by word or act their faith therein. If there are any circumstances which permit an exception they do not now occur to us."

True loyalty may require, in fact, what appears to the naïve to be disloyalty. It may require hostility to certain provisions of the Constitution itself, and historians have not concluded that those abolitionists who back in the 1840s and 1850s subscribed to the "Higher Law" were lacking in loyalty. We should not forget that our tradition is one of protest and revolt, and it is stultifying to celebrate the rebels of the past—Jefferson and Paine, Emerson and Thoreau—while we silence the rebels of the present. "We are a rebellious nation," said Theodore Parker, known in his day as the Great American Preacher, and went on:

Our whole history is treason; our blood was attainted before we were born; our creeds are infidelity to the mother church; our constitution, treason to our fatherland. What of that? Though all the governors in the world bid us commit treason against man, and set the example, let us never submit.

Those who would impose upon us a new concept of loyalty not only assume that this is possible but have the presumption to believe that they are competent to write the definition. We are reminded of Whitman's defiance of the "never-ending audacity of elected persons." Who are those who would set the standards of loyalty? They are Rankins and Bilbos, officials of the DAR and the Legion and the NAM, Hearsts and McCormicks. May we not say of Rankin's harangues on loyalty what Emerson said of Webster at the time of his championship of the Fugitive Slave Law of 1850: "The word honor in the mouth of Mr. Webster is like the word love in the mouth of a whore."

What do men know of loyalty who make a mockery of the Declaration of Independence and the Bill of Rights, whose energies are dedicated to stirring up race and class hatreds, who would straitjacket the American spirit? What indeed do they know of America—the America of Sam Adams and Tom Paine, of Jackson's defiance of the Court and Lincoln's celebration of labor, of Thoreau's essay on Civil Disobedience and Emerson's championship of John Brown, of the America of the Fourierists and the Come-Outers, of cranks and fanatics, of socialists and anarchists? Who among American heroes could meet their tests, who would be cleared by their committees? Not Washington, who was a rebel. Not Jefferson, who wrote that all men are created equal and whose motto was "rebellion to tyrants is obedience to God." Not Garrison, who publicly burned the

Constitution; or Wendell Phillips, who spoke for the under-privileged everywhere and counted himself a philosophical anarchist; not Seward of the Higher Law or Sumner of racial equality. Not Lincoln, who admonished us to have malice toward none, charity for all; or Wilson, who warned that our flag was "a flag of liberty of opinion as well as of political liberty"; or Justice Holmes, who said that our Constitution is an experiment and that while that experiment is being made "we should be eternally vigilant against attempts to check the expression of opinions that we loathe and believe to be fraught with death." ...[3]

It is easier to say what loyalty is not than what it is. It is not conformity. It is not passive acquiescence in the status quo. It is not preference for everything American over everything foreign. It is not an ostrich-like ignorance of other countries and other institutions. It is not the indulgence in ceremony—a flag salute, an oath of allegiance, a fervid verbal declaration. It is not a particular creed, a particular version of history, a particular body of economic practices, a particular philosophy.

It is a tradition, an ideal, and a principle. It is a willingness to subordinate every private advantage for the larger good. It is an appreciation of the rich and diverse contributions that can come from the most varied sources. It is allegiance to the traditions that have guided our greatest statesmen and inspired our most eloquent poets—the traditions of freedom, equality, democracy, tolerance, the tradition of the Higher Law, of experimentation, cooperation, and pluralism. It is a realization that America was born of revolt, flourished on dissent, became great through experimentation.

Independence was an act of revolution; republicanism was

---

[3] I cut a few pages on the impracticality of loyalty tests. For Commager, they are no protection from real dangers but only a threat to dissent.

something new under the sun; the federal system was a vast experimental laboratory. Physically Americans were pioneers; in the realm of social and economic institutions, too, their tradition has been one of pioneering. From the beginning, intellectual and spiritual diversity have been as characteristic of America as racial and linguistic diversity. The most distinctively American philosophies have been transcendentalism— which is the philosophy of the Higher Law—and pragmatism —which is the philosophy of experimentation and pluralism. These two principles are the very core of Americanism: the principle of the Higher Law, or of obedience to the dictates of conscience rather than of statutes, and the principle of pragmatism, or the rejection of a single good and of the notion of a finished universe. From the beginning Americans have known that there were new worlds to conquer, new truths to be discovered. Every effort to confine Americanism to a single pattern, to constrain it to a single formula, is disloyalty to everything that is valid in Americanism.

JOSEPH R. McCARTHY

Joseph R. McCarthy, United States Senator from Wisconsin from 1946 until his death in 1957, was the author of *McCarthyism: The Fight for America*, among other books.

COMMUNISTS IN
THE STATE DEPARTMENT

Fellow Americans, thank you very much for the opportunity to be with you tonight to discuss a subject which, in my opinion, towers in importance above all others. It is the subject of international atheistic communism. It deals with the problem of destroying the conspiracy against the people of America and free men everywhere. There are many phases of this subject which we might well discuss. However, the time is limited. Therefore, your program chairman and I have agreed that I shall briefly hit a few of the high spots and then will try to answer some of the many questions which I understand you editors want to ask about the anti-Communist fight in Washington.

Ladies and gentlemen, many of you have been engaged in this all-out fight against communism long before I came on the scene. You have been engaged in what may well be that final Armageddon foretold in the Bible—that struggle between light

---

From *Congressional Record*, Vol. 96, Part 15, pp. A4159-A4160. The speech runs on to p. A4162, but I cut away the part of it which dealt with specific cases with the pseudo-precision (to use Fender's word) so characteristic of the Senator from Wisconsin. The speech was first given on May 25, 1950, at the Catholic Press Association convention in Rochester, New York; hence, the "you editors" of the first paragraph.

and darkness, between good and evil, between life and death, if you please.

At the start, let me make it clear that in my opinion no special credit is due those of us who are making an all-out fight against this Godless force—a force which seeks to destroy all the honesty and decency that every Protestant, Jew and Catholic has been taught at his mother's knee. It is a task for which we can claim no special credit for doing. It is one which we are obligated to perform. It is one of the tasks for which we were brought into this world—for which we were born. If we fail to use all the powers of mind and body which God gave us, than I am sure our mothers, wherever they are tonight, may well sorrow for the day of our birth.

To fight, however, we must have facts. Those facts we do have. They stand as clear silhouettes, outlined by the fires of communism that are sweeping across Europe and Asia and flickering on the shores of America.

We know that the major aim of communism, as stated by its atheistic leaders more than thirty years ago, is to create a Red China, thence a Red Asia, wash it with a Red Pacific— and then enslave America.

In this connection let us take a look at the magnitude of Russian success and the enormity of our disaster in China. This is the disaster to which Mr. Acheson refers as the dawning of a new day; the disaster to which Mr. Lattimore refers as a "limitless horizon of hope."[1]

For whom is Mr. Acheson's new day dawning? Who faces Lattimore's limitless horizon of hope? Not China. Not the forces of democracy in America, but the military masters of the Soviet Union.

The question in the mind of a man elected to represent the people of this Nation and indirectly the people of the world is, Why is this so?

---

[1] For Owen Lattimore, see p. 218. Dean Acheson was Secretary of State.

Is it because we are less intelligent than the Communists? Is it because we can't match them in courage? Is it because their devotion to atheism is greater than our devotion to God? Is it because we are less willing to stand up and fight for what we think is right? Ladies and gentlemen, the answer to all those questions is "No." Then what is the answer? Is it in our leadership? To that my answer is "Yes," and I challenge anyone to find another answer.

I have been naming and presenting evidence against those leaders who have been responsible for selling into Communist slavery 400,000,000 people—those leaders responsible for the creation of Communist steppingstones to the American shores.

Those in power in Washington say that this is not so; that those are not the men. Now if I have named the wrong men, then the American people are entitled to know who is responsible for the tremendous Communist victory in Asia and the dismal American defeat—the greatest defeat any nation has suffered in war or peace.

It is essential, therefore, that we put the spotlight of exposure on those who are responsible for this disaster. This is important, not for the purpose of exposing past failures, but because those same men are now doing America's planning for the future. Unfortunately they have become so deeply entrenched that almost every power of the Government is used to sabotage any attempt to expose and root them out.

Let me give you one example of the difficulty experienced in pointing the spotlight of exposure on those who are a threat to this Nation. It is an example of the extent to which men honored with high positions will go to conceal communism, men whose shadows hover like vultures over the corpse of China and whose actions rip at the backbone of freedom in America.

It is an example of the extent to which the State Department will go in order to deceive and practice a deliberate fraud on the American people. In order to give you this example, it is necessary to publicly divulge information, which I had hoped could be properly presented to the committee. I am going to give you several reproductions of secret loyalty files.

I have first carefully eliminated any material which might in any way interfere with the workings of our investigative agencies.

The documents which are being given to you tonight should under no stretch of the imagination be kept secret. The secrecy label could only be applied to protect those who would cover up their incompetence or double-dealing. . . .

WHITTAKER CHAMBERS

Whittaker Chambers worked for the Communist Party from 1925 until 1938, first as an editor, then as a spy courier. He later worked for *Time*, was a senior editor at *Life*, and, after the Hiss case, was a senior editor at *National Review*. He died in 1961.

WITNESS

To be an informer. . . .

Men shrink from that word and what it stands for as from something lurking and poisonous. Spy is a different breed of word. Espionage is a function of war whether it be waged between nations, classes or parties. Like the soldier, the spy stakes his freedom or his life on the chances of action. Like the soldier, his acts are largely impersonal. He seldom knows whom he cripples or kills. Spy as an epithet is a convention of morale; the enemy's spy is always monstrous; our spy is daring and brave. It must be so since all camps use spies and must while war lasts.

The informer is different,[1] particularly the ex-Communist informer. He risks little. He sits in security and uses his special

---

From Whittaker Chambers, *Witness* (New York: Random House, 1952), pp. 453-57. Copyright 1952 by Whittaker Chambers. Reprinted by permission of Random House, Inc. In 1948 Chambers accused Alger Hiss of having passed documents to the Russians, thus triggering the most celebrated case of the 1950s. See note, p. 217. Chambers' book was generally accepted or attacked as an apologia for his part in the affair. This excerpt (Chapter 10, Section ii) is an indication of the mental processes that preceded Chambers' decision to expose Hiss.

[1] I am not speaking of such people as the F.B.I. and other security agencies send into the Communist Party. In the true sense of the word, they are not informers but spies, working in exposed, and sometimes hazardous, positions. [W.C.]

knowledge to destroy others. He has that special information to give because he knows those others' faces, voices and lives, because he once lived within their confidence, in a shared faith, trusted by them as one of themselves, accepting their friendship, feeling their pleasures and griefs, sitting in their houses, eating at their tables, accepting their kindness, knowing their wives and children. If he had not done those things, he would have no use as an informer.

Because he has that use, the police protect him. He is their creature. When they whistle, he fetches a soiled bone of information. He and they share a common chore, which is a common complicity in the public interest. It cannot be the action of equals, and even the kindness that seeks to mask the fact merely exasperates and cannot change it. For what is the day's work of the police is the ex-Communist's necessity. They may choose what they will or will not do. He has no choice. He has surrendered his choice. To that extent, though he be free in every other way, the informer is a slave. He is no longer a man. He is free only to the degree in which he understands what he is doing and why he must do it.

Let every ex-Communist look unblinkingly at that image. It is himself. By the logic of his position in the struggles of this age, every ex-Communist is an informer from the moment he breaks with Communism, regardless of how long it takes him to reach the police station.

For Communism fixes the consequences of its evil not only on those who serve it, but also on those, who, once having served it, seek to serve against it. It has set the pattern of the warfare it wages and that defines the pattern of the warfare its deserters must wage against it. It cannot be otherwise. Communism exists to wage war. Its existence implies, even in peace or truce, a state of war that engages every man, woman and child alive, but, above all, the ex-Communist. For no man simply deserts *from* the Communist Party. He deserts *against* it. He deserts to struggle against Communism as an evil. There would otherwise be no reason for his desertion, however long it may take him to grasp the fact. Otherwise, he should have remained within the Communist Party, and his failure to act at all against it betrays the fact that he has not broken with it. He has broken only with its organization, or certain of its forms, practices, discomforts of action or political necessity. And this, despite the sound human and moral reasons that may also paralyze him—his reluctance to harm old friends, his horror at using their one-time trust in him to destroy them —reasons which are honorable and valid.

But if the ex-Communist truly believes that Communism is evil, if he truly means to struggle against it as an evil, and as the price of his once having accepted it, he must decide to become an informer. In that war which Communism insists on waging, and which therefore he cannot evade, he has one specific contribution to make—his special knowledge of the enemy. That is what all have to offer first of all. Because Communism is a conspiracy, that knowledge is indispensable for the active phase of the struggle against it. That every ex-Communist has to offer, regardless of what else he may have to offer, special skills or special talents or the factors that make one character different from another.

I hold that it is better, because in general clarity is more maturing than illusion, for the ex-Communist to make the offering in the full knowledge of what he is doing, the knowledge that henceforth he is no longer a free man but an informer. That penalty those who once firmly resolved to take upon themselves the penalties for the crimes of politics and history, in the belief that only at that cost could Man be free, must assume no less firmly as the price of their mistake. For, in the end, the choice for the ex-Communist is between shielding a small number of people who still actively further what he now sees to be evil, or of helping to shield millions from that evil which threatens even their souls. Those who do not inform are still conniving at that evil. That is the crux of the moral choice which an ex-Communist must make in recognizing that the logic of his position makes him an informer. Moreover, he must always make it amidst the deafening chatter and verbal droppings of those who sit above the battle, who lack the power to act for good or evil because they lack any power to act at all, and who, in the day when heaven was falling, were, in Dante's words, neither for God nor for Satan, but were for themselves.

On that road of the informer it is always night. I who have traveled it from end to end, and know its windings, switchbacks and sheer drops—I cannot say at what point, where or when, the ex-Communist must make his decision to take it. That depends on the individual man. Nor is it simply a matter of taking his horror in his hands and making his avowals. The ex-Communist is a man dealing with other men, men of many orders of intelligence, of many motives of self-interest or malice, men sometimes infiltrated or tainted by the enemy, in an immensely complex pattern of politics and history. If he means to be effective, if he does not wish his act merely to be wasted suffering for others and himself, how, when and where the ex-Communist informs are matters calling for the shrewdest judgment.

Some ex-Communists are so stricken by the evil they have freed themselves from that they inform exultantly against it. No consideration, however humane, no tie however tender, checks them. They understand, as few others do, the immensity of the danger, and experience soon teaches them the gulf fixed between the reality they must warn against and the ability of the world to grasp their warnings. Fear makes them strident. They are like breathless men who have outrun the lava flow of a volcano and must shout down the smiles of the villagers at its base who, regardless of their own peril, remember complacently that those who now try to warn them once offered their faith and their lives to the murderous mountain.

By temperament, I cannot share such exultation or stridency, though I understand both. I cannot ever inform against anyone without feeling something die within me. I inform without pleasure because it is necessary. Each time, relief lies only in the certainty that, when enough has died in a man, at last the man himself dies, as light fails.

Sometimes, by informing, the ex-Communist can claim immunity of one kind or another for acts committed before his change of heart or sides. He is right to claim it, for if he is to be effective, his first task is to preserve himself. Sometimes, he can even enjoy such immunity, if he is able to feel what is happening to him in the simplest terms, impersonally, as an experience of history and of war in which he at last has found his bearings and which he is helping to wage. By the rules of war, common sense and self-interest, the world can scarcely lose by allowing him his immunity. It does well, provided by acts he makes amends, to help him to forget his past, if only because in the crisis of the twentieth century, not all the mistakes were committed by the ex-Communists.

I never asked for immunity. Nor did anyone at any time ever offer me immunity, even by a hint or a whisper. What immunity can the world offer a man against his thoughts?

THE REPORTER

THE ROAD TO DAMASCUS

A few days ago we read a speech by former Senator Harry Cain of Washington, now a member of the Subversive Activities Control Board. Before we had gotten through the first paragraph we found the Senator warning that this country had set up a security system which could "snuff out the lights of learning while making cowards and mental robots out of free men and women," and that "we had constructed an apparatus which can destroy us if we don't watch out . . ."[1]

Since Harry Cain has always been tagged as a buddy of Joe McCarthy's, we figured something must have happened and called at his office to find out what.

"I guess you wonder what happened to me," said the former Senator. "A lot of things. For one thing, I get to see a lot of people in this job. I listen to the organizations, and then I have to go around to the Justice Department and places like that. I talk to people. Even more important, for the first time since I got out of school, I have fifty per cent of my time to think.

"Then one day a man came in from my state. He was a

From *The Reporter*, XII (February 10, 1955), 4. Copyright 1955 by Fortnightly Publishing Co., Inc. Although the event and the article describing it came two years after *The Crucible*, I thought it might provide an analogy worth contemplating: try Harry Cain as John Hale.

[1] An abridged version of Cain's speech was published as "Security of the Republic," *New Republic*, CXXXII (January 31, 1955), 6-10. He gave the speech on January 15 before a group of Republicans in the Fifth Congressional District, Spokane, Washington. Cain had served as Senator from that state from 1946 to 1952.

scientist and a security case. He told me neither one of his
Senators nor his Congressman was interested in him. They
wouldn't touch his case with a ten-foot pole. He told me he
was a Democrat but he couldn't get any help from the Demo-
crats. I told him I'd look into it and see what I could do.
I'm not a lawyer but I defended that one.

"He was a scientist, working on cancer problems for the
government. What could be more important to the country?
But someone said he was a Communist organizer back in
1941. His maid said there used to be a lot of funny-looking
people around the house. And an old lady of eighty wrote in
—she never came to testify—and said he used to associate with
some funny people. Of course he did; he's a nonconformist."

Harry Cain tried to fight that one. "I couldn't believe we'd
lose," he said, "but we did."

After a year on the job, Harry Cain has concluded that
"whether in or out of the government, the orthodox mind
because of its strength and singleness of purpose maintains
and preserves progress, but the dreamer and nonconformist
makes progress. . . ." Moreover, the "eager beavers and Johnny-
come-latelies" who have become security officers cannot distinguish between nonconformity and security risk.

The Wolf Ladejinsky case,[2] he told us, was a good sample.
"Take the security officer over in Agriculture. One day he's a
farmer. Two weeks later he's the head of the security department. Now if that isn't a Johnny-come-lately, what is? I can
guess just what happened. He saw a few things: 'Amtorg,

---

[2] The Russian-born Ladejinsky was ousted from his position as agri-
cultural attaché in Tokyo in December 1954, after responsibility for such
positions passed from the Department of State to the Department of
Agriculture. Benson was Secretary of Agriculture. Ladejinsky was immediately hired by the Foreign Operations Administration and, after the
ludicrousness of the situation became public knowledge, cleared by
Benson in July 1955. Amtorg is the Soviet trading corporation, for
which Ladejinsky worked briefly as a translator in the early 1930s.

three sisters in Russia, two Communist fronts.' So what does he do? He doesn't have enough sense to ask any questions. He just calls him a security risk.

"And then it goes to Ezra Benson. Ezra's a pious man. So what does he do? He goes home and prays all night. And then he comes back satisfied that God is on his side. No questions. He didn't go over and talk to Dulles. He didn't talk to Ladejinsky. He didn't find out any more about it. He just went home and prayed all night."

Harry Cain thought about the situation for quite a while, then decided to get it all off his chest by making a speech. He worked on it nights at his kitchen table, and then a group of old friends in the State of Washington, conservative people, asked him to come home and make a talk. So he got it off his chest for an hour and fifteen minutes. No one squirmed, no one coughed, no one wriggled. They liked it.

Harry Cain is waiting for a White House reaction. If the White House doesn't like it, he says, he can quit. "But they might decide I'm right. They might just change this system. If they do I'd like to be in on it."

The Crucible:
SPIN-OFFS

BERNARD STAMBLER

Bernard Stambler taught music and drama at the University of Indiana and George Washington University, and has been a member of the literary faculty of the Juilliard School of Music since 1947. He is the author of *Dante's Other World* and has also written librettos for *The Lady from Colorado* and *The Servant of Two Masters.*

THE CRUCIBLE

Act III

Scene 1. Two days later. Woods, misty moonlight. The edge of Reverend Parris's house is barely visible. Abigail and John enter, she with a cloak thrown over a nightdress. She is tender and amorous. He is serious and under strain.

ABIGAIL: John, John, I knew you'd come back to me. Night after night I been waitin for you. (*She comes to be embraced. He extends his arms to hold her off, but she only nestles within them.*)

JOHN: No, no, you could not—

ABIGAIL: I cannot sleep for dreamin. I cannot dream but I wake and walk about, thinkin I'd find you comin through some door. Oh, John, my love, come to me now as you came before, like some great stallion wildly pantin for me. We are free now, free to love.

JOHN: No, Abby, we are not free.

ABIGAIL: John, surely you sport with me.

JOHN: You know me better. We are not free, I say. Elizabeth lies in jail, accused by you. The village lies under a curse, your curse. That is why I'm here, to tell you you must free them. You can, and you must.

ABIGAIL: Free them? But I am freeing them—from their own corruption. I am possessed by the Spirit. I open them to God—these psalm-singin hypocrites who say I danced for the Devil. Let them suffer for it now who must, but some day they will come to me and thank me on their knees.

JOHN: Abby, Abby, what do you say? You become a monster of evil. You whelp of the Devil, how can you do these things? Are you lookin to be whipped?

ABIGAIL (*She looks him full in the face and as she moves toward him drops her cloak from her shoulders*): No, no. I look only for John Proctor that took me from my sleep and put knowledge in my heart. For him that awakened me and taught me to love. Oh, John, John, you too are possessed of the Spirit of God!

JOHN: The Spirit of God?

ABIGAIL: Leave Elizabeth, your sickly wife!

JOHN: Speak nothin of Elizabeth.

ABIGAIL: Together let us do our holy work.

JOHN: "Holy work" you call it! It's fraud, pretense and fraud
—and I shall expose it.

ABIGAIL: Call it what you will. . . . Do what you like. But if
your sniveling Elizabeth dies—remember, remember, it is
you who kill her.

CURTAIN

JEAN-PAUL SARTRE

Jean-Paul Sartre, the French existentialist philosopher and playwright, has written scenarios for many of his own works, including *Les Mains Sales* and *Huis-Clos*.

ON *LES SORCIÈRES DE SALEM*

. . . As for the play, what troubles me is the ambiguity of the ending. Out of something that was a specifically American phenomenon, something universal has been made which at the same time signifies nothing more than that intolerance is everywhere and that everything always boils down to the same thing.

The mistake doubtless lay in entrusting to Marcel Aymé the task of adapting the play. Thus a whole violent, passionate side has disappeared from it. The emphasis is no longer on the "witches"; the social import of the affair is completely blurred.

Actually it is a question of a battle for the possession of the land between the old settlers and the new ones, between the rich and the poor. This we no longer recognize in Aymé's adaptation. There we see a man pursued one no longer knows

From "Jean-Paul Sartre *nous parle de théâtre*" in *Théâtre Populaire*, No. 15 (September–October 1955), 9, translated by Nora L. Magid. This excerpt is Sartre's answer to the one question about the French production of *The Crucible* (see note, p. 239) in a long interview (pp. 1-9) attempting to define, as the headnote says, "the conditions for the existence and the practice of a truly popular theatre." Bernard Dort was the interviewer. For other comments on *Les Sorcières de* Salem, see pp. 239-247. This selection might well have been placed with the others, but it seems a proper introduction to Sartre's film version of Miller's play, in which presumably he corrected the defects he found in the stage adaptation.

exactly by what, and the whole ending of *Les Sorcières de Salem* smacks of a disconcerting idealism. The death of Montand[1] and the fact that he accepts that death would have had meaning if they were shown as an act of revolt based in social conflict. But in the production at the Théâtre Sarah Bernhardt this social conflict has become incomprehensible, and the death of Montand seems like a purely ethical attitude, not like a free act which he commits to unleash the shame, effectively to deny his position, like the only thing which he can still do.

Thus rendered insipid, castrated, Miller's play seems to me precisely to be a mystifying play,[2] since each of us can see there what he wants to, since each member of the audience will find there the confirmation of his own attitude. That's because the political ideas and social bases of the witch-hunt phenomenon do not appear clearly there.

---

[1] Yves Montand played Proctor.

[2] This phrase is being used in a rather special sense. *Mystifiante* includes the idea of hoaxing, purposefully mystifying. Earlier in the interview, Sartre seems to dismiss the demystification theories of Bertolt Brecht, by which the audience is made privy to the process of putting on the play, in favor of a modified kind of demystification, in which the audience is allowed to experience the play in a traditional manner but in which that experience is not at the expense of the truth (which is to say the political point) the playwright wants to convey.

IN SALEM PRISON

JOHN (*harshly*): You wanted to see me before you die.

ELIZABETH: I am not going to die, John.

JOHN: Then . . . you have confessed? You? That's not possible.

ELIZABETH: I didn't have to confess. I'm pregnant.

JOHN: Pregnant? Then yes, you will live. You will live, you will raise our children, perhaps you will remarry. And that doesn't keep you from asking me to die?

ELIZABETH (*stunned*): To die?

JOHN: That's why you came, isn't it?

ELIZABETH: I came to beg you to live.

JOHN: You? . . . I will live if I confess.

ELIZABETH: Yes.

JOHN: You too! You too! Must I be contemptible!

ELIZABETH (*tenderly*): Be quiet! You know I can't speak. Pride stops my mouth. You must help me.

JOHN (*handing her the confession he has not yet signed*): Look.

ELIZABETH (*having read it*): Add that you killed Mr. Putnam's cows. You would only have to sign it. Sign, John! I'm your wife and I don't want you dead. My God, smash this wall of pride and shame, give me the words to convince him . . . You are the best of men, John, that's why you should live. Such goodness must not disappear from the world.

From *Les Lettres Français*, No. 631 (August 2-8, 1956), pp. 1, 10, entitled "*Dans la prison de Salem*," translated by Gerald Weales. As Henry Magnan points out in his headnote, there may be differences between the printed scene and the form it finally took. The emphasis, however, is that of the finished film. *Les Sorcières de* Salem once again directed by Raymond Rouleau with Yves Montand and Simone Signoret as the Proctors, was released in 1957. It reached the United States in 1958.

JOHN (*ironically*): The best! Then all mankind is roasting over the fire: the best of men is damned.

ELIZABETH (*intensely*): If God sends you to hell, I renounce my part of heaven. Everything is my fault. Ashamed of having a body, I made you ashamed to want me. I was ice and fire: I waited for your kisses and I hated being moved. I was tongue-tied, my heart sealed off, my body paralyzed; you were horrified at yourself because I ended frozen with horror. You thought me your judge and I was only your executioner. You would never have sinned if I had known how to keep you in my bed. For four months now my eyes have been open. Nobody should have done what you did for me. You shouted your sins in front of everyone, you destroyed yourself to save me. I love you.

JOHN: You asked God to pardon you for having married me.

ELIZABETH: Me? The only self-respect left to me is in being your wife.

JOHN: Look at me. You've never lied?

ELIZABETH: Never, except once, before the court, when they asked me if you were an adulterer.

JOHN: Then tell me what you came to say.

ELIZABETH: You are good, John! You are courageous! You are innocent. And you don't even know it, but the whole village knows it for you.

JOHN: My God! (*He throws himself on the table, sobbing.*)

.   .   .

JUDGE DANFORTH (*entering*): They tell me you want to confess.

JOHN: Yes. I confess that I wanted to lie to save my life and that I despaired of God because you forced me to despair of myself.

DANFORTH: Enough! Are you a witch, yes or no?

JOHN (*quietly*): No, sir. There have never been witches except in your mind.

ELIZABETH (*wanting to convince him to confess, passionately*): John!

JOHN (*to her, putting his arms around her shoulders*): Let me
lift up my head: I've held it down for so long. (*To Danforth*): She has given me back my self-respect!

ELIZABETH: I gave it back to you that you might live.

JOHN: Of course. You couldn't know that it would take away
my fear of death. (*To Danforth*): What do you think of
that, sir: I was determined to live because I was ashamed
of my life. That's over. A completely new self-respect makes
demands. (*To Elizabeth*): Tell me I'm right.

PARRIS (*the clergyman, silent since his entrance with Danforth*): Do your duty to your husband, Elizabeth. Tell him
he sins through pride.

JOHN (*to her*): Is it true?

PARRIS: Who will take care of your family if you die? Who will
feed them? Your duty is to live.

JOHN: Even at the cost of a lie?

PARRIS (*bursting out*): Who's talking about a lie? We ask
your signature. If you refuse to give it, you are killing yourself. Don't you know that God forbids suicide?

JOHN: Elizabeth! For the last time in my life, be my judge. I
am right, aren't I?

ELIZABETH (*bewildered, in an almost childish voice*): I can
no longer tell Bad from Good.

JOHN: This happiness that you have given me, is it possible it
comes from pride?

PARRIS: From pride, yes! Criminal pride: you will answer to
God for the blood that is going to flow.

DANFORTH (*imperiously*): Parris!

JOHN (*quickly*): The blood is going to flow? What blood?

DANFORTH: He means yours.

JOHN (*laughing freely*): The blood of a hanged man does not
flow. (*Pointing to Parris, who turns pale*): Look at him:
you can easily see that he's talking about his own blood.
(*From the window he sees the gallows set up on the square,
surrounded by farmers who have decided to prevent the*

execution. Then slowly, to himself): All my friends are there.

DANFORTH: Don't hope for anything from them: we will hang you in the prison.

JOHN (*without hearing*): All my friends. Armed. They were true friends. (*To Parris*): Do you still tell me my death is useless? If I agreed to lie, they would go away bowed down by the thought that you were right. But when the rope has been put around my neck, their anger will blow through Salem and you will be swept away like dead leaves. My children will live in freedom. (*To Elizabeth*): Tell me I'm right. I am also dying because I can no longer live, Elizabeth. Everything began so badly. My body embarrassed you.

ELIZABETH (*in a low voice, quickly*): If you live, I will love you with all my body.

JOHN: Your body, Elizabeth, your poor body. It has worn itself out. When I am dead, you will love my soul with all your soul. (*Taking her in his arms*): Tell me I'm right.

ELIZABETH: You are right.

JOHN (*to his executioners*): Let's go!

The Crucible:
ANALOGUES

BERNARD SHAW

Bernard Shaw wrote fifty-three plays, including *Arms and the Man,*
Man and Superman, Major Barbara, and *Pygmalion.*

SAINT JOAN

Scene VI

Rouen, 30th May 1431. A great stone hall in the castle, ar-
ranged for a trial-at-law, but not a trial-by-jury, the court being
the Bishop's court with the Inquisition participating: hence
there are two raised chairs side by side for the Bishop and
the Inquisitor as judges. Rows of chairs radiating from them
at an obtuse angle are for the canons, the doctors of law and
theology, and the Dominican monks, who act as assessors. In
the angle is a table for the scribes, with stools. There is also
a heavy rough wooden stool for the prisoner. All these are at

Reprinted by permission of The Society of Authors, for the Bernard
Shaw Estate. Shaw's play was first performed on December 28, 1923,
and first published in 1924. Scene VI is a dramatic unit in its own
right, so there is no need for any kind of explanation or synopsis. Besides,
Shaw being Shaw, your reading of this scene should send you to the
whole play if you haven't already been there.

427

the inner end of the hall. The further end is open to the courtyard through a row of arches. The court is shielded from the weather by screens and curtains.

Looking down the great hall from the middle of the inner end, the judicial chairs and scribes' table are to the right. The prisoner's stool is to the left. There are arched doors right and left. It is a fine sunshiny May morning.

Warwick comes in through the arched doorway on the judges' side, followed by his page.

THE PAGE (*pertly*): I suppose your lordship is aware that we have no business here. This is an ecclesiastical court; and we are only the secular arm.

WARWICK: I am aware of that fact. Will it please your impudence to find the Bishop of Beauvais for me, and give him a hint that he can have a word with me here before the trial, if he wishes?

THE PAGE (*going*): Yes, my lord.

WARWICK: And mind you behave yourself. Do not address him as Pious Peter.

THE PAGE: No, my lord. I shall be kind to him, because, when The Maid is brought in, Pious Peter will have to pick a peck of pickled pepper.

Cauchon enters through the same door with a Dominican monk and a canon, the latter carrying a brief.

THE PAGE: The Right Reverend his lordship the Bishop of Beauvais. And two other reverend gentlemen.

WARWICK: Get out; and see that we are not interrupted.

THE PAGE: Right, my lord (*he vanishes airily*).

CAUCHON: I wish your lordship good-morrow.

WARWICK: Good-morrow to your lordship. Have I had the pleasure of meeting your friends before? I think not.

CAUCHON (*introducing the monk, who is on his right*): This, my lord, is Brother John Lemaître, of the order of St. Dominic. He is acting as deputy for the Chief Inquisitor into the evil of heresy in France. Brother John: the Earl of Warwick.

WARWICK: Your Reverence is most welcome. We have no Inquisitor in England, unfortunately; though we miss him greatly, especially on occasions like the present.

The Inquisitor smiles patiently, and bows. He is a mild elderly gentleman, but has evident reserves of authority and firmness.

CAUCHON (*introducing the Canon, who is on his left*): This gentleman is Canon John D'Estivet, of the Chapter of Bayeux. He is acting as Promoter.

WARWICK: Promoter?

CAUCHON: Prosecutor, you would call him in civil law.

WARWICK: Ah! prosecutor. Quite, quite. I am very glad to make your acquaintance, Canon D'Estivet.

D'Estivet bows. (He is on the young side of middle age, well mannered, but vulpine beneath his veneer.)

WARWICK: May I ask what stage the proceedings have reached? It is now more than nine months since The Maid was captured at Compiègne by the Burgundians. It is fully four months since I bought her from the Burgundians for a very handsome sum, solely that she might be brought to justice. It is very nearly three months since I delivered her up to you, my Lord Bishop, as a person suspected of heresy. May I suggest that you are taking a rather unconscionable time to make up your minds about a very plain case? Is this trial never going to end?

THE INQUISITOR (*smiling*): It has not yet begun, my lord.

WARWICK: Not yet begun! Why, you have been at it eleven weeks!

CAUCHON: We have not been idle, my lord. We have held fifteen examinations of The Maid: six public and nine private.

THE INQUISITOR (*always patiently smiling*): You see, my lord, I have been present at only two of these examinations. They were proceedings of the Bishop's court solely, and not of the Holy Office. I have only just decided to associate myself —that is, to associate the Holy Inquisition—with the Bishop's court. I did not at first think that this was a case of heresy at all. I regarded it as a political case, and The Maid as a prisoner of war. But having now been present at two of the examinations, I must admit that this seems to be one of the gravest cases of heresy within my experience. Therefore everything is now in order, and we proceed to trial this morning. (*He moves toward the judicial chairs.*)

CAUCHON: This moment, if your lordship's convenience allows.

WARWICK (*graciously*): Well, that is good news, gentlemen. I will not attempt to conceal from you that our patience was becoming strained.

CAUCHON: So I gathered from the threats of your soldiers to drown those of our people who favor The Maid.

WARWICK: Dear me! At all events their intentions were friendly to you, my lord.

CAUCHON (*sternly*): I hope not. I am determined that the woman shall have a fair hearing. The justice of the Church is not a mockery, my lord.

THE INQUISITOR (*returning*): Never has there been a fairer examination within my experience, my lord. The Maid needs no lawyers to take her part: she will be tried by her most faithful friends, all ardently desirous to save her soul from perdition.

D'ESTIVET: Sir: I am the Promoter; and it has been my painful duty to present the case against the girl; but believe me, I would throw up my case today and hasten to her defence if I did not know that men far my superiors in learning and piety, in eloquence and persuasiveness, have been sent to reason with her, to explain to her the danger she is running, and the ease with which she may avoid it. (*Suddenly bursting into forensic eloquence, to the disgust of Cauchon and the Inquisitor, who have listened to him so far with patronizing approval*) Men have dared to say that we are acting from hate; but God is our witness that they lie. Have we tortured her? No. Have we ceased to exhort her; to implore her to have pity on herself; to come to the bosom of her Church as an erring but beloved child? Have we—

CAUCHON (*interrupting drily*): Take care, Canon. All that you say is true; but if you make his lordship believe it I will not answer for your life, and hardly for my own.

WARWICK (*deprecating, but by no means denying*): Oh, my lord, you are very hard on us poor English. But we certainly do not share your pious desire to save The Maid: in fact I tell you now plainly that her death is a political necessity which I regret but cannot help. If the Church lets her go—

CAUCHON (*with fierce and menacing pride*): If the Church lets her go, woe to the man, were he the Emperor himself, who dares lay a finger on her! The Church is not subject to political necessity, my lord.

THE INQUISITOR (*interposing smoothly*): You need have no anxiety about the result, my lord. You have an invincible ally in the matter: one who is far more determined than you that she shall burn.

WARWICK: And who is this very convenient partisan, may I ask?

THE INQUISITOR: The Maid herself. Unless you put a gag in her mouth you cannot prevent her from convicting herself ten times over every time she opens it.

D'ESTIVET: That is perfectly true, my lord. My hair bristles on my head when I hear so young a creature utter such blasphemies.

WARWICK: Well, by all means do your best for her if you are quite sure it will be of no avail. (*Looking hard at Cauchon*) I should be sorry to have to act without the blessing of the Church.

CAUCHON (*with a mixture of cynical admiration and contempt*): And yet they say Englishmen are hypocrites! You play for your side, my lord, even at the peril of your soul. I cannot but admire such devotion; but I dare not go so far myself. I fear damnation.

WARWICK: If we feared anything we could never govern England, my lord. Shall I send your people in to you?

CAUCHON: Yes: it will be very good of your lordship to withdraw and allow the court to assemble.

Warwick turns on his heel, and goes out through the court-yard. Cauchon takes one of the judicial seats; and D'Estivet sits at the scribes' table, studying his brief.

CAUCHON (*casually, as he makes himself comfortable*): What scoundrels these English nobles are!

THE INQUISITOR (*taking the other judicial chair on Cauchon's left*): All secular power makes men scoundrels. They are not trained for the work; and they have not the Apostolic Succession. Our own nobles are just as bad.

The Bishop's assessors hurry into the hall, headed by Chaplain de Stogumber and Canon de Courcelles, a young priest of 30. The scribes sit at the table, leaving a chair vacant opposite D'Estivet. Some of the assessors take their seats: others stand chatting, waiting for the proceedings to begin formally. De Stogumber, aggrieved and obstinate, will not take his seat: neither will the Canon, who stands on his right.

CAUCHON: Good morning, Master de Stogumber. (*To the Inquisitor*): Chaplain to the Cardinal of England.

THE CHAPLAIN (*correcting him*): Of Winchester, my lord. I have to make a protest, my lord.

CAUCHON: You make a great many.

THE CHAPLAIN: I am not without support, my lord. Here is Master de Courcelles, Canon of Paris, who associates himself with me in my protest.

CAUCHON: Well, what is the matter?

THE CHAPLAIN (*sulkily*): Speak you, Master de Courcelles, since I do not seem to enjoy his lordship's confidence. (*He sits down in dudgeon next to Cauchon, on his right.*)

COURCELLES: My lord: we have been at great pains to draw up an indictment of The Maid on sixty-four counts. We are now told that they have been reduced, without consulting us.

THE INQUISITOR: Master de Courcelles: I am the culprit. I am overwhelmed with admiration for the zeal displayed in your sixty-four counts; but in accusing a heretic, as in other things, enough is enough. Also you must remember that all the members of the court are not so subtle and profound as you, and that some of your very great learning might appear to them to be very great nonsense. Therefore I have thought it well to have your sixty-four articles cut down to twelve—

COURCELLES (*thunderstruck*): Twelve!!!

THE INQUISITOR: Twelve will, believe me, be quite enough for your purpose.

THE CHAPLAIN: But some of the most important points have been reduced almost to nothing. For instance, The Maid has actually declared that the blessed saints Margaret and Catherine, and the holy Archangel Michael, spoke to her in French. That is a vital point.

THE INQUISITOR: You think, doubtless, that they should have spoken in Latin?

CAUCHON: No: he thinks they should have spoken in English.

THE CHAPLAIN: Naturally, my lord.

THE INQUISITOR: Well, as we are all here agreed, I think, that these voices of The Maid are the voices of evil spirits tempting her to her damnation, it would not be very courteous to you, Master de Stogumber, or to the King of England, to assume that English is the devil's native language. So let it pass. The matter is not wholly omitted from the twelve articles. Pray take your places, gentlemen; and let us proceed to business.

All who have not taken their seats, do so.

THE CHAPLAIN: Well, I protest. That is all.

COURCELLES: I think it hard that all our work should go for

nothing. It is only another example of the diabolical influence which this woman exercises over the court. (*He takes his chair, which is on the Chaplain's right.*)

CAUCHON: Do you suggest that I am under diabolical influence?

COURCELLES: I suggest nothing, my lord. But it seems to me that there is a conspiracy here to hush up the fact that The Maid stole the Bishop of Senlis's horse.

CAUCHON (*keeping his temper with difficulty*): This is not a police court. Are we to waste our time on such rubbish?

COURCELLES (*rising, shocked*): My lord: do you call the Bishop's horse rubbish?

THE INQUISITOR (*blandly*): Master de Courcelles: The Maid alleges that she paid handsomely for the Bishop's horse, and that if he did not get the money the fault was not hers. As that may be true, the point is one on which The Maid may well be acquitted.

COURCELLES: Yes, if it were an ordinary horse. But the Bishop's horse! how can she be acquitted for that? (*He sits down again, bewildered and discouraged.*)

THE INQUISITOR: I submit to you, with great respect, that if we persist in trying The Maid on trumpery issues on which we may have to declare her innocent, she may escape us on the great main issue of heresy, on which she seems so far to insist on her own guilt. I will ask you, therefore, to say nothing, when The Maid is brought before us, of these stealings of horses, and dancings round fairy trees with the village children, and prayings at haunted wells, and a dozen other things which you were diligently inquiring into until my arrival. There is not a village girl in France against whom you could not prove such things: they all dance round haunted trees, and pray at magic wells. Some of them would steal the Pope's horse if they got the chance. Heresy, gentlemen, heresy is the charge we have to try. The detection and suppression of heresy is my peculiar business: I am here as an inquisitor, not as an ordinary magistrate. Stick to the heresy, gentlemen; and leave the other matters alone.

CAUCHON: I may say that we have sent to the girl's village to make inquiries about her, and there is practically nothing serious against her.

THE CHAPLAIN { *(rising and clamoring together)* } Nothing serious, my lord—
COURCELLES { } What! The fairy tree not—

CAUCHON (*out of patience*): Be silent, gentlemen; or speak one at a time.

Courcelles collapses into his chair, intimidated.

THE CHAPLAIN (*sulkily resuming his seat*): That is what The Maid said to us last Friday.

CAUCHON: I wish you had followed her counsel, sir. When I say nothing serious, I mean nothing that men of sufficiently large mind to conduct an inquiry like this would consider serious. I agree with my colleague the Inquisitor that it is on the count of heresy that we must proceed.

LADVENU (*a young but ascetically fine-drawn Dominican who is sitting next Courcelles, on his right*): But is there any great harm in the girl's heresy? Is it not merely her simplicity? Many saints have said as much as Joan.

THE INQUISITOR (*dropping his blandness and speaking very gravely*): Brother Martin: if you had seen what I have seen of heresy, you would not think it a light thing even in its most apparently harmless and even lovable and pious origins. Heresy begins with people who are to all appearance better than their neighbors. A gentle and pious girl, or a young man who has obeyed the command of our Lord by giving all his riches to the poor, and putting on the garb of poverty, the life of austerity, and the rule of humility and charity, may be the founder of a heresy that will wreck both Church and Empire if not ruthlessly stamped out in time. The records of the Holy Inquisition are full of histories we dare

not give to the world, because they are beyond the belief
of honest men and innocent women; yet they all began with
saintly simpletons. I have seen this again and again. Mark
what I say: the woman who quarrels with her clothes, and
puts on the dress of a man, is like the man who throws
off his fur gown and dresses like John the Baptist: they are
followed, as surely as the night follows the day, by bands
of wild women and men who refuse to wear any clothes at
all. When maids will neither marry nor take regular vows,
and men reject marriage and exalt their lusts into divine
inspirations, then, as surely as the summer follows the spring,
they begin with polygamy, and end by incest. Heresy at
first seems innocent and even laudable; but it ends in such a
monstrous horror of unnatural wickedness that the most
tender-hearted among you, if you saw it at work as I have
seen it, would clamor against the mercy of the Church
in dealing with it. For two hundred years the Holy Office
has striven with these diabolical madnesses; and it knows
that they begin always by vain and ignorant persons setting
up their own judgment against the Church, and taking it
upon themselves to be the interpreters of God's will. You
must not fall into the common error of mistaking these
simpletons for liars and hypocrites. They believe honestly
and sincerely that their diabolical inspiration is divine.
Therefore you must be on your guard against your natural
compassion. You are all, I hope, merciful men: how else
could you have devoted your lives to the service of our
gentle Savior? You are going to see before you a young girl,
pious and chaste; for I must tell you, gentlemen, that the
things said of her by our English friends are supported by
no evidence, whilst there is abundant testimony that her
excesses have been excesses of religion and charity and not
of worldliness and wantonness. This girl is not one of those
whose hard features are the sign of hard hearts, and whose
brazen looks and lewd demeanor condemn them before they

are accused. The devilish pride that has led her into her present peril has left no mark on her countenance. Strange as it may seem to you, it has even left no mark on her character outside those special matters in which she is proud; so that you will see a diabolical pride and a natural humility seated side by side in the selfsame soul. Therefore be on your guard. God forbid that I should tell you to harden your hearts; for her punishment if we condemn her will be so cruel that we should forfeit our own hope of divine mercy were there one grain of malice against her in our hearts. But if you hate cruelty—and if any man here does not hate it I command him on his soul's salvation to quit this holy court—I say, if you hate cruelty, remember that nothing is so cruel in its consequences as the toleration of heresy. Remember also that no court of law can be so cruel as the common people are to those whom they suspect of heresy. The heretic in the hands of the Holy Office is safe from violence, is assured of a fair trial, and cannot suffer death, even when guilty, if repentance follows sin. Innumerable lives of heretics have been saved because the Holy Office has taken them out of the hands of the people, and because the people have yielded them up, knowing that the Holy Office would deal with them. Before the Holy Inquisition existed, and even now when its officers are not within reach, the unfortunate wretch suspected of heresy, perhaps quite ignorantly and unjustly, is stoned, torn in pieces, drowned, burned in his house with all his innocent children, without a trial, unshriven, unburied save as a dog is buried: all of them deeds hateful to God and most cruel to man. Gentlemen: I am compassionate by nature as well as by my profession; and though the work I have to do may seem cruel to those who do not know how much more cruel it would be to leave it undone, I would go to the stake myself sooner than do it if I did not know its righteousness, its necessity, its essential mercy. I ask you to address yourself to this trial in that conviction. Anger is a bad counsellor: cast out anger. Pity is sometimes worse: cast out pity. But do not cast out mercy. Remember only that justice comes first. Have you anything to say, my lord, before we proceed to trial?

CAUCHON: You have spoken for me, and spoken better than I could. I do not see how any sane man could disagree with a word that has fallen from you. But this I will add. The crude heresies of which you have told us are horrible; but their horror is like that of the black death: they rage for a while and then die out, because sound and sensible men will not under any incitement be reconciled to nakedness and incest and polygamy and the like. But we are confronted today throughout Europe with a heresy that is spreading among men not weak in mind nor diseased in brain: nay, the stronger the mind, the more obstinate the heretic. It is neither discredited by fantastic extremes nor corrupted by the common lusts of the flesh; but it, too, sets up the private judgment of the single erring mortal against the considered wisdom and experience of the Church. The mighty structure of Catholic Christendom will never be shaken by naked madmen or by the sins of Moab and Ammon. But it may be betrayed from within, and brought to barbarous ruin and desolation, by this arch heresy which the English Commander calls Protestantism.

THE ASSESSORS (*whispering*): Protestantism! What was that? What does the Bishop mean? Is it a new heresy? The English Commander, he said. Did you ever hear of Protestantism? etc., etc.

CAUCHON (*continuing*): And that reminds me. What provision has the Earl of Warwick made for the defence of the secular arm should The Maid prove obdurate, and the people be moved to pity her?

THE CHAPLAIN: Have no fear on that score, my lord. The noble earl has eight hundred men-at-arms at the gates. She will not slip through our English fingers even if the whole city be on her side.

CAUCHON (*revolted*): Will you not add, God grant that she repent and purge her sin?

THE CHAPLAIN: That does not seem to me to be consistent; but of course I agree with your lordship.

CAUCHON (*giving him up with a shrug of contempt*): The court sits.

THE INQUISITOR: Let the accused be brought in.

LADVENU (*calling*): The accused. Let her be brought in.

Joan, chained by the ankles, is brought in through the arched door behind the prisoner's stool by a guard of English soldiers. With them is the Executioner and his assistants. They lead her to the prisoner's stool, and place themselves behind it after taking off her chain. She wears a page's black suit. Her long imprisonment and the strain of the examinations which have preceded the trial have left their mark on her; but her vitality still holds; she confronts the court unabashed, without a trace of the awe which their formal solemnity seems to require for the complete success of its impressiveness.

THE INQUISITOR (*kindly*): Sit down, Joan. (*She sits on the prisoner's stool.*) You look very pale today. Are you not well?

JOAN: Thank you kindly: I am well enough. But the Bishop sent me some carp; and it made me ill.

CAUCHON: I am sorry. I told them to see that it was fresh.

JOAN: You meant to be good to me, I know; but it is a fish that does not agree with me. The English thought you were trying to poison me—

CAUCHON } (*together*) { What!
THE CHAPLAIN } { No, my lord.

JOAN (*continuing*): They are determined that I shall be burnt as a witch; and they sent their doctor to cure me; but he was forbidden to bleed me because the silly people believe that a witch's witchery leaves her if she is bled; so he only called me filthy names. Why do you leave me in the hands of the English? I should be in the hands of the Church. And why must I be chained by the feet to a log of wood? Are you afraid I will fly away?

D'ESTIVET (*harshly*): Woman: it is not for you to question the court: it is for us to question you.

COURCELLES: When you were left unchained, did you not try to escape by jumping from a tower sixty feet high? If you cannot fly like a witch, how is it that you are still alive?

JOAN: I suppose because the tower was not so high then. It has grown higher every day since you began asking me questions about it.

D'ESTIVET: Why did you jump from the tower?

JOAN: How do you know that I jumped?

D'ESTIVET: You were found lying in the moat. Why did you leave the tower?

JOAN: Why would anybody leave a prison if they could get out?

D'ESTIVET: You tried to escape?

JOAN: Of course I did; and not for the first time either. If you leave the door of the cage open the bird will fly out.

D'ESTIVET (*rising*): That is a confession of heresy. I call the attention of the court to it.

JOAN: Heresy, he calls it! Am I a heretic because I try to escape from prison?

D'ESTIVET: Assuredly, if you are in the hands of the Church, and you wilfully take yourself out of its hands, you are deserting the Church; and that is heresy.

JOAN: It is great nonsense. Nobody could be such a fool as to think that.

D'ESTIVET: You hear, my lord, how I am reviled in the execution of my duty by this woman. (*He sits down indignantly.*)

CAUCHON: I have warned you before, Joan, that you are doing yourself no good by these pert answers.

JOAN: But you will not talk sense to me. I am reasonable if you will be reasonable.

THE INQUISITOR (*interposing*): This is not yet in order. You forget, Master Promoter, that the proceedings have not been formally opened. The time for questions is after she has sworn on the Gospels to tell us the whole truth.

JOAN: You say this to me every time. I have said again and again that I will tell you all that concerns this trial. But I cannot tell you the whole truth: God does not allow the whole truth to be told. You do not understand it when I tell it. It is an old saying that he who tells too much truth is sure to be hanged. I am weary of this argument: we have been over it nine times already. I have sworn as much as I will swear; and I will swear no more.

COURCELLES: My lord: she should be put to the torture.

THE INQUISITOR: You hear, Joan? That is what happens to the obdurate. Think before you answer. Has she been shewn the instruments?

THE EXECUTIONER: They are ready, my lord. She has seen them.

JOAN: If you tear me limb from limb until you separate my soul from my body you will get nothing out of me beyond what I have told you. What more is there to tell that you could understand? Besides, I cannot bear to be hurt; and if you hurt me I will say anything you like to stop the pain. But I will take it all back afterwards; so what is the use of it?

LADVENU: There is much in that. We should proceed mercifully.

COURCELLES: But the torture is customary.

THE INQUISITOR: It must not be applied wantonly. If the accused will confess voluntarily, then its use cannot be justified.

COURCELLES: But this is unusual and irregular. She refuses to take the oath.

LADVENU (*disgusted*): Do you want to torture the girl for the mere pleasure of it?

COURCELLES (*bewildered*): But it is not a pleasure. It is the law. It is customary. It is always done.

THE INQUISITOR: That is not so, Master, except when the inquiries are carried on by people who do not know their legal business.

COURCELLES: But the woman is a heretic. I assure you it is always done.

CAUCHON (*decisively*): It will not be done today if it is not necessary. Let there be an end of this. I will not have it said that we proceeded on forced confessions. We have sent our best preachers and doctors to this woman to exhort and implore her to save her soul and body from the fire: we shall not now send the executioner to thrust her into it.

COURCELLES: Your lordship is merciful, of course. But it is a great responsibility to depart from the usual practice.

JOAN: Thou art a rare noodle, Master. Do what was done last time is thy rule, eh?

COURCELLES (*rising*): Thou wanton: dost thou dare call me noodle?

THE INQUISITOR: Patience, Master, patience: I fear you will soon be only too terribly avenged.

COURCELLES (*mutters*): Noodle indeed! (*He sits down, much discontented.*)

THE INQUISITOR: Meanwhile, let us not be moved by the rough side of a shepherd lass's tongue.

JOAN: Nay: I am no shepherd lass, though I have helped with the sheep like anyone else. I will do a lady's work in the house—spin or weave—against any woman in Rouen.

THE INQUISITOR: This is not a time for vanity, Joan. You stand in great peril.

JOAN: I know it: have I not been punished for my vanity? If I had not worn my cloth of gold surcoat in battle like a fool, that Burgundian soldier would never have pulled me backwards off my horse; and I should not have been here.

THE CHAPLAIN: If you are so clever at woman's work why do you not stay at home and do it?

JOAN: There are plenty of other women to do it; but there is nobody to do my work.

CAUCHON: Come! we are wasting time on trifles. Joan: I am going to put a most solemn question to you. Take care how you answer; for your life and salvation are at stake on it. Will you for all you have said and done, be it good or bad, accept the judgment of God's Church on earth? More especially as to the acts and words that are imputed to you in this trial by the Promoter here, will you submit your case to the inspired interpretation of the Church Militant?

JOAN: I am a faithful child of the Church. I will obey the Church—

CAUCHON (*hopefully leaning forward*): You will?

JOAN: — provided it does not command anything impossible. *Cauchon sinks back in his chair with a heavy sigh. The Inquisitor purses his lips and frowns. Ladvenu shakes his head pitifully.*

D'ESTIVET: She imputes to the Church the error and folly of commanding the impossible.

JOAN: If you command me to declare that all that I have done and said, and all the visions and revelations I have had, were not from God, then that is impossible: I will not declare it for anything in the world. What God made me do I will never go back on; and what He has commanded or shall command I will not fail to do in spite of any man alive. That is what I mean by impossible. And in case the Church should bid me do anything contrary to the command I have from God, I will not consent to it, no matter what it may be.

THE ASSESSORS (*shocked and indignant*): Oh! The Church contrary to God! What do you say now? Flat heresy. This is beyond everything, etc., etc.

D'ESTIVET (*throwing down his brief*): My lord: do you need anything more than this?

CAUCHON: Woman: you have said enough to burn ten heretics. Will you not be warned? Will you not understand?

THE INQUISITOR: If the Church Militant tells you that your revelations and visions are sent by the devil to tempt you to your damnation, will you not believe that the Church is wiser than you?

JOAN: I believe that God is wiser than I; and it is His commands that I will do. All the things that you call my crimes have come to me by the command of God. I say that I have done them by the order of God: it is impossible for me to say anything else. If any Churchman says the contrary I shall not mind him: I shall mind God alone, whose command I always follow.

LADVENU (*pleading with her urgently*): You do not know what you are saying, child. Do you want to kill yourself? Listen. Do you not believe that you are subject to the Church of God on earth?

JOAN: Yes. When have I ever denied it?

LADVENU: Good. That means, does it not, that you are subject to our Lord the Pope, to the cardinals, the archbishops, and the bishops for whom his lordship stands here today?

JOAN: God must be served first.

D'ESTIVET: Then your voices command you not to submit yourself to the Church Militant?

JOAN: My voices do not tell me to disobey the Church; but God must be served first.

CAUCHON: And you, and not the Church, are to be the judge?

JOAN: What other judgment can I judge by but my own?

THE ASSESSORS (*scandalized*): Oh! (*They cannot find words.*)

CAUCHON: Out of your own mouth you have condemned yourself. We have striven for your salvation to the verge of sinning ourselves: we have opened the door to you again and again; and you have shut it in our faces and in the face of God. Dare you pretend, after what you have said, that you are in a state of grace?

JOAN: If I am not, may God bring me to it: if I am, may God keep me in it!

LADVENU: That is a very good reply, my lord.

COURCELLES: Were you in a state of grace when you stole the Bishop's horse?

CAUCHON (*rising in a fury*): Oh, devil take the Bishop's horse and you too! We are here to try a case of heresy; and no sooner do we come to the root of the matter than we are thrown back by idiots who understand nothing but horses. (*Trembling with rage, he forces himself to sit down.*)

THE INQUISITOR: Gentlemen, gentlemen: in clinging to these small issues you are The Maid's best advocates. I am not surprised that his lordship has lost patience with you. What does the Promoter say? Does he press these trumpery matters?

D'ESTIVET: I am bound by my office to press everything; but when the woman confesses a heresy that must bring upon her the doom of excommunication, of what consequence is that she has been guilty also of offences which expose her to minor penances? I share the impatience of his lordship as to these minor charges. Only, with great respect, I must emphasize the gravity of two very horrible and blasphemous crimes which she does not deny. First, she has intercourse with evil spirits, and is therefore a sorceress. Second, she wears men's clothes, which is indecent, unnatural, and abominable; and in spite of our most earnest remonstrances and entreaties, she will not change them even to receive the sacrament.

JOAN: Is the blessed St. Catherine an evil spirit? Is St. Margaret? Is Michael the Archangel?

COURCELLES: How do you know that the spirit which appears to you is an archangel? Does he not appear to you as a naked man?

JOAN: Do you think God cannot afford clothes for him?

The assessors cannot help smiling, especially as the joke is against Courcelles.

LADVENU: Well answered, Joan.

THE INQUISITOR: It is, in effect, well answered. But no evil spirit would be so simple as to appear to a young girl in a guise that would scandalize her when he meant her to take him for a messenger from the Most High. Joan: the Church instructs you that these apparitions are demons seeking your soul's perdition. Do you accept the instruction of the Church?

JOAN: I accept the messenger of God. How could any faithful believer in the Church refuse him?

CAUCHON: Wretched woman: again I ask you, do you know what you are saying?

THE INQUISITOR: You wrestle in vain with the devil for her soul, my lord: she will not be saved. Now as to this matter of the man's dress. For the last time, will you put off that impudent attire, and dress as becomes your sex?

JOAN: I will not.

D'ESTIVET (*pouncing*): The sin of disobedience, my lord.

JOAN (*distressed*): But my voices tell me I must dress as a soldier.

LADVENU: Joan, Joan: does not that prove to you that the voices are the voices of evil spirits? Can you suggest to us one good reason why an angel of God should give you such shameless advice?

JOAN: Why, yes: what can be plainer commonsense? I was a soldier living among soldiers. I am a prisoner guarded by soldiers. If I were to dress as a woman they would think of me as a woman; and then what would become of me? If I dress as a soldier they think of me as a soldier, and I can live with them as I do at home with my brothers. That is why St. Catherine tells me I must not dress as a woman until she gives me leave.

COURCELLES: When will she give you leave?

JOAN: When you take me out of the hands of the English soldiers. I have told you that I should be in the hands of the Church, and not left night and day with four soldiers of the Earl of Warwick. Do you want me to live with them in petticoats?

LADVENU: My lord: what she says is, God knows, very wrong and shocking; but there is a grain of worldly sense in it such as might impose on a simple village maiden.

JOAN: If we were as simple in the village as you are in your courts and palaces, there would soon be no wheat to make bread for you.

CAUCHON: That is the thanks you get for trying to save her, Brother Martin.

LADVENU: Joan: we are all trying to save you. His lordship is trying to save you. The Inquisitor could not be more just to you if you were his own daughter. But you are blinded by a terrible pride and self-sufficiency.

JOAN: Why do you say that? I have said nothing wrong. I cannot understand.

THE INQUISITOR: The blessed St. Athanasius has laid it down in his creed that those who cannot understand are damned. It is not enough to be simple. It is not enough even to be what simple people call good. The simplicity of a darkened mind is no better than the simplicity of a beast.

JOAN: There is great wisdom in the simplicity of a beast, let me tell you; and sometimes great foolishness in the wisdom of scholars.

LADVENU: We know that, Joan: we are not so foolish as you think us. Try to resist the temptation to make pert replies to us. Do you see that man who stands behind you (*he indicates the Executioner*)?

JOAN (*turning and looking at the man*): Your torturer? But the Bishop said I was not to be tortured.

LADVENU: You are not to be tortured because you have confessed everything that is necessary to your condemnation. That man is not only the torturer: he is also the Executioner. Executioner: let The Maid hear your answers to my questions. Are you prepared for the burning of a heretic this day?

THE EXECUTIONER: Yes, Master.

LADVENU: Is the stake ready?

THE EXECUTIONER: It is. In the market-place. The English have built it too high for me to get near her and make the death easier. It will be a cruel death.

JOAN (*horrified*): But you are not going to burn me now?

THE INQUISITOR: You realize it at last.

LADVENU: There are eight hundred English soldiers waiting to take you to the market-place the moment the sentence of excommunication has passed the lips of your judges. You are within a few short moments of that doom.

JOAN (*looking round desperately for rescue*): Oh God!

LADVENU: Do not despair, Joan. The Church is merciful. You can save yourself.

JOAN (*hopefully*): Yes: my voices promised me I should not be burnt. St. Catherine bade me be bold.

CAUCHON: Woman: are you quite mad? Do you not yet see that your voices have deceived you?

JOAN: Oh no: that is impossible.

CAUCHON: Impossible! They have led you straight to your excommunication, and to the stake which is there waiting for you.

LADVENU (*pressing the point hard*): Have they kept a single promise to you since you were taken at Compiègne? The devil has betrayed you. The Church holds out its arms to you.

JOAN (*despairing*): Oh, it is true: it is true: my voices have deceived me. I have been mocked by devils: my faith is broken. I have dared and dared; but only a fool will walk into a fire: God, who gave me my commonsense, cannot will me to do that.

LADVENU: Now God be praised that He has saved you at the eleventh hour! (*He hurries to the vacant seat at the scribes' table, and snatches a sheet of paper, on which he sets to work writing eagerly.*)

CAUCHON: Amen!

JOAN: What must I do?

CAUCHON: You must sign a solemn recantation of your heresy.

JOAN: Sign? That means to write my name. I cannot write.

CAUCHON: You have signed many letters before.

JOAN: Yes; but someone held my hand and guided the pen. I can make my mark.

THE CHAPLAIN (*who has been listening with growing alarm and indignation*): My lord: do you mean that you are going to allow this woman to escape us?

THE INQUISITOR: The law must take its course, Master de Stogumber. And you know the law.

THE CHAPLAIN (*rising, purple with fury*): I know that there is no faith in a Frenchman. (*Tumult, which he shouts down.*) I know what my lord the Cardinal of Winchester will say when he hears of this. I know what the Earl of Warwick will do when he learns that you intend to betray him. There are eight hundred men at the gate who will see that this abominable witch is burnt in spite of your teeth.

THE ASSESSORS (*meanwhile*): What is this? What did he say? He accuses us of treachery! This is past bearing. No faith in a Frenchman! Did you hear that? This is an intolerable fellow. Who is he? Is this what English Churchmen are like? He must be mad or drunk, etc., etc.

THE INQUISITOR (*rising*): Silence, pray! Gentlemen: pray silence! Master Chaplain: bethink you a moment of your holy office: of what you are, and where you are. I direct you to sit down.

THE CHAPLAIN (*folding his arms doggedly, his face working convulsively*): I will NOT sit down.

CAUCHON: Master Inquisitor: this man has called me a traitor to my face before now.

THE CHAPLAIN: So you are a traitor. You are all traitors. You have been doing nothing but begging this damnable witch on your knees to recant all through this trial.

THE INQUISITOR (*placidly resuming his seat*): If you will not sit, you must stand: that is all.

THE CHAPLAIN: I will NOT stand (*he flings himself back into his chair*).

LADVENU (*rising with the paper in his hand*): My lord: here is the form of recantation for The Maid to sign.

CAUCHON: Read it to her.

JOAN: Do not trouble. I will sign it.

THE INQUISITOR: Woman: you must know what you are putting your hand to. Read it to her, Brother Martin. And let all be silent.

LADVENUE (*reading quietly*): "I, Joan, commonly called The Maid, a miserable sinner, do confess that I have most grievously sinned in the following articles. I have pretended to have revelations from God and the angels and the blessed saints, and perversely rejected the Church's warnings that these were temptations by demons. I have blasphemed abominably by wearing an immodest dress, contrary to the Holy Scripture and the canons of the Church. Also I have clipped my hair in the style of a man, and, against all the duties which have made my sex specially acceptable in heaven, have taken up the sword, even to the shedding of human blood, inciting men to slay each other, invoking evil spirits to delude them, and stubbornly and most blasphemously imputing these sins to Almighty God. I confess to the sin of sedition, to the sin of idolatry, to the sin of disobedience, to the sin of pride, and to the sin of heresy. All of which sins I now renounce and abjure and depart from, humbly thanking you Doctors and Masters who have brought me back to the truth and into the grace of our Lord. And I will never return to my errors, but will remain in communion with our Holy Church and in obedience to our

Holy Father the Pope of Rome. All this I swear by God Almighty and the Holy Gospels, in witness whereto I sign my name to this recantation."

THE INQUISITOR: You understand this, Joan?

JOAN (*listless*): It is plain enough, sir.

THE INQUISITOR: And it is true?

JOAN: It may be true. If it were not true, the fire would not be ready for me in the market-place.

LADVENU (*taking up his pen and a book, and going to her quickly lest she should compromise herself again*): Come, child: let me guide your hand. Take the pen. (*She does so; and they begin to write, using the book as a desk.*) J.E.H.A.N.E. So. Now make your mark by yourself.

JOAN (*makes her mark, and gives him back the pen, tormented by the rebellion of her soul against her mind and body*): There!

LADVENU (*replacing the pen on the table, and handing the recantation to Cauchon with a reverence*): Praise be to God, my brothers, the lamb has returned to the flock; and the shepherd rejoices in her more than in ninety and nine just persons. (*He returns to his seat.*)

THE INQUISITOR (*taking the paper from Cauchon*): We declare thee by this act set free from the danger of excommunication in which thou stoodest. (*He throws the paper down to the table.*)

JOAN: I thank you.

THE INQUISITOR: But because thou has sinned most presumptuously against God and the Holy Church, and that thou mayst repent thy errors in solitary contemplation, and be shielded from all temptation to return to them, we, for the good of thy soul, and for a penance that may wipe out thy sins and bring thee finally unspotted to the throne of grace, do condemn thee to eat the bread of sorrow and drink the water of affliction to the end of thy earthly days in perpetual imprisonment.

JOAN (*rising in consternation and terrible anger*): Perpetual imprisonment! Am I not then to be set free?

LADVENU (*mildly shocked*): Set free, child, after such wickedness as yours! What are you dreaming of?

JOAN: Give me that writing. (*She rushes to the table; snatches up the paper; and tears it into fragments.*) Light your fire: do you think I dread it as much as the life of a rat in a hole? My voices were right.

LADVENU: Joan! Joan!

JOAN: Yes: they told me you were fools (*the word gives great offence*), and that I was not to listen to your fine words nor trust to your charity. You promised me my life; but you lied (*indignant exclamations*). You think that life is nothing but not being stone dead. It is not the bread and water I fear: I can live on bread: when have I asked for more? It is no hardship to drink water if the water be clean. Bread has no sorrow for me, and water no affliction. But to shut me from the light of the sky and the sight of the fields and flowers; to chain my feet so that I can never again ride with the soldiers nor climb the hills; to make me breathe foul damp darkness, and keep from me everything that brings me back to the love of God when your wickedness and foolishness tempt me to hate Him: all this is worse than the furnace in the Bible that was heated seven times. I could do without my warhorse; I could drag about in a skirt; I could let the banners and the trumpets and the knights and soldiers pass me and leave me behind as they leave the other women, if only I could still hear the wind in the trees, the larks in the sunshine, the young lambs crying through the healthy frost, and the blessed blessed church bells that send my angel voices floating to me on the wind. But without these things I cannot live; and by your wanting to take them away from me, or from any human creature, I know that your counsel is of the devil, and that mine is of God.

THE ASSESSORS (*in great commotion*): Blasphemy! blasphemy!

She is possessed. She said our counsel was of the devil. And hers of God. Monstrous! The devil is in our midst, etc., etc.

D'ESTIVET (*shouting above the din*): She is a relapsed heretic, obstinate, incorrigible, and altogether unworthy of the mercy we have shewn her. I call for her excommunication.

THE CHAPLAIN (*to the Executioner*): Light your fire, man. To the stake with her.

The Executioner and his assistants hurry out through the courtyard.

LADVENU: You wicked girl: if your counsel were of God would He not deliver you?

JOAN: His ways are not your ways. He wills that I go through the fire to His bosom; for I am His child, and you are not fit that I should live among you. That is my last word to you.

The soldiers seize her.

CAUCHON (*rising*): Not yet.

They wait. There is a dead silence. Cauchon turns to the Inquisitor with an inquiring look. The Inquisitor nods affirmatively. They rise solemnly, and intone the sentence antiphonally.

CAUCHON: We decree that thou art a relapsed heretic.

THE INQUISITOR: Cast out from the unity of the Church.

CAUCHON: Sundered from her body.

THE INQUISITOR: Infected with the leprosy of heresy.

CAUCHON: A member of Satan.

THE INQUISITOR: We declare that thou must be excommunicate.

CAUCHON: And now we do cast thee out, segregate thee, and abandon thee to the secular power.

THE INQUISITOR: Admonishing the same secular power that it moderate its judgment of thee in respect of death and division of the limbs. (*He resumes his seat.*)

CAUCHON: And if any true sign of penitence appear in thee, to permit our Brother Martin to administer to thee the sacrament of penance.

THE CHAPLAIN: Into the fire with the witch (*he rushes at her, and helps the soldiers to push her out*).

Joan is taken away through the courtyard. The assessors rise in disorder, and follow the soldiers, except Ladvenu, who has hidden his face in his hands.

CAUCHON (*rising again in the act of sitting down*): No, no: this is irregular. The representative of the secular arm should be here to receive her from us.

THE INQUISITOR (*also on his feet again*): That man is an incorrigible fool.

CAUCHON: Brother Martin: see that everything is done in order.

LADVENU: My place is at her side, my Lord. You must exercise your own authority. (*He hurries out.*)

CAUCHON: These English are impossible: they will thrust her straight into the fire. Look!

He points to the courtyard, in which the glow and flicker of fire can now be seen reddening the May daylight. Only the Bishop and the Inquisitor are left in the court.

CAUCHON (*turning to go*): We must stop that.

THE INQUISITOR (*calmly*): Yes; but not too fast, my lord.

CAUCHON (*halting*): But there is not a moment to lose.

THE INQUISITOR: We have proceeded in perfect order. If the English choose to put themselves in the wrong, it is not our business to put them in the right. A flaw in the procedure may be useful later on: one never knows. And the sooner it is over, the better for that poor girl.

CAUCHON (*relaxing*): That is true. But I suppose we must see this dreadful thing through.

THE INQUISITOR: One gets used to it. Habit is everything. I am accustomed to the fire: it is soon over. But it is a terrible thing to see a young and innocent creature crushed between these mighty forces, the Church and the Law.

CAUCHON: You call her innocent!

THE INQUISITOR: Oh, quite innocent. What does she know of the Church and the Law? She did not understand a word we were saying. It is the ignorant who suffer. Come, or we shall be late for the end.

CAUCHON (*going with him*): I shall not be sorry if we are: I am not so accustomed as you.

They are going out when Warwick comes in, meeting them.

WARWICK: Oh, I am intruding. I thought it was all over. (*He makes a feint of retiring.*)

CAUCHON: Do not go, my lord. It is all over.

THE INQUISITOR: The execution is not in our hands, my lord; but it is desirable that we should witness the end. So by your leave—(*He bows, and goes out through the courtyard.*)

CAUCHON: There is some doubt whether your people have observed the forms of law, my lord.

WARWICK: I am told that there is some doubt whether your authority runs in this city, my lord. It is not in your diocese. However, if you will answer for that I will answer for the rest.

CAUCHON: It is to God that we both must answer. Good morning, my lord.

WARWICK: My lord: good morning.

They look at one another for a moment with unconcealed hostility. Then Cauchon follows the Inquisitor out. Warwick looks round. Finding himself alone, he calls for attendance.

WARWICK: Hallo: some attendance here! (*Silence.*) Hallo, there! (*Silence.*) Hallo! Brian, you young blackguard, where are you? (*Silence.*) Guard! (*Silence.*) They have all gone to see the burning: even that child.

The silence is broken by someone frantically howling and sobbing.

WARWICK: What in the devil's name—?

The Chaplain staggers in from the courtyard like a demented creature, his face streaming with tears, making the piteous sounds that Warwick has heard. He stumbles to the prisoner's stool, and throws himself upon it with heartrending sobs.

WARWICK (*going to him and patting him on the shoulder*): What is it, Master John? What is the matter?

THE CHAPLAIN (*clutching at his hand*): My lord, my lord: for Christ's sake pray for my wretched guilty soul.

WARWICK (*soothing him*): Yes, yes: of course I will. Calmly, gently—

THE CHAPLAIN (*blubbering miserably*): I am not a bad man, my lord.

WARWICK: No, no: not at all.

THE CHAPLAIN: I meant no harm. I did not know what it would be like.

WARWICK (*hardening*): Oh! You saw it, then?

THE CHAPLAIN: I did not know what I was doing. I am a hotheaded fool; and I shall be damned to all eternity for it.

WARWICK: Nonsense! Very distressing, no doubt; but it was not your doing.

THE CHAPLAIN (*lamentably*): I let them do it. If I had known, I would have torn her from their hands. You dont know: you havnt seen: it is so easy to talk when you dont know. You madden yourself with words: you damn yourself because it feels grand to throw oil on the flaming hell of your own temper. But when it is brought home to you; when you see the thing you have done; when it is blinding your eyes, stifling your nostrils, tearing your heart, then—then —(*Falling on his knees*): O God, take away this sight from me! O Christ, deliver me from this fire that is consuming me! She cried to Thee in the midst of it: Jesus! Jesus! Jesus! She is in Thy bosom; and I am in hell for evermore.

WARWICK (*summarily hauling him to his feet*): Come come, man! you must pull yourself together. We shall have the whole town talking of this. (*He throws him not too gently into a chair at the table*.) If you have not the nerve to see these things, why do you not do as I do, and stay away?

THE CHAPLAIN (*bewildered and submissive*): She asked for a cross. A soldier gave her two sticks tied together. Thank God he was an Englishman! I might have done it; but I did not: I am a coward, a mad dog, a fool. But he was an Englishman too.

WARWICK: The fool! they will burn him too if the priests get hold of him.

THE CHAPLAIN (*shaken with a convulsion*): Some of the people laughed at her. They would have laughed at Christ. They were French people, my lord: I know they were French.

WARWICK: Hush! someone is coming. Control yourself.

Ladvenu comes back through the courtyard to Warwick's right hand, carrying a bishop's cross which he has taken from a church. He is very grave and composed.

WARWICK: I am informed that it is all over, Brother Martin.

LADVENU (*enigmatically*): We do not know, my lord. It may have only just begun.

WARWICK: What does that mean, exactly?

LADVENU: I took this cross from the church for her that she might see it to the last: she had only two sticks that she put into her bosom. When the fire crept round us, and she saw that if I held the cross before her I should be burnt myself, she warned me to get down and save myself. My lord: a girl who could think of another's danger in such a moment was not inspired by the devil. When I had to snatch the cross from her sight, she looked up to heaven. And I do not believe that the heavens were empty. I firmly believe that her Savior appeared to her then in His tenderest glory. She called to Him and died. This is not the end for her, but the beginning.

WARWICK: I am afraid it will have a bad effect on the people.

LADVENU: It had, my lord, on some of them. I heard laughter.

Forgive me for saying that I hope and believe it was English laughter.

THE CHAPLAIN (*rising frantically*): No: it was not. There was only one Englishman there that disgraced his country; and that was the mad dog, de Stogumber. (*He rushes wildly out, shrieking*) Let them torture him. Let them burn him. I will go pray among her ashes. I am no better than Judas: I will hang myself.

WARWICK: Quick, Brother Martin: follow him: he will do himself some mischief. After him, quick.

> *Ladvenu hurries out, Warwick urging him. The Executioner comes in by the door behind the judges' chairs; and Warwick, returning, finds himself face to face with him.*

WARWICK: Well, fellow: who are you?

THE EXECUTIONER (*with dignity*): I am not addressed as fellow, my lord. I am the Master Executioner of Rouen: it is a highly skilled mystery. I am come to tell your lordship that your orders have been obeyed.

WARWICK: I crave your pardon, Master Executioner; and I will see that you lose nothing by having no relics to sell. I have your word, have I, that nothing remains, not a bone, not a nail, not a hair?

THE EXECUTIONER: Her heart would not burn, my lord; but everything that was left is at the bottom of the river. You have heard the last of her.

WARWICK (*with a wry smile, thinking of what Ladvenu said*): The last of her? Hm! I wonder!

MARK TWAIN

Mark Twain (Samuel Langhorne Clemens) was the author of *The Adventures of Huckleberry Finn*, *The Tragedy of Pudd'nhead Wilson*, and *A Connecticut Yankee in King Arthur's Court*.

ADVENTURES OF TOM SAWYER

CHAPTER X

The two boys flew on and on, toward the village, speechless with horror. They glanced backward over their shoulders from time to time, apprehensively, as if they feared they might be followed. Every stump that started up in their path seemed a man and an enemy, and made them catch their breath; and as they sped by some outlying cottages that lay near the village, the barking of the aroused watch-dogs seemed to give wings to their feet.

"If we can only get to the old tannery, before we break down!" whispered Tom, in short catches between breaths, "I can't stand it much longer."

Huckleberry's hard pantings were his only reply, and the boys fixed their eyes on the goal of their hopes and bent to their work to win it. They gained steadily on it, and at last, breast to breast they burst through the open door and fell grateful and exhausted in the sheltering shadows beyond. By and by their pulses slowed down, and Tom whispered:

"Huckleberry, what do you reckon 'll come of this?"

"If Dr. Robinson dies, I reckon hanging 'll come of it."

From *The Adventures of Tom Sawyer* (New York: Harper & Row), pp. 89-93. By permission of the publishers. *Tom Sawyer* was first published in 1876 and is still doing well.

"Do you though?"

"Why I *know* it, Tom."

Tom thought a while, then he said: "Who'll tell? We?"

"What are you talking about? S'pose something happened and Injun Joe *didn't* hang! Why he'd kill us some time or other, just as dead sure as we're a laying here."

"That's just what I was thinking to myself, Huck."

"If anybody tells, let Muff Potter do it, if he's fool enough. He's generally drunk enough."

Tom said nothing—went on thinking. Presently whispered: "Huck, Muff Potter don't *know* it. How can he tell?"

"What's the reason he don't know it?"

"Because he'd just got that whack when Injun Joe done it. D'you reckon he could see anything? D'you reckon he knowd anything?"

"By hokey, that's so Tom!"

"And besides, look-a-here—maybe that whack done *him*!"

"No, 'taint likely Tom. He had liquor in him; I could see that; and besides, he always has. Well when pap's full, you might take and belt him over the head with a church and you couldn't phase him. He says so, his own self. So it's the same with Muff Potter, of course. But if a man was dead sober, I reckon maybe that whack might fetch him; I dono."

After another reflective silence, Tom said:

"Hucky, you sure you can keep mum?"

"Tom, we *got* to keep mum. *You* know that. That Injun devil wouldn't make any more of drownding us than a couple of cats, if we was to squeak 'bout this and they didn't hang him. Now look-a-here, Tom, less take and swear to one another—that's what we got to do—swear to keep mum."

"I'm agreed. It's the best thing. Would you just hold hands and swear that we—"

"O, no, that wouldn't do for this. That's good enough for little rubbishy common things—specially with gals, cuz *they* go back on you anyway, and blab if they get in a huff—but there orter be writing 'bout a big thing like this. And blood."

Tom's whole being applauded this idea. It was deep, and dark, and awful; the hour, the circumstances, the surroundings, were in keeping with it. He picked up a clean pine shingle that lay in the moonlight, took a little fragment of "red keel" out of his pocket, got the moon on his work, and painfully scrawled these lines, emphasizing each slow down-stroke by clamping his tongue between his teeth, and letting up the pressure on the up-strokes:

> "Huck Finn and
> Tom Sawyer swears
> they will keep mum
> about this and they
> wish they may drop
> down dead in their
> tracks if they ever
> tell and Rot."

Huckleberry was filled with admiration of Tom's facility in writing, and the sublimity of his language. He at once took a pin from his lapel and was going to prick his flesh, but Tom said:

"Hold on! Don't do that. A pin's brass. It might have verdi-grease on it."

"What's verdigrease?"

"It's p'ison. That's what it is. You just swaller some of it once—you'll see."

So Tom unwound the thread from one of his needles, and each boy pricked the ball of his thumb and squeezed out a drop of blood. In time, after many squeezes, Tom managed to sign his initials, using the ball of his little finger for a pen. Then he showed Huckleberry how to make an H and an F, and the oath was complete. They buried the shingle close to the wall, with some dismal ceremonies and incantations, and the fetters that bound their tongues were considered to be locked and the key thrown away.

A figure crept stealthily through a break in the other end of the ruined building, now, but they did not notice it.

"Tom," whispered Huckleberry, "does this keep us from *ever* telling—*always*?"

"Of course it does. It don't make any difference *what* happens, we got to keep mum. We'd drop down dead—don't *you* know that?"

"Yes, I reckon that's so."

They continued to whisper for some little time. Presently a dog set up a long, lugubrious howl just outside—within ten feet of them. The boys clasped each other suddenly, in an agony of fright . . .[1]

---

[1] If you want to find out more about that stealthily creeping figure and the howling dog, reread (that is the pedagogically polite verb to use) the novel. For our purposes, the swearing scene is enough—except of course that what Tom finally decides to do about his secret is relevant to what is going on in a number of the selections, particularly the Schulberg that follows.

BUDD SCHULBERG

Budd Schulberg is the author of *What Makes Sammy Run?*, *The Harder They Fall*, *The Disenchanted*, *Faces in the Crowd* (short stories), and, more recently, *Sanctuary V*.

WATERFRONT

. . . To gauge his time, Father Barry stepped out of the box a moment to see if the line of penitents was reaching its end.

Sitting in an empty pew was the young tough who had shown up at the basement meeting for Joey—Terry Malloy.

From Budd Schulberg, *Waterfront* (New York: Random House, 1955), pp. 237-44. Copyright © 1955 by Budd Schulberg. Reprinted by permission of Random House, Inc. The excerpt is part of a chapter ("Nineteen," pp. 228-44) which deals in its opening pages with Father Barry; since his problems are not as immediately relevant to this volume as Terry Malloy's, I have picked up the chapter at the moment when the two men meet. The novel as a whole, using waterfront corruption as a background, tells the story of Terry and the conflict within him, his struggle to overcome his ingrained allegiance to the self-destructive community practice of "D 'n D." The initials, as Runty Nolan explains at one point, stand for "Deef 'n dumb. No matter how much we hate the torpedoes, we don't rat" (p. 153). Schulberg's novel is a reworking of the material and the characters that he had already used in his screenplay for *On the Waterfront* (1954), the Academy Award-winning film directed by Elia Kazan. The film is more romantic than the novel (Terry survives in the movie, shored up by Leonard Bernstein's music), but it is essentially the same story of conscience versus convention. Some critics (for Eric Bentley's review see *What Is Theatre?* . . . (1968), pp. 258-61) assumed that the film was Kazan's explanation (apologia?) for having appeared as a cooperative witness before the House Un-American Activities Committee. See note, p. 208. The assumption that a personal statement is implicit in the informer-as-hero story in both movie and novel is strengthened by the fact that Schulberg, like Kazan, appeared before HUAC as a friendly witness. He testified on May 23, 1951.

He was crouched down, his face lowered and his hands pressed against his head. He seemed jumpy and rose quickly when he saw the priest. "Hey, I wanna talk to ya," he said gruffly.

"You mean you're waiting to be heard in there?" Father Barry said, thumbing toward the booth.

"Yeah, yeah. I guess so," Terry said uncomfortably.

"Wait a few minutes," Father Barry said. "That old lady's ahead of you."

He bent his head to pass through the black curtain into the box. With his ear against the screen he listened to the feeble voice struggle to think of a sin worthy of absolution. "Bless me Father, for I have sinned," she mumbled. "I lost my temper with the janitor for not coming up to fix the toilet. I scolded him something terrible."

Father Barry reminded her that a tenement janitor in the winter time can be a very busy man and that a little Christian understanding of his daily trials might get the faulty plumbing repaired more rapidly than angry words. He gave her one Hail Mary, absolved her in God's name, and dismissed her with a "God bless you, and pray for me."

Then he stepped quickly out of the almost airless booth, wiped the perspiration off his forehead, and hurried back to Terry.

"Lissen, I wanna talk to ya," Terry said impatiently.

Father Barry stared at him. The boy looked grimy, as if he hadn't shaved. The arrogant composure, the familiar, cocksure, street-corner smirk he had carried into the basement chapel the other evening were gone.

"That's no way to talk to a priest," Father Barry said. "I don't care for myself but . . ." He touched his stole.

"Okay, okay, but I gotta talk to somebody. I need a—. How's about you stick your head back in there"—Terry nodded toward the confessional—"and listen to me a minute."

"How long has it been since you've been in this church—any church?" Father Barry asked.

Terry shrugged. "I dunno. I think I come in with Charley Easter a year ago."

"You've been pretty far away from us," Father Barry said. "I don't think you're ready to go to confession. Why don't you get back in the swing, and start examining your conscience?"

"Lissen, Father, do you have to make such a big deal out of it? I got somethin' I wanna tell ya."

"What brought you here, Terry? Can you tell me that first?"

"I'm here, aint that enough? That stuff you was sayin' on the dock yesterday about Runty. Sure, I know Runty was gettin' ready to stool but"—he hunched his shoulders in an expressive helpless gesture again—"but he had balls. He got a lot of kicks out of life. And then this Doyle broad. And those goddamn pigeons of Joey's." He wiped across his mouth and nose with the back of his hand in the defensive gesture of a boxer trying to smear the blood off his face. "I tell ya, Father, it's got me so I gotta come in here and sit down to find out what gives with me."

"Kid, I've got to change into my street clothes and make a call," Father Barry said. "Sure, something's eating you. That's your conscience. It's been buried in there pretty deep. It's like a clean white tooth covered with green scum and grit. You don't brush that away in five minutes."

"You mean you won't buy me in there, huh?"

Father Barry shook his head. "Not yet. I've got to run now. Why don't you stay here and pray? Try St. Jude. He's sort of a specialist on fellers who've got evil deep-rooted in 'em. He converted plenty of barbarians."

"Yeah? And how did he wind up?"

"Beaten to death with a broadaxe," Father Barry said. "Stay here and think about him. Pray to him. He's a saint of desperate cases. Ask him to intercede for you. Maybe something'll happen." He started rapidly toward the sacristy. "I'll see you later."

"Hey," Terry called after him, but Father Barry was hurrying down the side aisle.

A few minutes later, when Father Barry came down the steps of the church, two at a time, on his way to the Glennons', Terry was outside waiting for him.

"What is this, a brush-off?" Terry said.

"That was a real quickie of a prayer," Father Barry said, crossing the street into the park. A common pigeon was perched on General Pulaski's head, which was turning a mottled green with oxidation. Father Barry had long legs and was moving them in such rapid strides that Terry had to trot occasionally to keep up with him.

"Lissen, Father, I don't wanna pray. Hell, why kid ya, I'd be fakin' it if I prayed. But I got somethin' that feels like it's bustin' me open inside—like a fist was in there beltin' me from the inside . . ."

Father Barry kept walking.

"Lissen to me, goddamn it, don't pull that high-and-mighty stuff," Terry half begged, half bullied. "Hell, the other night you was beggin' for someone to give you a lead on Joey Doyle."

Father Barry stopped and studied him.

"Oh? You got a lead?"

"Lead, hell." Terry almost shouted. "It was me, understan', it was me!" He grabbed the priest so fiercely by the arm that Father Barry thought for a moment he was going to attack him. Father Barry wrenched the arm of his overcoat free.

"You been up all night, on the bottle?"

"What difference?" Terry said, excited. It was like sticking a knife into your own carbuncle. You put it off as long as possible, but then it felt good to feel the pus ooze out. It hurt and felt good to squeeze the sore lips of the boil and empty out the infection. "I'm tellin' ya it was me, Father. I'm the one who set Joey Doyle up for the knock-off."

"Well, I'll be damned," Father Barry said.

"Now this is strictly between you and I," Terry said.

"I don't want it that way," Father Barry said. "When you're ready Father Vincent can hear your confession. I want to be free to use whatever you tell me."

"Listen, it's you I feel like tellin' this to. I'm takin' a chance you won't rat on me."

"I'm making no deals, Terry. I won't rat on you, as you put it. But you'll have to ride along on my judgment."

"Why can't I have it like confession?" Terry persisted. "What the hell difference does it make whether it's in that phone booth or out here with Palooskie lookin' over my shoulder?"

"Because you can't have it both ways," Father Barry said. "Now come on. Let's keep walking and give it to me straight. Fish or cut bait. Spill or button up. Go on, I'm listening."

"Well, it started as a favor," Terry began, and then the thumb of truth pressed against the sides of the inflamed lie and the pus oozed out in a relieving flow:

"Favor? Who'm I kiddin'? They call it a favor, but you know their favors—it's do it, or else. So this time the favor turns out to be helpin' them whop Joey. But, Father, I didn't know that. I figgered they was only goin' to lean on 'im a little bit. Honest t' God, Father, I never figgered they was goin' t' go all the way."

"You thought they'd just work him over, and that didn't bother you," Father Barry said.

"Yeah, yeah, I thought they'd talk to 'im, try 'n straighten 'im out, maybe push 'im aroun' a little bit, that's all."

"And what I said on the dock yesterday about silence, that's what brought you to me?"

"Well, sorta. I'll tell ya the truth, Father. It's that girl. The Doyle broad. She's got a way of lookin' at me. I wanna yell out the whole goddamn truth. All the girls I know are like the Golden Warriorettes, crazy kids. But this Katie is, well, I didn't know they made 'em like that. She's so square, it's funny. I walk down the street with her and I feel like—well, like I'm back in trainin' and I just stepped out of the shower. I'd come home with that liniment smell on me and I'd feel clean for a while."

"What are you going to do about this?" Father Barry cut him off brusquely.

"What d'ya mean, do? What d'ya mean?"

"You think you should know a thing like this and keep it to yourself?"

"I told ya, this was just between you and I," Terry said quickly.

"In other words you're looking for an easy out," Father Barry said. "You tell it to me so I can help you carry the load. But it's still an open cesspool for other people to fall into— and drown in. Like Runty Nolan. Isn't that right?"

"You're a hard man," Terry said.

"I'd better be," Father Barry said. "I'm having a hard day."

"You should talk," Terry said. "A week ago I was doin' lovely. Now I'm in more trouble than a one-armed fiddle player."

"What are you going to do about it?"

"What? What? About what?"

"The Commission? Your subpoena?"

"How come you know about that?" Terry said defensively.

"You know the waterfront Western Union," Father Barry said. "I heard they were looking for you. Well? What are you going to do about it?"

"I dunno. I dunno. It's like carryin' a monkey around on your back."

Father Barry nodded. "A question of who rides who."

They had reached the grilled fencing at the far end of the park. Beyond them at the river's edge a giant pile driver began pounding an ear-shattering rhythm. A new pier was under construction.

"I'm no rat," Terry said. "And if I spill, my life aint worth a home-made nickel."

Father Barry stopped walking and put it to him hard. "And how much is your soul worth if you don't? Who are you loyal to? Murderers? Killers? Hijackers? You've got the nerve to put the bite on me for absolution when you're still buddy-buddies with that human meat you think are men?"

"Lissen, what are you askin' me to do, put the finger on me own brother? And Johnny Friendly. I don't care what he done, he was always a hunnerd percent with me. When I was a snotnose kid, everybody lookin' to rap me in the head, Johnny Friendly used t' take me to ball games. He done that for a lot of us kids. Just pick us up off the street 'n take us in to the ball games. I seen Gehrig 'n Lazzeri. 'N Hubbell 'n Terry in the Polo Grounds."

"Ball games!" Father Barry exploded. "Don't break my heart. I wouldn't care if Johnny Friendly gave you a life's pass to the Polo Grounds. So you got a brother, huh? Well, let me tell you something. You've got some other brothers, and they're getting the short end while your Johnny's getting mustard on his face at the Polo Grounds."

Father Barry grabbed Terry's arm in a tight grip. "Listen, I think you've got to tell Katie Doyle. I think you owe it to her. I know it's a hell of a thing to ask you, but I think you ought to tell her."

Terry pulled his arm away angrily. "Hell, ya don't ask much, do ya?" Terry worked the fingers of his right hand into his scalp. "Ya know what you're askin'?"

"Never mind, forget it." Father Barry said abruptly. "I'm not asking you to do anything. It's your own conscience that's got to do the asking."

"Conscience . . ." Terry muttered as if he were trying to translate a foreign word. "You mean that bill of goods you fellas keep tryin' to sell? Conscience 'n soul 'n all that stuff? That stuff c'n drive you nuts."

"You're making me late for Mrs. Glennon," Father Barry said as he walked away from Terry, down the steps, out of the park. "Good luck," he said crisply over his shoulder.

"Is that all you got to say to me?" Terry called after him. He hated this smart-aleck priest, but he didn't want him to walk away. He didn't want to be left alone.

"You want to have it both ways, brother," Father Barry called back over his shoulder. "Well, you got it."

He took the small park steps to the street-level sidewalk three at a time at so rapid a pace he almost seemed to be running.

"The round-collar bastard leaves me standin' here with my ass hangin' out," Terry muttered to himself in a fury of confusion.

The pile driver had been silent for a few moments, but now it swung into action again, pounding pounding pounding its steel pilings down through the soft bottom muck to the river floor. Pound! Pound! Pound! Pound! It echoed through all of Port Bohegan.

"Goddamn the goddamn noise," Terry said, with his hand to his head. A cock pigeon on the frost-yellowed grass was fussing himself up for the benefit of a tacky female cull. He blew out his chest and spread his tail, cooed importantly and cakewalked around her. Terry watched the performance and thought of his own birds. Of Swifty with his powerful frame, his shiny blue-purple neck and his fine, powder-blue head. He wished he was a carefree kid again, running from the cops, swimming in the scummy river and watching his birds skim across the sky.

Topics
for Discussion and Papers

(*Malcolm Cowley*)

"Does *The Crucible* portray the Salem witchcraft trials accurately? Does its use of Salem provide a workable analogy for the American political situation in the early 1950s? These are the two questions most often asked about *The Crucible*," says Gerald Weales in his introduction to this volume. As regards the first question, Arthur Miller tells us that he changed several characters for dramatic purposes. "However," he adds, "I believe that the reader will discover here the essential nature of one of the strangest and most awful chapters in human history." (See his note preceding the text of the play.) The statement is amplified in his "Introduction to *Collected Plays*" and in his interview with Henry Hewes ("Arthur Miller and How He Went to the Devil"). Is it justified in the light of existing records?

Relevant material in the present volume includes David Levin's essay, "Salem Witchcraft in Recent Fiction and Drama," and the whole section "Contexts of *The Crucible*: Historical." Several critics, including Levin and Robert Warshow, say that Miller has distorted and simplified the Puritan experience. On the other hand, Stephen Fender thinks he has gone to the heart of the Puritan ethic (or lack of a real ethic). What is your judgment in this debate?

For a report or a paper on the witchcraft trials involving

library research, Weales provides a short bibliography in his
note preceding the section on historical contexts (p. 359). *The
Devil in Massachusetts*, by Marion L. Starkey, is the best one-
volume account of the trials, but it needs to be balanced at
some points by Chadwick Hansen's *Witchcraft at Salem*.
Starkey takes for granted that there were no witches in New
England. Hansen says, on the other hand, "There was witchcraft in Salem, and it worked. It did real harm to its victims
and there was every reason to regard it as a criminal offense."
He adds, however, that most of those hanged after the Salem
trials were innocent. A topic for discussion is whether Miller
presents some of his characters (Abigail Williams, Tituba,
Sarah Good) as "guilty" in the sense of trying to practice
witchcraft.

As regards the question whether Salem provides a workable
analogy for the American political situation in the early 1950s,
Miller leaves the answer to his audience. "I am not pressing a
historical allegory here," he says in the interview with Henry
Hewes, "and I have eliminated certain striking similarities . . .
which may have started the audience to drawing such an allegory. . . . My intent and interest is wider and I think deeper
than this." Early reviewers of the play took for granted, however, that he was thinking about Senator Joseph McCarthy's
campaign against people suspected of communism. Did that
campaign revive some features of the witchcraft trials? (See
especially the section "Contexts of *The Crucible*: Contemporary.") Or would there be a closer analogy between Salem
and the great purge trials in Russia (1936–1938)?

Several early critics of *The Crucible*—Eric Bentley, Warshow,
and the *New York Post*, among others—deny that there is
a real parallel between the witchcraft trials and the anti-
communist crusade of the 1950s. Communism and espionage
are real dangers to the nation, they say, whereas witches never
existed. There are historical anthropologists, however, who insist
that witches did exist, as members of a secret cult with thou-

sands upon thousands of adherents. (For library research, see especially Margaret A. Murray, *The Witch-Cult in Destern Europe*.) Murray says that many European members of the cult went to the stake proclaiming their belief in the god of the witches, who was an enemy of the Christian God. Thus, the seventeenth-century crusade against witches came to be regarded as a necessary defense of the social order. Does this suggest a closer analogy with the anti-communist crusade of the 1950s?

Largely owing to the fact that people drew political parallels, the original reception of the play (January 1953) was "decidedly mixed," as Miller says. The first-night audience rose with shouts of "Bravo!" but many critics condemned both the playright and his audience for what some of them called "political innocence." In the present volume one notes that the most enthusiastic comments on *The Crucible* are among those farthest removed in space or time from the original production: Jean Selz (France, 1955), Albert Hunt (England, 1960), Penelope Curtis (Australia, 1965), and Stephen Fender (Scotland 1967). All this suggests several questions. Was the appeal of the play weakened, in the beginning, by its assumed topicality? (Note that during its first production Julius and Ethel Rosenberg were under sentence of death for espionage. They would probably have escaped the electric chair if—as many accused of witchcraft did—they had confessed and recanted.) Again, was Jed Harris, the first director of the play, partly at fault for offering a realistic production that encouraged people to think of *The Crucible* in contemporary terms? Does the success of the play in revivals and adaptations suggest that it is less topical and more universal than its early critics were willing to admit?

Then there are questions about the play in itself: what, for example, is its central theme? Warshow says, "*The Crucible* was written to say something about Alger Hiss and Owen Lattimore, Julius and Ethel Rosenberg, Senator McCarthy, the actors who have lost their jobs on radio and television, in short the whole complex that is spoken of, with a certain lowering of the voice, as 'the present atmosphere.' " Is that a distortion of the playright's purpose? Richard Rovere seems to believe—in the light of Miller's subsequent refusal to "name names" when testifying before a Congressional committee—that the play is directed against informers. One of Miller's colleagues reported, after seeing *The Crucible,* "This play's about marriage." Marcel Aymé, the French adapter of the play, seems to share that view; at least he complains that Miller is unfair to the other woman.

There are still other interpretations of *The Crucible.* William Wiegand sees it as a study of the relation between the Man Who Knows, but is unable to communicate his knowledge (in this case John Proctor), and the Man Who Learns, but all too late (in this case the Reverend John Hale). Weales thinks that the essential conflict is between the hero's identity—his "name," to use a favorite word of Miller's—and the false image of himself imposed by social pressure. Does Weales's reading of the play seem closer than others to the author's intention as expressed in his "Introduction to *Collected Plays*"?

Still other questions concern the characters, and perhaps they are best considered in relation to the fourth act, when, to use another phrase of Miller's, "all the chickens come home to roost." John Proctor: does Miller succeed in establishing a connection between his private sense of guilt and his false confession to having committed a public crime? What are the moral implications of his tearing up the confession after having signed it? John Hale: how has he changed during the witchcraft trials, and why, and does he really take over the play, as Weales suggests? The Reverend Mr. Parris: what is the reason for his abject terror, and does it suggest a general change in the feelings of the Salem community Danforth: is he the figure of absolute evil that Miller hoped to present and is his character sufficiently explained? Elizabeth Proctor: when she says, "It needs a cold wife to prompt lechery," is she stepping out of character for a Puritan woman of 1692?

There are questions about the language of the play. Miller tries to suggest how people talked in colonial New England; sometimes he uses phrases copied from the transcript of the witchcraft trials; but at the same time he modernizes the idiom to keep it from being quaint or incomprehensible. Curtis thinks the result is highly effective. "The language seems to me," she says, "to avoid all dangers of quaintness or artificiality: not only in its cadences, but in the muscular way it keeps the Salem preoccupations and prejudices alive in our minds." Weales, on the other hand, questions whether it was a good idea to suggest the language of witchcraft days; "the lines," he says, "are as awkward and as stagily false as those in John Drinkwater's *Oliver Cromwell*." Faced by this conflict of authorities, the student will have to decide whether the language of *The Crucible* rings true in his own ears.

There are questions suggested by the "Analogues" at the end of this volume. How does John Proctor's conduct in the court-room scene compare, or contrast, with that of Shaw's Saint Joan before her judges? Budd Schulberg has chosen an informer, Terry Malloy, as the hero of *Waterfront* (1955). Can the novel (or the movie on which it is based, *On the Waterfront*, 1954) be taken as a rejoinder to *The Crucible*? In making this comparison, one should remember that Malloy was telling the truth about real criminals, at the cost of his life, whereas Proctor went to the gallows for obeying an old commandment: not "Thou shalt not inform," but "Thou shalt not bear false witness against thy neighbor."

Penelope Curtis says, "Although other plays by Miller are more overtly based on Greek models, *The Crucible* is the only one in which a whole community is directly, and tragically, implicated. . . . In this respect, *The Crucible* is closer in spirit to Sophoclean drama; for the fate of the Salem people actually depends, to a lesser or greater extent, on the choices of individual men." That suggests a final question, often argued in respect to *Death of a Salesman*, but seldom asked about *The*

Crucible: Is it a tragedy in the traditional sense of the word? Aristotle defines tragedy as "the imitation of an action that is serious [or noble, or important] and also, as having magnitude, complete in iteself; in language with pleasurable accessories . . . in a dramatic, not in a narrative form; with incidents arousing pity and fear, wherewith to accomplish the catharsis of such emotions" (Ingram Bywater's translation of the *Poetics*). Does *The Crucible* meet those conditions laid down by Aristotle? Has John Proctor the stature we demand of a tragic hero? "He have his goodness now," Elizabeth Proctor says as he swings on the gallows. Has he his greatness too?

Bibliography

Material reprinted in this volume is cited
in the respective title notes.

WORKS BY ARTHUR MILLER

The entries here are listed chronologically under genre. There is
no attempt to be all-inclusive, particularly in the listing of articles
and interviews. Material which deals too narrowly with plays
other than *The Crucible* has been passed over.

Plays (The date in parentheses is of the first production)

That They May Win (1943), in *The Best One-Act Plays of 1944*,
Margaret Mayorga, ed. New York: Dodd, Mead, 1945, pp. 45–59.

The Man Who Had All the Luck (1944), in *Cross-Section*, Edwin
Seaver, ed. New York: L. B. Fischer, 1944, pp. 486–552. (This
is a pre-production version of the play.)

All My Sons (1947), in *Collected Plays*. New York: Viking, 1957.
pp. 57–127.

Death of a Salesman (1949), in *Collected Plays*, pp. 129–222.

An Enemy of the People (1950). New York: Viking, 1951. (Adaptation of Henrik Ibsen's play.)

A Memory of Two Mondays (1955), in *Collected Plays*, pp. 331–
376.

A View from the Bridge (1955). New York: Viking, 1955.

A View from the Bridge (1956). Revised version; in *Collected
Plays*, pp. 377–439.

After the Fall (1964). New York: Viking, 1964. Final Stage Version, New York: Viking Compass, 1968.

Incident at Vichy (1964). New York: Viking, 1965.

The Price (1968). New York: Viking, 1968.

RADIO PLAYS

The Pussycat and the Expert Plumber Who Was a Man, in *One Hundred Non-Royalty Radio Plays*, William Kozlenko, ed. New York: Greenberg, 1941, pp. 20–30.
William Ireland's Confession, in *One Hundred Non-Royalty Radio Plays*, pp. 512–521.
Grandpa and the Statue, in *Radio Drama in Action*, Erik Barnouw, ed. New York: Farrar and Rinehart, 1945, pp. 267–281.
The Story of Gus, in *Radio's Best Plays*, Joseph Liss, ed. New York: Greenberg, 1947, pp. 303–319.

FICTION AND REPORTAGE

Situation Normal. New York: Reynal and Hitchcock, 1944.
Focus. New York: Reynal and Hitchcock, 1945.
The Misfits. New York: Viking, 1961.
I Don't Need You Any More, Stories by Arthur Miller. New York: Viking, 1967.
"Kidnapped," *Saturday Evening Post*, CCXLII (January 25, 1969), 40–42, 78–82.
In Russia (with Inge Morath). New York: Viking, 1969.

ARTICLES

"Tragedy and the Common Man," *The New York Times*, February 27, 1949, II, pp. 1, 3.
"Arthur Miller on 'The Nature of Tragedy,'" New York *Herald Tribune*, March 27, 1949, V, pp. 1, 2.
"Journey to 'The Crucible,'" *The New York Times*, February 8, 1953, II, p. 3.
"University of Michigan," *Holiday*, XIV (December 1953), 68–70, 128–143.
"A Modest Proposal for Pacification of the Public Temper," *Nation*, CLXXIX (July 3, 1954), 5–8.
"The American Theater," *Holiday*, XVII (January 1955), 90–104.
"A Boy Grew in Brooklyn," *Holiday*, XVII (March 1955), 54–55, 117–124.
"On Social Plays," Preface to *A View from the Bridge*. New York: Viking, 1955, pp. 1–15.

Untitled comment, *World Theatre*, IV (Autumn 1955), 40–41.

"The Family in Modern Drama," *The Atlantic Monthly*, CXCVII (April 1956), 35–41.

"The Playwright and the Atomic World," *Colorado Quarterly*, V (Autumn 1956), 117–137.

"Arthur Miller Speaking on and Reading from *The Crucible* and *Death of a Salesman*" (recording). Spoken Arts, No. 704, 1956.

"Concerning the Boom," in *International Theatre Annual*, No. 1, Harold Hobson, ed. New York: Citadel, 1956, pp. 32–35.

"Global Dramatist," *The New York Times*, July 21, 1957, II, p. 1.

"The Writer's Position in America," *Coastlines*, II (Autumn 1957), 38–40.

"The Shadow of the Gods," *Harper's*, CCXVII (August 1958), 35–43.

"Bridge to a Savage World," *Esquire*, L (October 1958), 185–190.

"The Bored and the Violent," *Harper's*, CCXXV (November 1962), 50–56.

"On Recognition," *Michigan Quarterly Review*, II (Autumn 1963), 213–220.

"Lincoln Repertory Theatre—Challenge and Hope," *The New York Times*, January 19, 1964, II, pp. 1, 3.

"Our Guilt for the World's Evil," *The New York Times Magazine*, January 3, 1965, pp. 10–11, 48.

"The Role of P.E.N.," *Saturday Review*, XLIX (June 4, 1966), 16–17.

"It Could Happen Here—And Did," *The New York Times*, April 30, 1967, II, p. 17.

"Arthur Miller Talks," *Michigan Quarterly Review*, VI (Summer 1967), 153–184.

"Broadway, from O'Neill to Now," *The New York Times*, December 21, 1969, II, pp. 1, 7.

INTERVIEWS

Schumach, Murray. "Arthur Miller Grew Up in Brooklyn," *The New York Times*, February 6, 1949, II, pp. 1, 3.

Wolfert, Ira. "Arthur Miller, Playwright In Search of His Identity," New York *Herald Tribune*, January 25, 1953, IV, p. 3.

Griffin, John and Alice. "Arthur Miller Discusses *The Crucible*,"

Theatre Arts, XXXVII (October 1953), 33–34. (The interview introduces the published play, pp. 35–67.)

United States House of Representatives, Committee on Un-American Activities. *Investigation of the Unauthorized Use of United States Passports*, Part 4, June 21, 1956. Washington: United States Government Printing Office, November, 1956. ("Interview" is not exactly the word for this item.)

Gelb, Philip. "Morality and Modern Drama," *Educational Theatre Journal*, X (October 1958), 190–202.

Allsop, Kenneth. "A Conversation with Arthur Miller," *Encounter*, XIII (July 1959), 58–60.

Brandon, Henry. "The State of the Theatre: A Conversation with Arthur Miller," *Harper's*, CCXXI (November 1960), 63–69.

Gelb, Barbara. "Question: 'Am I My Brother's Keeper?'" *The New York Times*, November 29, 1964, II, pp. 1, 3.

Feron, James. "Miller in London To See *Crucible*," *The New York Times*, January 24, 1965, p. 82.

Morley, Sheridan. "Miller on Miller," *Theatre World*, LXI (March 1965), 4, 8.

Gruen, Joseph. "Portrait of the Playwright at Fifty," *New York*, October 24, 1965, pp. 12–13.

Carlisle, Olga, and Rose Styron. "The Art of the Theatre II: Arthur Miller, an Interview," *Paris Review*, X (Summer 1966), 61–98.

Evans, Richard I. *Psychology and Arthur Miller*. New York: Dutton, 1969.

WORKS ABOUT ARTHUR MILLER

The entries here, listed alphabetically, include books, articles, and reviews about *The Crucible* or about Miller in general with some relevance to that play.

Atkinson, Brooks. "'The Crucible,'" *The New York Times*, February 1, 1953, II, p. 1.

———. "'Crucible' Restaged," *The New York Times*, June 1, 1958, II, p. 1.

Bentley, Eric. *The Theatre of Commitment and Other Essays on Drama in Our Society*. New York: Atheneum, 1967.

Bergeron, David M. "Arthur Miller's *The Crucible* and Nathaniel Hawthorne: Some Parallels," *English Journal*, LVIII (January 1969), 47–55.

Beyer, William H. "The State of the Theatre: the Devil at Large," *School and Society*, LXXVII (March 21, 1953), 183–187.

Brown, John Mason. "Witch-Hunting," *Saturday Review*, XXXVI (February 14, 1953), 41–42.

Cassell, Richard A. "Arthur Miller's 'Rage of Conscience,'" *Ball State Teachers College Forum*, I (Winter 1960–61), 31–36.

Cohn, Ruby, and Bernard F. Dukore. *Twentieth Century Drama: England, Ireland, the United States*. New York: Random House, 1966. (Preface to the play, pp. 537–538.)

Douglas, James W. "Miller's *The Crucible*: Which Witch Is Which?" *Renascence*, XV (Spring 1963), 145–151.

Driver, Tom F. "Strength and Weakness in Arthur Miller," *Tulane Drama Review*, IV (May 1960), 105–113.

Duprey, Richard A. "The Crucible," *Catholic World*, CXCIII (September 1961), 394–395.

Eissenstat, Martha Turnquist. "Arthur Miller: a Bibliography," *Modern Drama*, V (May 1962), 93–106.

Esslin, Martin. "Team Work," *Plays and Players*, XII (March 1965), 32–33.

Fast, Howard. "I Propose Arthur Miller as the American Dramatist of the Day," *Daily Worker*, November 8, 1955, p. 6.

Fruchter, Norm. "The Development of Arthur Miller," *Encore*, IX (January–February 1962), 17–27.

Funke, Lewis. "'The Crucible,'" *The New York Times*, March 12, 1958, p. 36.

Ganz, Arthur. "The Silence of Arthur Miller," *Drama Survey*, III (Fall 1963), 224–237.

Gassner, John. *Theatre at the Crossroads*. New York: Holt, Rinehart & Winston, 1960.

Gibbs, Wolcott. "The Devil to Pay," *New Yorker*, XXVIII (January 31, 1953), 47–48.

Hartley, Anthony. "Good Melodrama," *Spectator*, CXCVI (April 20, 1956), 547.

Hayashi, Tetsumaro. *Arthur Miller Criticism (1930–1967)*. Metuchen, New Jersey: The Scarecrow Press, 1969. (Use this bibliography with caution: it is full of errors.)

Hayes, Richard. " 'The Crucible,' " *Commonweal*, LVII (February 20, 1953), 498.

Hill, Philip G. *"The Crucible: A Structural View,"* *Modern Drama*, X (December 1967), 312–317.

Hogan, Robert. *Arthur Miller*. Minneapolis: University of Minnesota Press, 1964. (Pamphlets on American Writers, Number 40.)

Hope-Wallace, Philip. "Theatre," *Time and Tide*, XXXV (November 20, 1954), 1544.

Kerr, Walter F. " 'The Crucible' Retells Salem's Violent Story," New York *Herald Tribune*, February 1, 1953, IV, p. 1.

Kirchway, Freda. " 'The Crucible,' " *Nation*, CLXXVI (February 7, 1953), 131–132.

Lawson, John Howard. *Theory and Technique of Playwriting*. New York: Hill and Wang, 1960.

Lemarchand, Jacques. "Les Sorcières de Salem," *Nouvelle Nouvelle Revue Française*, année 3 (February 1955), 309–331.

Lewis, Allan. *American Plays and Playwrights of the Contemporary Theatre*. New York: Crown, 1965.

Maulnier, Thierry. "Les Sorcières de Salem," *Revue de Paris*, LXII (February 1955), 137–140.

Moss, Leonard. *Arthur Miller*. New York: Twayne, 1967. (Contains a good Miller bibliography.)

Mottram, Eric. "Arthur Miller: the Development of a Political Dramatist in America," in *American Theatre*. London: Arnold, 1967, pp. 127–161. (Stratford-upon-Avon Studies 10.)

Murray, Edward. *Arthur Miller, Dramatist*. New York: Ungar, 1967.

Nathan, George Jean. *The Theatre in the Fifties*. New York: Knopf, 1953.

New York Theatre Critics' Reviews, XIV (1953), 383–386; XXV (1964), 295–298.

Newman, William J. "Arthur Miller's Collected Plays," *Twentieth Century*, CLXIV (November 1958), 491–496.

Pandolfi, Vito. "Il Crogiuolo," *Il Dramma*, XXXI (December 1955), 57–58.

Payne, Darwin R. "Unit Scenery," *Players Magazine*, XXXIII (December 1956), 59, 62.

Peck, Seymour. "Growth—and Growing Pains of an Actor," *The New York Times Magazine*, February 15, 1953, pp. 20, 34–36. (On Arthur Kennedy.)

Popkin, Henry. "Arthur Miller: The Strange Encounter," *Sewanee Review*, LXVIII (January–March 1960), 34–60.

———. "Arthur Miller's *The Crucible*," *College English*, XXVI (November 1964), 139–146.

Prudhoe, John. "Arthur Miller and the Tradition of Tragedy," *English Studies*, XLIII (October 1962), 430–439.

Quasimodo, Salvatore. *The Poet and the Politician*. Tr. Thomas G. Bergin and Sergio Pacifici. Carbondale: Southern Illinois University Press, 1964.

Raphael, D. D. *The Paradox of Tragedy*. Bloomington: Indiana University Press, 1960.

Raymond, Henry. " 'The Crucible,' Arthur Miller's Best Play, Dramatizes Salem Witchcraft," *Daily Worker*, January 28, 1953, p. 7.

Small, Christopher. "Theatre," *Spectator*, CXCIII (November 19, 1954), 608.

Steinberg, M. W. "Arthur Miller and the Idea of Modern Tragedy," *Dalhousie Review*, XL (Fall 1960), 329–340.

Taubman, Howard. "Return of 'The Crucible,' " *The New York Times*, April 7, 1964, p. 30.

Trewin, J. C. "Blanket of the Dark," *Illustrated London News*, CCXXV (November 27, 1954), 964.

Tynan, Kenneth. *Curtains*. New York: Atheneum, 1961.

Watts, Richard, Jr. "Introduction," Arthur Miller, *The Crucible*. New York: Bantam, 1959, pp. ix–xiv.

Weales, Gerald. *The Jumping-Off Place*. New York: Macmillan, 1969.

———. "Plays and Analysis," *Commonweal*, LXVI (July 12, 1957), 382–383.

Weber, Eugen. "The Crucible," *Film Quarterly*, XII (Summer 1959), 44–45.

Welland, Dennis. *Arthur Miller*. New York: Grove Press, 1961.

West, Paul. "Arthur Miller and the Human Mice," *Hibbert Journal*, LXI (January 1963), 84–86.

Worsley, T. C. "A Play of Our Time," *New Statesman and Nation*, XLVIII (November 20, 1954), 642.

———. "Producers at Play," *New Statesman and Nation*, LI (April 14, 1956), 370–371.

Wyatt, Euphemia Van Rensselaer. "Theatre," *Catholic World*, CLXXVI (March 1953), 465–466.

FOR THE BEST IN PAPERBACKS, LOOK FOR THE Ⓟ

In every corner of the world, on every subject under the sun, Penguin represents quality and variety—the very best in publishing today.

For complete information about books available from Penguin—including Penguin Classics, Penguin Compass, and Puffins—and how to order them, write to us at the appropriate address below. Please note that for copyright reasons the selection of books varies from country to country.

In the United States: Please write to *Penguin Group (USA), P.O. Box 12289 Dept. B, Newark, New Jersey 07101-5289* or call 1-800-788-6262.

In the United Kingdom: Please write to *Dept. EP, Penguin Books Ltd, Bath Road, Harmondsworth, West Drayton, Middlesex UB7 0DA.*

In Canada: Please write to *Penguin Books Canada Ltd, 90 Eglinton Avenue East, Suite 700, Toronto, Ontario M4P 2Y3.*

In Australia: Please write to *Penguin Books Australia Ltd, P.O. Box 257, Ringwood, Victoria 3134.*

In New Zealand: Please write to *Penguin Books (NZ) Ltd, Private Bag 102902, North Shore Mail Centre, Auckland 10.*

In India: Please write to *Penguin Books India Pvt Ltd, 11 Panchsheel Shopping Centre, Panchsheel Park, New Delhi 110 017.*

In the Netherlands: Please write to *Penguin Books Netherlands bv, Postbus 3507, NL-1001 AH Amsterdam.*

In Germany: Please write to *Penguin Books Deutschland GmbH, Metzlerstrasse 26, 60594 Frankfurt am Main.*

In Spain: Please write to *Penguin Books S. A., Bravo Murillo 19, 1° B, 28015 Madrid.*

In Italy: Please write to *Penguin Italia s.r.l., Via Benedetto Croce 2, 20094 Corsico, Milano.*

In France: Please write to *Penguin France, Le Carré Wilson, 62 rue Benjamin Baillaud, 31500 Toulouse.*

In Japan: Please write to *Penguin Books Japan Ltd, Kaneko Building, 2-3-25 Koraku, Bunkyo-Ku, Tokyo 112.*

In South Africa: Please write to *Penguin Books South Africa (Pty) Ltd, Private Bag X14, Parkview, 2122 Johannesburg.*

FOR THE BEST DRAMA, LOOK FOR THE 🐧

☐ **"MASTER HAROLD"... AND THE BOYS**
   Athol Fugard

A stunning exploration of apartheid and racism, *"Master Harold"... and the boys* "is beyond beauty." (Frank Rich, *The New York Times*)

60 pages   ISBN: 0-14-048187-7

☐ **CONTEMPORARY SCENES FOR STUDENT ACTORS**
   Edited by Michael Schulman and Eva Mekler

Containing more than 80 scenes by major modern playwrights, *Contemporary Scenes for Student Actors* includes dialogues for two men, two women, and one man and one woman.

438 pages   ISBN: 0-14-048153-2